MW01595147

A Whack On the Head

A Story of Faith, Family,
Friends, and Forgiveness with a
Dash of Weird

Chris E Beemer

authorHOUSE®

AuthorHouse™
1663 Liberty Drive, Suite 200
Bloomington, IN 47403
www.authorhouse.com
Phone: 1-800-839-8640

© *2009 Chris E Beemer. All rights reserved.*

*No part of this book may be reproduced, stored in
a retrieval system, or transmitted by any means
without the written permission of the author.*

First published by AuthorHouse 4/16/2009

ISBN: 978-1-4389-6018-0 (sc)

Library of Congress Control Number: 2009903662

*Printed in the United States of America
Bloomington, Indiana*

This book is printed on acid-free paper.

‏✦✦ One ✦✦

Colby Allen Duncan is about to discover he is having a really bad day, when he wakes up...dead!

The intensive care unit at Mercy Hospital can be quiet as a tomb even when it is full. This evening only one bed is occupied, and the only patient there has not spoken or made any intelligent sound for two days. At this moment his mother, Helen, who has kept vigil for over forty hours of his two-day stay, is running a quick errand for his sister, Caitlyn. Candy Striper Kristy Lamb is making her rounds, checking rooms, emptying waste cans, getting fresh water, chitchatting with patients—in her words, "being useful." Kristy is not supposed to be in the ICU, but she had been checking on the mother, who had been going crazy waiting for "something" to happen. She seemed like a nice lady, and Kristy thought this patient was fortunate to have someone who cared so much for him. Thus, Kristy was surprised to see the room empty when she walked by. She stopped for just a moment, then decided to step in and make sure everything was in order. Kristy did not realize that Helen had done some rearranging, so while she was staring at the young man with the bandaged head, she bumped a side cart, knocking a stainless steel bed pan to the floor.

It only dropped a few inches, but when it hit the tiled floor, it sounded as though a gun had fired. Kristy's immediate response was, "Oh shhh..." She stopped just before the bad word escaped; employees were strictly forbidden to use inappropriate language at work. However, even before she had time to utter another word, the "dead" boy lying behind her jumped, started to sit up, and plainly stated, "What the..." then moaned, may have groaned, "Ohhh..." and collapsed back on the bed. For just a moment the room was silent again. Kristy had just about wet her pants; her heart was beating a hundred miles an hour. What had she done? A nurse was already running toward the ICU. Kristy took just a moment to check on the young patient; his eyes were open and he appeared conscious. Without thinking, Kristy decided to cover her tracks by announcing to the approaching the nurse, "He's conscious; he spoke to me." The nurse immediately buzzed the nurse's station, and the level of activity began to accelerate. Kristy made a quick retreat.

For a while Kristy was so distracted she hardly realized what she was doing. She wondered how the young man was progressing; it angered her she could not remember his name but was almost positive the mother had mentioned it. She found it strangely amusing that many of the staff referred to the ICU as the "dead room" since it could be so quiet, and sadly, many patients died there. Obviously, this "dead" boy had come back to life, and Kristy was dying to know what was happening.

By the time she had completed her rounds, it was much quieter in the "dead" room. The young man's mother had returned. Since she appeared to be talking, Kristy assumed her son was conscious; however, the mother had been talking to him almost constantly for the last two days. Friends and relatives are encouraged to talk or read to comatose patients; familiar voices are a strong connection to their conscious world. She moved a little closer, and Helen must have heard her because she turned. "Oh, it's you. I have great news; Colby's come back to us."

"That's fantastic. Is he okay?"

"Yes, the doctors think so; he's resting again, but he seems to be out of his coma. I only hope he suffered no permanent damage; blows to the head can be scary."

"Well, I'm sure he'll be fine." Kristy was relieved by the good news, but still somewhat shaken. "Except for the bandage on his head he looks pretty healthy to me. Sometimes the patients we get in here...well, they don't look that good...if you know what I mean."

Helen looked at her. "I know, the only place worse than the ICU is the cemetery. It's one step from the grave."

"Oh, I know; it sounds morbid, but it's true."

"Well, I want to thank you for your concern; you've been really nice. I already told the head nurse how much I appreciate your efforts."

"Thank you." Kristy smiled as she left the room.

Mrs. Duncan had not let it show, but she was still very concerned about Colby; he had not spoken since he "awoke;" he lay with a vacant stare that unnerved his mother. She had been talking to him, but he was much the same as before...except his eyes were open. The nurses had assured her this was not unusual; sometimes it takes time for the brain to adjust from one state to the next. Mrs. Duncan was not convinced and genuinely worried about her child.

Colby was more than just a son to Mrs. Duncan; she loved him more than life. She had never been able to explain it, Colby was the perfect child. He looked like his mother, but acted like his dad. Rational and not impulsive, Colby tended to be calm and collected and had the most delightful personality. Total strangers had stepped forward to compliment the Duncans regarding his behavior and demeanor; he was bright and did exceptionally well in school. Helen had told friends she could not have ordered a better child; his only flaw, which she considered trivial, was his lack of musical talent. Mrs. Duncan was skilled in music and had hoped her children would be so blessed. Colby liked music, but his "so-low" voice was better seen than heard, and he had never taken any interest in playing an instrument except beating on an old pan when he was a toddler; Mr. Duncan made an extra contribution at church when Colby finally outgrew this activity.

Since Colby was now conscious, one of the nurses asked Mrs. Duncan if she would allow him to have visitors. Helen had been so preoccupied she hadn't even thought about notifying Colby's high school friends; in addition, she did not want anyone to see him lying there looking more dead than alive. Now that Colby was more himself, she knew he would welcome guests and gladly agreed. When the nurse left, Helen's emotions overwhelmed her and she began to cry quietly at Colby's side. After a few minutes, Helen thought she heard a stir, then nearly jumped out of her seat. "Mom, what's wrong? Why are you crying?"

Helen almost screamed; her first impulse was to hug Colby like he'd never been hugged before...then realized he had been hurt and it might cause him pain. This idea abandoned, she did the next best thing. "Oh, Colby, you can talk...I've been so worried...how do you feel? Are you okay? Oh, Colby, I've been so worried..."

"Mom, calm down; I'm okay. By the way, where am I?" Colby seemed confused.

"Colby, you're not okay. You're in the hospital. Someone tried to kill you."

"What? Someone tried to kill me? What are you talking about?"

"You were run down by a car; the police still don't know who did it. Do you remember anything?" Mrs. Duncan was becoming agitated.

"Well, I remember you...we live in the same house..."

"No, silly...I mean about the accident."

"So it wasn't attempted murder...just an accident?"

"No one really knows, but who ever did it had to drive up on the sidewalk to hit you...do you remember anything?"

"Mother, I told you. I don't know what you're talking about." Colby was exasperated.

"It's okay; I just wondered. We all want to know what happened."

"Who's we?"

"The authorities...you know, the police; they're looking for the person who did this. It's against the law to run people

4

down with a car, especially when it's my son!"

"You've got a point; I guess I need to be extra careful when I drive and not take out any pedestrians...they could end up in the hospital..."

His mother interrupted. "Or at the morgue."

By now the nurses had descended upon the room and a doctor was on his way. Things looked better; Colby was obviously cognizant although slightly confused. Mrs. Duncan was relieved. In a few minutes another familiar face appeared. Detective Johnson arrived; word had spread that Colby was back...and talking. "Hi, Deb, what's up?"

She was her usual self. "I'm up and you're down, but it looks like you're on the mend. Can we talk?"

"Sure, but do you think we should talk in front of my mom; she doesn't know about us."

Mrs. Duncan looked curiously at the detective, who quickly responded, "Mrs. Duncan...I mean, Helen, Colby and I have been having an affair for some time now; apparently he has a thing for older women who carry guns. We haven't said anything because of the obvious age difference, but we love each other and that's all that matters. I hope you'll not have me thrown in jail before we locate the scumbag who ran him down!"

Mrs. Duncan listened to Deb's comments; her first reaction was minor shock quickly followed by the realization that Deb was a joker and this was all nonsense. Colby was about to die trying to keep from laughing. Mrs. Duncan played along. "Look, I want Colby to be happy. If he loves you, with or without your gun, so be it, but I want you to get the dirty so-and-so that did this and nail his hide to the wall."

"I promise you, we will."

Deb turned to Colby. "I need to know everything you can remember; it may not be much, but anything is better than the nothing we have now."

Colby looked at her with a confused expression; he hesitated. "Okay, it was Friday night; I should have gone to youth group with Patti, but I wanted to finish the research on my term paper. I went to the library at the juco hoping to find more references, and I found several. It was almost exactly 9:45 because the clock is right above the checkout desk. I remember thinking the library would close at 10:00 and I was cutting things a bit close. I put everything in my backpack, put on my coat, and headed out of the building on the sidewalk leading to the street. I remember hearing a car behind me, then something hit me; I vaguely remember falling, but not hitting the ground."

"That's very good, Colby; you've done really well. We now know what time it was when the accident happened. This is important. Do you remember seeing anyone at the library about the same time you checked out...anyone at all?"

"It's funny you should ask that...yes, I do remember. There were couple of guys leaving while I was in line, and I had to wait for a girl who was ahead of me."

"Do you remember anything about them?"

"The guys...no, I have no clue; I wasn't paying much attention to the girl, but I think she had dark hair, not too long, not too short."

Deb was brusque. "Colby, you've been a great help. I'm going to catch the person who did this and we will throw the book at him; some people shouldn't be allowed to drive. I'm sorry I can't stay; there's much to do." She said farewell and quickly left the room.

Colby's mother now resumed her position on the seat next to the bed. "How do you feel? Do you hurt anywhere?"

"Mom, I'm okay. My head aches a bit, my left arm is sore, and my butt hurts...I'm sure I'll live. Where are Patty and Geoff or my other friends?"

"Well, I suppose they're in school."

"In school? Why would they be in school on Saturday?"

"Because your Saturday is their Monday. You've been unconscious for over two days."

"Mom, cut it out! I just left the library last night...it's Saturday morning!"

"No dear, its Monday morning; I'm afraid you've lost the entire weekend."

"Oh no, it can't be! I have schoolwork to finish. What am I going to do?"

"Colby, don't worry about it. The junior class will survive without you, and I'm sure your teachers will understand. I don't think anyone will believe you did this on purpose."

"What a mess! Mom, I'm hungry; I can't remember my last meal."

"Honey, it's been a while; I expect you are hungry, and obviously feeling a lot better!" Moms are so smart.

The doctor's report was excellent. Colby had no broken bones or fractures. He had suffered a mild concussion. The car had hit him in the right hip and he fell to his left. He must have hit his head when he landed. The doctor felt very good about him and even thought he could go home the next day and then to school by Wednesday. They just wanted to watch him and make sure nothing unexpected happened. His vision and other senses seemed to work; he was able to talk rationally. They wanted to check his motor skills, but there was no reason to believe he could not stand and walk.

Exhausted, Mrs. Duncan told Colby she had to go home, get some rest, and report all the good news to his dad, who was out of town. After she left, the ICU was quiet again and Colby thought silence was indeed golden. He had closed his eyes to rest, then heard footsteps near his bed. He opened them to find Nurse Bender standing and smiling at his side. "Hey, sleepy head, I heard you finally woke up.

When you take a nap, you go all the way."

"Yeah, nothing like sleeping for a whole weekend to get rested for a week of school." Colby tried to smile.

"I can't stay, but I wanted to say hi and check on you. You had us worried, but it looks like you're back and ready to rumble...or at least, rumble lightly."

"Well, maybe very lightly."

"Listen, you take care and I'll see you later; I'm sure Patti will be here after school. Go back to sleep so the nurses can wake you up."

Colby sighed. "Ain't life grand?" Nurse Bender smiled and left the room.

Her idea of rest sounded like a good plan so Colby drifted into dreamland...but not for long. One nurse came to take his temperature, another to take his blood pressure, then another to check his bandages and dressings. Colby was reminded of that line from *MASH*. "This is no hospital; it's an insane asylum!" Colby knew he was a little crazy, but this place would definitely push him over the edge. Things finally calmed down, but by then he was wide awake.

After he ate his lunch, one of the staff from physical therapy came to check his motor skills; the therapist helped Colby turn in bed and then sit up; Colby felt a little funny, but said nothing. As he slid off the bed and onto his feet, he could feel his knees start to buckle; he also felt stiff. The therapist steadied him and he was soon walking unaided in his room. His balance was off, but the therapist insisted he was fine and should keep walking. Colby made every effort to comply and felt better the more he moved. The therapist encouraged him to be as mobile as possible, but not be in any hurry...unless the prospects of falling really appealed to him. Colby agreed to take it easy.

After walking around for some time, Colby decided to rest and sat down. He was just getting comfortable when a nurse stuck her head into the room and announced he had a visitor...a certain young lady would like to see him. A few moments later another familiar face appeared. "Hey, Colby, how are you doing? I've been kind of worried; I missed you at school today!"

"Patti, it's great to see you. Believe me, I would rather have been at school; this place is a nut house."

"Well, now you know why my mother spends so much time here."

"Ah, Patti, that was mean; your mother's no nut."

"Hey, you don't know her as well as I do."

"That's true, but I still like your mom."

⤛ Two ⤜

Kathy's story began about eighteen years ago, a year before Patti was born...

Kathryn Bender was a girl of great promise; at least, that is what people who knew her said. She was the oldest of three children, and her parents were very proud of her. She had always done well in school, been involved in numerous activities, and planned to become a registered nurse—to help people. She was in line to receive several scholarships and as the saying goes, "had the world by the tail." Then she met Brandon Linder.

She met Brandon in May backstage at West Wood High's annual awards banquet. The honorees gathered there to avoid the steps up to the stage and to speed up the process of handing out awards. Brandon was receiving an award in athletics; Kathryn was to be honored for her grades and forensics. They were both juniors but did not know each other very well. However, that night Brandon charmed her, and she was hooked. He called the next day for a date, and she accepted almost before he asked; they were inseparable for the next several weeks.

In late June, Kathy called one of her closest friends, Sherry, and asked if she could come by and visit. Sherry was rather shocked since Kathy had seemed only to have eyes for Brandon lately and had suddenly ignored her other friends. When Sherry arrived, Kathy asked her to walk to the park so they could visit privately. Sherry was about to go crazy wondering what Kathy wanted to tell her and did not really notice that Kathy was not her usual self. Once at the park, seated on a shady bench, Kathy burst into tears. "Oh, Sherry, I've just done the dumbest thing in the whole world."

"What are you talking about?"

"Last night Brandon and I had planned to go to the movies. On the way he wanted to stop by the drive-in and get a soda. While we were waiting, he mentioned it was such a nice evening; we should just drive around and enjoy it. We ended up at the state park just as it was getting dark. He stopped the car, turned to me, and told me he loved me. I kissed him, he kissed me back, one thing led to another, and all I can say is that my blood was on fire, and I had to have him." Kathy tried to hold back her tears.

Sherry seemed puzzled. "What are you saying?"

"We made love right there in the front seat, and, Sherry, it was wonderful...but I'm afraid. What if I get pregnant?"

Sherry's eyes grew big. "Oh my God! He used no protection?"

"None."

"What are you going to do?"

"What can I do? It's too late to change what happened. I just can't believe I was so stupid."

Sherry tried to calm Kathy's fears. "Let's not panic right now; I mean, having sex doesn't mean you're pregnant. Let's just hope you're lucky this time, and everything will be okay."

10

"Oh, I hope so...and Sherry, you can't tell anybody; I mean it, no one until I know for sure." Kathy spoke in the firmest tone she could muster.

"I promise; I won't tell a soul." For the record, Sherry never did.

Kathy saw Brandon again a few days later and attempted to explain the possible consequences of their actions. Brandon seemed to understand and suggested they cool their romance a bit—just to be on the safe side. Kathy agreed they could still go out, but no more front seat activity. June ended well and the summer got hotter. Kathy and Brandon had planned to go out for the Fourth of July; it was their first date since their night at the park. Brandon was full of questions. Obviously, he wanted to know if Kathy was pregnant; she did not yet know, but was due for her period anytime. By mid-July Kathy had not begun her monthly cycle; she was worried, but still knew nothing for sure. However, by mid-August, with her senior year only days away, Kathy discovered she was pregnant. She had gone to a clinic for a pregnancy test; it was positive. She now knew the price she'd paid for one moment of lust.

Kathy called and asked to meet Sherry privately; Sherry came by and they went for a drive. "Sherry, I wanted you to the be the first to know; I'm definitely pregnant. The clinic contacted me this morning."

Sherry started to gasp but was not shocked by the news. "Oh, Kathy I'm so sorry. What are you going to do?"

"Well, I'm going to have a baby—that's what happens when you get pregnant—unless I take the easy way out."

Sherry's eyes got big. "Oh no, you're not thinking about an abortion are you? I don't want you to kill your baby."

Kathy's voice took a very somber tone. "No, Sherry, I would never consider abortion. I think I'll kill myself." Sherry was appalled. "Think about it. I wouldn't have to tell anyone, there would be no embarrassment, and I wouldn't have to worry about motherhood and a baby. It's the perfect solution."

Sherry started to cry. "Kathy, you can't kill yourself; if you did that you'd be be killing your baby too. I don't want to lose you. Is there anything I can do? You've got to face this."

Kathy sighed and her head dropped. "I know, Sherry, I know. It was my first thought. The way I figure, I've got two choices. I kill myself and break my parent's hearts, or I tell them I'm pregnant and break their hearts. If I'm dead, I don't have to live with the shame, but you're right, I've also killed my baby...somehow I don't think murder-suicide will win me any brownie points in heaven."

Sherry nodded and seemed relieved. "Oh, Kathy, I feel so bad about this; I can't imagine all the things that must be going through your head. Who would have thought one little fling would cause so much trouble?!"

They talked it over and decided they would visit with Mrs. Bowman, the school counselor. Sherry had wanted her to visit with the pastor of her church, but Kathy chose not to. Obviously, she had to tell Brandon, her parents and teachers; then she had to face her classmates and friends. Kathy cried herself to sleep that night.

She decided to tell Brandon first; he took the news rather well. He wanted to know what he could do. Should they get married? What actions should be taken? He told her he would stick with her and do the right thing. They decided to continue dating, and there was no need to restrain themselves since, in Brandon's words, "If you are already pregnant, you can't get pregnant again." Kathy tried to laugh but felt strange, almost sick, inside.

By the time school had started, Kathy felt she must tell her teachers; she had no idea how her pregnancy might affect her, and she just wanted them to know she fully intended to have her baby, complete all of her classes, and graduate in May with her class.

Things had gone very badly at home. She told her mother

first; she listened in disbelief and then began to cry. When she was able to speak, she told Kathy she would talk to her brother and sister in order for Kathy to avoid that embarrassment. Her father did not take the news well at all. He almost slapped her and actually called her a little whore; Kathy immediately broke into tears; her father quickly apologized and hugged her. "Daddy I'm so sorry; you and mother deserve so much better than this." Little more was said that night, but nothing was the same for a long time; Kathy became a stranger in her own home.

By September everything was deteriorating all around Kathy. There were whispers at school, silence at home. She and Brandon continued to date, but she could tell he was uncomfortable around her in public; they had made love a couple more times, but it wasn't the same. Brandon had been flirting with other girls at school and supposedly told some of his friends the baby wasn't his. Kathy almost confronted him, but decided it wasn't worth the effort. Then there were rumors about Kathy, that she'd been running around, chasing boys and being slutty. It was enough to turn the toughest stomach and hurt her deeply.

She had told everyone she intended to marry Brandon; they had agreed to that, but she realized Brandon had no intention of marrying her; he had plans, and they did not include a wife and child. Kathy had thought she loved Brandon but it was becoming increasingly clear that she had been a victim of infatuation, more like a middle schooler than a high school honor student. The problem was the baby; it deserved a name—legitimacy—and what chance was there if they were not married? The issue was finally resolved by the two fathers, Mr. Linder and Mr. Bender, in December. Brandon would acknowledge he was the father; it would be on the birth certificate. The Linders would pay any expense not covered by the Benders' medical insurance. Mr. Linder would establish a gift trust in the amount of $5,000, available when the child finished high school at age eighteen. That would be the end of it; all parties would go their separate ways.

The year ended Kathy's first semester of school, her relationship with Brandon, and what she later called the

13

happiest days of her life. She was seventeen years old, pregnant, and getting sicker every day. The baby was thankfully small and Kathy was grateful she had not gotten huge, but it was little compensation for her misery, loneliness, and shame. On the outside she played with a game face; on the inside she cried all the time. Kathy pondered her reaction should some poor soul wish her a "Happy New Year." Pow! Right in the kisser.

Kathy was working to get ahead in all of her classes; she hoped to be gone for no more than a week, assuming no complications. She kept thinking if she only felt better, she would be fine. In the meantime, her only friend, Sherry, was driving her crazy with what seemed like a thousand questions! "What will you name the baby?" "Do you want a boy or girl?" "How are you going to care for it and stay in school?" Sherry just went on and on. Finally, near the end of January, Kathy decided to share as much as she knew.

"If the baby is a boy, I'd like to name him Jeremy...Jeremy Donald; if it is a girl, I'll call her Patricia Anne. I don't really care if the baby is a boy or a girl, but I think I would rather raise a son—I just don't want him to look like Brandon. As soon as school is out, Dad wants me out of the house; I don't know what I'm going to do about that. Mother has agreed to take care of the baby until I leave home; she really wants me to finish school, and I agree. I've decided to nurse the baby; I know there will be issues, but it is the right thing to do. Mother nursed all three of us, and I heard her say it established a bond that can never be broken. Obviously this will make more sense after the baby is born. I want to be conscious during delivery; I want to suffer whatever pain I must—I view it as another part of my punishment for being such an idiot." Kathy was forcefully blunt; Sherry began cry.

In February many things began to change. Kathy was less nauseous and actually felt better. However, around that time, her baby had decided to become a gymnast and kick boxer. Without any warning, Kathy would feel the baby jerk, kick, and almost somersault. Sometimes it hit a nerve, kind of like the "crazy bone" in an elbow; other times when a sharp kick occurred, it hurt, but not unbearably. It was difficult to pay attention in class with all of that going on. In addition, all of this activity made her want to cry out, wince, or flinch, and the last thing she needed was to call extra attention to herself. Her mother finally made her go to the doctor. He politely listened to her observations and responded by saying, "This baby wants to be born; don't be surprised if it arrives early."

Kathy smiled slightly and thought, "the sooner, the better."

By the end of February, Kathy figured the baby could come any day. She was also getting a lot of attention from too many people. She had not gotten huge, but she was big and felt like a cow at times. She and Sherry would "moo" at each other as their private joke, and at this point, anything that made Kathy laugh was a blessing. The real problem was all of the comments she was getting from well-meaning, but often complete, strangers.

"You are so lucky the baby isn't big."

"Just be thankful that it's not July and 100 degrees."

"If you are going to nurse the baby, I sure hope you don't have any complications; my breasts were raw, and I didn't have enough milk."

Kathy would nearly gag and decided morning sickness wasn't so bad after all. But some of these comments frightened her: Women do die in childbirth, and what would become of the baby? For the first time since becoming pregnant, Kathy really wanted this baby—to hold it, love it and, most importantly, be its mother.

Folklore states if March comes in like a lion, it will go out like a lamb, or vise versa. This year the lion roared and roared—then roared again. It had been windy; it stormed and rained; then it stormed and snowed. Likewise, the baby continued its gymnastic routine, and Kathy felt as if she were going to explode. The weather was miserable and so was Kathy. Her mother assured her this weather would surely "trigger" the birth, and each day Kathy was convinced that it would happen, but little Jeremy or

Patricia may have figured it was safer inside and was not interested in a "coming out" party. Her family was supportive, but they could not cater to all her various problems, ignoring their lives and work, and quite frankly, Kathy knew this was her mess, and her responsibility. On March 10th Kathy asked Sherry if she would take her to the hospital if necessary. Sherry gladly agreed, and told Kathy she would like to be there when the baby was born.

They did not have long to wait. As a senior, Kathy could leave school early on Fridays; on this particular Friday, Sherry had agreed to take Kathy home. Her mother had been picking her up at school because she didn't think Kathy should be driving in her condition. As they drove out of the school parking lot, Kathy told Sherry she felt strange inside. "I think the baby is coming."

"Oh my God, Kathy, what should I do?"

"How about a quick trip to the hospital; you're so goofy...remember, moo." Kathy almost laughed as she tired to calm Sherry.

"Well, moo yourself; we're just a couple of goofballs, you know."

"Oh, how well I know, but I've got the big belly!"

"Well, not for much longer, our mooing days are almost over." Sherry giggled.

On the afternoon of March 11, Kathy was admitted into the hospital. Sherry called Kathy's family, and her mother arrived shortly thereafter. Sherry faithfully stayed with Kathy. Her water broke, and her labor continued throughout the evening. By 11:00 pm Kathy was exhausted and was beginning to wonder if she would survive. Her mother and Sherry stuck with her, but they were exhausted too. The doctor had been in and out, but by midnight he determined her labor must end; shortly thereafter, Kathy accommodated everyone, but she was not conscious when her daughter, Patricia Anne, was born on March 12.

A new chapter was beginning in Kathy's life and the mold

for a new life had begun; their future was about to
unfold...and it was anything but certain.

⤜ Three ⤚

When Kathy came to, she was in the recovery room;
Sherry and Mrs. Bender were with her, and they
immediately rang for the nurse, who went to get her
daughter. Kathy was not exactly aware of everything, but
the moment they brought Patricia to her, she seemed to
revive. Her baby was perfect although her fingers and toes
were blue from the stress of labor and delivery; she
weighed almost exactly six pounds and was nineteen inches
long. As Kathy held her, she was so thankful she had
decided to have her. Perhaps something good could come
from her mistake.

Sherry needed to get home, so she was the first "stranger"
to hold Patricia. She was uneasy about holding the baby,
but finally relaxed. "Oh, Kathy, she's so beautiful." Sherry
paused, admiring the baby. "But I just can't stay any
longer; I'm exhausted. I'll see you later." Sherry appeared
relieved as she passed the baby to Kathy's mother.

Mrs. Bender held her close; it had been quite a while since
she cradled a baby in her arms, and here was her first
grandchild—not exactly when she had expected it, but a
darling baby girl; it was impossible not to thrill over her.
Kathy realized that perhaps this could heal the rift in her
family; if her mother could be won over, it might help win
back her father's heart.

The nurse soon arrived and asked if Kathy was ready to try
to feed the baby; Kathy's response was quick and direct,
"Yes, I'd like that very much." She soon realized she was
definitely her mother's daughter; holding little Patricia to
her breast and feeling the tiny lips sucking there warmed
Kathy from head to toe; she finally knew the meaning of
bliss. The baby seemed content also; Kathy had difficulty
getting her to switch breasts. In the midst of this feeding,
Kathy's mother announced she just had to get home and
get a some sleep; the family would not tolerate her sleeping

17

all day, and she had plenty of chores that wouldn't get done by themselves. "When the doctor releases you, call home, and your father will come and pick you up." Mrs. Bender then excused herself and left the room.

"Father," thought Kathy. "What would he say? How would he act?" Kathy shivered a bit then her thoughts returned to the baby. "I love you, Patricia," but she had fallen asleep.

Kathy only vaguely remembered the nurse coming in to take Patricia away; she was dead to the world. The nurses let her sleep, checking periodically to make sure she was okay. Around 6:00 am when the shift changed, the nurse on duty told her replacement, "Keep an eye on her; she paid quite a price to bring that baby into the world; it was a long labor and difficult delivery; we could have lost her." Kathy had wanted to pay a price for her "foolishness," and she did.

The doctor was to make his rounds at 8:00, but like Kathy, he had been up late the night before and needed his sleep too. The baby needed to be fed, and the nurses held off as long as possible to wake Kathy. By 9:00 they could wait no longer and sent for the baby. One nurse roused Kathy; another one held the baby. It was curious; Patricia had been fussy—right up to the moment the nurse stepped into the room. This baby already knew where her meal ticket was, and Mother was quick to oblige. "We'll bring you a late breakfast when you're done; you need to eat too." The duty nurse then left them alone. Kathy didn't care; she was in heaven again, and this was something she was definitely doing right!

The doctor arrived right before 10:00, just after Kathy's breakfast. "We had a tough one last night. How are you feeling?"

"Like I was hit by a truck—one with lots of wheels!"

"Well, other than that, how do you feel?"

"Everything seems to be working and no one has rushed me to the ER and put me on life support."

"Then you must be fine!" The doctor laughed.

"I guess so; I do feel lighter today." Kathy did her best to smile.

"I noticed you had lost some weight, but you know women are sensitive about that; I didn't want to say anything to upset you."

"I think that's when they're gaining weight—not losing it."

The doctor grinned. "Are you ready to go home?"

"No, but Mother says it's important for me to get back on my feet as soon as possible, and I've got school next week before spring break."

The doctor spoke sternly. "Now listen, young lady—you had a difficult delivery and you need rest. Remember that little one is going to want to eat, and your life is going to be very different from now on. Your mom's right, but I want you to take it easy, and if you don't, we'll have you back here so fast Superman will envy your speed."

"That fast?"

"Maybe faster."

"Okay, I'll be good; I promise. I'll check with you before making any big decisions."

"That's what I wanted to hear. I'll have the nurse call your folks to come get you; we'll check you out of this place, and I don't want to see you for a while—except to say hi—fair enough?"

"Fair enough."

After the doctor left, the realization again hit Kathy—it was her father that was coming to pick up her and the baby; she was uneasy about this. About a half hour later, the duty nurse came into the room to see if Kathy was dressed and ready to leave.

"You've got a visitor here that we are going to have to restrain if he doesn't get to see you. Can I send him in?"

"Sounds like you'd better; we don't want anyone arrested for disturbing the peace." Kathy was apprehensive.

Moments later, her dad entered the room with a handful of flowers, boldly demanding, "Where's Patti?"

"Dad, there's no Patti here; the nurse will bring Patricia any moment." Her father's bold manner made Kathy wonder if he might have been drinking more than his usual cup of coffee.

"Look, no granddaughter of mine is going to have a prissy, fancy name like Patricia; I haven't called you Kathryn since you were born. Your mother named you and that was fine, but you're my Kathy and that is who you will always be. So I repeat myself, where's Patti?"

"Right behind you, Mr. Bender." Kathy's father was taken by complete surprise; he turned, held out his arms, and the nurse handed him the baby. "Here's your granddaughter, sir."

"Thank you, ma'am." He held the baby and just whispered, "Patti." Kathy started to cry and later admitted she never heard the baby called Patricia again.

They bundled everyone up, got Kathy in a wheelchair, holding Patti, and rolled toward the exit. As they were leaving, Mr. Bender leaned over and told Kathy that once they got into the car, he needed to talk with her before they left the parking lot. Did this mean all hell was going to break loose? Had all this been an act to fool everyone outside the family? Kathy was scared. Her dad had gone on ahead and pulled the car into the entrance. The nurses assisted Kathy with the baby and sample packs of every baby product known to man. Once inside the car, her father pulled into the parking lot, stopped and turned to Kathy.

"Honey, there are a few things I want to say, and I need to

tell them to you privately before we go any farther; this is no one else's business." Kathy sat there dreading an outburst. "I've been a fool; I've said things, done things, and thought things I had no business saying, doing or thinking. I've been angry with you and I've been wrong. Your mother and I have always been proud of you; we didn't deserve to have a child as wonderful as you—you are so special. I know things will never be quite the same; we can't change what happened, but we want you to know we love you, and we will move heaven and earth to do anything we can for you. We have two more kids to raise and we can't let them think what happened to you is okay for them, but we can't stop loving you just because you made a mistake; we all make mistakes. I'm asking for you to forgive us; I know it will be hard. I want you to know Patti is a part of our family and no one will ever say anything against her in our presence; she will be special because she is a part of you—and that's enough. I hope you understand, but I think you do." Tears were streaming down his cheeks, and Kathy sat there stunned by what she had just heard. Tears flowed down her face also—Patti didn't seem to care.

"Oh, Daddy, I do forgive you; I'm so sorry about all of this. I love you and Mom so much; you have always been good to me and made sacrifices for all of us. Thank you. I want to make you proud of me again; Patti and I will never disappoint you—I promise."

"Did they give you any sample tissues? I could use a few."

"Me too." Kathy rummaged through her stockpile of treasures. It was curious; Kathy couldn't remember a time when she'd seen her father cry, and now she fully understood why their conversation had to be private.

Kathy had not even thought about going home; that is, what possible homecoming she might face, but she should have been suspicious when her Dad pulled into the driveway, and she saw her whole family, brother, sister, and mother standing on the front porch. "My God, have they lost their minds; this is March—it's cold outside," thought Kathy; the very thought made her shiver. In reality, no one on the porch had given any thought about the temperature, and certainly no one was cold; they were feeling warm from within—sadly, they had forgotten to hire someone to quietly sing or play, "I've Got My Love to Keep Me Warm" in the background. In any event, even before the car had stopped, they all rushed forward and Kathy thought for sure her dad might run over someone.

"Daddy, watch out! They've all gone crazy!"

"They're your family!"

Her brother reached the car first and opened her door. "Get out! Come inside where it's warm."

"These crazy people should be taking their own advice," mused Kathy.

Someone said, "We'll unload the car later...let's get inside."

Kathy might have guessed but never expected what happened next. Walking into the entry, adjoining the living room, she looked up and saw a huge banner, "Welcome home, Kathy" in large print as its first line followed by, "Welcome to our family, Patti" in smaller print on the second. The last line, in large print again, summarized it all, "We Love You!"

Kathy stood there, her mouth dropped, "Well I...I mean...I don't know what to say...I just wasn't...," her voice trailed off and the sentence was never finished; everyone was crying except for Patti who had managed to sleep through all of this "insanity."

"Well, close the door and come inside. It's winter you know; this isn't a barn!" shouted Dad.

"Yup, I'm home now." Kathy smiled. "I'm definitely home!"

Her sister, Maggie, stepped forward. "Give the baby to Mother; I've got something to show you."

"That's a good idea. You need to listen to your sister," Mrs. Bender added.

"Okay, okay...this place has become a nut house," retorted Kathy.

Maggie grabbed Kathy. "Wait, let me get my coat off; I'm starting to bake; it might curdle my milk."

"Kathy!!" exclaimed her mother.

"Mama, it's all right; she's got a point—formula is expensive," said Dad, looking amused.

"Well, I never...what's this family coming to?" stammered Mrs. Bender.

"Kathy had it right; it's a nut house," chimed her brother, Jake.

Maggie pulled Kathy down the hall to their bedroom. They had shared this room since Maggie was little. The sisters got along remarkably well considering there was a six-year difference in their ages. They were nothing alike. Maggie was not pretty like her sister, nor was she exceptionally good in school, but she had a delightful personality, liked to rough house and get dirty in a tomboyish sort of way, and really enjoyed the outdoors. Kathy would not have been caught dead doing such things. Both girls enjoyed reading, although not the same kind of books, and both liked to sing. Kathy had always been serious; Maggie was a little "goofy."

When Maggie opened the door and Kathy stepped in, she was immediately aware this was not their room. Where was Maggie's bed? When Maggie turned on the light, even more surprises awaited. There was the family crib with a new mobile, numerous balloons, and a sign displaying "Patti" on its headboard.

"Oh Maggie, what have you done? You shouldn't give up your room. Patti doesn't have to be in here with me."

"Yes, she does."

"But where will you sleep?"

"In the bathtub."

"Maggie, why you're not going to...no, we can't have this!"

"Sis, it was a joke."

"Oh, Maggie, I ought to punch you right on the nose."

"Go ahead and try!"

"No, I'm serious, you shouldn't have to lose your room...or at least, your half of it; we can fit Patti in almost anywhere—in a drawer, on a shelf, or in the sink!"

"You're sick!"

"You started it, bathtub girl! Come on, what are you going to do?"

"Okay, Mom bought a nice air mattress and I'm going to sleep on the floor in the living room until you graduate; it's only two months. I can tough it out that long."

"But you shouldn't have to."

"Maybe so, but it was my idea, and I don't what to argue about it anymore, okay?"

"Okay, come here." Kathy put her arms around Maggie and gave her a hug; they stood there for a long time, then looking intently into each other's eyes, simultaneously stated, "I love you, Sis." They laughed and hugged again.

Maggie said, "I hope you like the room; I'll be okay...and before I forget, I'm glad you lost some weight. You've been looking sort of 'tubby' lately."

"Hey, bathtub girl, you be quiet or I'll swat you." Kathy reached out as if to gave Maggie a whack.

"Mama! Kathy's going to hit me." Maggie raced down the hall with Kathy hot on her trail. The whole living room replied, "Shhh..., you'll wake the baby!"

Maggie wanted to hold the baby and Mrs. Bender needed to visit with Kathy, so Patti was traded and Kathy went with her mother to the kitchen.

"Mom, I want to thank you for everything."

"It was your father's idea; the rest of us just chipped in. Your father has had a lot of..."

"Mom, you don't need to explain, Dad and I already had this conversation. I love you."

They hugged, smiled and cried. After a few moments, Mrs. Bender continued, "There is a lot going on this weekend, and you need to be aware of it."

"What do you mean?"

"Well, first of all, Sherry wants to come over and see the baby; I think she has forgotten what Patti looks like, the poor child. Then you have other family members who want to see your child and share their support for you. I don't think you understand how much we are all behind you; there were so many bad options you rejected and the fact you decided to keep this baby, for better or worse, makes grandparents out of your father and me. We weren't exactly ready for this, and raising a baby in this day and age is no walk in the park.

"I didn't want to tell you at the hospital, but your doctor wants you to stay home from school on Monday; he's worried you might overdo, and you can't take care of your little one if you're confined in some hospital. Sherry said some of your school friends want to see the baby; I thought they could come over early Monday night, then you could get a good night's rest before school on Tuesday.

"I've made arrangements with your principal to bring Patti to school for you to nurse during your lunch period and homeroom for the rest of the week. You can meet us in one of the empty offices; it shouldn't disturb anyone. Some of the secretaries and office people may want to see the baby too, so that should work nicely. Finally, I think we need to eat lunch; you'll need to feed the baby; and then I want you to go bed and get some rest. You look like you've just had a baby."

"No duh, Mom! Let's do this before I fall asleep standing up."

Lunch was great; Mrs. Bender was very capable in the kitchen and her husband boasted it was one of several reasons why he kept her. Kathy was never sorry she had spent many hours in the kitchen helping her mother fix meals and clean up; she enjoyed cooking. As everyone was cleaning up their plates, they could hear a rustling in the living room and an occasional murmur and blubbering. Mrs. Bender went to check on Patti and returned a few minutes later to announce that her plumbing was working, but she was changed and dry now...and hungry. Maggie wanted to watch the baby nurse so she went with Kathy to the bedroom; Maggie was fascinated and Kathy was in heaven. Kathy and the baby both fell asleep; Maggie put Patti in her crib and covered her with a blanket; then she buttoned Kathy's blouse and arranged her on the bed, covering her with a blanket. Maggie left the bedroom and returned to front of the house announcing, "The children are both asleep." Grandma and Grandpa smiled.

Kathy jerked and suddenly awoke. The last thing she remembered was holding Patti and feeding her. Patti was gone and she was in bed as if nothing had happened. She started to yell, but wisely held back; it was her room and Maggie's bed was gone...the crib, look in the crib she thought. Sure enough, there was her little one sound asleep and looking ever so content. Kathy quietly left and started down the hallway. She could hear Sherry talking to someone in living room. Sherry had been waiting since 4:00 to see her and the baby. She needed to visit with Kathy about other matters as well.

"Kathy, several of the girls from school want to come over

and see the baby..."

"Patti, not *the baby*; Dad insists we call her *Patti.*"

"Okay then, *Patti*; they want to see Patti. I wanted to check with you before I extended any invitations; I know you're not on the best of terms with some or maybe all of them. I'd like your opinion."

"Look, I've been thinking about this for a long time. I'd like to tell the whole bunch of them to go to you know where, but that isn't the "nice" thing to do. On the other hand, for them to go along with some of the rumors and other hateful things they did really galls me. I didn't steal anyone's boyfriend or make up things about any of them; they had no reason to treat me that way. We were supposed to be friends, and friends don't stab each other in the back." Sherry nodded like one of those bobble-head dolls. "Anyway, here is what I think. You tell them they are welcome to come see Patti...if they are also willing to apologize to me face to face. I'll forgive anyone who shows up and we'll just forget about it, but they're going to tell me they're sorry or no deal."

"Do you think any of them will show?"

"Only if they want to see Patti; I already know they don't care much about me."

"Okay, I'll spread the word, and we'll see what happens. If no one comes, we'll get to eat all of the refreshments!" Sherry laughed; Kathy shook her head.

Maggie heard the baby and insisted on checking her and changing a diaper if necessary. As soon as the all clear was given, Kathy and Sherry went to the bedroom to feed Patti. "Kathy, I've never seen you so happy."

"I simply cannot describe how awesome breast feeding is. Would you like to give it a try?"

"Are you nuts? I'm not thinking about children or a family now; I don't even have a boyfriend." Sherry started to fuss.

"Don't forget; neither do I."

Sunday dawned; the family had considered going to church, but it was chilly and with company coming, lots of things around the house needed attention. The morning went smoothly, and Patti proved the other side of her plumbing worked too...so everything was in order. After lunch, close friends and local relatives began to arrive. Everyone oohed and aahed over Patti, who was manhandled the better part of the afternoon; the baby took it all in stride and slept most of the time. Kathy could tell she had a polite and considerate baby. Patti never fussed or said anything bad to anyone all afternoon...at least, that's what she told her mother after everyone was gone.

Kathy had done nothing all afternoon, but she was worn out by the time everyone had left; usually full of energy, she was puzzled by this sudden attack of exhaustion. "Mother, I can't understand why I'm so tired. I've never been a nap taker, what is wrong with me?"

"When was the last time you had a baby, silly girl?"

"I guess it has been a while."

"Yeah, quite a while, deary...quite a while. Look, why don't you take a nap until I get supper. Maggie and I will look after for Patti, and if she gets hungry, you're on your own." Kathy didn't have to reply; she was halfway down the hall before her mother even finished.

After supper, everyone discussed their plans for Monday; Kathy's mother had taken the week off to help with Patti. Jake and Maggie were back in school, and Mr. Bender had to go to work to support their "extravagant" lifestyle. Kathy had no idea how many of her "friends" might show up, and after the ultimatum Sherry was supposed to deliver, there might be a "no show." They decided to keep everything simple and not break out too many refreshments.

Sherry called right after school and wanted Kathy to know she had done her part; she had told everyone not to show up before 7:00 and that by 9:00 anyone left would be shot as trespassers.

"How was your news received?"

"I think your point came across; I could tell several of them looked pretty sheepish and even tried to apologize to me, but I would have none of it. I don't know what to think, but I can hardly wait to see who shows up."

"Look, why don't you come over for supper and you will be here and not miss a thing; we're not going to pig out tonight, but if you don't get enough to eat we'll serve you twice!"

"Well, I...don't know...but I would like that...I don't want to make any extra work for anyone; you guys have a lot on your hands."

"They'll wash; get your butt over here and you can work for your supper; I'm tired of being nice." Kathy was firm.

"Yes'm, Missa Kathy, yo wish is ma command; jessa don't yo beat me, Missa Kathy, I jes hates it when yo beats me; I lives to serve yo." Sherry gave her non-Oscar winning imitation of a plantation slave.

"Sherry, you're going to miss your own party if you're not careful; now get over here and stop telling lies. You know you love it when I beat you. Ta, ta."

"Kathy, what in the world was that all about?" gasped her Mother.

"That was a joke, Mother, just a joke!"

Kathy hadn't told anyone, but she was just as anxious to discover who might show up as Sherry. As promised, Sherry helped get things ready, and they had Patti on display. At 7:00 everything was quiet, but they didn't have long to wait for the doorbell to ring, and quite frankly, they were rather surprised when they opened the door and discovered two guys from Kathy's government class. They didn't necessarily want to see the baby; they just wanted to say hi and wish everyone well. Word had spread that Kathy had endured a tough delivery, and they hoped she was okay. Kathy appreciated their concern. The boys had only been gone a moment when the doorbell rang again. This time when the door opened, two of Kathy's "friends" were standing on the porch holding packages and trying to maintain a game face.

The first girl stepped forward. "Kathy, we didn't have to be told; we're really sorry. There is absolutely no excuse for the way we behaved. We knew those rumors were not true, but we made no effort to stop them..."

The second girl interrupted. "Yeah, you are probably the nicest girl in high school, and well, we feel bad about everything; we owe you an apology for our callousness. Please forgive us. We'd like to see your baby; we brought gifts."

Kathy looked hard at them. "Your humble apology is accepted; it wasn't necessary to bring anything, but thank you anyway. You're welcome to come in and see Patti and you can stay as long as you want, but we have to shut this down by 9:00."

The girls came in and passed poor Patti around like a football; she seemed to enjoy the attention; on the other hand, it could have been gas. This scenario was repeated several more times during the evening; they stayed a long time and seemed to have fun. Kathy was both pleased and appeased; she hoped the girls had learned a lesson in common decency and friendship. When everyone left, Kathy asked Sherry if anyone who could have been there had not shown up; Sherry mused that she had been thinking the same thing. The girls restored order, and Sherry started to leave. She reached for the door handle and stopped. "Wait, I know who wasn't here; I figured Alicia would come."

"That's right; I would have thought she would want to see Patti. Oh well...thanks for helping out; I'll see you tomorrow." Sherry headed out the door.

"What in the world?...Kathy, come out here...I don't believe this."

At the end of the driveway, blocking Sherry's car, was another vehicle; it had obviously been there quite a while because the windows were fogged over, and it appeared cold. Kathy inquired. "Whose car is that?"

Sherry's face lit up. "Whose car indeed...it's Alicia's...and if I didn't know better I'd say she was in there with someone trying to make her own baby!"

"I didn't know Alicia even had a boyfriend; this doesn't make sense."

The girls charged the car then held up; it was obvious they wanted to be ornery and surprise whoever was inside. On the finger count of three they each opened one of the front doors, preparing to confront anyone inside. And what to their wondering eyes did appear? It sure wasn't Santa or any reindeer! "Alicia! What in the world are you doing...how long have you been out here...what is going on?" chimed the duet of investigators.

Alicia nearly jumped through the windshield; she screamed, gasped and sputtered, "Oh my gosh, oh my gosh, oh my gosh." Alicia was shivering and shaking, her seat filled with crumpled tissues. A package lay on the passenger seat, and it was more than obvious she was an absolute wreck. Alicia looked at Kathy and attempted to speak, but she was having difficulty. "Kathy, I...I came...I came over to bring your baby...I wanted to do something nice...I...Oh, Kathy, I'm so ashamed..."

"Alicia, stop! You've got to calm down. We can't stay out here in the cold. Help me get her into the house, Sherry; we need to thaw her out."

Mrs. Bender didn't ask; she immediately brought Alicia a cup of hot coffee. Alicia held it in her hands for a long time, then finally sipped and sipped again. They wrapped the afghan from the back of the sofa around her shoulders and Sherry and Kathy each tried to warm her hands between sips of coffee. Finally, Alicia stopped shaking; her head had been down, but she looked up at Kathy and began to cry; the tears flowed, and the crying evolved into sobbing that seemed to rack her very core. The girls sat in stunned disbelief; they could not imagine what was wrong. Finally, Alicia seemed to gain some composure. She took deep breaths and sipped more coffee.

"Kathy, I don't...I just don't...I don't know how to say this; I've been out there for nearly an hour. I wanted to send my gift with someone else; I just couldn't face you. I tried to leave but I was crying so hard I didn't think I could drive. It occurred to me I might freeze to death, or I could run the car and get carbon whatever it is poisoning. I wanted to die; I really did."

"Alicia, are you crazy? You have your whole life ahead of you; you'll soon graduate and go to college. I don't understand." Kathy was confused and felt sorry for her.

"It's you, you're the reason...I couldn't face you."

"Me? What did I do?" Kathy was becoming more bewildered each second.

"You had Brandon's baby, that's what! You got what I wanted."

"You wanted to have Brandon's baby?"

"I know you don't understand, no one can. I've loved Brandon since we were in the fourth grade; I've gone to sleep with him so many nights I can't count them; I would kill for him."

"Alicia, do you hear what you are saying? You sound like someone who's lost her mind."

"But you don't know the half of it; you don't realize what I've done. I'm the one; I'm the one who started rumors about you. I was jealous; I wanted to hurt you. You of all people, undoubtedly the nicest girl in school, the kindest person I know...and Kathy I'm so sorry, so very sorry.

That's why I wanted to die; that's why I was ashamed to face you. And Kathy, here's the worst part—I know you'll forgive me, but I don't deserve it."

Kathy and Sherry were dumbstruck. They had known Alicia for years; they'd run around together, acted silly, even a bit crazy, but never, not once, had they known Alicia had feelings for Brandon, nor were they aware of any jealously or hard feelings she had for Kathy. However, this did explain the mystery of the source of the rumors that swirled about Kathy shortly after school began. It seemed good to clear the air, but what were they going to do with Alicia?

Kathy drew Sherry aside. "What should I do about this?"

Sherry's quick wit was sharp. "Shoot her; we can dump her body in the quarry, and no one will know the difference. She wants to die; have her write a suicide note, and we'll take care of the rest!"

"Sherry, stop that! We aren't going to kill anybody." Kathy paused. "I do like the idea about the quarry." Sherry's frown turned back to a smile. "Okay, let's try this." Kathy and Sherry held a whispered conference.

Kathy turned to Alicia, who now seemed more calm and rational. "Sherry wants to kill you. Would you consider writing a note expressing deep remorse? You don't have to mention why. Just say that you've decided to end it all, and we'll throw you into the quarry. We don't want to be charged with your murder."

Alicia looked up aghast; her mouth dropped. She tried to speak, but nothing came out. She finally stammered. "You wouldn't...you wouldn't kill me, would you? Just a moment ago you told me I had my whole life ahead of me."

Taking a cue from Kathy, Sherry shot back. "That was before we knew the whole story."

Kathy spoke calmly. "That's right. We can take you out to quarry, throw you in and be back in time to feed the baby."

Alicia sat nodding, accepting her fate. "Okay, that's what I deserve; I'll write the note. I'd ask for mercy, but I extended none to you, so I deserve none now..."

Sherry interrupted. "But the quarry is merciful; between the fall, the cold temperature, and the deep water you won't last more than ten minutes, if that long; and if you're lucky, you'll be dead when you hit the water!"

"On the other hand." Kathy paused. "I could do exactly what you would expect me to do; I could forgive you; after all, you have certainly apologized, and no one here could doubt your sincerity, but what's in it for me? How can I go to bed tonight, knowing this matter is finally settled?" Alicia looked up and started to cry again. Kathy later told her mother she had never felt so sorry for anyone as she did at that moment...even Sherry was crying...and she wasn't the crying type.

Finally, Alicia looked right into Kathy's eyes and reached out for her hand. "Kathy, as God is my witness, I swear I have learned my lesson. I'm terribly sorry; it was wrong of me to hurt you. I promise you I will do better; you will see a change in me."

"And if we don't?" queried Sherry.

"Then you can throw me in the quarry." Alicia tried to smile.

"So be it," said Kathy. "You are forgiven, but you must promise me two things."

"Name them; I'll do anything."

"Okay, I want you to talk to the youth director of my church; I want you to visit with him about forgiveness. None of us deserve to be forgiven for our transgressions. Forgiveness is a gift, and I give that gift to you.

"Secondly, I want you to come see me after school before spring break. You set the time. We're going to talk about Brandon; he is not the person you think he is. He's no

knight in shining armor. You need to understand I have no
reason to lie about it. I have forgiven Brandon and bear
him no ill will. Do you agree?"

"Kathy I'll do both of these things for you and for me;
thank you so much; I've always loved you if you know what
mean; you are truly special..."

Sherry interrupted. "And 'we always hurt the ones we love'
or so goes that song."

Kathy sighed. "So true, Sherry, so very true."

The girls noted the 9:00 deadline had long passed, and
they needed to leave so Kathy could get to bed. Alicia
wanted to get a quick look at Patti and "officially" present
her gift. Sherry took off first, but then remembered Alicia's
car was in the way. Alicia was still trying to apologize for
her stupidity while Kathy attempted to nudge her toward
the door. "What an evening," thought Kathy as she finally
got everyone out the door. Kathy shouted to her friend.
"Sherry, don't forget you're taking me to school in the
morning." Sherry's response was a big "thumbs up." At that
moment Kathy knew she was exhausted, and she still had
to change and feed the baby—oh, the joys of motherhood!

⋙ Four ⋘

Kathy was apprehensive about going to school. Anyone
with eyes could tell she had been pregnant on Friday; it
was obvious she was not that way today. She felt
uncomfortable when people stared at her; it bothered her
they might be thinking things that were not true; and even
worse, it made her feel guilty and somewhat ashamed. She
had to focus on just one thing: she had made a mistake;
she was not the only one to blame; and she was "paying for
this sin" as best she could. Surprisingly, the kids seemed to
pay little attention to her; she was relieved. Alicia had
wanted to know if tomorrow after school would be a good
time to talk about Brandon, and Kathy thought that would
be fine. Everything was going quite well until the activity
period at the end of the day when the intercom interrupted

the relative peace and quiet. "Will Kathy Bender please come to the office and bring your school materials with you."

"Oh my, now what have I done?" thought Kathy.

As she gathered her things and headed down the hall, she realized this was the first time in four years she had been called to the office. The principal's secretary asked her to please sit down; Mr. Ashton was on the phone. "Do you know what he wants?"

"No, he didn't say, but I don't think you're in any trouble." She smiled.

"Well, that's a relief," thought Kathy.

"How is that baby doing?"

"Oh, Patti is doing great; I've been really lucky...but then, she's only four days old."

"Well, get all the good days you can; they grow up really fast."

Kathy was gracious. "You can come see her if you like. She will be here tomorrow; I'm feeding her in the empty counselor's office right before lunch."

"That would be nice; babies are so cute until they learn to talk...you'll figure it out." Just then the intercom buzzed and the secretary pointed to Mr. Ashton's office.

Kathy didn't know Mr. Ashton very well. Sometimes if you stay out of trouble, you don't get to meet administrators on a one-to-one basis. "Kathy, come in. You know, I've had several nice conversations with your mother over the last two or three weeks, and I feel like I know her better than you. I apologize for that. I understand you are one of our top students, and when I checked your discipline file, I discovered it was empty. I would kill to have a hundred more like you. Thank you for your fine record and hard work here." Mr. Ashton seemed very sincere.

"Well, thank you." Kathy was pleased and somewhat embarrassed.

"I know you are anxious to get home and be with that new baby, but I need to visit with you about something. As you know, last semester you finished all your course work in our nurse's aide program, but due to circumstances beyond our control, you were unable to complete the onsite portion; we cannot certify you without that credit. Your mother tells me you are still interested in pursuing a career in nursing, so it seems to me you could really use this certificate to get your career rolling. As you may know, we only offer the onsite training during second semester, and it is too late to enroll now, so I made a few calls to see if something could be worked out during the summer. The folks at the hospital are willing to give you a try on the condition you don't make it an issue; they don't want to be obligated to provide summer training."

"In other words, they are making an exception for me as a favor to you."

"Something like that." Mr. Ashton smiled. "The important thing to remember is that if you would like to have your nurse's aide certificate, we can award it to you at the end of the summer. Can you decide before spring break so they will have time to propose a schedule? I know it might affect your summer plans."

"Mr. Ashton, thank you for helping me. I figured I would have to start over at the juco. I can answer right now; yes, I am very interested and you are right, it will affect my summer plans...although to be really honest, I haven't had time to think much about them lately; I'm kind of up to my armpits in diapers and a hungry baby." Kathy grinned.

Mr. Ashton nodded. "Good enough, I'll contact the hospital and get back to you as soon as I have something definite. You have a nice day and enjoy that baby."

"Thank you again; I really appreciate it." Kathy left the office.

Alicia met Kathy at the end of school and took her home. They had a long talk about Brandon and the circumstances leading to Kathy's pregnancy. When Kathy had finished, Alicia remarked, "I guess I've been sleeping with the wrong man. Brandon seemed like such a dream boat; I was always attracted to him."

"And you might be exactly where I am now if that boat had sailed. I was swept off my feet. I don't believe Brandon set out to seduce me or add me to a collection of conquests. What happened to us...just happened; it was stupid."

"Well, you deserve better, and Kathy, I want to tell you again how very sorry I am; I should have come to you at the very beginning; I made an awful mistake. I've thought so much about what you said on Monday. I mean this, if there is anything I can do for you, anything at all, you name it, I'll do it."

"I believe you, and there may be a time when I'll need someone to watch Patti. Mom and I have scheduling conflicts, and I seem to be the only one with right baby formula."

"Why, I'd love to help; I can keep her dry by giving her nothing to drink!"

Kathy laughed. "I just hope you're that lucky!"

Alicia needed to run, and yes, she had made an appointment with the youth director at Kathy's church on Saturday, but had already learned much about forgiveness, and the lesson seemed to hit home. Sometimes things actually work.

The week ended quickly and Kathy wondered if she had not had Patti, what she might be doing over spring break. Sherry was leaving right after school but thought she would be back in time to see Kathy and the baby later in the week. Kathy had a little school work to do, and she still needed to better organize the baby things and tidy her room. She felt bad that Maggie was sleeping on the living room floor, but Maggie didn't seem to mind, and it was nice to have privacy at feeding time.

When Kathy got home from school on Friday, her mother remarked that her dad had called, and wanted to make an appointment with her that evening or early in the weekend. "What does Dad want?"

"He didn't say, but he's been talking with someone about a place for you to stay after you graduate."

"He really wants me out of here, doesn't he?"

Mrs. Bender bristled. "Kathy! Don't you say that even if you're not serious; your dad thinks the world of you, but you know you can't stay here, and you don't really want to...I mean, well, you know what I mean."

"I know, Mom, but this is the only home I've ever known; this place means a lot to me and I don't want to leave my family."

"Of course you don't, and we don't want you to leave, but you have your own family now."

"That's something I haven't gotten used to." Kathy looked sad.

Mrs. Bender sighed. "I know, dear, I know."

When her dad got home, she told him after supper would be fine to discuss his ideas; she was curious about what he wanted. Finally, after the table was cleaned and the new dishwasher loaded, they strolled into the living room. "First of all, do you think the dishwasher will sufficiently replace you in the kitchen when you leave?"

"Ah, Daddy, why are you so goofy?"

"Hey, who are you calling goofy? I bought that dishwasher to help your mother after you leave; you've been the best kitchen servant we've ever had. It won't be easy to replace you."

Kathy didn't want to think about all the dishes she and her mother had washed. "Well, let's put it this way; there probably isn't anything that can replace me, but I know Mother is thrilled to not worry about the dishes; I guess a little good comes out of everything."

Mr. Bender got down to business. "Okay, enough dishwasher talk. I've been talking with Al Mitchell...I don't know, do you know him?"

"I might have heard his name, but I'm not sure."

"He used to work for the railroad, and he got an early retirement when he was injured at the rail yard. Anyway, about five years before this happened he received an estate settlement from an aunt he'd never met. Apparently, she married some older, rich man and they lived high on the hog for several years until he died; then by golly, she turned around and did it again. Anyway, she had two husbands, apparently numerous lovers, but no children. She also didn't have much of a will, so her estate was divided among her relatives.

"When Al got his money, he decided to spend most of it and bought the old Thompson Mercantile building in the warehouse district as an investment. It was one of the few buildings down there still in pretty good shape. Al has been fixing up the downstairs for a couple or three store locations for several years, and here's the deal, he wants to make apartments upstairs. That's where you come in. He needs someone to live in the warehouse, maybe take some calls, and keep an eye on the place; his insurance people are concerned that the building is vulnerable when it's vacant, and they are going to up his insurance if he can't provide a night watchman. Now before you say we're crazy, let me remind you that the warehouse is close to town; the juco and library are nearby and so is the hospital. I thought since you don't have a car, you could walk almost anywhere you needed to go. What do you think?"

Kathy was almost shocked. "You want me to live in a warehouse?"

40

"I didn't say that; it's not what I want; you will be making that decision, but there is one more thing."

"What's that?"

"You can live there for nothing; it won't cost you one thin dime. He'll cover all of your expenses: gas, electric, water, phone...everything, just for helping out and keeping your eyes and ears open."

Kathy didn't believe it. "You're kidding, aren't you?"

"No, Sis, I'm not kidding...and Mr. Mitchell will be there in the morning. He said he'd be glad to show you around if you would like to see the place. I know it's not the Ritz, but the price is right!"

"Wow, Dad, it sure is; it's awesome. Let's take a look tomorrow." Kathy was intrigued.

The so called "warehouse district" had become the community's "slum;" no one lived there, and it had been an eyesore for years. However, this had not always been the case. Years ago shops and businesses lined Broadway Street, representing most of the community's commerce. Sadly, in the 1950's Broadway was unable to live up to its name; the state wanted to widen the highway, and Broadway was too narrow, so the highway moved, taking the traffic and business with it. Within ten years, only a few commercial supply companies and service businesses were left. As Kathy and her dad gazed at this old building, it was sad to see what had become of a once thriving area.

"Well, what is your first impression?" asked her dad as they pulled up to the building.

"It's big, really big!"

"That's for sure; if you don't have enough room here, you've got too much stuff!"

"What stuff?" Kathy felt quite deficient in the home wares department.

"Mr. Mitchell should be here any moment, and you'll get the tour. I know it's not what you or perhaps anyone would want, but the benefits are incredible, and Al will treat you right."

At just that moment, an old pickup pulled in front of the building, and a short but sturdy-looking older man with gray hair got out and stretched; he looked up at the building in awe and shouted to Kathy and Mr. Bender. "This is my baby!"

Kathy thought half smiling. "Wow, his baby is a lot bigger than mine!"

"Hey, Jim, this must be Kathy; I'm pleased to meet you. If you are anything like your dad, you're one in a million!"

Mr. Bender waved him back. "Hey, let's not talk like that; I can't afford to buy a new hat every time I meet you, and besides, a big head is hard to hold up!"

"Okay, follow me, and I'll show you the place; you don't have to make a commitment now, but at least you'll know what you're getting into."

Mr. Mitchell showed the downstairs first; he was trying to make three store locations, but he had a problem: There were only two entrances in the front. Kathy was impressed with his workmanship; the stores were taking shape and looked like they would be ready to occupy in no time. The other problem was just as serious; the only interior stairway to the second floor was near the back of the building, which had a series of large overhead doors designed for unloading trucks. The only way to easily get upstairs was to use the metal fire escape on the side of the building. He would be working on a front stairway at the same time he built the third front entrance. The upstairs seemed huge after viewing the areas downstairs. Kathy thought, "Wow, if you like bricks and steel, rust included, this is the place!" However, Kathy was genuinely impressed with the flooring in the front half of the building; it was oak, and considering its age and the amount of activity that transpired there, it was in remarkable shape. It could be cleaned up,

42

refinished, and beautiful.

Mr. Mitchell explained she would have the entire upstairs to work with as she pleased; he had no intention of doing work there until he had finished below. The upper level only had a toilet and sink; obviously Kathy would want to bathe or shower. He would have something ready if she was willing to accept this offer by the time school was out. Kathy's mind was in a whirl; she was trying to visualize what might be done with all this space, but she had no idea how to place things she didn't even have.

As they were leaving, Mr. Mitchell added, "By the way, the wife and I have several furniture items you are welcome to use if you live here; we hate to throw nice things away, but it's hard to just give someone your extra sofa. It was very nice meeting you; I hope you can help me out, but I realize if I had offered my Mrs. the upstairs to this building as our little love nest when we got married, my life would have ended right then and there...so believe me, I will understand if you're not interested."

"Well, Mr. Mitchell, I can tell you this kind of offer doesn't come around every day. You're right, it will definitely be different, but it has lots of potential!"

Mr. Mitchell smiled. "Yup, huge potential."

"Thank you for showing us your 'baby' and giving me a chance to have a roof over my head; I'll make a decision within the next week and give you a call."

"You're welcome, miss, I'm glad to help out."

On the way home, Kathy's dad asked, "Well, what do you think?"

"I think I'm going to have to think about this one, Dad; this is different!" After a few minutes, she spoke again. "Do you think I can make a home out of that place?"

"You know, Kathy, you can make a home anywhere; you just have to be happy there. I think your home should be a special place where you can escape from your work day, take off your shoes, relax, and be yourself. You really need that in life, and I don't think a lot of people understand it. I know Mr. Mitchell didn't mention this, but he does plan to make four apartments up there so you won't really have all of the space, probably only about 25%...on the other hand, I don't expect that to happen for a long time, and you would have some control over the whole process since you'd already be there. I know he would work with you to keep you happy."

"That's good to know, Dad; this could be interesting."

⋙ Five ⋘

Spring break flew by like the March wind. Kathy couldn't believe it when Sherry called around 9:00 pm and announced it was Thursday; she wanted to come by tomorrow and see everyone but wanted to make sure it would be okay. Kathy told her to stop by anytime, but not too late; there was news on the home front.

Sherry arrived around 10:00 am...early for Sherry on a non-school day. Kathy always wondered how Sherry ever got anything done because it sure didn't happen in the morning!

Sherry was disappointed Patti wasn't walking and talking; she was almost the same as she was when Kathy brought her home from the hospital. "Sherry, Patti is only two weeks old; she hasn't had time to grow up and finish high school. Besides, we've been on spring break; you know...no school for one week."

"Well, I thought maybe you'd home schooled her; I can see it now, Kathy Bender, Teacher of the Year, darling of the local media." Sherry waved her arms in grand flourishes.

"Sherry, we should have your head examined, but I'm pretty sure there's nothing there; you haven't been taking any 'medications' without a prescription have you?"

"Ah, come on, give me a break; you knew I vas crazy before vee vas luvahs, sweetheart." Sherry demonstrated her best gangster dialect.

"How well I know; now I have you...and the baby to take care of."

After Sherry had checked on Patti, Kathy told her she had an offer on a place to live. Sherry was fit to be tied. "Kathy you've got to tell me more."

"I can't. I've got to show you; I really want to know what you think, okay? Can we take your car? Mom will stay with the baby."

"Sure, no problem."

The girls were out the door in a flash and under way in seconds. Kathy directed Sherry to Broadway and then toward the old warehouse district. As they neared the area, Sherry said, "I sure hope you aren't going to live around here; this place is a dump!"

"Thanks, Sherry; pull over by that building, Thompson Mercantile, and stop the car."

"Why?"

"Because I've got to punish you!"

"What?" Sherry was trying to figure out what was happening.

"I'm going to make you suffer: torture you, revel in your screams, and watch you bleed." Kathy flashed a cruel, sardonic grin.

"Why? What did I do?" Sherry was becoming unnerved.

"You parked in my spot!"

"What spot?"

"My parking spot!"

"Parking spot! You don't even own a car; why do you need a parking spot?" Sherry was completely confused.

"It comes free with the apartment...my new home."

"This is your new home...oops, I think I am coming down with foot-in-the-mouth disease."

"A little...no, forget that...a lot of torture can cure your problem..." Kathy couldn't hold back any longer; she started to laugh and just kept laughing; pretty soon Sherry was laughing too, but she wasn't sure why.

"I'm a little bit confused."

"Of course you are; in fact, you're a lot confused, but that's why we brought dear old Kathy along to straighten you out; I think the rack should do it, and don't you think you'd look better if you were six inches longer?"

"Ah, Kathy, come on, what's the deal here?"

"Well, this place you call a dump just may be my home"

"What!? Here?" Sherry pointed at the Thompson building.

"Well, not exactly there, raise your arm...higher...a little more...there...up there."

"You mean upstairs?" Sherry appeared amazed.

"I mean the whole upstairs."

"My God, it's as big as a gymnasium!"

"Maybe bigger."

Kathy tried to explain as best she could about the place: no walls, no tub or shower, no front door, but a great escape—fire escape, that is—no wall paper or paint, but lots of brick and steel, a great location, and best of all, no cost whatsoever to live there. "Honestly, what do you think? I mean for me. I know you would never live there. I really want to know."

"Okay, you've tortured it out of me. I'm going to tell you the God's honest truth. I'd bet a million dollars you and your mom could make a home here that would be the envy of the neighborhood, and you're right; I would never live here, but I want to come and visit."

"Sherry, I love you; I'd like to give you a great big kiss..."

Sherry cut in. "Whoa there, big girl, not here in public; people will talk."

"Where? I don't see anyone." Kathy quickly leaned over and pecked Sherry on the cheek.

"Kathy, control yourself. You must be in need of a man."

"I don't need any man when I've got a friend like you who knows just what to say to make me happy."

"What did I do...I mean...say that has turned you into a psycho lesbo?"

"You told me to take the deal and make this my home."

"I did...I, well...are you sure? When did I say anything like that?"

"Oh be quiet, and take me home"

Once there, Kathy announced, "Mom, I'm going to accept Mr. Mitchell's offer and live in the warehouse."

"Why, honey, are you sure that's what you want to do?"

"Well, I am now; Sherry says you and I are going to fix up the place, and it will be the envy of the neighborhood...that cinched it for me."

"What? What did Sherry say?" Mrs. Bender exited the

kitchen holding a rather large knife.

"Oh, Mother, why must I repeat myself...Sherry says you and I are going to fix up the place..."

Mrs. Bender scowled. "That's what I thought you said." She turned to Sherry, who was looking rather bewildered. "Why it's so thoughtful of you to think about me and decide I should be spending my free time decorating Kathy's apartment...er, warehouse, as if I didn't have anything else to do." She then turned to Kathy. "I'm so glad you brought Sherry back; we can have her for lunch." Mrs. Bender approached Sherry with the knife. "Come dear, let's go into the kitchen and see what I can cook up, and because you have been such a good friend to Kathy, I will kill you before I slice you up." Mrs. Bender was doing her best not to laugh.

"You guys sure know how to make a body feel right at home when she comes for lunch."

"Yup, it's old fashioned Bender hospitality," replied Kathy with a grin.

"And, if you girls don't want lunch at 2:00, you'd better get your backsides into the kitchen and help out; I can't cut Sherry up all by myself!" Mrs. Bender tried but could not hold her laughter any longer.

"Come, Sherry, the kitchen awaits us. By the way, this is the perfect time to introduce you to the world of kitchen appliances...why over there, that's a refrigerator...and, look, here's a range..."

Sherry sighed. "Oh Kathy, give me a break."

After lunch, the girls chatted about school issues. "What are you going to do about prom?" asked Sherry; "Last year we had so much fun going stag; I'll never forget the look on the doorman's face when the limo pulled up and four girls got out holding hands. It was a riot!"

"We did have fun that night. You know I'd like to go again

this year, but I just don't feel right about it; I don't feel as connected to high school as I used to...it's not the same now. None of the other girls are mothers."

"Look, Kathy, I had a date, but it fell through; I don't think Alicia has one either; I'm not sure about Megan, but what say we try to get the gang from last year together and do something. We don't have to go to the school; I'll bet the other girls wouldn't mind—it would be fun. I can talk to them if you want me to."

"Hey, it's okay with me, but what are we going to do?"

"Leave it up to me; I'll talk to them and we'll think of something."

"Well, let me know; I don't want to go bungie jumping or skydiving; I have a daughter to live for...so let's not get crazy."

"I promise we'll keep it safe and simple, and have you home by midnight!"

A couple of days later Sherry told Kathy she had some tentative plans for prom, but wanted to make sure Kathy approved them. They agreed to meet after school and Sherry would take Kathy home and get everything finalized. Sherry had talked to the girls and they had all agreed it would be fun. "Okay, the plan I have revolves around you, so let me start there. The problem we have is finding a place to go where we can enjoy our evening and not have to worry about anyone fouling up things. Do you think Mr. Mitchell would let us use your warehouse apartment to meet for the evening? All we need is an electrical outlet and a bathroom. I've got some portable tables and chairs; we can have our own food; we can bring a CD player for music; and I can get a TV and a VCR so we can watch a chick flick or two. The girls don't care what we do; they just like the idea of having a casual, fun time. What do you think?"

"Well, I don't know. Mr. Mitchell seems like an okay guy; I would guess he wouldn't mind. I was trying to remember if I saw any outlets up there. I know there's a bathroom, but no tub or shower. You weren't planning some groupie thing in the bathroom were you?"

"No, but now that you mention it, it sounds like a good idea." Sherry grinned.

"You know, you need professional help."

"Oh, my folks tried that; it didn't work. You're stuck with me just like I am." Kathy shook her head.

"Heaven help us, but it does sound like fun—not the groupie business. I will contact Mr. Mitchell to see if he's agreeable. If we clean up after ourselves, I don't think he'll mind. We need to get this decided. Prom is next weekend."

While many of the seniors busied themselves renting limos and formal wear, ordering flowers and corsages, making reservations and appointments, Kathy and her three friends gathered what they needed and took it to the warehouse. Mr. Mitchell had not even flinched about letting Kathy use the upstairs, and he told her to have good time but not invite any police by jumping out of the windows or throwing fireworks in the street. Kathy assured him they would behave although they might have to throw Sherry in the street just to calm her down. Mr. Mitchell laughed and told her if things got that interesting, he would bring his video recorder for the judges to score Sherry's landing. Kathy told him to keep the recorder handy; she never knew about Sherry.

The girls had everything ready by Thursday. Sherry was so excited that Kathy was afraid they might have to knock her out to calm her down. On Friday the girls decided to show up around 5:00 pm and go as long as they could; if they saw the sun come up on Saturday morning, it was because they had been up all night. If not, it really didn't matter. They had plenty of time to get the food ready after school, and Kathy arranged to feed Patti around 4:00 and then leave milk for another feeding at bedtime. Her mother and Maggie agreed to watch and care for Patti until she got back, but made no promises if the milk ran out.

On Friday the girls managed to arrive at almost the same time. They unpacked quickly and got situated in the apartment; they agreed they had plenty of room so if anyone got mad, she could easily find a distant corner and just stay there. Once they got everything in order, Sherry took over by producing a bottle of champagne which caught everyone by surprise. "Look I know we are not all 18 yet, so I am smart enough to know none of us is 21, but I figure we deserve to have a toast; in fact, several of them, so if we're going to do it, we might as well do it right."

There followed, "Here, here!"

After considerable effort and more time than necessary, Sherry got the bottle opened and poured four half glasses. She then asked the girls to taste the champagne so they wouldn't spit or gag when the toasts were made. Everyone managed a sip without any problem. "Now to the best darn class that ever graduated from West Wood High, I say!"

The girls responded, "Here, here," then tipped and sipped.

"Now to the best of the best right here, the four of us united again, I say!"

"Here, here." The girls sipped the champagne.

"And finally, to Kathy, the best friend I'll ever have, I say!" finished Sherry.

"Here, here." They sipped again.

Kathy now raised her glass and said, "To Sherry, the craziest girl I know, who stuck with me through the worst time in my life, I say!"

"Here, here." Everyone took a drink.

"And this isn't a toast, but I just want say that I love you all; you're the best!"

By now it didn't matter, the girls responded, "Here, here," and drank again.

Finally, Alicia and Megan stepped forward, and speaking together said, "To Kathy, for caring enough to forgive us and for being the nicest person we've ever known, we say!"

"Here, here." They tipped and sipped for the final time.

Their glasses were empty so Sherry filled each about half full again. "Okay, before we finish this second glass, we must perform this sacred act...Group hug!!"

The girls reached for each other and there wasn't a dry eye in the room; they cried and kissed and hugged. Yes, it was so good they had done this thing; they would remember this evening for as long as they lived.

When they finished, Sherry announced, "Let's drink this champagne before it gets warm; I have more for later, so don't hold back."

The champagne was having an effect on their empty stomachs; the warming was delightful, but it was getting harder to stand. The girls hurried as best they could to get their food and sit down; they decided too much of the bubbly could end their evening before it began. They hadn't spent a fraction of what their classmates had, but they were having just as much, if not more, fun. After eating, the girls debated whether they wanted to watch a video or dance; they decided to dance a time or two and then watch a movie. After dancing to several of the songs from their junior prom, they chose to watch a tear jerker first and armed themselves with tissues. As expected, the movie produced a flood of tears, but the tissues saved the day. When it ended, Sherry suggested they pop some corn. No one can watch movies and not eat popcorn. She then wondered if champagne would go with it. The other girls weren't sure, but were willing to give it a try. No one was going to be driving and they could always sleep on the floor; while that didn't sound very comfortable, it certainly made sense.

They had planned to watch three movies. The next one was an action flick, so they set the tissues aside and got ready for a wild time. When this movie ended, they stopped again to snack and be silly. The last video was a horror movie. Sherry and Megan were not as fond of this venue, but they were finally persuaded to give it a try; the girls would all sit on the floor and huddle together. In addition, Sherry came up with the "brilliant" idea of finishing the champagne to help everyone relax, and then the movie wouldn't scare everyone as much. Kathy had her doubts, but she kind of enjoyed the bubbly, and it appeared the other girls did too. They decided to give Sherry's idea a try. Sherry had brought three bottles, the first of which was nearly empty; she graciously decided to finish drinking it...right out of the bottle. Alicia nearly fainted and called Sherry a wino. The second bottle was not as empty as the first, but had more than anyone wanted—at least out of the bottle—so two of the girls split it. The last bottle was full so they could all share it. After everyone had drunk at least a glassful, they split the remaining champagne and started the movie.

Near the half way point, Sherry asked to stop the movie for a few moments because she had to pee; Alicia agreed this was an excellent idea and would go just as soon as Sherry returned. Unfortunately, Sherry couldn't get up; she tried twice, falling down both times. Alicia immediately accused her of being a drunk, or even worse, a falling-down drunk. She said if Sherry wasn't able to go then she would take her turn. Not surprisingly, she discovered she couldn't stand either, and in the meantime Sherry had begun crawling on her hands and knees to the bathroom with Alicia crawling right behind her. Kathy and Megan got so tickled that they fell over, insisting they weren't going anywhere. It took quite awhile for the girls to get back together, and even when they started the movie again, they couldn't stop laughing. As it turned out, Sherry was right. If she drank enough champagne, she wouldn't get scared—she was too busy laughing or in the bathroom.

When the show ended, the girls were still trying to collect themselves. The question that tortured them was whether or not any of them could get up and do anything. Kathy gave it the first try, starting up and standing gingerly to steady herself; she seemed to have it, but had to move slowly. Alicia tried next with similar success, but stumbled and nearly fell. Sherry tried to jump up but simply fell over and Megan managed to get to her feet, but discovered she could not make them walk. The girls all began laughing again and decided they should probably sit down longer. They picked up what they could on their hands and knees, then stopped to jabber for awhile. They agreed their forthcoming graduation would put an end to their high school days and perhaps separate them forever. Someone decided another group hug was in order; there were a few tears, a quick kiss or two, and their "prom" was over.

Generally speaking, once prom is over, the seniors are a lost cause. Two big ceremonies remained, the awards banquet and graduation. The week after prom the senior counselor, Mrs. Bowman, called Kathy to her office. Kathy did not know her very well, but she had been so kind at the beginning of school when Kathy had to announce her pregnancy. Kathy assumed Mrs. Bowman wanted to finalize everything before graduation, which turned out to be correct. She went over a check list of the things that had to be done. In Kathy's case nearly everything was complete, but Mrs. Bowman needed to verify her records. When they finished, she noted Kathy had won numerous awards and scholarships. Kathy thanked Mrs. Bowman for everything and also for her support during her pregnancy and even after Patti was born. Mrs. Bowman thanked her for making a positive contribution to her class and the school. Kathy left feeling pretty good about herself.

The school had a long tradition of honoring seniors for their many accomplishments. The Honors Banquet was the grand school event of the year; any student invited considered it an honor. This year the school had brought in a well known and respected speaker, but due to the length of his presentation, a few of the awards normally handed out had to wait until graduation. No one seemed disappointed and the banquet went like clockwork. Kathy had the opportunity to stand and be recognized or to step forward to pick up an award several times. Her mom and dad beamed at their table, very proud of her.

As the practices and preparations for graduation increased, so did the anticipation of being out of school. Everyone was beside themselves as the big moment rapidly or, for some, slowly arrived. Kathy had mixed feelings; she really wanted out, and yet, she knew she would miss high school and had already figured a way to hide a wad of tissues under her gown.

This year after the seniors filed into the auditorium and the opening remarks were made, the principal, Mr. Ashton, announced that before they presented diplomas, several other awards were to be presented. He noted that no previous class in recent history had been awarded more scholarships and honors. This statement brought a roar of approval from the seniors.

Mr. Ashton announced these final honors were not as momentous as some of the others but, in his opinion, were the most important of all. He then named all those seniors who had perfect attendance and asked them to step forward and receive their certificates. With that concluded, Mr. Ashton stated that the office and counselors had created a new award for a very special senior who had dealt with difficult personal and health issues, but had overcome them and never missed a single day of school. He was truly honored to be able to present this high honor to Miss Kathy Bender. Would she please step forward? Kathy was completely stunned; she could not move. Her classmates all around her applauded and chanted, "Kathy, Kathy, Kathy..." She finally rose and moved forward. Everyone began to applaud and Kathy was crying so hard she could barely see. When Mr. Ashton handed her the certificate, she just kept saying, "Thank you, thank you so much," and managed to get back to her seat. Her classmates were still standing and chanting. Kathy had finally achieved some respect, but never dreamed it would come like this.

Following graduation, in their reception line, Mr. Ashton tried to meet and shake each hand again. When he got to Kathy, she held on to his hand. "Mr. Ashton I can't tell you how honored I am to receive your new award, but there has been a mistake."

"A mistake, what do you mean?" Mr. Ashton appeared puzzled.

"I missed a day of school right after my baby was born; the doctor didn't think I should overdo; it would have been on March 14."

"You know, it's odd you should bring this up. The attendance records for that day were lost; we can't find hide nor hair of them. I guess it's too late to do anything about it now; I sure hope it's okay." Mr. Ashton half smiled.

Kathy was almost sure he winked at her as he moved to the next senior...funny thing. This had been a very special day; it's said that graduation marks a new beginning, much like jumping out of a plane. The jumping was easy; it was the landing that caused concern. In Kathy's case where would her new beginning take her and what kind of "landing" could she expect? Sometimes the future is hard to predict and if she had known, she might never have jumped.

Six

Just before graduation Mr. Ashton had sent Kathy a note telling her to talk to the hospital nursing supervisor regarding her onsite hours. Kathy also needed to contact the juco about summer classes. She had received a top scholarship, primarily related to her interest in nursing. She had not intended to go to juco, but after becoming pregnant with no husband or resources, she resigned herself to staying in the community. Her scholarship was remarkable according to her counselor, Mrs. Bowman. She had received a full ride on all tuition and fees, including books; it was renewable for up to four years as long as she maintained a 3.5 gpa and at least half time student status. This would allow her to receive a free associate's degree in pre-nursing and also become a certified LPN.

On Monday after graduation she went to the hospital early in the morning. The nursing supervisor was well aware of her situation and even remembered when she had been in the hospital; she inquired about the baby and was pleased that Kathy and her daughter were well. She explained the onsite situation, adding she hoped Kathy would consider working there after completing her training.

Kathy, who had not expected a job offer, was thrilled. Could she start the first Monday in June and work Monday through Thursday each afternoon until the middle of July, a total of six-weeks? If her progress was satisfactory and she decided to continue working for the hospital, they would give her a lump sum payment for one half of the hours she had worked, plus an increase in salary when she became "officially" employed. Kathy could hardly believe her ears; she almost cried when she shook the supervisor's hand and thanked her for this opportunity.

As she headed to the juco, she thought she was really having a good day; maybe the old Bender luck was back. It brought a little more confidence, and she walked a bit taller. The juco had already assigned her an enrollment counselor, who was quite pleased Kathy had chosen to enter the nursing program. There were no requirements on the number of hours she had to take in summer school. Kathy wanted six; she already had nine hours from high school, and this would give her a full semester of credit...before school began in the fall. For her scholarship program, she had to take eight or nine hours to be considered enrolled half time. She thought she could handle it but knew she would have to work hard to maintain her grades, earn a living, and take care of Patti. They finally found two three-hour classes Kathy could take in the morning; she would be done by 11:30, giving her an hour and a half to get to the hospital. She could make that work, and it was only for six weeks. The summer school also used a Monday through Thursday schedule, which began two days after she started working at the hospital. This would leave Kathy with three-day weekends.

When she got home, her mother had more news. A friend had a relative who worked in one of the local nursing homes; apparently they were having problems finding people to work weekend shifts. Kathy was incredulous; she had just worked out a schedule with a three-day weekend, and here was a chance for a weekend job. She updated her mother about the morning and asked her advice.

Mrs. Bender was thrilled by Kathy's news but had one big concern. "Honey, all this is fine; in fact, it's wonderful, but you have absolutely no income. How can you live without any money? Your dad has agreed to help you until you get paid, but I don't know if he will wait for six weeks. If you could get this weekend job, at least you would have a little income to buy food and necessary items; and it would go a long way toward convincing him to stand by you. He wants to help any way he can, but you know your dad, and if we can keep him happy, it will make everything run so much smoother. I think you should check it out." Kathy nodded and asked to borrow the car to drive to the nursing home.

This nursing home was fairly new; Kathy could remember when it was built and her dad had laughed that she could visit her parents there when they could no longer take care of themselves. After going inside, she asked to speak to the personnel manager. When this lady arrived, Kathy explained her situation. She was impressed with Kathy's situation. Would Kathy consider working approximately one and a half shifts between Friday afternoon and Saturday night? She would be employed as a temporary employee, then have ninety days to meet any specific requirements, in her case, certification. She would also receive an automatic raise on or before that time. Before Kathy could reply, she added, "You can start this coming weekend; I can give you a schedule today." Kathy could not believe it; someone up there loved her...or wanted to work her to death!

When Kathy returned home for the second time with even more good news, her mother nearly fainted. "You mean they hired you without an application?" Her mother was in complete disbelief.

"No, I have the application; I wasn't sure about all of the names so I thought I would check with you first. I have to take it back after lunch and feeding Patti."

"Your dad is not going to believe this; maybe I should fix him a drink before supper to calm him down. Kathy, this is wonderful; I know he will go along with you now, if you need help. I think he is really rooting for you and was so

58

proud at your graduation. You have much to be thankful for, and I know things will work out. You started in a bit of a hole, but you are proving you're not going to stay there."

"Thank you, Mom. You and Dad are my biggest fans; I really appreciate everything you've done. I want you to be proud of me; you deserve that much."

After lunch, Kathy needed to feed Patti. Her schedule had been so hectic she could only give Patti about five minutes on each breast, then lay her aside and go about her business. It would be nice to have time with Patti and not have to rush, rush, rush, but it was going to be short-lived because everything was starting again...very soon.

Kathy completed her application and delivered it to the nursing home; she was scheduled to report at 3:00 pm on Friday and work until about 8:00 pm. Saturday was a regular shift from 7:00 am to 3:00 pm. She couldn't believe she was going to work so soon, but in some ways it was good to start and learn the ropes. When she returned from delivering her papers, she and her mother sat down to discuss their strategy for getting her apartment ready. Mr. Mitchell was working on the plumbing, and her dad had volunteered to help him install the tub. The girls were in charge of cleaning. Mr. Mitchell had already delivered a stove and refrigerator. He had located a washer and dryer, but they couldn't be used until the wiring and plumbing were completed. Various family members had made offers of beds, chairs and other accessories. Kathy wanted to move by the first full week in June, so they couldn't tarry.

Organizing and basic cleaning went well; Mr. Mitchell focused on the plumbing and wiring and ways to divert heating and air conditioning from the offices downstairs to the apartment area. The real problem was reducing the volume of the upstairs; the ceilings were nearly twelve feet tall and heat would rise quickly to the roof, letting every one on the floor freeze. Air conditioning would be a similar failure. Mr. Mitchell wanted to wall off the back of the apartment area and then put in a suspended ceiling, which he called his first line of defense. He admitted it might be uncomfortable for a while, but his efforts would pay off and the place would be cozier. By Wednesday the space was clean enough to begin moving "Kathy's belongings"; nothing matched or went together, but it was all hers—and, as her mother said, "You have to start somewhere." At the end of the day Thursday, the place definitely looked like a home and it appeared Kathy would meet her deadline. She didn't want to leave her real home and family, but it was exciting to have a place of her own, much closer to work and school.

Kathy was wise enough to understand that life "on her own" was going to be a lot different from living with her parents. There were the big things like earning an income to support herself; she would have to do her own shopping for food and other consumables; and she had the lone responsibility for her daughter. It would difficult to sleep in since Patti would wake up early and be hungry. However, Patti wouldn't be a baby forever, and then there would be no one to rouse her. She decided to get an alarm clock that worked without electricity. She also decided she needed to keep some kind of weekly schedule to plan her day. She needed to nurse and spend time with Patti, and complete her school work. As she put these things together, she realized the only time she really had for herself was also "nap" time. If she were going to have any fun in her life, it would have to be in her dreams. As this reality began to emerge, so did a few tears. No doubt about it; her life had changed, and it was hard to see right now how it had gotten any better—her few tears began to multiply and divide...this kind of math was very discouraging.

The nursing home had approved Kathy's application, so Friday was her first day of work. Her mother and Maggie had agreed to take care of Patti while she worked, provided she left enough milk for Saturday. Kathy had no idea what to expect; she was not familiar with nursing homes, but after her first half day she told her mother it had been quite interesting. She decided she really liked older people. Most of them were sweet and actually quite helpful. Of course, there were exceptions, but that was to be expected. Saturday also went well and Kathy concluded working wasn't all bad. Her mother agreed, but noted she would be working in three different places and environments, if school was included. The old adage, "variety is the spice of life," was certainly true; it was doing the same old thing over and over that drove everyone crazy, except for people who were already that way. Her final words echoed in Kathy's ears. "Do what you love and love what you do...and always do your best. Never leave ashamed of your work. You'll rest better and live longer."

The "official" move-in took place on Sunday; her family brought the last load of smaller items and left her to herself. Kathy was amused at Patti, who lay in her carrier staring in awe at her new surroundings. Mrs. Bender had found one precious item in their garage she knew Kathy could use; the same stroller Kathy and her siblings had ridden in for miles was now hers. Kathy decided she and Patti would enjoy the park as often as possible; Patti needed to be outdoors in the sun; Kathy needed time to escape her hectic life.

Her hospital work began on Monday. The hospital had a childcare and nursery center, and even though Kathy was not an employee, the hospital had agreed to keep Patti for no charge. In Kathy's case, they would even allow her to tend and nurse Patti if necessary; they took great pride in their pro-family programs. The hospital had been founded and maintained by the Catholic church until they sold it to the city just a few years after Kathy was born. The more Kathy saw of it, the more she felt she was in a good place. Much of the Catholic tradition remained and Kathy already had strong pro-life feelings and no objection if someone mentioned God. After all, He was responsible for life, and hospitals are dedicated to preserving it. How could the two issues be separated?

Kathy's training went well and she was looking forward to working the next day. Everything was proceeding smoothly, except once she almost forgot to pick up Patti. She was not worried about school; after all, she had only been out of high school for two weeks and had not forgotten how to be a student. Somehow she didn't feel college would be much different, but she was serious about keeping her scholarship and getting this part of her education out of the way as quickly as possible. She knew she would make a lot more money as soon as she became an LPN. It would take more than two years to complete her degree even if she took summer school. One nice benefit at juco was a day care offered for their students with children to coincide with a new program to train and certify baby-sitters. Having free child care was a real plus for Kathy and, no doubt, also helped the would-be sitters.

By the end of her first full week of work and school, Kathy told her mother she could handle this. She was walking with Patti in the park and Patti seemed to enjoy being outside. Kathy was amused watching Patti's expressions; she would stare at things for the longest time and even coo and make funny sounds. In many ways Kathy enjoyed being a mother; she had always wanted children; she just hadn't planned one quite so soon, especially without a dad. She would soon be a certified nurse's aide and a "real" hospital employee. Summer school would be over shortly thereafter, and she would get a break, albeit a short one. Things were looking pretty good, or at least, Kathy was pretty, and Patti was good.

At the end of her six-week onsite work, the nursing supervisor presented Kathy with her nursing certificate, then as promised, a lump-sum payment, which just happened to be a little more than originally planned, and finally, notification that she was a regular employee of the hospital. The issue was when she could work. Kathy explained she would only need time out for school and wondered if she could have hours scheduled more in the afternoon and early evenings. She also wanted to continue at the nursing home; she really enjoyed working with the elderly. The nursing supervisor agreed it was good experience and would be helpful when she applied for her LPN. They finally agreed to have her work Monday through Thursday, compatible with her school schedule. As their conference broke up, the nursing supervisor told Kathy. "I'm not supposed to tell you this, but we are very pleased with your work. We hope you'd be interested in working here after you complete your LPN program. The hospital would help you continue your nurse's training if you decide to 'stick' with us."

Kathy was very pleased. "Why thank you; I hadn't really thought about it, but I do enjoy working here. Yes, I will certainly consider your offer."

The end of summer school was hectic. Her one "easy" class was a cinch. The other class was harder; she had not got into a rhythm with it. Her grade was borderline A/B, and she decided to really hit the books and do well on the final. It paid off for her, but she had learned a lesson about managing her time and keeping up with her work. She also enrolled for the fall semester, scheduling a five-hour science class with a lab and another three-hour course.

After school ended, Kathy picked up another half shift at the nursing home; she now worked full shifts on Friday and Saturday. She continued to enjoy her work there although one of the residents passed away during the summer, which was sad. She got lots of attention; the old men would flirt, and the women would comment on how pretty she was. Many of the residents were fascinating, and she hoped when she got old, she would be as spry as some of them.

By Labor Day weekend, Kathy finally had a schedule that might last for a while; she had juco in the mornings for two to three hours except for Friday, when she only had one class. She had the option of working one and a half to two shifts on Friday and Saturday at the nursing home, then five or six hours every afternoon at the hospital Monday through Thursday.

Patti had suddenly begun to grow and required what seemed like gallons more milk; at times Kathy felt like a cow. She wondered just how much longer she could continue nursing; she had the option of giving Patti solid food, but wanted to put it off as long as possible. She had talked to her mother and the doctor, who both agreed Patti would function better the longer Kathy could nurse. Kathy did feel good about what she was doing, but she was busy Monday through Saturday. Thankfully, God made the seventh day for rest because by then Kathy really needed it; even the baby slept in on Sunday morning!

The first semester ended and she continued her record of excellent grades. Patti's first Christmas was not very exciting, but she was mobile now. Kathy had to keep an eye on her because she crawled everywhere. The apartment was far from child proof and Patti had no fear to poke her head anywhere it might fit. Kathy had little contact with anyone outside of work; there was always something to do and even when she got home, nothing got done if she didn't do it.

In March right before Patti's birthday, Kathy decided to wean her. Patti would sometimes drink from a cup, but often spilled much more than she drank and didn't seem interested; however, she had taken to solid food very well. Patti was standing and trying to walk, but not quite there; she seemed to actually prefer crawling, which she did well and quickly. She wore Kathy out trying to keep up with her. She did have a fabulous first birthday bash at the Benders where the whole family discovered, and had pictures to prove it, that Patti had a taste for cake; she demolished her birthday cake, and they finally had to take it away before she ate too much and got sick.

The end of the spring semester brought Kathy some good news. First of all, she had completed thirty-one semester hours at the juco, which meant she had the equivalent of one year of college. She then discovered her work at both the hospital and the nursing home would qualify as the onsite hours needed to receive her LPN. This would not shorten her class load, but would eliminate the need to do supervised work outside of class and would earn class credit when approved. The juco program required more hours and onsite time than were needed, but this was offset by the fact a student could transfer immediately to an RN program and not lose any credit or have to make up any work. Kathy was especially pleased because she fully intended to move on and didn't want to do any more than necessary. She decided to enroll in only one three-hour summer class. There was no reason to work herself to death, but if she could find a class she needed, it was probably best to get it out of the way.

The arrival of spring and warmer weather made the trips to

the park with Patti more interesting. As Patti became more mobile, Kathy turned her loose on the grass. Patti loved the park and the outdoors; she tried to chase squirrels and birds. She even hugged the trees. Kathy often got so tickled she would still be laughing when they got back to the apartment. Patti provided all the entertainment Kathy needed, and she marveled at the things Patti tried to do. In addition, she was also trying to talk; she would babble and yell, then grin as if she had really accomplished something. Kathy wondered what she was trying to say but figured she wouldn't have to wait much longer to find out.

The next year roared by so quickly Kathy almost didn't realize Patti had reached her "terrible twos" until her mother reminded her they wanted to have another birthday party. Patti was quite a charmer; she had never been a cute baby and wasn't pretty at age two, but she had spunk and more energy than a team of horses. She was independent and fearless; Kathy worked hard to keep her under control, and Patti got an occasional swat. She didn't like to be punished, so it didn't take her long to figure out she needed to follow directions. In public, people remarked how well she behaved; Kathy was grateful, but did not know how long the good times would last. One thing for sure, it was unlikely Patti would ever be spoiled by her grandparents. Kathy well remembered bits of wisdom like, "children need to know their place" and "you can make up your own rules when you pay the rent."

Kathy had completed fifty hours by the end of that spring semester. At first, she decided not to take any summer school, but at the last minute a class she needed opened. Fall enrollment was not finalized, but it appeared she had a chance to complete her degree requirements and graduate in December; the availability of her classes would make all the difference. Kathy made up her mind not to be disappointed; she knew her education would not be finished one way or the other. However, if she could get that LPN certificate, the extra income would let her buy a vehicle so she would not have to borrow her mother's car to go to the nursing home.

Summer rushed by. Kathy contacted her advisor on numerous occasions regarding the availability of the three final classes she needed. They had already enrolled her in two of them; the third was pending. At the very last minute, things fell into place, and the last class was offered. Kathy was thrilled; all she needed was to pass these courses and her first big step toward becoming a registered nurse was complete. The fall semester raced to the finish line, and Kathy was once again eligible for graduation, but if she wished to attend, it would have to wait until May—the only time the juco held formal ceremonies.

Christmas was very merry that year. Patti was old enough to understand about Santa; Kathy talked with her dad about buying a car, and of course, everyone was thrilled she was officially a nurse...though not yet registered. She was the first member of her family to have a college degree, and they were proud of what she had accomplished. The only dilemma was what to do for next year.

Kathy talked to the nursing supervisor at the hospital and discovered they would cover a large share of her expenses providing she would work full time when she finally became an RN. Kathy debated and finally decided to enroll during the regular fall semester; spring and summer would be a nice break from school. She looked forward to just working and saving money for future expenses. There would also be more time for herself and Patti.

Patti turned three in March. Kathy wondered if it was child abuse to tie Patti up and throw food at her two or three times a day. She had more energy than Superman. Kathy was often frazzled at the end of the day and in no condition to chase Patti around the apartment or race with her at the park. In addition, Patti had mastered several challenging words like "why," "no," and "when." She knew how to behave, but she was bright and not easily fooled by adults who often made the mistake of thinking little kids were dumb. Patti knew what she wanted, and Kathy learned she sometimes needed to compromise to keep the peace.

Spring rolled into summer and Kathy soon found herself enrolling in school. The RN program was a cooperative effort between the hospital, the juco, and a nursing school upstate. The hospital and juco provided the facilities; the nursing school provided instructors and support. Kathy had a big advantage by already working at the hospital and accumulating several years of experience. She also had the support of the hospital, which made it easier to have flexible hours and a "friendly" work schedule. However, Kathy had another two years plus of education with no guarantee she would be able to keep up with students who had no other obligations; it would be tough.

The pattern of study in the RN program was different. Some of the classes were more intense and Kathy found everything more serious and formal. She enjoyed her studies but struggled to adjust to the different environment. She worked hard during the fall semester and for the first time she could remember, she was genuinely thankful when it ended. She hadn't anticipated the pressure and intensity required day after day.

Over the Christmas holidays she debated with herself whether she could continue this pace; she did not have to take a full load of classes, but if she didn't, she would have to go to school for at least an extra year. She was growing weary of school, then going back to school, and so on. She finally decided to talk to her nursing supervisor, who fully understood her level of frustration; she'd been down that road. She told Kathy to hang in there for one more semester, then she would be over the hump. Next year would include the hands-on and onsite work Kathy could do blindfolded. What most encouraged Kathy was her supervisor's parting words. "Kathy, you can do this; I know you can." That was all anyone needed to say.

The spring semester was better. Kathy couldn't explain it. Maybe she was more focused, maybe she had a better sense of everything. As winter wound down, she was thinking about Patti's forthcoming birthday, four years old and quite the little lady. Total strangers would comment on how well Patti conducted herself; they couldn't believe she was not even four. In some circles she was known as a miracle child. Kathy wasn't that impressed, but Patti had always seemed older than she actually was; she had been around more adults than children. The first part of March had worn Kathy down and she was looking forward to their midterm break. All she really needed was a week or two of sleep and she would be fine; on the other hand, even one good night's rest would be welcome.

✙ Seven ✙

As Kathy readied for bed, a multitude of questions flashed through her mind. Was it even conceivable Patti would be starting to school in one more year? Should she be enrolled in preschool? Kathy was overwhelmed with thoughts and responsibilities. "If I can only make it to the weekend, I have Saturday off and maybe I can think through some of this." It was almost 10:00 pm, Patti was asleep, and Kathy could already feel the warm covers wrapped around her as she got into bed. She had decided to take her shower in the morning and go to bed before she fell asleep and collapsed somewhere in the apartment. "Oh, this bed feels good," she thought, pulling the covers up to her chin. She turned, twisted, and finally settled in just the right position; she would be asleep in just a few moments. "Life is goo..." This thought was interrupted by the phone. "Who on earth would be calling at this hour?" she thought, startled and apprehensive. "Hello? Who is this?" said Kathy, fumbling with the phone. No response. "I say, hello. Who's there?"

"Kathy, is that you?" said a garbled, unknown voice.

"Yes, this is Kathy Bender. Who is this?"

"I...well...Kathy, this is Sherry."

"Sherry, do you know what time it is? Don't you know working people have to go to bed because they have to get up in the morning?"

"Yeah, I know it's late...I'm in trouble...I called to say goodbye."

"You called to say goodbye; I don't understand; your voice

sounds funny. Are you okay?"

"No, I'm not okay; I'm drunk. I can't do what I've got to do sober."

"What have you got to do?"

"I can't say; I just want to say goodbye...I love you..." The phone went dead.

Kathy lay there confused, stunned, and frightened; suddenly, she was wide awake, and her nursing instincts seemed to take over. "Oh, my God! She's going to kill herself; that's why she wanted to say goodbye; that's got to be why she called." Kathy paused to collect her wits. "Be calm, Kathy, be calm. Think. How can I stop her? She's over 60 miles away!" Kathy remembered she had a contact number for Sherry; Sherry was never around, and she had given Kathy a number to call if there was something really pressing. Kathy rushed to her desk and rummaged through various papers until she found that note. The number was for a girl named Carol; Kathy didn't even know if Carol was still around, but she decided to call her instead of the police. She had no evidence to prove anything; Carol could at least check on Sherry. She dialed the number; the phone rang and rang. Finally, a response, "Hello, this is Carol; may I help you?"

"Yes, Carol, I hope you can. My name is Kathy Bender. I'm a good friend of Sherry Hughes..."

Carol interrupted. "Sherry has spoken of you."

Kathy's voice had tones of urgency. "Listen carefully. Will you check on Sherry, right now? Can you get into her room even if it's locked?"

"Yes, I'm an RA; I have a pass key."

"Okay, good. Listen, Sherry called me just a few minutes ago; she was drunk; and we got cut off. Could you check on her, then come right back and talk to me?"

"Sure, just a minute; she's only a few doors down the hall. I'll be right back..." Kathy waited.

"Kathy, are you still there?"

"Yes."

"She's passed out on the floor." Carol was out of breath, but not frantic.

Kathy remained calm. "Is she breathing? Did you happen to notice if she was alive?"

Carol was shocked. "What? Still alive! What do you mean?"

"Exactly what I said. Is she breathing?"

"Why I don't know. I think so. I'll go check..."

"Yes, she's breathing." Carol seemed much relieved.

"Okay, listen. I believe she is going to, or perhaps has already tried to, kill herself; I can't explain it right now. She told me she was drunk, and that may be our only problem. Can you go sit with her until I get there? I'm sure you've been trained on what to do; if you can get her to throw up, that would be helpful. I'm a nurse and I can be there in about an hour. I'm sorry to put you through of this, but that's why you get a free room in the dorm."

"Oh yeah, I get great perks for this job; I'll watch her." Carol sighed. "I don't want to call the police..."

Kathy interrupted. "Oh, I know, too much paper work."

Kathy called her mother to see if she could watch Patti and briefly explained the emergency. She bundled up Patti and had her delivered in short order; Patti hadn't even woke up...she would be surprised to wake in a different bed. Kathy was soon headed out of town half angry and confused. "What in the world had Sherry gotten herself into?"

As she drove, it was Sherry's life that flashed before her. Kathy had known Sherry forever. They had been chums since grade school, but it was funny; they had so very little in common. They both had two siblings, a brother and sister, but Kathy was a first born, and Sherry was the last hurrah. They both enjoyed music and liked to read. The Benders were hard working, simple people; Sherry's family had money. In fact, while Kathy grew up working at home, doing chores, and helping with her siblings, Sherry hardly knew the meaning of work. She was lost in a kitchen, would have starved to death in the Garden of Eden, and was helpless around anything mechanical.

Kathy, on the other hand, had learned to cook and sew at home. She had helped her mother in their garden. She was no mechanic, but she was not afraid to tear into anything and try to fix it. The Benders were generally faithful in their church attendance, and Sherry hardly knew what the inside of a church looked like. One thing Sherry did like to do was shop and spend money; she could spend more money in one day than Kathy spent in six months. The more Kathy thought about it, the more she wondered why they had ever been friends. And yet, Kathy loved Sherry; she was the only friend who had stood beside her, offering support and counsel, while Kathy was pregnant.

Between thinking about Sherry and the fact she probably broke every speed limit along the entire route, she arrived at State University in record time. Fortunately, she found a vacant visitor parking space, and the dorm was still open. She announced herself at the front desk and proceeded to Sherry's room; she knocked and Carol came to the door. "How's our patient?"

"Well, I'm no doctor, but I've seen my share of drunks, and I'd say she'll live."

Kathy reassured Carol. "She's no drunk, but I appreciate your staying with her. What has happened since we spoke on the phone?"

"Well, I got her on the bed. She started to gag, then threw up in the waste basket."

"Did she throw up any pills or unusual solids?"

Carol made a yuck face. "I really didn't look."

"Has she said anything that makes sense?"

"She mumbled a few words and then kept repeating the word 'goodbye;' I heard her say your name once, maybe twice; she is pretty well out of it."

"Carol, what I have to do may get ugly. If you need to go, I understand, but if you stay, I may need help. It's your choice."

"I'll stay; I want her to be okay."

"Good enough."

Kathy walked over to Sherry, grabbed her shoulders, and shook her firmly. No response. Kathy repeated the process with the same result. She reached out and slapped Sherry sharply across her cheek. This time Sherry twitched a bit and seemed to respond; Kathy slapped her again. This time it had the desired effect. Sherry opened her eyes and raised up somewhat. "Kathy, what are you doing?"

"I'm here to beat you within an inch of your life, and Carol's going to help me. Right?" Carol nodded.

Sherry was obviously confused. "Why are you going to do that?"

Kathy was frank and blunt. "It will make both of us feel better."

Sherry moaned. "I want you to leave me alone; I don't feel well."
"Of course you don't; you're drunk and sick and smell like vomit."

"You don't have to be nasty."

"Nasty! What I'd like to do is kick your butt and then kick it again just for fun. I've got to ask you some questions, and I need straight answers. Can you handle that?"

"I'll try."

"Okay, did you take anything...like pills, or drugs?"

"Noooo..."

"Did you drink anything besides the alcohol, anything else?"

"Just the vodka...that's all."

"Have you eaten anything since supper?"

"The vodka was my supper."

"Okay, Carol, we need to get her up and walking, then I think a cold shower might help. After we get her dressed, I'm taking her home for the weekend. Will you be here Sunday?" Carol nodded. "Good, I'll talk with you then. You've been great."

Carol was impressed. "Hey, girl, when you take charge; you don't fool around."

Kathy made an attempt to smile. "Thank you; I'll take that as a compliment."

They walked Sherry and kept her talking as best they could; it seemed to help, but she had trouble standing unassisted. The girls decided she was ready for the shower so they stripped her to her underwear and led her to the bathroom. It took one girl each holding one of Sherry's arms to keep her standing. The shower scene was ugly. Sherry screamed and pulled, then pulled and screamed. A couple of girls came in to investigate, but left promptly when they realized it was therapy and not murder. Soon Sherry was turning blue and shaking badly. The girls decided she would get hypothermia if they continued, so they got her out and dried off as quickly as possible. She was still shaking as they removed her wet clothes and got a heavy bathrobe around her. Kathy suggested. "Let's get her back to her room and dressed; I think she'll be okay now."

"She's much more responsive." Carol then paused. "I can help you get her to the car when she's ready."

"Thank you. You've been a good friend."

Kathy found some warm clothes and got Sherry dressed; she gathered a few toiletries and some casual wear and put them in bag. "Sherry, you're coming with me."

"I know." They loaded Sherry into Kathy's car and were soon on their way.

It was quiet for a long time, then Sherry broke the ice. "Kathy, I need to talk to you; it's important."

"And I need to talk to you."

"Okay, you go first."

"All right, I want to know some things; Do you remember calling me tonight?"

Sherry nodded. "Yes, I called you to say goodbye."

"Do you know how strange that sounds? You want to say goodbye to me now because you're going to graduate in two months, and we won't see each other for a long time?" Kathy was confused.

"No, I called you to say goodbye because I planned to kill myself, and I wouldn't be seeing you or anyone else again."

Thankfully, before Kathy lost control of the car, the turning lane for a rest area appeared; she awkwardly pulled into the parking area, slamming on the brakes, then turned to Sherry. "What? You're going to kill yourself; I ought to kill you just for thinking it! What has gotten into you!?"

Sherry's face filled with sadness. "Kathy, I'm no good and worthless; I just realized it tonight. The world will be better off without me."

"Good grief! What makes you think that!?"

Sherry had been looking down; she looked up, turned to Kathy, and her voice broke. "Kathy, I...I'm...I'm going...I'm pregnant."

Kathy was appalled. "You're what!?"

"I'm pregnant." Tears started to flow down Sherry's cheeks. "What's more, and there is more, I don't know who the father is; I don't know for sure when it happened, and I didn't even get to enjoy the sex! I don't want a baby; I don't want an abortion; and I don't want to live. Will you kill me? You're a nurse; you know about these things; please kill me."

Aghast and speechless, Kathy sat in a state of complete shock. Her mind was going forward at a hundred miles per hour, but her body was in reverse. Finally, without thinking, the word "no" escaped from her mouth, then again, only louder. Sherry was crying so loudly she didn't hear anything. Then it came out loud and clear. "No, I'm not going to kill you! I'm a nurse; I'm supposed to help people, not kill them!"

Sherry was taken back. "Well, you don't have to shout; I knew you wouldn't do it."

Kathy was very annoyed. "Then why did you ask?"

Now it was Sherry's turn to shout. "I'm desperate! You know I can't do it myself; I'm a coward!"

"Sherry, I've slapped you twice tonight, and so help me, I want to drag you out of this car and beat you within an inch of your life...but I will not kill you. Here is what we are going to do. You're coming home with me; we're going to sleep in the same bed so I can keep an eye on you. I'm going to take tomorrow off, and we're going to sit down and figure out this mess. If you even mention suicide or killing yourself to me one more time, you're going to wish you were never born; I'll have none of it!" Kathy was very intense.

Sherry, who was still crying gathered herself and looked at Kathy. "You don't want me to die. You still love me. We're still friends, aren't we? You care for me. How can you do it?"

Kathy sighed. "Cause that's what friends do; they care for each other...I shouldn't have to tell you."

Kathy and Sherry didn't say another thing as Kathy drove home. Sherry continued crying, occasionally sniffling and blowing her nose; Kathy felt tears trickle down her cheeks, but tried to concentrate on her driving. She couldn't help Sherry if she killed both of them, wrecking the car. Kathy was relieved when she saw the familiar outskirts of her hometown, and only a few minutes later they pulled up in front of the warehouse. They quickly ascended the old fire escape and entered the apartment. The heat felt good, and Kathy had a chill inside that needed warming. "Okay, I don't know about you, but I'm not doing my pajamas; you need to understand that even though I'm really tired, I don't sleep the way I used to...it's a baby thing...so if you do anything weird, it will wake me up."

"I'll be good; I promise. I don't have pajamas either so don't worry about that; we're both in the same boat...or should I say, bed."

With that, the girls climbed into Kathy's bed, seeking its warmth and security. Once there, Kathy felt Sherry reach for her hand; Kathy pulled her closer. They hugged for a few moments, and Kathy kissed Sherry the same way she kissed Patti when she tucked her in bed.

"Kathy, thank you for coming to get me; you may have saved my life. You're probably the only person I know who cares enough to do that. I'm sorry about this; I love you."

"Sherry, thank you for being my friend; it has meant a lot

to me. We'll work everything out tomorrow; I promise. I'm so tired right now...I'll see you the morning..." If she intended to say more it would have to be in her sleep.

The next morning Kathy opened her eyes to the light streaming into the apartment. She needed to call her mother to see if she could continue watching Patti, at least for the morning; she needed to call work and tell them she simply could not be there. Of course, she needed to talk with Sherry and figure out how she managed to get pregnant. She also realized she had something in her hand; it felt like another hand...in fact, there was someone in her bed, and even though she knew it was Sherry, it was strange not to wake up alone. She could tell Sherry was sleeping and didn't want to wake her; she needed to rest. Kathy slipped out of bed and decided they would start their day with a good breakfast. Sherry was not an early riser so there was no rush, but she had to be awake enough for them to visit and make some sense of this.

Kathy set the table and prepared breakfast, then went to Sherry and tried to rouse her. Sherry finally yawned and told Kathy, "I'll help you with breakfast; I'm starved."

"You mean last night's vodka didn't stick to your ribs?"

"No, it's stuck in my head; do you serve aspirin with breakfast?"

"Not usually, but I can get you a couple if you'd like."

"Oh, I'd very much like, if you don't mind."

"Well, breakfast is ready; I see you're already dressed."

"Oh, yes, it's the latest thing at State; you should try it." Sherry smiled.

"Why, yes, I must do that." Kathy posed making grand flourishes. "Let's eat!"

Breakfast was wonderful. Not that the food was any better or worse than usual; it was nice to enjoy eating and not be

77

on the way to somewhere else. Both girls were hungry, so not much was said during their meal, but as soon as the dishes and food were put away and the table cleaned, Kathy motioned for Sherry to come to the living room. "Let's talk." The girls sat down. "Sherry, I've been thinking about your situation; we need to figure out what happened before we try to decide what to do. Is that all right?"

"It's okay with me, Kathy, but you'll have to do all the figuring; I'm totally confused."

"Try to clear your head and let's see what we can come up with. Let's go back to the first of the year. Have you had a date or gone out with anyone this semester?"

"No, this is my last semester and I had to take an extra class in order to graduate; I've just been too busy."

"Okay, have you gone to any parties or been out with friends since this term began?"

Sherry brought her hand to her head. "Well, not really, I went to a couple of dorm parties, but I didn't stay very long and no men were present."

"Are you sure you haven't been..."

"Wait a minute! I came back to school a couple of days early, and some of the girls told me about this party; they invited me to come along. At first I didn't want to go, but the more I thought about it, I figured why not have a good time; it's going to be tough semester."

"Okay, what happened there?"

"Well, Kathy, that's just it; nothing happened. I mean there was music; people were dancing; people were drinking; you know, it was just a party—nothing rowdy."

"What did you do?"

"I remember I had a couple of drinks; I talked with a girl I hadn't seen for a while; one of the guys asked me to dance;

78

I think I had a couple more drinks. Then I remember I just felt tired and sat down; I tried to talk to this girl sitting next to me, but I couldn't keep my eyes open. I must have gone to sleep because the next thing I knew I woke up on the same sofa I'd been sitting on. It was kind of weird; that had never happened before. Several other people were lying around asleep, and I'm sure other people were there...you know, doing a variety of disgusting things. I decided I'd go back to the dorm."

"Okay, now think carefully about this. What time did you go to the party?"

"Oh, it must have been between 10:00 and 11:00 pm; let's just say 10:30."

"What time did you go home?"

"Well, I remember looking at the clock and thinking I was glad I didn't have to get up the next day; I think it was almost 4:00 in the morning."

"Okay, so you left the party around 3:30, you would have been there about five hours."

"I guess so."

"Do you have any idea how long you were you asleep?"

"Well, I'm not sure; I can only guess, but I'd say two to two and half hours."

"Okay, I'm going to change the subject. When did you find out you were pregnant?"

"Yesterday morning, the day I called you."

"When did your have your last period?"

"In late December; it was over before New Year's Eve."

"So you didn't have a period in January and none in February. What made you think you were pregnant?"

"Well, duh, you're a nurse...I didn't have a period for a couple of months; I haven't been sick; and while this semester has been stressful, I'm a senior, you know, been there, done that!"

"Okay, Sherry, here's what I think happened; I wasn't there, and in some ways you weren't either, but I think you were drugged at that party; while you were unconscious someone took advantage of you. You probably weren't the only one, based on what you told me. In other words, to be very blunt, you were raped!" Kathy's words ripped into Sherry.

Sherry looked at Kathy; her expression indicated little surprise, but a sadness seemed to engulf her. "I was afraid you'd say something like that; it's kind of like two plus two is four. We solved the problem, but I'm still screwed..."

Kathy quickly interrupted. "And we can't change that. The question is what are we going to do about it?"

"What can we do? There's no evidence to present two months after the fact, and there's no real proof...except that I'm pregnant."

"Agreed, but I think you still need to report it and see if the authorities will investigate. My bet is the perpetrator is still around and doing the same dirty work; one way or another he should be neutered with no anesthetic."

"What do you think I should do?"

"Well, first of all I think you need to report it to the university authorities and try to find out if anyone else has reported a similar incident. Then I think I'd go see the police there and do the same thing. Finally, I think we should go see our law enforcement people; we have a pretty good police department and they might be more sympathetic to your case than the police in a college town. I can't imagine what things are like there, but I'm sure it's a mess. What do you think?" Kathy was feeling more like Nancy Drew, the detective, than a LPN.

"Well, I guess. I don't want the dirty 'so and so' to get away with this, but I think we're probably wasting our time." Sherry looked a bit woebegone.

"You want me to go with you, don't you?"

"Kathy...I feel silly...I mean, I don't know what I mean...yes, I'd like you to come with me; I'm sorry I'm such a bother." Sherry started to cry.

Kathy was now crying too. "Sherry, if you don't stop this, I'll be too dehydrated to go anywhere, and you'll turn into a prune." Kathy attempted to laugh.

They looked at each other crying and laughing, held out their arms, and then said almost simultaneously, "I love you," followed by a long, firm hug.

The girls, or at least Kathy, thought they should get changed and go the police right then and get it out of the way. They could get an official opinion on what to do since Nancy Drew wasn't 100% right on every case. When they got to the police station, they were referred to the new officer assigned to vice, Detective Johnson, who appeared to be in her mid twenties. She listened intently to what they had to say. "Sherry, I want you to know that I really feel bad for you. I have no idea what you plan to do, but no one should have to be making life decisions under these circumstances. You need to know one of the main reasons I am sitting here is to get scumbags like this off the street!"

Sherry and Kathy were surprised at her frankness and sincerity. Detective Johnson added, "This will be a difficult case, but I am going to do everything I can to investigate it and get justice for you. I do have some questions. Sherry, have you ever had any legal malfeasance? Have you ever been arrested or cited for any crime?"

"No, ma'am, I've never even had a speeding ticket; I've not had any problems at State either."

"Good, that's very good. How well do you remember that evening?"

"Well, Kathy and I have been going over it, and it has helped a lot. I feel pretty comfortable with my memories although it was a long time ago, and of course, if I was drugged, I can't be certain about everything."

"No, Sherry, you're doing fine. Can you give me the names of any of the people there; did you know any of them?"

"Why yes, I knew quite a few."

"Oh, Sherry, that's great. I want you to write down all of the names you can remember. We'll rattle this tree and see what falls out. I feel really good about this; I mean it. You have been so helpful. I'm convinced there were witnesses to your assault and if I can get them to talk, we'll catch this bastard...er, pardon my French."

Sherry tried to clarify the situation. "That's okay, this rat is a bastard...but I'm pretty sure that "bastard" is an English word; you know, from the British Isles."

Kathy looked at detective Johnson who looked back to see Kathy tapping her temple and glancing at Sherry; the detective nodded and smiled. "Sherry, you're one in a million!" Kathy and the detective started to laugh.

Detective Johnson agreed that Sherry needed to report her assault to the university authorities; she doubted they would do much investigating, but they could provide valuable information without one hundred pounds of red tape. She then told Sherry to go to the police station at State and inform them she had reported the crime to the authorities here, and Detective Johnson would contact them to coordinate her investigation and maybe use their facilities to question witnesses and suspects. Kathy asked if it would be possible for her to get information on how the case was progressing since she felt involved and wanted to be kept up to date. Detective Johnson then asked Sherry if that was okay, and she had no problems with it. They both thanked the detective for her help and support.

On the way back to the apartment, Kathy asked Sherry, "Do you think we did the right thing?"

"Yes, I feel better about it; at least I know I have support that carries a little weight. I have just felt so helpless in this and, Kathy, thank you for being my friend and caring; it means so much to me."

⌲ Eight ⌲

When the girls got back to the apartment, Kathy called her mother to see about picking up Patti. Her Mother said Patti wanted to eat lunch with them because she had helped prepare it; Patti didn't get an opportunity to work in the kitchen very often, and she enjoyed helping. Mrs. Bender could bring her home after they had eaten. With that problem settled, Kathy asked Sherry, "Okay, can we talk some more or would you rather have lunch?"

"I'm not hungry yet; let's get this over with so we can dwell on more pleasant things like root canals and gall stones."

"Oh boy, just what the doctor ordered!" Kathy groaned. "Okay, this is the part that's going to be tough for both of us, but not for the same reasons. I know you said you could not abort the baby, and I'm glad you feel that way. I can't help being pro-life and I know you appreciate my position. As I see it, the question is what are you going to do with the baby? You have about seven months worth of pregnancy to deal with and some really hard decisions; I don't want to sound mean, but I'm not sure you want to make any of them, and if I were in your shoes, I might feel the same way. Does that make any sense to you?"

"I think so...Kathy, I don't know what to do; I just found out yesterday I was pregnant, which about blew me away, and now I have to decide what I'm going to do with a baby that doesn't really belong to me...if you get my drift."

"Sure I get your drift; at least I knew who the father was, but I sure as heck did not want a baby. It doesn't matter how good the sex was; neither Brandon nor I had any intention of starting a family. And Sherry, it's unfair; we both know plenty of girls who go out and sleep with anything on two legs and don't get pregnant. Here I had

83

sex one time, just one lousy time and, bingo, I'm knocked up; then look at you! For crying out loud, you had sex and didn't even know it, and you're pregnant!" Kathy was almost screaming. "It's just not fair!"

"What do you think I should do?"

"Listen, Sherry, you're over twenty-one, and you don't have to pay any attention to what I think, but here goes. Priority #1, you've got to finish this semester and graduate from college. No one wants to hire someone that 'almost' got her degree. You only have two months left, and you won't even be showing by then. Can you do that?"

"Absolutely, I want to. I can do that."

"Okay, the next thing is, you need a summer job, a place to stay, and probably someone to look after you; you can be pretty irresponsible at times. For example, some people would say that getting drunk when you're pregnant could be called child endangerment..."

Sherry whined. "Ah, come on, Kathy, I wanted to die."

"I'm not accusing you; I'm just saying sometimes you're kind of crazy."

"I suppose I am a bit crazy; I get it from being around you." Sherry smiled.

"Probably so, but I'd like for you to stay with Patti and me after you graduate. We can help each other. Patti likes you, and I could teach you a thing or two about managing a home; you do know you are going to be on your own around mid-May, don't you?"

"I don't want to talk about it; I won't last a week on my own, and you know it," Sherry's voice conveyed sadness.

"Well, what do you think about living here; I've got plenty of room; you don't really need anything but a bed, and we can surely find one around here some place. If you get a job, you can help out with our expenses, and maybe even watch Patti when I'm in a pinch. I think it would be good for you to get this experience, and after the baby is born, you can focus on getting a permanent job and relocating. What do you think?"

"Well, it's the best offer I've had, and probably the only one I'm going to get. I'll take it."

"Oh, Sherry, that's great; I'm excited about it. We'll make it work; I know we will. Oh, by the way, just one more word...moo!" Kathy sort of laughed.

"Hey, that's not as funny as it used to be, but I guess you're right...moo!" Sherry tried to smile, but it was not easy.

The girls prepared lunch and tried to forget about their immediate problems. They talked about old times, looked through some pictures of Patti, and just acted silly. Kathy couldn't remember having so much fun, and Sherry seemed comfortable and relaxed. They were good for each other, but it worked best when one of them was pregnant. Mrs. Bender brought Patti home around 2:00; they had enjoyed "doing" lunch. Kathy was always pleased when her mother could take Patti because she had more free time to spend with her. She also knew Patti was in good hands and her mother would make Patti behave. Kathy worried about being a failure as a parent because she didn't want to raise a rebellious child; she'd seen enough of those to know she didn't want to come home to one every night.

Patti liked Sherry and was excited to learn she would be living with them during the summer. The girls didn't mention the details of this extended stay, but it would certainly have to be explained when Sherry began to show; Patti was aware of mommies and babies, so she would not be fooled long. Patti and Sherry played for a while, then Patti wanted to watch a kiddy show on television. This gave Kathy and Sherry a chance to discuss forthcoming plans. "Sherry, what do you think? I have been trying to decide if I should send Patti to preschool; I have several options, one of which would not cost anything. I just don't know what to do, especially now that you're going to be here."

Sherry looked puzzled. "Gosh, how would I know? It doesn't look to me like Patti is behind or has any learning problems; in fact, she has always seemed quite bright. I think I'd skip it and let her start kindergarten next year."

"Well, Mom doesn't think she needs to go, and you don't think she needs to go, so I think we'll just forget it, and I'll give her another year at home. I just wondered what you thought since you're part of the family now."

"Kathy, I suppose this will sound silly. I have never felt like I was part of any family. I was a tail ender and to be honest, I don't think my folks wanted me. I was an accident. My older brother and sister were gone from home by the time I started school. My folks let me do whatever I wanted. I felt closer to your family than mine. I don't see any reason to tell them about my situation. I guess they would be concerned, but they would just tell me to make the best of it or get an abortion and move on."

Kathy frowned and nodded. "Sherry, I feel bad for you; it's hard to imagine being in your situation."

Sherry looked straight at Kathy. "I've never told you this, but the reason I liked you was because you had a family; you guys care about each other, and I think that attracted me to you. I mean, you know we are nothing alike, and yet I have always considered you my best friend. Maybe I thought being around you would help me; you are so sensible and make good decisions. I suppose I secretly wanted to be more like you; I'm such a goofball, and sometimes I even scare myself, but you have always been there, and this is another example to prove it. I can't thank you enough."

"You humble me with your comments. I just want you to know that even though we are very different, I have always felt close to you. I used to feel sorry for you because I know your family didn't seem to care if you were dead or alive. You were always welcome in my family; you made us laugh, and I'm not sure we did enough of that. You know my parents are more serious than a lot of people, but you brought sunshine in our lives. We owe you our thanks for that. I don't want you to ever feel like you have no value; you are very special."

"You know, we should talk like this more often; it makes me feel good."

"I agree. I know you think highly of me, Sherry, and I sincerely appreciate it, but I have never felt more ashamed than five years ago when I told you, and only you, that I was pregnant. Here I was, in your eyes, the perfect Kathy Bender, but in my eyes I felt no different from a cheap whore. Now before you interrupt me and tell me to not be so hard on myself, we both know I'm no cheap whore; I've only had sex three times, all with the same boy, in my entire life...but I got caught, and she's sitting right over there watching TV."

"And, Kathy, she's a wonderful little girl." Sherry now had tears in her eyes.

"I know, Sherry; that's why you've got to keep your situation in perspective and not dwell on the negative; it can spoil all the good that comes from a bad situation."

About this time Kathy realized that even though she had called the hospital about work, she hadn't been to school either. She was trying to remember what she might need to do. It finally occurred to her they were doing onsite work; it would all be review, so she hadn't missed anything important. When she began her RN program, she had been forced to quit working on Fridays at the nursing home; she now worked either Saturday or Sunday, and occasionally both when needed. She did not want to quit working there because she liked the older people; she had become friends with many of them and it would be difficult to leave. This weekend she was to work on Sunday, so she could spend time with Sherry and restore a little normalcy to her life before going back to school.

The girls talked about their evening and finally decided to fix a nice supper and have a glass of wine. Sherry suggested they rent a couple of movies and just chill. Kathy thought that would be okay, so Sherry took Patti to pick up the movies and Kathy started supper. By the time they got back, the apartment began to smell like someone might be working in the kitchen. They decided to watch the first movie before supper to get an early start and not have to stay up late. Sherry had picked out one video she thought Patti would like so they watched it first. The movie was funny; it was nice to be together and laugh after a difficult day. When supper was ready, they stopped the video and ate; everyone managed to eat too much so there was no talk of popcorn or treats to go with the second movie. The evening was delightfully peaceful.

As Kathy put Patti to bed, the girls visited. "Well, have we got things settled?"

"Oh, Kathy, I hope so; I'm a wreck, but I think we have things figured out. I need to finish school, spend the summer and fall with you, have my baby, and try to find work. It sounds simple, but I have to tell you I'm scared."

"Well, you have very right to be; I know I was scared before Patti was born. Gosh, here I was pregnant, trying to finish high school, sick as a dog part of the time, and getting bigger by the second. It was scary; I don't care what anyone says. If you want to get really morbid, consider that, at one time, more women died from childbirth than any other condition. If that doesn't frighten you, you may already be dead!"

"Hey, thanks for cheering me up." Sherry looked somewhat forlorn.

"What are friends for, if not to support you in your hour of need?" Kathy flashed a smile.

"Yeah, but in my case, it's going to take longer than an hour." Sherry started to grin.

"Oh, yeah, days...maybe weeks...or months, heaven forbid!"

"Say, Kathy, I guess I have one more question for you?"

"Shoot."

"Well, I was wondering, you know...I just wondered if I could sleep with you again tonight?" Sherry looked a bit sheepish.

"Now, Sherry, what do you think people will say if word gets out that we're sleeping together? Patti is only a few yards away. What will she think?"

"Look, I'm not going to tell anyone, and to be honest, I don't think Patti gives a hoot what we do. I just think I'll feel better sleeping with you."

"Why?"

"Because...well, you...I mean...you've got warm feet!"

"Oh Sherry, I'm going to bop you right on the head." Sherry avoided Kathy's attempt to swat her by running and jumping in her bed.

Everyone slept in for a while Saturday morning. As they did rouse, they decided to have brunch and just take it easy for the rest of the morning. Mrs. Bender called to ask if Maggie could take Patti to the park in the afternoon. That would not be a problem, and it would give Kathy and Sherry more time together.

After brunch, they sat down to chat. "Are you going to be okay?" asked Kathy.

"Yes, I think so. To be really honest, I'm not sure it has all soaked in yet, but I'm dealing with it."

"I don't want you to think you are in this alone, and I'm certainly not going to talk to anyone about it, but Sherry, I know you, and you frighten me sometimes. The idea you were going to kill yourself nearly ripped me in half. I don't want anything bad to happen to you. Promise me you will make this work. If there is anything I can do, please give me a chance. Is that clear?"

"Kathy, I'm awfully sorry I got you in this mess; I was drunk. I don't think I could ever kill myself, but I called you...I guess because somehow I knew you wouldn't let anything bad happen to me. I know I stood by you when you were pregnant, and now it looks like the tables have turned. I promise I will be good; I promise I will have this baby. Beyond that I can't say. I know this will sound funny, but I truly do love you. Thank you for caring about me." Sherry began to cry.

"Sherry, I love you too; you've been a good friend." Kathy reached for and hugged Sherry.

Very shortly, Maggie arrived to pick up Patti, noting that the adults in the room were not even dressed for the day. Kathy threw a sneaker at her as she scurried out the door with Patti, who laughed at this little escapade. During the quiet moments after they left, Kathy realized Maggie and Patti had much in common. They both enjoyed the outdoors, running around and being crazy. They were both rough and tumble and never cried unless they were really hurt. Kathy was amazed at the pounding Patti would take and just come back for more. Maybe it was good to be more that way, to be tough. The world outside could be very dangerous; she, Sherry, and Patti all had to live there.

Kathy and Sherry lounged and relaxed; Sherry wanted to bathe before they traveled. Kathy gathered everything she could find belonging to Sherry and added a surprise or two. By the time Maggie brought Patti home, and they had her clean and dressed, it was time to "hit the road." Sherry entertained Patti, Kathy kept the car rolling, and they were soon at school saying goodbye. They agreed to keep in touch. Kathy told Sherry to stay focused on school; it would be silly to blow everything now. Sherry assured her she would roll up her sleeves and work hard. Kathy's final advice was insightful, "Sherry, remember, no one knows you're pregnant; you have no reason to be embarrassed. Square everything with Carol so she doesn't add you to the loony list and I think you will be okay. After you graduate, you can move in with us, and we can help each other. Keep your head screwed on straight...no drinking to excess and no skydiving. If you need me, you know my number. I love you. Moo."

Sherry glanced quickly at Kathy and smiled. "You guys are the greatest," and kissed them both on the cheek.

Patti, still trying to understand everything, added, "I luv you too...moo."

Sherry was so amused she bumped her head as she got out of the car and Kathy was about to burst. Patti had to be wondering about these strange adults.

On the way home, Kathy told Patti Sherry would be living with them for a while after school was out in May. Patti was excited because she liked Aunt Sherry. Kathy never asked but wondered where Patti had connected the word *aunt* with Sherry, but guessed it didn't matter...*Aunt Sherry* had a nice ring to it...just like *Aunt Maggie* did.

Toward the first of April, Kathy got a call from Detective Johnson; she apologized for not communicating sooner. They had been working Sherry's case and had gotten numerous leads, many of which seemed to be checking out; they had narrowed down the suspect list to two or three people. In addition, they had witnesses willing to testify. They hoped to break the case within the next week or so because they wanted to wrap everything up before school ended. She would share more details when they arrested the perpetrators. Kathy thanked her for the info and said she would forward it to Sherry, saving the detective some time. Kathy in turn called Sherry, who surprisingly was in her room, and told her the news. Sherry was pleased they might catch the dirty so-and-so. She also told Kathy school was going well and she had been approved for graduation, assuming she passed her classes. Yes, she was feeling okay; no problems had developed and she was getting used to not having her period. Kathy had to admit it was one of the few perks of pregnancy.

Almost like clock work, the detective called about a week later and asked if she could meet with Kathy and Sherry the next evening when Sherry was out of class. Kathy called Sherry and finally managed to catch her. Yes, she could come. Early the next evening they met at the police station. The detective thanked them for being there; she knew they were busy. She began her report, "I know this is going to shock you. If you want me to stop at any point, just ask. I apologize for having to share this information, but I know ultimately you'll both want and need to know it.

"First of all, Sherry, we caught these SOB's, and no matter what you think of them right now, I can guarantee you will think even less when I'm through. There were three of them: two who did the deed, and an accomplice. They've been at this for a while and in order to be 'fair,' they rotated their responsibilities so each could get in on the action. The accomplice spiked the drinks; his two buddies committed the assaults. We cannot say for sure but as many as six of the girls who attended that party were raped by these guys; we think some of you were probably raped by both of them.

"In any event, on the night in question, while they admitted to wearing condoms, they have no idea whether any of them failed—because they were drunk and didn't pay any attention. In fact they cannot remember who had who or who did what. When we asked them to identify from pictures whom they assaulted, they only managed to get one right...and for the record, Sherry, it wasn't you. Regrettably, I have no way of knowing which of these 'boys' assaulted you; it's possible they both did. I'm just sorry the whole thing ever happened.

"We may have some really good news though. They are going to plead guilty. We have so much evidence against them it is an open and shut case. There will be no trial, no testifying, no further embarrassment to any of their victims. I don't think their guilty plea will lessen their sentencing; they will be going away for a long time; they won't even get to finish school, and we are granting them no leniency at our end. Do you have any questions?"

"Why did they do this?" asked Sherry, looking very sad.

"I think because they could; I don't even think it was the sex. They thought they could get away with it so it was okay; to be honest, it makes me sick."

Sherry looked at the detective stunned. "So I was just a piece of meat."

"That's what I think."

"Well, I hope the bastards rot in jail, and I'm not making any excuse for my French."

Kathy looked at Sherry, shocked to hear her respond in such a way, but she was fighting back tears and decided to keep her mouth shut. Sherry had said enough. The girls thanked the detective for her help and support; she in turn informed them these young men could be held responsible for this situation and ordered by the court to pay for her medical expenses. Sherry said she was covered by her parents' health insurance; they had already paid for her preliminary examinations, but she would keep it in mind.

On the way back to their cars, the girls were silent. Sherry opened her door and sat in the seat. She looked up at Kathy and started to cry. "Oh, Kathy, why did this have to happen?"

"Sherry, I've asked myself that same question a thousand times; I still don't have an answer, but I have Patti, who now calls you Aunt Sherry." Sherry smiled through her tears. "I only know there has to be some good that comes from it. I don't know what it will be, but I believe it will work out for the best. Remember, Patti and I love you and want to help."

"I know you do and I thank you for it every day. Look, I'll be seeing you again soon; I've only got about a month of school. I love you guys. I'd better get back and get my head straight. You take care; I may need a full time nurse just to take care of me, and you're my first choice."

"Well, thanks, thanks a lot." Kathy pondered. "I guess."

⟡ Nine ⟡

The tears from April did indeed bring the blossoms of May. First of all, Kathy completed her third year of nursing school was pleasantly surprised when the nursing supervisor advised her she would be receiving an in-house promotion accompanied by a salary increase. Kathy would not have any more school until the fall semester, giving her more time to focus on Patti, and on her newest addition, a second child, who was not only older than Patti, but even older than she was! Despite the tragedy that had befallen Sherry, Kathy was thrilled to have her with them and influence her decision about the baby. Kathy was indeed conflicted. On the one hand, she knew Sherry did not want to keep the baby, even though she had never said so. On the other hand, she really believed Sherry needed this responsibility; Sherry had a lot of growing up to do. Would being a single mother make any difference?

Kathy finally decided to attend Sherry's graduation; she didn't figure anyone from Sherry's real family would be there. Kathy was amused that Patti was awed by the pomp and circumstance of this ceremony, then realized Patti had probably never seen so many people in one place at the same time. A lady sitting next to them complimented Patti on being so well behaved; Kathy assured her Patti was very normal at home. They laughed. Patti was the first to spot Aunt Sherry, who had no idea they were there. Thankfully, the ceremony was short, and when the president of the university invited everyone to step forward and congratulate the graduates, Kathy had to restrain Patti from charging forward and doing the entire job by herself. When they finally did break through the mob, Sherry was surprised to see her new sister and mom. Patti spoke first, "Aunt Sherry, I like your hat."

Sherry was unprepared for these remarks, but managed to thank Patti for the compliment. "Patti, this is just a costume we have to wear for graduation, and if you like my hat, I'll let you wear it later."

Patti was almost more excited than she had been at

Christmas. "Oh, Aunt Sherry, you're the best; I love you!"

Kathy followed. "Can I wear the hat too?"

"I think you guys are a bit too caught up in this. You need to calm down." Sherry tried not to laugh.

"But I want to wear the hat too."

Sherry turned to the girl next to her. "What do you do with friends like this?"

The girl looked at them and smiled. "You've got to love 'em."

Sherry turned and looked at Patti and Kathy with a tear in at least one eye. "Hey, thank you for coming; I love you."

There followed a group hug; even the girl who offered advice joined the celebration.

Kathy asked if Sherry needed any help with her things, but Sherry had been packing her car for the last two days, and nothing was left, probably a good thing since her car barely had room for her! She had to check in with some of the staff people to verify addresses and complete a checklist. Sherry "checked out" fine, and they were soon on their way to the biggest apartment in their hometown.

After they arrived and emptied Sherry's car, Kathy attempted to share information that would help Sherry survive in their apartment. Kathy had found a nice bed frame with an almost new mattress and springs, locating it near her bed opposite the room from Patti. There were virtually no walls in the apartment which afforded little privacy. Kathy had gotten used to running around half dressed in her underwear, especially when it was warm. If that offended Sherry, she needed to let them know. Mr. Mitchell had finished building the walls around the bathroom, so it offered some seclusion. She wanted Sherry to feel comfortable and enjoy her surroundings. Sherry insisted she was okay with everything; in the summer a lot of people run around half naked to keep cool, so why not be comfortable in your own home. Sherry was at ease in the apartment and was grateful for their support.

Once they had most of Sherry's things unpacked and moved near her living area, the girls began to chat. Kathy said, "I want to congratulate you again on finishing your degree and getting out of school; I have to wait one more year...and it can't come too soon. How are you feeling? I noticed you aren't getting big yet, which is good."

"Kathy, I know how sick you were with Patti, but except for occasional flutters in my stomach, I have been fine. I haven't even gained much weight."

"You don't want to...unless you are going to name the baby Horse or Hippo. You may start having cravings for different kinds of food; you have to hold back and not pig out. I'm hoping we can take long walks in the park. Patti loves it there, and I think you'll enjoy being outside. Not to change the subject, but I thought we might do something special for your graduation, maybe a favorite meal. Please think about it and let me know. I can't tell you how happy Patti and I are to have you here; I wish it were under better circumstances. If something bothers you, please let me know. You stood by me all year when virtually everyone else turned their back; I never dreamed I might be able to do the same for you, but now that I can, there isn't anyone in the world I'd rather help."

"Kathy, I have thought about you and Patti over and over for the past two months. At first I thought it was wrong of me to impose on you guys. The more I thought about it, the more I realized you were not offering me a handout or a place to stay; you were offering me a home, a sanctuary. I know I am not like you. I don't think I can raise a baby right now, but I know we will do the right thing. What happened to me is not the baby's fault; it shouldn't be punished because someone else was stupid. I know everything will work out for the best, and I think for me, it can only happen here. I love you both so much."

They sat quietly looking into each other's eyes; whether they chose to admit it or not, they were quite a team...best friends.

In the meantime Patti had found Sherry's "hat," better
known as a mortar board, and she paraded up and down
the room. The hat kept slipping all over her head. When it
fell forward, she could not see anything and if it rocked
backward, it perched at the back of her head. Kathy and
Sherry got so tickled watching Patti graduate they could
only stammer and sputter, so they gave up trying to talk
and just watched the parade. Kathy looked forward to the
day the mortar board might fit better, and she could watch
a grown Patti cross the stage and receive her diploma.

Sherry did come up with a special meal and Kathy bought
a bottle of wine...only one glass for Sherry and grape juice
for Patti. The girls had a delightful dinner then decided to
take short walk in the park. Patti really appreciated these
trips; she loved to romp and "chase her tail." It was fun to
be outside. On the way back to the apartment Sherry told
Kathy she wanted a break before she looked for a job; she
would be glad to take care of Patti during the day.

Sherry used the next few days to get to know Patti better;
they would go to the park and visit. Sometimes Patti liked
to sit and quietly watch the birds; Sherry would get her to
identify them and was surprised at the number of different
birds Patti could name. "What is your favorite bird?"

"I like the red birds, the cardinals, and the birds with the
orange breasts, the robins. Robins are always busy,
scratching and pecking at the ground."

"Are there any birds you don't like?"

"I don't like blue jays; they're pretty, but they're mean and
chase away other birds; I don't like that."

Even though Sherry told Kathy she was in no hurry to find
work, she did make a few calls and discovered several
places were interested and wanted to schedule an interview.
Sherry was surprised how nice everyone seemed and was
sure she could find a job, preferably where she wouldn't

have to show her stomach all the time. It would be embarrassing to explain any or all of her situation. Kathy was pleased to hear Sherry had possible offers and noted things seemed to be working out satisfactorily.

A local company was expanding and looking for a full-time receptionist who could type and file. Sherry would only work three days a week, Monday, Wednesday, and Friday. Then in a couple of weeks, when their remodeling was completed, she would work every weekday. Thankfully, she could work primarily from her desk, and there was no lifting or strenuous activity. Sherry accepted their offer and looked forward to having income and something to do.

June rolled around and summer with it. Everyone was working. Sherry and Kathy made sure Patti got a chance to explore the park's sights, sounds, and activities. Sherry seemed to fit in with their schedule and soon discovered the open format of the apartment left few corners in which to hide. Sherry was not particularly modest, but she did find Patti's interest in her belly somewhat annoying. Patti was thrilled Sherry was going to have a baby even though she understood Sherry would be leaving after it was born. Kathy cautioned Patti not to pester Aunt Sherry, but it was hard for Patti to ignore. Kathy envied the fact Sherry had never been sick and seemed to deal easily with pregnancy; Kathy did not even like to think about how she had felt when she was carrying Patti. It was hard for her to imagine ever having any more children even if she found a man.

As August approached, Kathy was mentally preparing for her last year of nurse's training. It was exciting to think she would soon be through, but it would be a long time until next May. Kathy continued to be amazed that a year from now Patti would be starting to school; it made her feel old, but she decided being 22 was a long way from retirement. Sherry enjoyed her job and continued to have no problems with her pregnancy.

Late one afternoon Kathy and Sherry discussed her baby. "Kathy, I know this will not please you, but I want to give the baby up for adoption; I admit I have mixed feelings about it, but I really believe it's for the best. Does the

98

hospital have access to adoption agencies, or can they direct me to someone who can help?"

"Sherry, I think we can take care of it locally. The hospital encourages unwed mothers to keep their babies or give them to people who can't have children. I will try to get the ball rolling. I don't know all the details, but I will try to see what we can do. I hate for you to do this, but I understand. More importantly, if you can make some couple happy, then we will have turned this mess into something glorious. I do have one request; I hope you'll consider. I'd like for you to keep the baby for a few days, nurse, and care for it so you can feel what it is like to be a mother. I think you need that experience and it might help you better adjust to what you have to do...kind of provide closure."

"I agree; I think I need to hold my baby and know it is part of me. I know it will be hard, but in my case, it's the right thing to do."

Kathy's school began; it was soon September. Sherry was getting bigger and complained she didn't really enjoy dragging this baby around. Kathy continued to remind her that the more she ate, the bigger both she and the baby would likely be. It helped keep her focused, and for Sherry that was important. Her doctor reported everything was going well; the baby seemed healthy and normal. She was due near the end of October, and Kathy kept telling her she would probably have a little Halloween baby; Sherry wasn't so sure she really wanted a spook, so she found little humor in the Halloween nonsense. The hospital did have an excellent prospect to adopt Sherry's baby, but there might be complications. The adoptive mother had been on some kind of hormone therapy in an attempt to get pregnant, with no success. She wanted to nurse the new baby, but needed to flush this material from her system before attempting to feed a child. They would have to wait and see what happened.

Kathy had arranged to be with Sherry in the delivery room and Patti insisted she had to see Aunt Sherry's baby. Sherry continued to work but planned to go on maternity leave around the 25th of October if the baby had not come by then; she had promised her employer she would come back and help train her replacement after the baby was born. As it turned out, Sherry worked through the 26th and then stayed home the next day. Apparently it did the trick because around 6:00 am on the morning of the 28th Sherry went into labor. Kathy got her to the hospital and her baby, a little girl, was in her arms by noon.

After the baby was born, the nurse, who had been in and out of the delivery room, commented that she knew Kathy. Of course, Kathy worked at the hospital, but she didn't know all of the staff since they were never all there at the same time. This nurse did not realize Kathy worked in the hospital either; she remembered her from when Patti was born. "You know, we nearly lost you during delivery. Your baby was all tangled up with the cord and we didn't know if we would be able to save both of you. You and your daughter are a couple of tough cookies; we were mighty proud of you. I'm pleased to know you're on our staff." Kathy was a bit shocked; she had known there were problems with the delivery, but the doctor had never been specific. She told the nurse her daughter, Patti, was in the waiting room in case she wanted to see her. The nurse promised to see Patti and say hi.

Kathy was with Sherry when the nurses brought her the baby. Kathy wondered how she would react and was surprised Sherry held her and helped her find a breast. She seemed uneasy about the nursing, but the baby knew what to do, and soon Sherry appeared to relax and get a feel for it. The hospital had made all the arrangements for the adoption. Sherry would stay with the baby at no charge until the adoptive mother could attempt to nurse. It might be three or four days. The adoptive parents would not show up until the actual transfer of the baby was made. Sherry had the option of being in an observation room when her baby was delivered to its new mother; Kathy encouraged her to view this event. Kathy would come and see her everyday. They brought Patti in and she thought the baby was tiny; when her mother told her she had once been that small, Patti was amazed. "Aunt Sherry, you have a lovely baby."

Kathy now had two issues. First, she had to explain to Patti that Sherry was not going to keep her baby. When they got home, Kathy asked Patti to listen. She did her best to explain what Aunt Sherry was doing, making another couple who could not have children very happy. Patti looked sad. "But you kept me and you're not married."

"I know, honey. I never thought about giving you up for one minute; you were my special Patti. Everyone in my family wanted you, Grandpa and Grandma, Maggie and Jake. Sherry doesn't have any family here to support her."

"But she's got us; we're her new family. We can help her."

"That's right, but Sherry is not going to stay here; she'll be leaving and won't be able to care for the baby by herself." Kathy tried to be patient.

"I'll miss the baby." Patti frowned and lowered her head.

"Me too, honey, me too." Kathy managed not to cry.

The second issue involved transferring the baby from Sherry to its new mother. Sherry agreed to go to the observation room, feed her baby for the last time, then see her given away. On the morning of the transfer while Sherry was nursing, the new parents entered the receiving room. They waited impatiently while talking with one of the administrative staff. Shortly, a nurse came and apparently informed them the baby would be there soon because they seemed to perk up and be more in control. The same nurse came to see if Sherry was finished. Sherry kissed her baby, said good bye and gave her to the nurse, who left immediately. Sherry cried quietly, and Kathy began to tear. The nurse entered the receiving room and handed the baby to the new mother, whose expression would be forever etched in Kathy's mind; Sherry also watched in awe. The new mother simply glowed; neither girl had ever seen anyone happier. Sherry looked at Kathy and spoke through her tears. "See, I've done the right thing; just look at that woman's face!"

"Oh, yes, I see it; it's wonderful." Kathy paused. "But I

think you broke Patti's heart."

Sherry gasped. "My gosh, I never thought about Patti. What am I going to do?"

"Just be honest; I don't know if she will understand now, but don't lie to her. We've already talked about it."

When they finally got home, Patti welcomed Sherry. "I miss the baby."

Sherry looked at Patti engulfed with sadness. "I do too."

Patti didn't say much of anything for the rest of the evening. Later when Kathy went to bed, she could hear Sherry crying. She went to her. "Are you okay?"

"No, I'm not. I'm not okay. I didn't want to hurt anybody; now Patti hates me for giving away my baby. You hate me for the same reason, and I'm beginning to hate me too."

"Sherry, nobody hates you. Maybe we're disappointed, but I could never hate you, and I know Patti loves you dearly. You've made your decision, and I suspect it was the right one. I have no right to judge you. We both saw the look on that lady's face. The problem is living with your decision; I'll be okay and so will Patti. You need to understand that and deal with how you feel."

"Kathy, would you stay here with me tonight? I don't want to be alone. I know you will never believe this, but what I did today was the hardest thing I've ever done. I loved my baby, but I loved her enough to know I could never do what you've done with Patti. You are a good mother; you care about Patti and she loves you. I just don't have that in me, and you need to know I'm ashamed of it. I can live knowing I gave up my baby; it will be hard to live knowing I'm the reason I had to. I hope you can forgive me; I love you so much." Sherry started to cry again.

Kathy leaned over and kissed Sherry on her cheek, then kissed her again; she slid next to Sherry in the bed and made an effort to put an arm around her. "I do forgive you, and you don't have to be alone tonight...but keep your cold feet to yourself!" Kathy smiled.

Sherry didn't realize it, but Kathy was crying too. She knew things would never be the same, and she was convinced Sherry knew it too. Kathy realized she had so little in common with Sherry, and there was no doubt Sherry was a different person than she had been in May, but they were still miles apart in who they were. It was truly sad; in a few weeks Sherry would be leaving, and they very likely would never see each other again.

Life soon returned to normal, but it was not the same. A hint of tension surrounded them. Sherry went out of her way to be nice to Patti, and Patti never mentioned the baby. Sherry had been contacting companies regarding full-time employment relating to her degree in marketing; she found a couple of prospects back East and finally arranged to head there after Thanksgiving. Kathy was happy for her; she knew Sherry had a lot of talent. It would be great to see her put it to use and get credit for it. Kathy planned a big Thanksgiving send off, and Sherry accepted Mrs. Bender's invitation to have Thanksgiving dinner with them. She could not say enough about all the things everyone had done for her, and she would never forget them. Patti and Kathy were both crying, but still managed to tell her how much they would miss her. They would all do their best to keep in touch, but it might be hard to make connections. Sherry was to drive carefully, and Kathy was not to have a breakdown until she at least finished school and became an RN. Patti was to be a good girl in kindergarten next year. Everyone had high hopes as Sherry began another chapter in her life.

Kathy completed her semester of school. Santa brought Patti some new toys, a warm winter coat, and sweets to eat; the year ended quietly. Patti frequently mentioned how much she missed Aunt Sherry, and Kathy tried to keep up with Sherry's adventures. She did receive the good news that Sherry had found a job and seemed happy in her new surroundings. All in all, it had been a good year...albeit stressful at times.

The new year roared by like a runaway train. Patti reached her fifth birthday; she wasn't very big, but she could be mighty feisty. The school district had pre-enrollment for new kindergartners. Kathy had talked to her about it, but Patti did not have any real feelings about school. She had always taken an interest in learning and had picked up much from the people around her. She knew her letters, she could count to twenty and even further with a little assistance; she recognized a lot of words, and she could identify almost every animal imaginable. Patti even knew the names of most of the trees in the park. Kathy was never worried about her ability to learn; she only hoped Patti would not be bored with school. The school district had started an enrichment program during the other half of the day when a child was not in kindergarten. It started after Labor Day and Kathy thought if Patti liked school, it would be an option.

Kathy was flying through her final semester of the RN program; she would be done with classes in May, but the program required a ninety-day internship for certification. Kathy would be exempt from this since she already worked at the hospital and had been employed there for almost five years; however, she still had to wait for ninety days like everyone else. The hospital agreed to promote her with all of the benefits of her new title as soon as she completed her classwork. She would officially graduate in August.

The summer also flew by. The trips to the park were still exciting as Patti chased away blue jays and tried to catch squirrels. Some days she enjoyed the play areas since she had always liked to climb on virtually everything, but other days she was just a nature lover and free spirit. Kathy sometimes felt she had a bit of eagle in her genes; Patti would have loved to fly like those birds and even tried—with no success.

Kathy's graduation took place at almost the same time Patti started kindergarten. Kathy was perhaps as happy as anyone had seen her in years. No more school. Hallelujah! However, there was one downside to Kathy's new title and licensure; she could no longer work at the nursing home.

They would have to pay her as an RN, and they could not afford that salary without releasing other employees. She could only work on an emergency basis if needed. She would really miss the elderly patients and working there.

While Kathy's formal education had ended, Patti's was just starting. Kathy hated to put her on a bus to go to school, but it was simply too far to walk and there was no other way to get her there on time every day. Patti did not really like school; she loved the learning and activities but did not seem to care much for her classmates. The other children soon learned to leave her alone; Patti would stand right up for herself and not be intimidated. As time passed, Patti seemed more at ease, and a talk with her teacher convinced Kathy the enrichment program would probably benefit Patti's interest in learning. Kathy felt it was important for Patti to like school and get the best education possible; it had paid off handsomely for her.

The holidays came and Santa proved especially nice to Patti. Kathy now had a respectable income; she and Patti could live comfortably. She considered moving to another location, but the warehouse apartment had grown on her; it was easy to walk to work, and she had been spoiled by all the space. The winter that year was cold, but without much snow. The hospital had asked Kathy if she would coordinate their inservice program; she would initiate new employees and conduct periodic programs to update the staff. She also would be the hospital representative at public meetings or educational settings. Kathy felt strongly that better communication with staff and community greatly strengthened the hospital's image.

Patti soon turned six and was flourishing in school; she had apparently inherited her mother's love of learning and easily applied herself to school tasks. However, she was not very social. While it was not unusual for children to be that way, Patti was fiercely independent and resisted efforts to improve her relationship with the other kids. They encouraged Kathy to work with her on this problem, but Kathy did not see Patti as unsociable nor unfriendly. She was just more mature, and therefore, had other interests; if she was more interested in learning her alphabet than playing tag, why was that a problem?

⟶ ⟵

School ended, summer arrived, and the two girls, Patti and her mother, tried to spend more time together. The park was their favorite place and they had many heart-to-heart talks there. One day, Patti, seemed quite reflective and after some stuttering and stammering finally asked, "Mom, I have a question about us."

"Okay, honey, go ahead; I'll try to answer it."

"There's something I don't understand. Why is your last name Bender, and my last name Linder? I mean, shouldn't they both be the same like the other kids in school?"

"Gosh, Patti, this is confusing, but I'll try to explain. You know most kids have a mommy and daddy. When they get married, they usually take the father's last name because that's what we do in our society...like Grandpa and Grandma Bender. I have never been married..."

"Then how did I get born if you weren't married?" Patti seemed quite puzzled.

Her mother was somewhat disheartened. "Oh, Patti, I wish we hadn't got into this...babies are made when a man plants a seed in a woman and it grows..."

"Like what happened to Aunt Sherry."

"Yes, just like Aunt Sherry...she wasn't married either; a man planted a seed in her without permission, which is against the law. That's why she didn't keep her baby, because it hadn't been planned, and she wasn't married."

"Then how did you get me?" Patti was still confused.

"Well, I made a mistake, I let a man, your father, plant a seed in me; we weren't married and we didn't think it would grow...but it did grow and became you. Your father and I decided we did not want to get married, but I wanted to keep you because you were part of me. Your Grandpa Bender and Grandpa Linder made a deal. Grandpa Linder would pay all my medical expenses if I gave you your father's last name. So you are Patti Linder. Does that make any sense?" Kathy was relieved she had managed to explain this without going crazy.

"I guess so. My daddy didn't want me?"

"Well, no, I guess you could say that...he didn't love your mommy either. I'd say he was pretty stupid not to love a couple of good looking gals like us; don't you think?" Kathy smiled, trying to paint the best picture she could on this canvas.

"I don't care if my daddy didn't want me; I've got the best mommy in the world." Patti beamed.

"And I've got the nicest little girl in the world." But, that little girl's mother still cried herself to sleep that night.

If the previous year had been uneventful, the coming year was even less so. Patti went about being a first grader; her mother went about being a nurse. They were happy together and Kathy thanked God every chance she got that Patti was such a pleasant child to have around even if she didn't socialize enough at school. They tried to do as much together as they could and Patti never tired of being with her mom or going places where there were lots of adults and few, if any, kids. They sometimes took drives in the car, usually to the country where Patti could see bigger animals like cows and horses; Patti was always thrilled by animals. One time they visited a farm and Patti just took off to see a cow up close; there was no fear and the cow sensed no harm from Patti. They were like a pair of old friends. Despite the trauma and stress involved, Kathy never regretted her decision to have Patti; she was truly a special child with considerable gifts to share with the world.

Kathy did sense Patti needed a friend; perhaps the second grade would provide one.

⤳ Ten ⤲

Colby Duncan was Patti's first and oldest friend. The Duncans had moved during the summer before Colby was to enter the second grade. Mr. Duncan's work in sales had expanded, and he needed a more central location for his travel. Considerable family discussion surrounded this decision; everyone had agreed the family would be better off in a larger community with more access to the "finer" things of life, especially shopping and entertainment. Mrs. Duncan was pleased there was a well-established community college which initiated many cultural activities; she liked to think of herself as a patron of the arts. Mr. Duncan often mused that the local hospital had an outstanding psychiatric ward that could care for her when she slipped over the edge.

In any event, the move happened, and the Duncans located in a new environment. The only problem they faced was finding a place to stay; housing was difficult to come by. They did not want to build a new home since there was no guarantee how long they might stay. Mrs. Duncan wanted a nice older home, a place that had history and did not look new. Mr. Duncan was much less choosy; all he wanted was running water and indoor plumbing. The Duncans had spent nearly two weeks looking at homes, and neither of them had been satisfied with what they saw. Finally, out of desperation, Mr. Duncan suggested they simply find a temporary house and live there until something came available that everyone liked. Mrs. Duncan agreed; she wanted to get Colby enrolled in school and acquainted with the new community.

The house they finally settled upon, and within, was not at all what they wanted. It was not in the "better" part of town; and the property was in need of both care and repair. Mr. Duncan proclaimed he would work on the outside, and Mrs. Duncan would be the official interior decorator. The kids would do their best to stay out of the way and assist if needed. Colby helped his dad a little, but his main task was watching his little sister, Caitlyn. Colby needed no justification for why Romans left little girls out to die, especially if they were Caitlyn's age. Additionally, he told one of his elementary teachers he had skipped being two and three years old to avoid his family that embarrassment. His teacher had been so amused she called Mrs. Duncan, and they laughed about it every time they saw each other.

When school started, Colby was the only "newbie;" that is, he was the only student in his classroom who had not been in that school the previous year. Many of the kids knew each other, and Colby was often "out of the loop." He felt bad no one seemed to pay attention to him. However, it did not take long to notice he was not alone in this regard. The other "outcast" was a little girl named Patti. Colby felt sorry for her; she did not seem to fit in with the rest of the kids. She was plain, a little boyish, and not like the other girls. She was clean and neat but never wore nice clothes. The other kids did not pay much attention to her.

Colby decided to sit with her at lunch; she never spoke to him, but he could tell she was pleased to have him there. He did his best to be her friend, but she was unresponsive. However, about a week after school began, Colby was on his way home. On this particular day Colby was about a block from school when he very distinctly heard his name called. He turned around, but no one was there. He was puzzled but decided it was someone on the playground waiting for the bus, teasing him. As he continued his walk, the voice sounded again, "Colby, I'm over here." This time Colby turned toward the plantings around the retaining wall that helped level a softball and soccer field. Hiding amongst the bushes was Patti; he recognized her dress.

"What are you doing in there?"

"I'm waiting for you. Can I walk with you?"

"Sure, but I'm confused."

Patti emerged from the shrubbery and began to walk with him. "Well, you shouldn't be. I don't like to walk alone." Colby was genuinely puzzled; here he was walking home with a girl who had never spoken so much as one word to him—now they were having an actual conversation.

"Why don't you speak to me at school?"

"I was afraid you might not talk back."

"Patti, that's silly. Why would I not talk to you?"

"I don't know; I'm stupid, I guess."

"No, you are not stupid; you're just weird."

"Well, so are you!"

"I know; everyone in my family is weird." Colby started to laugh.

"Friends?" Patti questioned.

"Yes, friends...that would be nice." They shared a big grin.

From that day forward Colby and Patti walked home together. Colby assured his mother he had a friend to walk with; she did not need to pick him up at school, but if she did, she had to take Patti too. Mrs. Duncan was not terribly impressed with Patti; that is, Patti was not the kind of girl she envisioned Colby taking to prom or heaven forbid, marrying! On the other hand, when you're a second grader such things are a long way off, and more importantly, Patti and Colby were friends; it was good for both of them.

Colby did not know at the time that Patti went several blocks out of her way to walk with him. She lived nearly two miles from school and could have ridden the bus to within three blocks of her home, but she wanted to walk with Colby, and he liked to walk with her. He liked to think he could protect her from anyone who might harm her; of course, in reality, Colby knew it was probably Patti who would protect him. Something about her suggested "don't mess with me." Colby found that fascinating.

They had walked together for several weeks when Colby learned that Patti came home to an empty apartment. Her mother sometimes worked until 5:00 pm or later. This explained why Patti walked; she did not particularly like being home alone; there was not much to do but watch television, and Patti found that boring, so she found ways of "killing time" without being home or getting into trouble. Colby suggested she come home with him, where they could play outdoors or even practice spelling. Mrs. Duncan would have none of it without written permission from Patti's mother. She did not want to be responsible for someone else's child; she already had two of her own.

Patti liked the idea of staying with Colby after school; she knew she couldn't do it every day, but being with Colby and not having to be home waiting for her mother or playing in the park would be fun. She talked to her mother about it, and Kathy agreed to visit with Mrs. Duncan. If it was okay, Patti could tell her what days she would be with Colby, and she could pick Patti up at his house. She was pleased that Patti had finally found a friend and knew it would be good for her to be more social. The next day Kathy picked up Patti and Colby and took them to the Duncans. Mrs. Duncan had difficulty believing Patti belonged to Kathy. They talked for a while and Mrs. Duncan was pleased to know Kathy was a nurse, a professional person; she would not have said it, but she didn't want Colby associating with riffraff. Mrs. Duncan was willing to give her a chance; Colby needed a friend. She was also pleased that both children were willing to work on their studies and not spend all their time playing.

There were lots of things to do at the Duncan's and it would be fun to explore them together. Mrs. Duncan was shocked at the effect Patti had on Colby. Colby had never been one to get very dirty. Patti rarely got filthy, but she liked to play outside and usually required a bath before supper. One night after school, they were so grimy Mrs. Duncan made them take a bath...Patti first since she was a lady. Mrs. Duncan was not exactly pleased by Colby's change in behavior, but acknowledged that he was a boy, and boys are supposed to get dirty. Mr. Duncan thought Patti was good for Colby; Mrs. Duncan reluctantly agreed.

When Kathy met with Patti's teacher that year, it was the first time she did not have to listen to the "Patti's not very friendly" speech. She was pleased. In addition, it appeared

Patti was having more fun at school and doing better than ever. By pure coincidence she saw Mrs. Duncan, who shared that Colby was also having a good year; she had been worried their move and new location might cause a problem for him, but he was doing quite well. The two mothers began to think Colby and Patti were good for each other. Mrs. Duncan shared her earlier misgivings, and Kathy understood that Patti did not look like the person she really was; she told Mrs. Duncan Patti always said nice things about Colby and called him a "little gentleman." Mrs. Duncan laughed and told Kathy that while she had dreamed about having such a child, she never thought she would get one. She told Kathy to come by and have coffee any time she picked up Patti, and even though these two kids seemed about as mismatched as any two could be, they were quite a pair.

Kathy liked Mrs. Duncan. Yes, she was a bit—well, maybe more than a bit—crazy, but she was a good woman and said what was on her mind—no sweet talk or games. Kathy admired people who were honest and unafraid to speak their mind.

Second grade was the best ever. When Santa brought holiday snow that year, Patti had to go to the park and try to make a snowman; Kathy supervised, and they finally created one that made Patti happy. When the weather warmed, Kathy suggested to Mrs. Duncan that the kids could play at the park after school. It would be a change for them, and the park was safe. Mrs. Duncan was a bit concerned, but agreed it would probably be good for Colby, and Kathy promised she would stay with them if they wished to extend their play time. The plan worked well except one day a storm forced them to go the apartment for shelter. Colby had never seen such a big room, and he talked about it for several days; he hoped he would get a chance to come back and explore the place. Patti hoped so too.

During the middle of May, Patti realized school was about over and she and Colby would be on vacation. Patti really liked having no school...but this would mean she would not see Colby every day...and perhaps not until school started in the fall. They needed some kind of plan for the summer. Patti visited with her mother and Colby with his. Would it be okay for them to go to each other's house occasionally? Colby could come and they could go to the park and play, or maybe explore Patti's apartment; Patti could go see Colby and maybe spend the day with him and play outside or they could find something to do inside. Both mothers agreed it was a good idea.

Patti and Colby enjoyed that summer. They explored many of the secrets in the back of the apartment and climbed every tree in Colby's yard. Even the mothers had to admit these two kids were easier to manage and more fun when they were together; they were an odd pair, but they truly loved being together and with school starting, they would have another year as best friends.

Third grade can be big step for many children; the very basic concepts learned at the primary level begin to expand, and some students have difficulty adjusting to harder work. Patti and Colby discovered they could work together and learn more easily...so they cut back their play time to do homework and go over their studies. This paid dividends at test time, and their grades soared. In many ways they both liked the harder work. Trying harder meant learning more, and both seemed to understand the value of their efforts. It also seemed the harder they worked, the easier everything became, and it was neat when other kids had to ask them for help. Intelligence is one thing, but real learning requires effort and work...even for third graders.

Third grade turned out to be the best grade yet. Patti and Colby figured if they got their studies done first, they had all kinds of time to play and have fun, but when they played and had fun first, they were too tired to think straight. Their school year went well and Mrs. Duncan was especially pleased with Colby's work. She had high hopes for him, and it was difficult for her not to micromanage his life. Mr. Duncan remained the calming influence, insisting that Colby, like all children, needed the opportunity to just be a kid. Perhaps Colby's success was related to the fact that he got outside, ran around in the yard, climbed trees, and acted crazy; after all, he was a boy, and boys...like to

113

have fun too!

Kathy was always busy and didn't have time to think much about Patti's success; she was a believer in hard work and its benefits. Patti was capable of hard work and she seemed full of common sense. Patti had always been fascinated by so many things; she loved animals and the outside, but she also liked to read and work in the apartment. While Kathy might have wished for a more feminine girl, she was learning to really appreciate the one she had. Patti may not have been a "little lady," but she was certainly a very special child. Aunt Sherry would never see the joys of knowing her daughter. Life had been tough, but Kathy felt good about the life they had.

The school year ended and summer began. Once again Colby and Patti had their rendezvous at Colby's house, at the park, or in Patti's apartment. Most importantly, they had fun; this summer they went to a few of the Saturday afternoon matinees at the theater. Patti said they were on a date when they went out, but Colby shied away from that nonsense; he didn't see their relationship in any romantic fashion, but he did admit that holding hands with Patti when a movie got scary or suspenseful felt pretty good. Patti agreed, but made little issue of it. One weekend after they had gone to a show, Kathy had given Patti some extra money to go to the ice cream shop; it was Patti's favorite place in all the world. She told her mother once she would like to go there and eat ice cream until she froze to death; Kathy was a bit shocked until she realized it wasn't such a bad idea. When they finished their treats, Patti asked Colby if they could go by the park; she wanted to ask him a question. They headed for Patti's favorite park bench.

"Colby, what would you do if I died?"

Colby looked at her, very concerned. "Patti, you aren't sick or something are you?"

"No, I'm not sick; I just wondered how you would feel if I died."

"Oh, Patti, I don't want to think about it; you're my best

friend in the whole world. It would be awful to lose you. Why do you ask?"

"Well, I thought about it once. I wondered what I would do if you died."

"What would you do?"

"I'd die; it would kill me."

"Oh, I wouldn't want you to die...not for me, not for anyone; you're too special."

"Do you really feel that way?"

"Yes, I wouldn't lie to you."

"Colby, I don't know how to say this and I'm not trying to be funny. I love you. I know you don't like all the lovey dovey stuff, but I don't know any other way to say it. I don't think I could live without you; we have to take care of each other so we can be best friends forever."

Colby looked at her and, for just a moment, something flashed through him that made him warm inside; he reached for her hand and shook it firmly. "Yes, best friends forever."

Colby couldn't see that Patti had a tear or two in her eye. "Colby, would you kiss me?"

Surprised, Colby started to blush. "You mean here...right now?"

Patti pointed toward her cheek. "Yes, right here and right now."

Colby, still in disbelief, whispered quietly. "You won't tell anyone, will you?"

"Of course not, silly; this is between you and me." Patti was very serious.

Colby looked around to see if the coast was clear, then

leaned in and kissed her on the cheek. Patti smiled and quickly returned his kiss. Colby was terribly embarrassed, but enjoyed kissing Patti, and even more, having her kiss him back. Squeezing each other's hand, they looked at each other and whispered quietly, "Friends, forever."

⟫⟩   ⟨⟨

Fourth grade started as a near disaster. When enrollment time arrived, they discovered they where going to be in different classes. Everyone was shell shocked. Kathy and Mrs. Duncan planned to call the school, but were stopped in their tracks by a letter received two days later. The schedules had been completely mixed up; someone had pushed the wrong button and the kids were assigned classes in an alphabetic arrangement. The error had been corrected and the proper schedule for the year was included. Patti and Colby had the same fourth grade teacher. There was great joy in "Muddville" that night!

The fourth grade played out like the previous two years. Patti and Colby liked their teacher, especially when she read to them right after lunch. It was a year they would long remember. However, storm clouds were brewing as winter ended. Colby told Patti his mother really wanted to move and depending upon the location, he might have to change schools. Patti had heard Mrs. Duncan complain about their home, so she was not surprised when Colby told her, but in the back of her mind she worried she might lose him. She recalled their conversation in the park; if she lost Colby, she would surely die.

⟫⟩ Eleven ⟨⟨

Although Patti didn't realize it at the time, her world was falling apart. It began late in April as the fourth grade was ending. The weekend had been delightful, and most fourth graders had enjoyed time outdoors. Patti had gone to the park once with her mother and again with one of her cousins, who were visiting the Benders. Even though she had a lot of fun, she was still anxious to see Colby and get back to school.

When she got to school, she looked anxiously for Colby

116

but could not find him. Soon, however, she saw the Duncans' car pull up to the curb; Colby jumped out and ran toward the building. Patti intercepted him, and they walked in together. Colby was out of breath; his mother had misplaced her keys, and they were beginning to think she would never find them. She was all excited because she had finally found a house for them to buy, and she was beside herself thinking about moving and redecorating. Colby wasn't enthused; he liked where they lived and didn't want to relocate.

Patti was curious about the new home. Mrs. Duncan had always wanted to live in an older, Victorian home. Mr. Duncan was less particular; he was more interested in a roof over his head—a kitchen would be nice. Colby and Caitlyn couldn't care less, but they enjoyed a big yard and playing outdoors. In any event, Mrs. Duncan had driven by a house she liked; it was listed for sale, but it really wasn't. It had been tied up in an estate dispute for several years and could not be sold until its title could be transferred to the heirs. When prospective buyers inquired about it, the local realtors could only say that it would be available in the near future. Thus, most people had lost interest. However, Mrs. Duncan had learned the problems had been resolved, and her family took a tour of the house over the weekend; the realtor had difficulty getting Mrs. Duncan to leave. She really wanted this house.

Colby was not as impressed as his mother, but there were things he did like. The property had a huge yard and lots of large trees. The house had several stories and probably many secret places he would need to explore. He would also no longer have to share a bathroom with Caitlyn; she spent a lot of time in there, and he got tired waiting on her. The house was in good condition so they would be able to move in without much extra work, a big improvement over their current home. Patti wanted to know where the house was. Colby only knew it was close to downtown; he would be able to walk to the library and other places without any problems. He thought he might be closer to where Patti lived, but he didn't know that area of town very well so he was not sure.

117

There were other things of which he was unaware. A new location meant he might have to attend a different elementary school; Patti wasn't moving. What did this mean to their relationship? Were their days together really numbered? If they were, that number was less than thirty, and time can slip away before anyone knows it, stealing something more precious than gold.

Mrs. Duncan was moving heaven and earth to make the best possible offer on the old house. The clincher came on the first of May when Mr. Duncan brought home some "good news"; he had received a promotion. He would be in charge of training new personnel then managing the accounts of several other salesmen. This would greatly reduce his road time and allow him to be home more often; the company had also agreed to let him open a small local office. It would now be possible for people to come to him instead of the other way around. His extra salary and benefits were more than enough to let the family afford a more expensive home. Mrs. Duncan sprang into action, notifying the realtor she was able to make an offer and was confident she could purchase the property.

Colby didn't discover until about a week before school was out that he would have to change schools. Mrs. Duncan had found out by accident while talking with one of their new neighbors; all students in that area attended Carson Elementary; Colby and Patti attended Jackson Elementary. Colby broke the news after school. "Patti, I'm pretty sure my folks are going to get the house Mom likes; I guess I'll be moving."

She took it rather well. "I'll bet your mom is really excited; we both know she wants to move. I guess you don't have much choice; you'll have to go too."

That night before going to bed, her mother caught her crying, and she almost never cried. "Patti, what's wrong? Why are you so sad?"

Patti told her about Colby's move and Kathy shared her concern. "Oh, honey, that's too bad. Does this mean Colby will be going to a different school?" Patti nodded. "Well, listen, I promise you'll still get to see him; please don't feel bad." Patti didn't want to argue, but she was not sure everything would work out that simple.

In the next few days Patti and Colby made many promises, promises over which they had no control. *Sure we'll see each other; I can come over this summer; we can meet at the park.* But there was no way to know it would happen.

On the last day of school, they arranged to walk home together. Patti spoke first. "Colby, you know I'm going to miss you."

"I was about to say the same thing, but we'll go to middle school together in sixth grade."

"It won't be the same; we may not be in the same class, and even if we are, it would only be for one period; that's less than an hour!"

"Look, we're friends, and things will work out; I know they will."

"Maybe, but I've got to know something. Do you remember in second grade when we first walked home and pledged we would be friends?"

"Sure, I remember, and we've been best friends since."

"Good, can we do that again?"

"What do you mean?"

"I mean will you tell me again that we are friends?"

"I thought I just did."

"No, you said we have been best friends since second grade. I want you to make that pledge again."

"Okay. Patti, will you be my friend?"

"Yes I will. Will you be my friend, Colby?"

"Yes, absolutely; I will be your friend."

"Forever?"

"Yes, friends forever—best friends; I promise."

"Colby, can we stop for a moment?"

"Sure, but why?"

"So I can do this." Patti leaned over and kissed Colby on the cheek.

"Patti, what are you doing!?" Colby was embarrassed and pulled away.

"I'm sealing my pledge. Would you kiss me to seal your pledge?"

"Well, I...I don't...I'm not sure, well, I mean, I don't usually go around kissing girls."

"It's okay; you can kiss me to seal your pledge."

"I guess...it's okay; you won't tell anybody will you?"

"Of course not."

Colby leaned over, started to wince, then managed to relax and kiss Patti on her cheek. They looked at other and reached out a hand; their hands met as they stared intently into each other's eyes; it could have been a hug, but they only managed a weak handshake. They were both certain they heard each other say, "Friends, forever," and those were the last words spoken until they got to Colby's house.

Once there, Patti would have liked to stay and play, but both of them were already committed to other plans. Colby had to go someplace with his mother, and Patti was to meet her mother for some summer shopping. Patti was to get right home, but she had walked with Colby anyway; she felt she would not get a chance to see him for quite a while, and she was right on target.

Patti loved the summer; there was always so much she could do because she had so much more time. During June she was passed around between her grandparents and aunts and uncles; she even went on vacation with her Uncle Robert, Mrs. Bender's brother, and his family. By the end of the month she was actually glad to be home.

Colby spent his time in June moving. The Duncans had taken possession of their new residence on the first of June, but many little things needed to be repaired, cleaned up, or replaced. Mrs. Duncan had contacted a retired handyman to help with the work, but things never go as fast as they should. In the meantime, one day while Mrs. Duncan was loading her car with items to move, a couple passing by stopped to ask if their home might be for sale. These folks had been looking for a place to buy and had not found anything they liked or could afford. Mrs. Duncan nearly passed out; they hadn't even considered putting their home on the market until sometime in July.

The couple scheduled an appointment for later in the week, and when they toured the house, they were very impressed and wanted to purchase it. Mrs. Duncan called her husband who was on the road, and they discussed an appropriate selling price. When Mrs. Duncan relayed their final decision to the other couple, they agreed immediately to buy the house but needed possession as quickly as possible, finally agreeing on July 1. Thus, everyone was in a frenzy to get the new home ready and the old house emptied. Colby thought his mother would go crazy, but somehow with everyone's help, they met the deadline on time. The work on the new home progressed slowly, so the sights and sounds of remodeling were still evident when Colby started to his new school in August.

In June, Colby called Patti and told her his new address. Kathy and Patti had driven by the house a couple of times, and it was beehive of activity. Patti's schedule had been so erratic she decided not to bother Colby until later, so she waited until after the Fourth of July to call him. They talked for a while. Colby was trying to get used to his new room and laughed that he would get confused going to the

121

bathroom, and end up in a large closet by mistake. Patti told him he'd better not store anything of value on the floor there; accidents happen! He liked the neighborhood but didn't know anyone. He was glad she called. It was okay to come over just about anytime; maybe she could help him arrange his room. It was a mess.

Patti and Colby got together a few times during July. Patti was amazed at how big the house was; she thought it was neat that Colby had his own bathroom...even if it didn't have a tub or shower. All four of the upstairs bedrooms had some kind of bathroom or washroom as Mrs. Duncan called them. Caitlyn's bedroom had a full bath, which she was now responsible for maintaining. Colby got to use the big bathroom upstairs, which had both a tub and a large shower; it made him feel pretty important. Patti wanted to know if he had found any secret passages. Colby had discovered nothing so far, but there were closets inside of closets, and he thought that was strange. The master bedroom where his folks slept even had a built-in safe no one could open. Everyone thought it was empty, but arrangements had been made that if anything of value was discovered, it belonged to the estate. Mr. Duncan knew an old locksmith who thought he could open the safe and not hurt it, but no one was interested in it right now.

Patti was glad Colby was happy, and it didn't take long for anyone to realize that Mrs. Duncan was in heaven. Mr. Duncan liked the house, but he was getting tired of all the confusion and mess as they went through room after room papering, painting, or repairing. Patti got the impression Mr. Duncan enjoyed his peace and quiet, and right now this place was anything but peaceful. Caitlyn was still pretty young, so for her it was just a great big place in which to play. Colby assured Patti she was welcome anytime; he did not want to lose touch with her, but Patti could already sense things were not going to be the same.

In no time at all it was August and school began. Patti felt very much alone. She tried to make the best of it, but life without Colby became increasingly difficult. She knew almost everyone in her fifth grade class, but none of them could safely be called friends. School became increasingly less fun, and her grades slipped. Her mother asked her about the problem and received a most profound, "It's boring," as a response. Kathy was unimpressed and told Patti no one can have fun every day; she should remember that and make the most of her school work; it would be very important some day. Patti knew all that, but it didn't make any difference; she was uninspired without Colby.

As the year continued, Patti noticed she and Kathy spent less and less time together. It seemed she had not only lost her best friend but was also losing her mother. Early on Mrs. Bender had warned Kathy she needed to spend extra time with Patti; children crave attention from their parents and Patti would need it, especially without a father. Kathy was too busy to see the problem, and the rift widened. Patti began to do little things she knew her mother would not approve; she wasn't always honest and didn't follow the directions her mother provided. Her rebellion was subtle, but it was there; she wanted attention, and maybe one way to receive it was to get into trouble.

As Patti's dark side began to emerge, a major player was thrust into the game. In March right before her birthday, Patti went to school on Monday and discovered a new student in her class. Melissa was, to say the least, different from the rest of the kids. During lunch, Patti managed to sit with her and tried to get her to talk. Melissa was not a big talker, but she told Patti her parents had just moved into town; she had a younger brother, she hated school, and most importantly she was a Goth—which explained her black hair, black clothes, black fingernails, and "black" attitude. Patti was curious about this Goth stuff. She tried to get Melissa to explain it, but she put Patti off. Later in the week Melissa asked Patti to meet her after school.

The girls met and started walking toward Patti's home. "Do you live this direction from school?" asked Patti.

"No, I live in another part of town," replied Melissa.

"Well, how did you know to come this way?"

"I know things; the spirits of darkness talk to me...I know

123

about you."

"You do? What do you know about me?"

"I know you're a kindred spirit; I sense your anger and force. You're a perfect candidate."

"I am?"

"Look, you wanted to know about me and I am going to tell you, but what I say stays between us; don't even talk to yourself about it. Understand?" Melissa was quite blunt.

"No problem."

"Okay, first of all, my name isn't Melissa; you can call me that at school, but I am Raven, a spirit of the night. I believe in the forces of darkness. When the world was created there were two forces, one of light and one of darkness, one to rule by day, the other by night. This way they didn't have to oppose each other. I follow the spirits of the night."

"You mean like vampires, witches and demons?"

"Well, sort of...you've got to separate yourself from all those horror movies and not associate my beliefs with evil; evil is in the eye of the beholder. For example, I might say it is evil to kill a bee because bees make honey and honey is sweet and good. On the other hand, you might say killing a bee is good because you are allergic and a bee sting might kill you. In the same way vampires don't have to be evil; they could just as easily be hunting and destroying evil by killing bad people. Like I said, it's in the eye of the beholder."

"Gosh, I've never thought about it like that."

"Okay, here's the deal. In the middle school there's a secret club called the Gypsy Goths, all girls; obviously they meet at night. They get together with other groups and have parties and rituals to celebrate the darkness. I've already gone to one of their meetings."

"But you're not in middle school."

"I know; I didn't say I belonged to the group, I just went to one of their meetings. I can't join until summer, but I've got to pass fifth grade. If you'll help me with my grades, you can go with me to all the meetings for the rest of the school year. What do you think?"

Patti thought for a moment; she knew her mother would be displeased. "Sure, why not? I can help you in school, and you can take me to the Gypsy Goths; it's a deal."

Thus, Patti entered a new world, a world that never seems dark in the light of day, but how could she fool her mother to get want she needed?

Patti asked her mother if she was getting her a birthday gift soon. Kathy told her she wanted to take her shopping and get something. Patti said she would like a pair of black jeans and if possible, a black jean jacket to go with it. When questioned about this fascination with the color black, Patti explained it was her new favorite color. She also asked her mother for a favor. If she raised her grades during the last nine-weeks, would she make her something to wear with the jeans...like a black jean vest? Kathy told her if she was really serious, she would do it for her. Patti was thrilled; step one in her transition phase was complete. She knew Raven would love her outfit.

Now, could she pull off getting in and out of the apartment without her mother knowing? She thought long and hard before determining it wouldn't be easy, but with several possible avenues of escape and her mother's schedule, she was pretty sure she could come and go as she pleased and no one would be the wiser...and, if she did get caught, there were multiple excuses she could use; no one would know the difference.

As agreed, she helped Melissa at school, then Raven after school. Raven was bright enough to do well, but she didn't care; Patti wondered what would become of her if she didn't apply herself. Patti had seen first hand from her mother the value of an education. They now had more money and a car; they ate better and even went out to eat occasionally. The apartment was better furnished and more comfortable. Raven might be fooled about school, but Patti wasn't. Looking back, she didn't like being poor. She and her mother now had a better life, although they were paying a higher price for it than they realized.

Raven took Patti to the next meeting of the Gypsy Goths. It started at 10:00 pm on a Thursday night. Since Patti's mother was working, Patti had no problems getting away. The location was a mile away, in an abandoned building. There was only candlelight, so it was difficult to see. They began each meeting with a blood ritual, pledging their loyalty to each other and the spirits of the night. The girls stood in a circle and held out their arms, palms down; the leader, called a queen, stood inside the circle, leading a chant. When she finished, each girl lowered her right arm, and the leader went around the circle pricking the back of their left hands with a lancet. Then each girl turned to her right and licked the blood from the back of the hand next to her. The queen would then lance herself several times and all the girls would lick her blood. The blood pledge was now complete. The ritual continued with more chanting, not always in English. Following this, the leader would ask if anyone wished to join the club. Patti later learned the only way a girl could belong was to receive a unanimous vote of approval from the current members. The candidate would then receive an invitation of membership requesting her presence at the next meeting. That evening two girls had been approved, and they stepped into the circle.

This initiation was called the bond of wax, which was meant to seal a pledge of loyalty to the group. The first girl was asked in responsive form if she would now pledge her loyalty to all members present; she then had to pledge obedience to the group and agree to follow their rules without question. Upon completion of this, the girl removed her blouse and unfastened her jeans. Members of the group surrounded her, picked her up, and carried her to a nearby bench were she was laid in a prone position. A gag was placed in her mouth and her arms stretched back over her head. Her jeans were pulled down to her panty line, completely exposing her midriff, and her feet were held to stretch out her legs. The remaining members formed a circle and began walking around the new initiate. Each girl carried a candle. The leader of the group produced a large candle with multiple wicks then announced the ceremony would begin.

As they performed a chant, the girls moved closer to their victim. When signaled, each girl began dripping her candle on the bared girl, who writhed and twitched as the hot wax splattered on her skin. Following another signal, the girls stopped and held their candles in front of them. The girls holding the victim were now given candles and continued the dripping; they returned their candles and again made a firm grip on the girl. The leader spoke, "Each member has sealed her pledge and affirmed her oath with this wax. As Queen of the Gypsy Goths, I hereby complete this ritual of wax by uniting these seals as a pledge of our loyalty and unity."

She immediately poured the wax from the very large candle onto the midriff of the girl below, who was now in considerable pain. The leader produced a horsetail-like whip, checked to see if the wax was firm, then struck the initiate across her midriff, saying, "The wax is sealed." Then she passed the whip to another girl who repeated the ritual, until everyone had used the whip; then they repeated the process from the other side of their victim and announced she was a full member of the Gypsy Goths. It didn't appear as though this new member heard the pronouncement; she had gone limp and passed out.

Patti thought for sure the second girl would have run for the hills, but she stepped forward and the entire process was repeated except this victim bit through her gag and cried out while being whipped; she remained conscious, but obviously had suffered considerably as she writhed on the bench. When this was completed, the queen announced that due to the extra time initiating the new members, they would adjourn for the night; it was approaching 11:30, and they could never stay past midnight. A chant was repeated and all were excused.

Patti and Raven left together. Raven was near ecstasy; she told Patti she could hardly wait to become a member. She had already approached some of the girls in order to curry favor and get their vote; other girls might be more difficult and require certain tests or tasks. Patti was afraid to ask what kind of tests, but learned later they usually involved groveling and pain. This did not appeal to Patti, but it was a way to get back at her mother, and she could see no harm in watching other people make fools of themselves.

The school year and a couple of Goth meetings ended. Patti had helped Raven improve her grades, and in the process she finished the quarter and semester with the best grades she'd had all year. Proud of her, Kathy told everyone in the family how well Patti had done. Patti was pleased to have the attention, but it was no big deal for her to do well; she knew she was smart, and getting good grades was only a bit harder than just getting by. In addition, her mother remained completely unaware she was playing right into Patti's hands; Patti would have her vest made just the way she wanted in less than two weeks.

In the meantime Raven was excited she had done well in school. If Patti decided to join the Gypsy Goths, she would have Raven's full support. There would be another vote in June to accept new members to replace the eighth grade group moving on to other clans. Raven was hoping she would be accepted but told Patti to hold off for a while, since she was new to all of this. That would give Raven more time to lobby on Patti's behalf. Patti was not sure she was interested in becoming a Gypsy Goth, but she wasn't saying anything about it to Raven.

Summers slip by quickly. Patty heard from Raven that her membership had been accepted; she wanted Patti to be there for the ceremony. Patti promised she would. It was well into June before she realized she would be attending middle school in August. She was out of elementary school at last and maybe, just maybe, might be with Colby again. She wouldn't know until they held their sixth grade orientation around the first of August. They would tour the building, receive a copy of their schedule, have a chance to meet their teachers and enjoy cold refreshments. It would be a new experience because there would be lots of students instead of the usual twenty-five or so. The whole affair was simultaneously exciting and frightening, but everything would be fine if she could be with Colby.

Raven called to remind her about the Gypsy Goth meeting. As usual, they arranged to meet and go together. Eight girls had been accepted into the group; they would initiate four this night and the rest during a special meeting a few days later. The ceremony was exactly the same except they had built a small fire and melted wax in a small black kettle. When the group seal was to be done, a ladle of hot wax was to be poured on the victim instead of using the large candle. Raven was the third person to complete the ceremony; Patti could tell she was anxious and nervous. One of the first two girls had passed out and the other seemed a bit dazed as she recovered outside of the circle. Raven stepped forward and the ritual began. She seemed surprised by the pain but appeared to hold up well. She jerked violently when the wax from the ladle was applied and the whipping took its toll, but she did not pass out. They helped her to the side and completed the initiation. When the meeting officially adjourned, Patti went to help Raven peel off the wax and get her clothes arranged. In the dark it was hard to say, but Patti figured Raven's stomach had to be sore. She told Raven to rub some aloe vera on it before she went to bed to soothe the pain. Patti wondered why anyone would want to suffer like this to join a club.

Patti tried to contact Colby but could only get him occasionally; he said the same thing about her. They did meet a couple of times in July, but Patti realized that being away from him for a year and the fact that she was a girl—fifth grade boys aren't always fond of the opposite sex—put a strain on their relationship. Things were no better at home. Patti continually felt left out of her mother's life. She knew her mother loved her. No one would work so hard only for herself, but it seemed as if Patti didn't exist and she resented being alone and forgotten. Thoughts crossed her mind that frightened her; she had considered running away, but where would she go? Who would take her and not send her back to her mother? Patti began to understand the conflict raging in Kathy—no matter how great or wonderful Patti was, nothing erased the blot of getting pregnant. Patti felt bad for her mother almost as much as she did for herself. If she could just get her mother to see things differently, their world would change dramatically, but what could she do?

⟫⟫ Twelve ⟪⟪

By August Patti was beside herself waiting for middle school orientation; she so wanted to be with Colby. There was something about him she needed, now more than ever. Her mother drove her to school and Patti quickly spotted him. He was with a new friend he'd met in fifth grade, a boy named Geoff; she had never met him, but Colby said he was a goofball, and Patti thought it was funny she had been replaced by a goofball. Boys can be pretty silly, but that didn't change her feelings for Colby. When she pledged "friends forever," she really meant it, and she had to believe Colby did too.

Colby had been waiting. "Hey, Patti! Where have you been?"

Patti waved at him. "My chauffeur overslept this morning; it's not my fault!"

Colby laughed. "It's hard to find good help these days; my dad says that all the time."

"Well, your dad is pretty smart. Is this your friend Geoff?"

Colby pointed to Geoff. "Yeah, he's my weird friend. Go ahead, say something Geoff."

Geoff looked at Colby, then at Patti. "Something!"

Colby shook his head. "See what I mean?"

Patti laughed and Colby was still shaking his head as the three students entered the auditorium where they would be given instructions for the day. They were more interested in seeing their schedules than listening to a bunch of talk, but sacrifices have to be made, so they endured several welcomes and other propaganda. They were to leave the auditorium and pick up their schedules in the foyer. Each schedule was color-coded with a letter. All holders of yellow schedules were to go to the lunchroom where they would be separated by their respective letters and assigned an instructor who would give them a tour of the building and answer questions. Colby and Patti had the same color, but their letters were different. When the tours were completed, the students went to the lunchroom for sodas and/or ice cream; they were then allowed to recheck their room assignments, and it was important to look for errors so their schedules could be fixed before school began.

Patti enjoyed the tour, and the fact that sixth graders were all in the same area of the building. Their hallways were trimmed blue; if you were in a hallway with a different color, you were in the wrong place. Even so, the sixth grade attendance area was large, and most of the kids were unfamiliar with the building. Patti went back over her schedule twice and found all of her rooms; she even met a couple of her teachers. Colby got lost during his schedule review because there was a mistake; they had enrolled him in two classes at the same time. Even sixth graders know this creates attendance problems, so Colby would have to fix his schedule.

When the three friends met after their tours, they sat down to compare schedules. They all had the same courses but generally different teachers. Colby had two classes with Geoff, no classes with Patti; Geoff had one class with Patti. Patti tried to be brave about it, but she nearly cried in front of the boys. There was one hope. If the problem in Colby's schedule was resolved the right way, it was possible he could be with her. They all went to office and showed the defective schedule to one of the secretaries; she managed to contact one of the counselors who escorted them to her office. They explained their situation, and she apologized for the error; she would do everything possible to place Colby in the same class with Patti during one of those hours. She thanked the students for being so polite and told them to come see her anytime they had a problem.

Patti expressed some relief. "Well, maybe we can be in one class together."

Colby nodded. "That would sure be better than nothing."

Geoff grinned. "You guys were probably troublemakers and they wanted to keep you separated."

Patti shot back. "Hey, Geoff, thanks a lot!" Colby nodded his support.

Colby noted. "It sure is nice to have someone on our side."

"Ah, come on, I was only trying to be funny." Geoff looked a bit sheepish.

Patti laughed. "It's okay, we already know you're crazy."

The kids were supposed to be going home, and cars were pulling up everywhere. Geoff saw his mother's car and said goodbye. Colby had agreed to meet his mother a couple blocks away to avoid the congestion. He asked Patti if she would like a ride, and it was hard to refuse such an offer on a hot August day.

When Patti got home, she sat down in one of the two soft chairs in their living room. She thought about her day, the empty apartment, her mother, Colby's schedule and middle school. She leaned back in the chair and a few tears formed and rolled down her cheeks. Could this day have been any worse? She thought briefly about throwing herself off the roof, but the way things were going, it could never work; she'd end up some broken up cripple, still alive and suffering even more. As she was leaving enrollment, she thought she saw Raven. Maybe Raven was right, maybe the spirits of the night were her real friends; she sure wasn't getting much help from the ones in the daytime!

Not all was doom and gloom. The sixth grade orientation had reminded Kathy school was starting and Patti might need more than paper and pencils. They took the school's supply list and attempted to figure out what Patti might need. When they finished, her mother asked if she needed any other things before school started. Patti hadn't grown much, but she did have some clothing items that needed to be replaced...more importantly, she had found a pair of shoes she really wanted. In reality Patti had not found them; Raven had discovered the shoes, bought them, then told Patti she should get a pair too. Patti told her mother she really wanted these shoes, which Raven had called boots. They were black, ankle high with nickel accents and very "Goth"; they were also rather heavy and stiff looking, not the least bit feminine. Patti was concerned her mother would not even consider the purchase and was surprised when she commented, "Big, black, butt-kicking shoes...just what I'd expect a Hell's Angel's Mama to wear; I suppose you'll be wanting a motorcycle for Christmas?"

"Ah, come on, Mom, you know I'm not old enough to drive a motorcycle. Besides, who wants to drive around and get bugs on your face." Patti laughed, trying to suppress her excitement about getting the shoes.

There was another bit of good news. When the first day of school rolled around, Patti discovered she and Colby had the same English class; they were also in the same assembly and activity group. In addition, there was a possibility they could be in the same exploration class next semester, so things were better, but far from ideal. Patti also had classes with Raven, so at least she was with a few friends. However, anyone who didn't feel strange about being in middle school had probably been dropped on the head too many times. It was embarrassing having to find your locker or the restroom, plus remember a stupid schedule or feel silly ending up in the wrong class. That kind of attention was totally unwarranted.

While it was nice to be back with Colby, she almost never got to talk with him. They had different lunch schedules, and talking in English class was not exactly encouraged by their teacher. There might be an assembly or school activity about once a month, but there was no guarantee she could find or sit by Colby. She would see him after school, but she had to catch the bus, and he either walked or his mother would pick him up. It was a mess. They would call each other occasionally, but a phone visit wasn't the same as being together. Patti continued to run around with Raven although it was impossible to keep up with her, and Patti began to feel she wasn't cut out to be a Goth.

In October Raven and Patti met and walked together after school. Raven told her the Gypsy Goths would be having their first combined meeting with other Goth groups right before Halloween; the meeting was followed by a big Halloween party. Patti could not attend the meeting, but each member was allowed to bring a guest and Raven asked Patti to come with her. Patti was curious. "What do you do at these parties?"

"Well, to be honest, I don't know. Usually, they have music, dancing, and refreshments; of course, most people will dress up. There will be lots of fake blood and probably some real blood; they may have a program and I'm pretty sure they'll make a sacrifice."

"You mean they're going to kill someone?" Patti was appalled by Raven's casualness.

"No, not a real sacrifice; it will be fake, but it will look real. It will be fun!" Raven was excited.

Patti thought about it and decided to give it a try; she was certain her mother would not approve, and that motivated her to go. Over the next few days they made arrangements and shared ideas about costumes. Patti decided upon an "Elvira, Mistress of the Night" look and Raven chose to be one of the "Brides of Dracula." October flew by and Patti soon found herself on her way to meet Raven. The hospital had called in extra staff for Halloween; they tried to save as many vampires, werewolves, witches, and weirdoes from themselves as possible. The party was absolute insanity. The music was loud; the dance floor was crowded; and many of the older kids, who had been drinking, were rude and obnoxious. It was more fun to watch than participate. The program was good; it scared a lot of people, with two sacrifices and lots of blood. Raven had well described what would happen. Patti kept watching the time; she knew she couldn't stay much past 1:00 am. She found Raven and asked if she were ready to leave; Raven didn't want to go but agreed it was a long way home and they had better get started. Patti noticed she acted funny, and Raven told her she had a couple of drinks containing more than just soda. Patti worried that maybe Raven was digging a hole for herself. She told Raven to take it easy and not start something leading to trouble. Raven agreed she had probably gone too far, but she'd had a great time and could hardly wait for the New Year's party.

By the end of first semester Patti felt much better about middle school, but all she really wanted was for the year to be over and hoped to have more time with Colby next year. She sensed Colby felt the same way; at times he seemed to feel the need to be close to Patti. They meant a lot to each other. Patti had worked hard; she wanted to keep up with Colby and not end up in different classes. She had continued to help Raven off and on, and Raven was grateful enough to invite Patti to the New Year's party. However, Patti's mother had committed them to attend a youth gathering at Uncle Robert's church. She had volunteered to help sponsor it. Patti got the details from one of her cousins. It started after lunch; kids would watch videos, play games and have activities. The evening meal was a big barbecue, followed by more games, singing, and activities. The event was for middle school and up, so Patti could go along with her mother and enjoy the fun. She was looking forward to it, but hated to tell Raven she could not go to the Goth party.

Patti's year ended well and she was ready to finish the sixth grade. On the first day back she discovered she and Colby were in the same exploration class, so they now shared two classes; the best part was they could visit in exploration, which meant they could actually communicate every day if necessary. Patti thought this was going to be a better semester. Maybe her luck was changing. In many ways, she was more correct than she realized; the spirits of darkness were about to turn on her.

Toward the end of February, Patti asked Colby if there was any way they could get together privately after school; she had something she wanted to share. Colby thought he would have to walk home in a couple of days because his mother had to take Caitlyn somewhere; it was cold, but they could walk together, and maybe his mother would take Patti home. The next day he had everything worked out; she could walk home with him and they could visit. Patti was thrilled.

They met after school and started walking. "What do you want to tell me?"

"Well, it's not exactly what I want to tell you; I want to tell you and show you...sort of," explained Patti. "Have you noticed anything different about me lately?"

"Well, I...really...I mean...no, not really; you've seemed happier, but you look the same to me."

Patti stopped, unbuttoned her coat and opened it up. "Are you sure you haven't noticed anything; I thought boys were interested in this kind of stuff."

"I don't understand; what kind of stuff are you talking about?" Colby was puzzled.

"Breasts!"

"Breasts?...I don't understand; I mean, I know about breasts...but I'm just, well, I don't understand...wait, you mean your breasts. What about them?"

"Mine are growing; I'm growing breasts! Would you like to touch them?"

Colby was shocked. "What? I can't go around touching your breasts; you shouldn't even ask!"

"I didn't mean I wanted you to get all lovey dovey and rub on me. Boys don't get them; I figured you would be interested, that's all. It means I'm becoming a woman."

"Look, that's girl stuff I don't care about, but I'm happy you're excited about it. I guess I would like to touch you, but I don't think I should; I hope you're not mad at me."

"No, it's okay; I'm not mad at you. You're a gentleman; some boys aren't. And just so you'll know, I'm not going to let anyone touch me there...just remember though, you had your chance." Patti gave Colby an ornery smile.

"Well, thanks for the offer." Colby felt good; he liked the sound of the word *gentleman* when it came from someone outside of his family.

About one week before her twelfth birthday in March, Patti noticed she felt a little strange inside; she couldn't explain why. It wasn't like she was sick, yet she felt queasy low in her body; like when your lower digestive tract is upset and you worry about "soiling your shorts." It was an uneasiness she didn't understand. She decided she would talk to her mother about it after school. Following lunch, she felt better and decided maybe this was just another one of those mystery pains that come and go but mean nothing.

However, later that afternoon when she decided to walk home because it was a beautiful, sunny day, the pain returned. It felt as though she was leaking or as her Grandpa Bender would say when he fixed engines, "She's losin' oil." When Patti reached the apartment, she went straight to the bathroom...it wasn't oil; she had spotted her panties three or four times. The blood was in various colors, which meant it had been happening off and on most of the day.

Patti had told Colby she was becoming a woman; lo and behold, it came true. In many respects she was excited; she could get pregnant and have children; she would be growing hair in odd places, hopefully, not her face. On the other hand, she wasn't even twelve years old; she didn't want to be woman; she enjoyed being a girl. And one thing she knew for certain: she definitely did not want to get pregnant! She didn't want any whiny baby to take care of; nope, none of that; she'd seen her mother suffer to take care of her, go to school and go to work. No, she didn't want any baby and found it hard to understand why anyone would.

Patti found one of her mother's panty liners and changed

her clothes; she treated and soaked her bloody underwear and put it in the laundry. She was anxious, sort of, to tell her mother the news. Kathy got home late and in a rush. Patti asked to visit, but her mother put her off. Patti was annoyed her mother never seemed to have time for her, so later when she asked Patti about her news, Patti told her to forget it; it wasn't that important. Her mother didn't press the issue and they were soon in bed.

It wasn't until two or three days later that Patti felt like talking about her period. Kathy had come home really tired so Patti had fixed and warmed some leftovers for supper. While they were eating, Kathy said, "Patti, I just don't know what I would do without you; you are such a big girl and are so helpful. Thank you for fixing supper."

"It's okay, Mom, I like to help out; I know you're busy, and I feel sorry for you. By the way, I had my first period this week."

"You what?" Kathy nearly dropped her fork.

Patti was very nonchalant. "I had my first period this week."

Kathy showed concern. "Why Patti, are you okay? Why didn't you say something?"

"Look, you were busy and didn't have..."

Kathy interrupted. "Now listen to me, young lady! When you have something important to share, I want you to tell me; I'm not so busy that I don't have time for my own daughter!"

"But, Mom you don't." Patti paused. "You're welcome for supper."

Kathy was angry, and Patti was hurt. Their little family was teetering on the edge. Patti knew it, and somehow she felt her mother did too. There was no more talking that evening, but the next day her mother promised they would discuss Patti's womanhood and other related matters. Patti wasn't exactly ignorant about such things. She had taken health in school, and the girls in her classes talked about such things as casually as breathing. Patti thought she had handled things quite well. Perhaps she didn't need her mother as much as her mother thought, and yet, her mother claimed to need her. Patti worked hard around their apartment. She did most of the laundry, kept the floor swept and mopped, picked up after her mother and herself, fixed meals for herself or both of them, kept the bathroom clean, and tried to give her mother the "space" she needed. One thing for sure, Patti knew her mother could not survive without her. Patti thought. "Boy, if I were dead, my mother would be sorry; I'd like be at my funeral and just see how she'd feel then. Yeah, that would be fair, she could suffer for a change." Such wishful thinking held dim prospects for her future. Little did she know how much her mother had suffered and was suffering, and little did she know that her wish just might come true.

Kathy forgot about Patti's birthday or at least did not mention it. Patti didn't really care; no one ever made a big deal about her birthday anyway. Sometimes she wondered if they were ashamed and didn't want to acknowledge she was alive. Of course, she knew that wasn't true. All of her mother's family loved her and went out of their way to be nice; she knew her mother loved her, but more and more, she realized her mother did not know how to show it. Sometimes, when Patti went to bed, she would feel tears rolling down her cheeks. "Tough girls don't cry," thought Patti, who would continue crying. Maybe she wasn't such a tough girl after all; maybe she was a normal girl with real emotions and feelings. Maybe that was her problem...and maybe it explained a few things.

Right before spring break Raven reminded Patti of their Rites of Spring party, the biggest party of the year. There would be lots of blood—virgin blood, a celebration of womanhood; she would love it. Patti was impressed. Celebrating womanhood, hmm, how interesting; she would definitely be there. Raven was thrilled, and even Patti was anxious to go.

During spring break, Patti and her mother did visit, but not about what Patti expected. Her mother actually sat down and shared some things Patti had never known. First of all, her mother wanted to assure her that being a woman was okay; it meant she was growing up. Since kids want most of all to grow up, she should be happy about it. However, with it came a host of responsibilities. "God doesn't give us something just to have and then disregard; He expects us to be responsible for what He has given us, in this case, the gift of life. I gave life to you, but your father and I were not responsible; we, in that one moment, failed to honor God by having sex before we were married and I paid the price by having to raise you without a father. I want you to understand God did not punish me because of what we did. I believe conception is a chance, like rolling dice. You can't always roll a 7; in the same way, having sex doesn't necessarily mean you will get pregnant.

"I have to believe God allowed your conception; He wanted you to be born. You are the special creature God intended; you must believe that. I hope you feel it is wrong to kill any of God's special people, the born or unborn. I could have chosen to have you killed in my womb; Aunt Sherry could have done the same thing. I couldn't do it because I believe it's murder; Sherry couldn't do it because she had no stomach for it. There's a difference, but the result was the same; we both had our babies. I kept mine and Sherry didn't, but we both shared God's gift to us. Patti, it's important to believe in something or you will never be anything; believe in life. I've tried to teach you, but I know I've been a lousy mother. I just hope you understand and can forgive me for my foolishness; I promise I am going to do better. I love you so much, and Patti, you are truly special. I can see so much in you that is good and wholesome; you are the best mistake anyone ever made." Kathy wiped away tears and tried to smile.

"Mama, I love you too; I admire the way you have tried to take care of me; you are special too, and I'm not sure you realize just how special. Can we talk like this more often?"

"Yes, Patti, I'd like that very much." They reached out and hugged each other, both crying, both ashamed. Maybe, just maybe, something good would come of this.

∞ Thirteen ∞

When school started, Raven and Patti began plans for their big night. They would meet as always; Raven was pretty sure she had a ride home, so Patti could leave whenever she wanted. Patti had to be home well before 2:00 am; she couldn't afford to let her mother discover she was sneaking out so soon after their tête-à-tête. The day of the party, Raven was absolutely beside herself; Patti kept reminding her to calm down or she might wet her pants, but it didn't help. When the bell rang at the end of school, Patti found Raven and they finalized their plans. The party started around 8:00, but Raven suggested she meet Patti at 9:00. They would easily be there by 9:30 when things started to "heat" up.

All was set. Patti dressed in her black jean outfit with her black shoes; she also wore a black hat Raven had not seen. When they met, Raven really liked the hat, and they headed on their way. The party was as expected. She and Raven tried to enjoy the music over the noise, or it may have been the other way around. They danced a couple of times, including a group dance where no one knew with whom they were dancing. One of the older boys offered Patti a sip of his beer; she had never tasted beer; her mother only drank wine, which could be tolerable, but Patti almost spit it out. "Yuck," she thought; it reminded her of a dog drinking out of the toilet. When Raven came back with a small glass of beer, Patti asked, "How do you drink that stuff?"

"It's wet," she chirped.

The girls lost track of time and nearly missed one of the shows; as usual, Raven was right—lots of blood and gore. They had a short break before they went back on the dance floor. Patti had to go to the bathroom, and when she returned she told Raven she'd seen several couples celebrating the rites of spring. If they continued, they would likely find a most unusual gift in their Christmas stocking; one that cried, needed to be fed, and changed. Raven laughed and told her not to worry; there wasn't much anyone could do about it. Raven left for a minute and came back with two drinks, giving one to Patti, who sipped it. "This tastes kind of funny. What is it?"

"I don't know. Just drink it and have fun."

Patti sipped the drink, which seemed to get better the more she drank. Raven had already finished hers and was going for another. Patti began to wonder if Raven had an alcohol problem. When she got back, they went to another show and Patti finished her drink. She had to admit it did relax her; she felt warm inside. Raven wanted to get her another, but Patti reminded her she had to walk home. Then it struck her. "Gosh, what time is it?"

Raven shrugged. "I have no idea."

They finally found someone with a watch; this person wasn't sure, but thought it was about 1:00, maybe a little later. They found another person who confirmed the time. "Look, I'd better be going; thank you for inviting me...it's been fun," said Patti, starting to turn away, then stopping to turn back. "Listen, Raven, be careful; watch yourself. I think you drink too much, and when you do, you are vulnerable; my mother had a good friend who went to a party and came home with more than a hangover. I was at the hospital when she gave birth. Don't let anyone take advantage of you; you'd probably make a lousy mother."

Raven looked rather shocked. "Patti, I guess I'd never thought of it that way; I'll watch myself, I promise. You're right about the mother part. Thank you...and hey, be careful going home in the dark. I don't want you running into a tree or something." Raven smiled.

"I'll be careful; see you at school, Monday."

It took a little while to get out of the building. When Patti stepped outside in the fresh air, she began to worry more about the time. She had to get home before her mother, or there would be trouble...big trouble. If she cut across the park she could save several minutes. It was darker through there, but the sky was clear and a half moon helped. She decided to risk it. About a third of the way through she decided to run; that would save additional time. At first she kind of jogged, but soon she found herself running faster and faster. She tried to keep focused and, as Raven had said, not run into any trees. Just then a large tree loomed to her left; she adjusted right to avoid it and...BOOM! Something hit her right across the chest.

The upper part of her body stopped completely; her legs continued running but they were no longer on the ground. She might have said something like "What" or "Hey," but it didn't matter; she could see her feet in front instead of under her. Her whole body began to fall; she felt buttons pop from her vest. Her rear end hit the ground first. The ground was damp and softer than usual because it had rained the day before, but the landing knocked the wind out of her; her feet hit the ground next, bouncing in front of her; finally her head landed with a resounding thump. For a moment everything went black; then she saw stars; unfortunately they were not the ones in the sky. She lay there stunned, barely conscious. What in the world had happened? She knew she had missed the tree; there were no low branches. What hit her?

Patti lay very still as if she were dead. As she recovered her senses, several things came into focus. Her butt hurt, she was having trouble getting her breath, and her head was buzzing like a hive full of bees. Somehow instinctively, she knew she had to lie still and play dead. As she continued to get a grip on her senses, she slowly opened her eyes. She could see real stars in the sky through the branches of the tree. The streetlight she saw before still provided security from the night. But directly between her prostrate body and that light stood a giant, a monster standing at her feet. She looked up and could not even tell whether or not it had a head, but she saw its arms resting at its waistline and she thought it might be fumbling with its belt. Patti immediately understood what was about to happen; she was terrified at the thought of being violated and left for dead. Her mind flashed with thoughts of escape and safety, then like a bolt of lightning, it struck her.

Silhouetted at the base of the giant was an almost perfect

inverted V. Patti knew what she had to do; drawing upon every ounce of strength and every bit of courage she could muster, she lurched forward and kicked the vertex of this inverted shape as hard as she could. The nickel studs on her black boot twinkled as it drove straight to the mark. The giant, caught completely by surprise, issued a muffled groan, followed by a series of deep moans, then dropped to its knees, but Patti never saw it.

She was on her feet, flying across the park at record speeds; she didn't look back, just ran as fast as she could, not even slowing down for the fire escape at their apartment. She managed the door and rushed inside to safety, closing it behind her. She ran to her bed and sat there, and as she did, she began to shiver, then shudder. She tried to cry but there were no tears, only more shudders. Her breathing was rapid, her lungs hurt, her legs were sore...her boots were lousy running shoes. Her head hurt and her bottom was sore and worst of all, for the first time in Patti's life, she was really scared...afraid. She curled her knees to her chest and rolled into a fetal position on her side in the bed. She fell asleep almost immediately.

The next thing Patti remembered was waking up on her bed; sunlight broke through the high windows in the apartment. It was very quiet; her mother was still asleep. She lay there trying to explain this awful dream; she remembered running, something hitting her, being on the ground, a giant, escaping and running home. What an awful dream. If she had to dream that dream, she would rather not fall asleep. At that moment she realized she was all curled up in bed; she didn't sleep like that...and why was she wearing her day clothes? She always wore pajamas to bed. Something was wrong. Patti started to uncurl. She was stiff and sore; her bottom hurt; her head ached. What was going on? She sat and straightened her clothes, then noticed buttons missing from her vest; she remembered wearing a hat but did not see one anywhere near her bed.

She shuddered, then did it again; she was starting to shake, then started to cry as a hand of fear enveloped and almost crushed her. She needed to go to the bathroom, but her feet wouldn't move. She couldn't understand what was

wrong, but it occurred to her that the giant had been real.
Had she come within minutes of being raped and killed?
Had she really escaped this monster? Was she safe in her
own bed? Patti was confused; she sat there a long time and
finally tried to stand up. She was okay; she took a few steps;
she could walk. She made it to the bathroom. On the way
back, Patti could see her mother sleeping; standing there
looking at her, she suddenly began to cry. The tears
poured down her face and dripped about her; she began to
sob. Without even realizing it she called out, "Mama," then
just a little louder, "Mama."

Her mother groaned and moved in her bed. "Patti, is that
you? What do you want? I'm trying to sleep."

"Mama, I've got to talk to you; I've done something
terrible. Can we talk?"

Her mother finally rolled over to look at her. "Why,
Honey, what's wrong? Are you sick?" It only took a second
for Kathy to see that something was horribly wrong. Patti
stood there crying and shaking, looking like a whipped
dog; Kathy noticed her missing buttons. "Oh, you've lost
some of your buttons; it's okay, I can fix that. Don't cry."
But wait...Patti never cried like this, and she was very upset.
"Patti, there's something else, isn't there?"

"Yes, I told you; I've done something terrible, and you will
probably send me away. Oh, Mama, I'm so sorry." Patti
cried even harder.

"Why Patti, how can you feel that way? I would never send
you away. I love you." Kathy reached out her arms to Patti,
who rushed into her embrace. She held Patti for what
seemed like an hour. Patti continued to cry and sob; her
mother was soon crying too.

Finally, Patti seemed to calm down and pulled away,
looking her mother right in the eye. "Mama, we've got to
talk, and what I'm about to say is shameful. When I'm
finished I know you will want to punish me, and I deserve
whatever you decide, so don't spare me."

Kathy held back a smile; she could not imagine what Patti could have done to make her feel this way. Patti went back to the fifth grade and told her mother about sneaking out of the house, going to parties and secret meetings, tricking her into buying the very clothes she was wearing...all of her secrets. Kathy sat there listening, surprised and concerned, but not exactly convinced that what Patti was saying related to her emotional state. "You know, Patti, I have always trusted you; we have been a team, and you know how important trust is in any relationship. I guess you're saying I can no longer trust you. Is that correct?"

"Yes, I guess so. Would you like to beat me and make it right?" Patti was crying again.

"Patti! Why do you say that? How would beating you restore my trust? You've done bad things, and worse yet, you knew they were bad."

"I'm really sorry, Mama, I promise you it will never happen again...cross my heart and hope to die."

"I know you're sorry, but what are we to do?"

Patti hesitated. "Maybe you'd better hear the rest of the story before you decide."

Patti then related the specific events that had occurred since 9:00 the evening before right to the moment Patti rushed into the apartment and latched the fire escape door. This time Kathy was absolutely stunned; if someone had hit her in the head with a two by four, it would have only been a tap compared to how she now felt. "Oh my God, Patti, you could have been killed! I could be in the park right now identifying your body. Oh Patti...I feel so bad for you..." Kathy stopped. 'Wait one minute, young lady, are you telling me the truth? Or are you making this up to get me to forgive you for being dishonest and sneaky?"

"No, Mother, it's the God's honest truth as best I remember it."

"Okay, take your clothes off so I can examine you; if what

you say is true, I can verify it."

Patti complied instantly; she stood before her mother in her underwear while she examined her. Yes, it appeared that Patti's bottom had mild discoloring; it was tender to the touch. The back of her head appeared to have a bump; it was also tender. Buttons were missing from her vest and the remaining threads suggested they were pulled off, and grass had stained the backside of her jeans. Kathy looked sternly at Patti. "Okay, I want you to fold these clothes and put them in a sack; I want you to take your shoes and put them in another sack; then I want you to put on some clean clothes; we're going to see the police."

Since Patti rarely got into trouble, she had no idea how to interpret or process her mother's demands. "You're going to have me put in jail aren't you?"

"Is that what you want?"

"No, but I told you I will accept any punishment I deserve; if you think I should go to jail, then that's were I'll go; if you decide to have me shot, my life is over." In Patti's mind, her days were numbered.

Her mother got on the phone and asked if Detective Johnson were there. Kathy was in luck. The detective was filling a shift for another officer and would be there all morning. Kathy told them she would be right down. Carrying the sacks of evidence, they drove directly to the police station. Kathy told Patti she and Detective Johnson were old friends, and she wanted to talk to her alone for a few moments before the detective talked to Patti. Patti, terrified, willingly agreed to anything her mother proposed. When they got to the police station, they were ushered to Detective Johnson's office. Patti waited outside while her mother talked to the detective; soon the detective opened the door and called for Patti to come in; Patti entered, ready to "face the firing squad." "Patti, have a seat."

"Yes, ma'am." Patti quickly sat down.

"Your mother tells me you've had a terrible experience and

147

have been a bad girl. Is that correct?"

"Yes, it is."

"Okay, I'd like for you to tell me about how you were bad. Take your time and tell me everything."

Patti immediately related exactly what she had told her mother about sneaking out of the house and going places without her mother's permission. Detective Johnson listened intently. "All right, now tell me about last night."

Once again Patty told the detective everything she remembered about what had happened in the park. Ms. Johnson looked through the clothes in Patti's sack and examined her shoes. "Okay, I'd like for you and your mother to come with me; we need to take a drive."

Patti knew this was it; they were taking her to be shot; her mother would be a witness. They got in Detective Johnson's car and she radioed for another squad car to meet and follow them. Patti figured these guys would do the shooting. She was quite surprised when they pulled up to the park and got out of the car. "Patti, I want you to show me where this happened. Can you do that?"

"Yes, I think so." Patti led them into the park.

She wasn't exactly sure, but she thought she found the right tree and location. Detective Johnson ordered the other officers to look for evidence. One of them found her hat, then Patty spotted one of her buttons; the detective found the other one. The detective told the officers that this was crime scene and turned to Patti. "Do you have a job?"

"Why, no, ma'am, I'm only in the sixth grade; no one would want to hire me."

"Well, let me say you have the makings of a good detective. How about coming to work as my assistant?"

"Why gosh, I don't know...I mean...you'd have to ask my mom."

148

"Well, Kathy, what do you think about having Patti work for me?"

Kathy thought a moment. "I think she's pretty young to go to work; she probably needs to finish school first."

Deb sighed. "Okay, but I could sure use an assistant. Let's go back to the station."

Patti was confused; she was surprised she hadn't been shot, then the detective wanted her as an assistant. It didn't make sense. When they got back to the office, Detective Johnson had everyone sit down. She looked right at Patti. "You, young lady, are a very brave girl, and I'd like to shake your hand." The detective reached out her hand and Patti did the same; they shook hands and smiled. "You did a very brave thing and I want you to know we are going to catch this bas...er, scumbag so he doesn't go around hurting anyone else, and we are going to have you to thank for it." Patti smiled, feeling rather proud. "However, we still have this other problem; I think you know the one I mean."

"Yes, ma'am, I do." A bit of fear crept into Patti's voice.

"Well, your mother has left it up to me to decide what to do with you; she thinks you should be punished for your dishonesty, and even though you are a hero, I have to agree with her; I think it's really important to be honest. How do you feel about it, Patti?"

"I agree; I know I did a bad thing sneaking out of the house and not being honest with my mother, and I told her she has every right to punish me; I'll accept whatever you say. If you're going to send me away, I'd like to say good bye and tell her I'm sorry one more time." Patti began to cry.

Patti had not noticed her mother crying next to her, and even Detective Johnson was having trouble holding back tears. "Okay, we can do that. I just have one more question before we take you away."

"Okay."

"Do you like ice cream?"

"Why yes, it's my favorite dessert."

"Good." The detective continued. "Do you like big banana splits with all the trimmings?"

"Yes, ma'am! Banana splits are awesome."

"Okay, I've decided your punishment." The detective paused. "Your mother and I are going to take you to the ice cream shop and buy you the biggest banana split they make, and you are going to eat...every...single bite. Do you understand?"

"I sure do!" Patti paused. "What if I can't eat it all?"

Her mother injected. "Then we'll shoot you." Detective Johnson nodded and grinned.

When they arrived at the ice cream shop, everyone ordered a banana split. While Patti dived into hers, the older girls talked. "I thought policemen only ate doughnuts." Kathy grinned.

"You've been watching too much TV. You show me a policeman that won't eat a banana split and I'll bet you're in a graveyard looking at his tombstone. The problem is it takes too long to eat them!"

"Isn't that the case? It takes time to enjoy, enjoy, enjoy." Kathy smiled.

"How right you are! It seems like all I do is run around and wind up no better off than when I started. I know my eating habits are a disgrace; I'll probably pay for it when I get old." The detective made a face.

"I completely agree. The hospital is always rush, rush, rush...I don't even have time to eat a meal, let alone enjoy it. Then when I finally get home, I'm too tired to fix anything, and if I do manage something, I'm too tired to chew." Kathy sighed.

"Sounds like you and I are in the same work...saving other people but killing ourselves. Say, not to change the subject, but I hate crying while I'm eating. I don't think I ever told you the whole story about your friend...er, I forget...her name, it started with an S..."

"Sherry, her name was Sherry."

"Yeah, Sherry, I should have remembered. Well, I have you two to thank for saving my department." Ms. Johnson looked pleased.

This surprised Kathy. "Saving your department? I don't understand."

"Well, this is what happened. The state had been encouraging communities our size to add additional departments and have more manpower available. Our station did not have a vice squad; two or three of our guys handled these cases, but no one was in charge, and there were no guidelines to handle vice crimes. I was the new kid on the block and only the second female officer to make detective at this station; as you can imagine, the "guys" weren't very happy about having me around, so when I suggested we organize a vice unit, they jumped on the bandwagon to get me out of their hair; they figured if they put me in charge and everything fell through, I would be discredited and leave the force, jump off a bridge, or try to catch bullets with my teeth.

"Anyway, when you and Sherry showed up with the proverbial "impossible" case that only gets solved on TV, I knew I had a chance to give our department a big—no, make that a huge—win. When Sherry remembered so many of the people at that party, I was absolutely convinced we could nail those SOB's, and Kathy, we did it; we got them, and I'm pretty sure they're still in prison where they belong. When we won that case, no one could turn around and say I had failed. One of the older detectives came to me secretly and told me I had won the support of most of the guys; he told me if I didn't make a big deal about my success, no one would oppose me when we came up for review. Hey, what can I say; here I am still in charge of vice and kicking ass. By the way, we're going to get this guy too...you mark my words! I owe all this to you and Sherry. Thank you for coming forward and giving me that opportunity; you guys were the best."

Kathy sat shocked, her ice cream melting and her eyes watering. "I didn't realize...I never even thought about it; I just wanted some justice for Sherry. No one deserves what happened to her. She was no virgin, but she was not a bad girl. It's bad enough when you really want a baby, then to go through all that pain when you don't...it's just not fair."

Deb opined. "And in Sherry's case, rape is against the law."

Kathy's face brightened. "Well, listen, I know we thanked you at the time, but let me say it again. Thank you for helping and not forgetting about us, and thank you for what you are going to do for Patti; you're the best too!"

The detective flashed a grin. "Hey, it's okay; I'm glad to help, and by the way, I assume you know you can get free counseling for Patti if she needs it; some people can go on with their lives and some can't; I want her to be okay."

If Patti lived to be one hundred, this would be the best banana split she would ever eat. She had learned forgiveness can taste superb, and she did eat every bite. She liked Detective Johnson and trusted the detective would get her "man." Kathy seemed so happy, and Patti loved when her mother smiled. Patti suggested she could probably eat another banana split, but the mean old adults laughed her down. She had to settle for watching them eat "soupy" splits; adults just don't know when to shut up and eat their just desserts.

When they got home, Kathy admitted she was tired and needed a nap; she reminded Patti she had been up late the night before and might need some rest also. Patti was not a napper, so the suggestion fell flat...until her mother invited her to sleep with her; in no time at all both girls were sound asleep in each other's arms. Patti had always felt safe and secure around her mother, and Kathy didn't really get that connection, but maybe things were starting to sink in.

152

Patti hoped so because somehow she sensed her fear would return to haunt her...when she was alone.

When the girls awoke, Patti was surprised at her mother's attitude. "Patti, what would you like for supper? Make it something special."

Patti thought a moment. "Spaghetti, spaghetti with meat sauce and cheese and a big green salad."

"Will you help me with it?"

"You bet I will."

"Okay, what would you like to do this evening? Would you like to go someplace?"

"No, I'd like to stay home with you, but maybe we could rent a couple of movies and eat popcorn; I'd like that."

"Then that's what we'll do."

"Okay, just one thing, Mama. I pick one movie and you pick one. I won't get any cartoons, if you won't get any lovey dovey stuff."

"It's a deal; I've cried enough for one day. I'd prefer a good comedy!"

They were very close now and Patti began to see that being attacked in the park was not all bad. She'd gotten a big banana split; her mother was fixing a great supper; and they were going to rent movies. Perhaps even more important, Kathy was being a real mother to Patti, who thought, "Why can't it be like this all the time...or at least, most of the time?"

While Patti helped her mother with dinner, Kathy wanted to visit. "Patti, I want to tell you how much I love you and how special you are...even Detective Johnson thought so. Today, I also learned how brave and tough you can be. I feel bad about this because, well, some of it is my fault. I haven't been a good mother lately and you deserve better.

I don't tell you often enough how much I appreciate all you do around here or how well you do in school. It seems like we only get attention when we've done something wrong, and it shouldn't be that way; we need to get credit for what we do right...to balance things out. I know we've had this conversation before, but I'm going to do my darnedest to be a better mother, and I want you to make me a promise. Will you do that?"

"I'll try."

"Promise me if I ever honestly neglect you or refuse to listen to your concerns again, you will slap me across my face as hard as you can."

Patti was shocked. "But I can't hit you! You're my mother."

Kathy was adamant. "No, Patti, I mean it; maybe it will knock some sense into me. We're going to make this work; we both know it hasn't been working, and we're going to fix it, and fix it so well we won't ever want it to change. Now, do you promise?"

Patti was tentative. "Okay, I guess...no, I promise...but will you hit me back?"

"No, Patti, I won't hit you back." Her mother smiled. "I'm sorry to be so windy, but I wanted to get this out of the way before we eat and enjoy our movies. Are you okay?"

"What do you mean?" Patti didn't understand.

"I mean, how do you feel? How's your bottom?"

"Oh, I feel better. My head is okay; it's a little sore. My bottom still hurts when I sit, but I'll be all right."

"Good, I'm glad to hear that." Kathy paused. "We have a problem."

Patti's face wrinkled. "We do? What's wrong?"

"We have to decide how we are going to handle this mess.

Right now the only person who knows what happened to you is Detective Johnson. I'm not sure we should be blabbing all over town that you were attacked in the park; we don't want to call attention to this until she has a chance to investigate; I don't want to hinder any chance they might have catching this guy. What do you think?"

"I want her to catch this bum so he can't hurt anyone else. I think we should keep quiet."

"Okay, how about this? I'll talk to my mother and fill her in. I want to contact Mrs. Martin, one of the counselors at the middle school. If you have any problems you can see her; she's a nice lady. I'm going to tell my supervisor at work that I might have to be gone if any problems arise; she'll understand. I think that's it."

"Can I tell Colby? He won't say anything if I tell him not to."

"Yes, you can tell Colby, but no one else. Is that okay?" asked Kathy.

"Sure, I don't really want to talk about it anyway."

It's funny how banana splits, spaghetti, and your mother can help you forget about things you wished had never happened. Right now Patty was miles and miles from a park only blocks away from her home, a park where she and her mother had spent many hours walking, talking, laughing, and playing...a place associated with good times and fun. Could Patti ever go back there and enjoy its pleasures? More importantly, could she ever go back by herself?

Supper, actually dinner, was just what Patti ordered, and it tasted wonderful. Patti admired her mother's talents; it often seemed she could do anything. Patti resented her mother was not there to teach her more about the kitchen or sewing or even about what she did at work. Patti wanted to learn because she knew someday she would be on her own and have to take care of herself, and even though she was only twelve, her time was coming.

After dinner, they went to town and rented two movies. They had a great evening together, a couple of "wild and crazy" girls. When the second movie ended around 11:30, it was time for bed. As they changed, Kathy asked, "Will you be all right tonight?"

"What do you mean, Mom?"

"Well, I shouldn't have to remind you, but you had a difficult time last night. Are you going to be okay?"

"Yeah, I'm okay." Patti's voice showed a bit of hesitation.

"Well, I was just wondering; I thought you might want to sleep with me tonight. I..."

She didn't get a chance to finish before a human torpedo landed in her bed, triggered by the secret code, "sleep with me." There was safety in her mother's arms, and right now that meant more than all the banana splits and spaghetti in the entire world!

The weekend ended too quickly. Kathy contacted Mrs. Martin at home and asked to see her briefly before school on Monday to alert her to Patti's situation but without details. Patti enjoyed riding with her mother to school; the school bus was often crowded and noisy in the morning, and Patti didn't care for all that confusion so early in the day. In fact, she often thought if she were in charge, school would start around 10:00 am...after she was more awake. They went to see Mrs. Martin, who told Patti in no uncertain terms that if she were having any problems—any problems at all—she was to come immediately to her office and they could talk or she could just sit and recover. Patti felt a little better knowing she had somewhere to go. Patti talked to Colby briefly in English class and they arranged to meet the next morning before school. Patti wanted him to know what had happened.

The next morning Kathy brought Patti to school early so she could talk to Colby. He listened intently to Patti's description of the events in the park. When she finished, Colby looked at her in astonishment. "You mean you kicked this guy right in the..." Colby just couldn't say the missing word because during the summer, not too long after he had moved to his new home, he had endured the dreaded "boys bicycle" accident when his foot slipped and he suddenly found himself straddling that bar of pain supporting the seat and the steering column. He grimaced and started to reach down before he realized other students were around—some things are best done in private. Patti was slightly amused, but did not give herself away. Colby was quite surprised by Patti's revelation. "Are you all right? You had to take a nasty fall."

Patti's response was short and perhaps not entirely true. "Yes, I'm fine." She did not want to admit that her heroism in the park was followed by a death grip of fear, nor did she want anyone to know that when other people were around she was fine, but home alone was an entirely different matter.

The week ended quickly and for all outward appearances Patti seemed her old self. She was getting all kinds of attention; even Detective Johnson had called and talked to her. Mrs. Martin at school had checked on her two or three times. Her mother had been driving her to school so she only had to ride the bus home. Grandmother Bender had called to arrange a dinner for her over the weekend. Her mother had changed shifts so she was home earlier in the day, which meant they could spend more time together. All of this was fine, but inside Patti knew she was not the same. Something was wrong; something seemed to be eating at her, and it was not going away.

⤞ Fourteen ⤝

The only thing missing during the next week was Raven; Patti had not seen her since the party. She asked around, and no one seemed to know much. Then later in the week Patti heard Raven was sick. By the end of the week she understood Raven had been in school, but Patti had not seen her in the classes they shared. She hoped Raven was okay, but knew she had a tendency to abuse herself, and such behavior has a way of striking back.

The dinner at the Benders held several surprises for Patti. First of all, many of her seldom seen relatives were there. It was good to see Maggie; she had graduated from high school and was working. Patti missed their fun times at the park. She was also surprised to see her Uncle Robert, or Bob, as Mr. Bender called him. Patti liked Uncle Bob because he was always nice to her. He was not like his sister, Patti's grandma; he was outgoing and friendly, always joking about something. Patti thought everyone had more fun when he was around. Uncle Bob had not come for dinner; he had come to see Patti. "Well, young lady, I understand you're someone not to be messed with. How about it?" asked her uncle.

Patti grinned. "I have to protect myself from all those crazies; I can't afford a bodyguard."

"I can't either; I was wondering what you are going to be doing in June?"

"Hey, I'm going to be celebrating being out of school and enjoying my summer vacation."

"Good, how would you like to go to a summer camp?"

Patti looked curious. "What kind of camp?"

"It's called Fun Camp." Her uncle made a face. "You have to do awful things like go swimming, hiking, exploring, and playing games. Whoops, I forgot, you don't like any of those things...I guess I'll have to give this award for a free week of camp to someone else."

Patti's eyes got big. "Hey, hold it a minute! You mean I get to go to camp for a whole week, do all those awful things, and it won't cost anything?!"

"Yup, not one thin dime." Bob smiled.

Patti didn't hesitate. "You talked me into it; I'd love to go."

"Good, I'll get you signed up."

The next week was a chance to clear up a few loose ends. Raven had been sick with a serious intestinal disorder. For the first couple or three days, she couldn't keep anything in her stomach; then after she was finally able to eat, she couldn't keep anything in the other end. She tried to come to school, but only lasted a couple of hours before she had to go home. Her doctor finally decided she had food poisoning and was lucky to not end up in the hospital. The experience put a damper on her goth activities; she decided to cool it for a while, and Patti thought that was a good decision.

The middle school did pre-enrollment for all the sixth and seventh graders. Patti and Colby enrolled in the same classes and got their schedules approved. They had a better chance of being together in the seventh grade, plus Patti visited with Mrs. Martin in the office and mentioned it would be nice if she and Colby could share as many classes as possible. She explained they had been friends since second grade and meant a lot to each other; she also made it clear she did not want to be with Colby to just gab or cause trouble. Their friendship suffered when they could not be together. Mrs. Martin was surprised at how well Patti sold her argument and told her she would see what she could do. Mrs. Martin said it was easier to help students who wanted to do things for the right reasons and thanked Patti for coming to see her.

Things seemed to be working out nicely, but there was one secret Patti had not shared with anyone. On two or three occasions she had awakened in the middle of the night lying in the same fetal position she had assumed on the night of her attack. On one occasion she was also shaking. She did what she could to ignore the problem, but that did not change the fact it happened. Patti was puzzled; she had worried about bad dreams or nightmares, and even though they had not materialized, it was obvious that her mind had not forgotten the park...nor had her fear gone away.

When Patti got home from school on the following Monday, roughly two weeks since her assault, there was a phone message from Detective Johnson. When Patti called her, the detective said she would like to visit about some news in her case. Patti told her she would be home all evening and her mother would be home by supper time. She invited Detective Johnson to come by when her shift was over to eat with them. The detective did not want to impose, but Patti insisted, telling her she was fixing supper, and it would be special, her way of thanking the detective for all she had done. Detective Johnson paused, then remarked that a home-cooked meal sounded great; she would come by as soon as possible and maybe help out...or at least, not get in the way. Patti was thrilled.

When Detective Johnson arrived, she and Patti discussed school and how Patti was doing since the attack. Finally, the detective asked, "May I inquire what we are having for supper?"

"You may," Patti asserted. "We are having pizza."

"Really?" The detective could hardly believe it. "You can make pizza from scratch?"

"Absolutely! You have to learn how to make the things you like or you may never get them."

"Hey, that's right! What kind of pizza do you like?"

"My favorite is supreme; you know, everything but the kitchen sink and lots of cheese!"

"Oh, Patti, are you sure you can't move in with me? I could really use a good cook."

"Well, I don't know; I only know how to fix about six different things, but Mom is teaching me; maybe you should give me a little more time, and I'll get better." Patti grinned.

"I know you will. Say, when you eat pizza, do you drink beer?" The detective flashed an ornery smile.

"Nope, I don't like beer; it tastes nasty, but you probably already know that. Mama drinks wine sometimes; she says it relaxes her. Do you like wine?"

Ms. Johnson frowned. "I'm not a big wine drinker, but tonight I might make an exception. We'll see when your mother gets here."

No sooner were these words spoken when they heard some fumbling at the door. Kathy was in the process of entering their apartment, loaded with grocery bags. She managed to get the door open, and started into the front room. "Patti, honey, are you here? I've really got my arms full. I could use your help."

Patti glanced at Detective Johnson and put her finger to her lips; Ms. Johnson understood, smiled and played along. "Sure Mom, I'll be right there." She rushed to help.

"Patti, I thought I saw Detective Johnson's car out front. Have you seen her?"

"No, I sure haven't." Patti took some bags from her mother and started for the kitchen.

Kathy seemed puzzled. "Well, that's odd. I'm sure her car is outside; I figured she was here." She rearranged her load and followed Patti, who was trying not spoil the surprise.

"I haven't seen her for quite a while," Patti's voice raised. "It sure would be nice for her to come visit—she could even stay for supper."

"Say, your supper smells great; Detective Johnson doesn't know what she's missing." Kathy was still struggling with the bags.

The detective shouted. "Pizza!" She then appeared to assist Kathy.

"What? Who's this...Patti, is someone here?" Kathy started to drop one of her bags, which the detective deftly retrieved.

Ms. Johnson beamed. "Why, ma'am, it's your helpful law enforcement officer here to protect and serve, and just in time to rescue you from a grocery bag assault." The detective attempted to aid Kathy.

Kathy scolded Patti. "Why you little scamp! You told me you hadn't seen the detective."

She defended herself. "Mama, I wanted to surprise you; Detective Johnson is staying for supper. I made her an offer she couldn't refuse."

"Patti, did you threaten the detective? How many times have I told you it's not nice to hit people in the knees with a baseball bat just to get them to go along with your half baked ideas, er...pizza." Detective Johnson reached for her knee and winced.

"No Mom, I didn't threaten her; she has a gun...and you don't mess with anyone packin' iron." Patti growled using her best "bad guy" imitation.

Kathy turned to Patti. "Well, then, what offer did you make?"

"Pizza, ma'am...just the facts; it was pizza...and you don't turn down an offer like that from...a pretty little lady." The detective was trying hard not to laugh. Jack Webb and John Wayne would have been proud, and the girls got so tickled they were fortunate not to drop the groceries.

Patti finished in the kitchen while her mother and Ms. Johnson talked at the table. "Hey, you've got quite a place here." The detective glanced around and over her head.

"It's a work in progress. I've been here ever since Patti was born...I guess that's twelve years now. We used to have the whole upstairs, but my landlord finally got the hallway completed so we only have about half the space now. The best part is that we did get a front door; we used to have to use the back stairs or the fire escape. This front entrance means a lot after a long day on your feet." Kathy rubbed her toes.

"Look, I called and left a message that I wanted to talk to you guys; Patti returned my call and invited me to supper.

I couldn't turn her down...never turn down an offer for pizza even if it's six o'clock in the morning, but alas, no beer."

Kathy quickly added. "I've got some wine in the frig."

"That would be okay; we've got some celebrating to do and a little wine wouldn't hurt a thing. I've got some good news, but Patti will want to hear it too...so let's get this meal ready and celebrate!" Kathy could hardly wait, but she had a pretty good idea what the detective wanted to share.

The pizza was almost done and the wine glasses chilling. Kathy was both amused and intrigued that Patti had taken an interest in cooking; she hadn't learned how to cook very many things, but she knew how to make them taste good. Kathy knew she watched "cooking shows" occasionally on television and perhaps that had piqued her interest. In any event she had put together her own special pizza, and everyone was getting hungry waiting for it to come out of the oven. When everything was ready, the girls sat down to eat, but Detective Johnson lifted her glass. "I'd like to propose a toast to good friends and our brave little cook."

"Here, here." Kathy raised her glass and sipped the wine. "And I'd like to propose a toast to our special guest, who has always been there when we needed her."

"Here, here," stated Patti, asking her mother for a little sip...which made her pucker.

As they were eating, Detective Johnson explained that she was almost certain she had captured the man who attacked Patti. On the Monday after Patti had been assaulted, the detective had contacted local hospitals and clinics to determine if any of them had treated a man with a peculiar male problem. Interestingly, such a patient had shown up and told the emergency room personnel he had slipped on his exercise bike, landing hard on his "privates." Apparently, he had been injured rather severely...Patti's boot had hit the mark. The detective got his name and address, then conducted a background check; he had been involved with minors in the past and had always managed

163

to skirt the law. However, his wife had left him, and the company he worked for had phased out his job so he had relocated to this community.

"He managed to get along for a while, but apparently had reverted to his "old habits." We kept him under surveillance, hoping to catch him and finally get him off the streets. On Friday night a youth group had met in the park for a cookout. One girl attending got home and realized she had left a jacket there and went back to find it. Our man used a similar MO on this girl; he clothes-lined her and had her down before she realized what had happened. "I guess you could say our officers caught him with his pants down; they pretty much witnessed the whole thing. With his prior record, we are certain we can get him put away and let the penal system handle his retirement. You guys will not be involved in any way; I just wanted you to know before you read it or saw it on the news. I also wanted Patti to know she is responsible for this; her actions allowed us to catch this guy and put him behind bars."

Having explained her visit, Detective Johnson continued, "One more thing, I have a request. I'd like to think of us as more than a crazy policewoman and a pair of good looking babes. My birth name is Deborah. When I was little, everyone called me Debbie, then just Deb. You pick. I just don't feel we need to be so formal; I hope we're friends."

Kathy was touched by her comments, and Patti was thrilled to think she had a detective for a friend. Kathy replied, "You honor us; thank you for saying so...Deb."

"You guys make it easy; you're good people."

Patti injected, "Does this mean you'll come and have supper with us again?"

"I'd like that; I'd like that a lot." Deb grinned.

"Oh boy, that would be great; we could rent some movies, fix popcorn and just have fun!" Patti was trying not to get too excited. "But you'll have to bring your own beer."

Deb laughed. "That's okay, I'll just stick with soda."

The meal was great; Patti thought the very center of the pizza was not quite done, but it did taste good and she received a round of compliments. Patti agreed to clean up and take care of the dishes because, as she put it, "adults always need to talk...blah, blah, blah." Kathy and Deb did want to visit and neither one of them knew why until they actually discovered they had much more in common than they realized. They were about the same age; they had graduated from high school the same year; both were single and very lonely...but too busy to know it. Kathy commented, "Well, at least you finally got your man; that is, Patti's giant in the park."

"Yeah, I can get the crooks; I just can't find a man for me."

"Hey, I know; I've had similar problems. I had a man, well, a boy once, and now I have Patti to raise with no father."

Kathy explained her situation, and Ms. Johnson listened intently, then appeared shocked by a revelation. "You know if I didn't know better, I'd say we were living the same life."

She went on to say that after graduating from high school she had attended junior college to major in criminology. During her second year while taking her first criminology class, she met a man ten years or so older than she was. They had sat together off and on and made idle chitchat. She had taken a liking to him and was pleased one afternoon when he suggested they study for their mid-term exam together. They met after class, studied, went to dinner, and studied some more. Deb liked that he seemed to respect her, and they could have a more "adult" relationship. She'd had her fill of "boys" in high school.

He started bringing her little gifts and even a bouquet of flowers for her birthday in November. One day, he suggested they get together and study for finals. However, right after Thanksgiving, he called to say there was a problem; he had to be out of town for a meeting. When she inquired where he was going and learned it was less than an hour's drive away, she suggested she could meet him to study there. Arrangements were made, and she met him at his motel; they studied, went to dinner, then back to his room, and mostly studied in bed...but not criminology, even though a "crime" was taking place. She stayed over an extra day, and they spent most of it in the bed or the shower. Needless to say, she was hooked; they continued their affair throughout the Christmas holiday and into the next semester. One evening, following a raucous "study" session, she found his billfold and decided to return it.

She made several observations as she parked across from the address shown on his driver's license. Numerous children's toys littered the yard, and as she was about to get out of her car, a vehicle pulled into the driveway. An attractive young woman stepped out and helped two small children out of their car seats. After they went inside, Deb sat there for a long time. At first she was angry, then she laughed, then she thought seriously about murder, then she calmed down and got out of her car, walked up to the front door, and rang the bell. The same lady came to door; why yes, she was Mrs. so and so, and yes, the man whose name appeared on the driver's license was her husband, and yes, he would be thrilled she had found and returned his wallet; could the wife pay a reward? No, it was not necessary; she was happy to return it. Deb walked back to her car, and managed to throw up in the street before driving away. She never saw her "lover" again; he dropped the class they were taking, and she had no idea whatever became of him and quite frankly didn't care. She found out about a week later she was pregnant.

Kathy sat awed by her story. "My God, what did you do?"

"I'd rather not say. To be honest, I'm not very proud of myself."

"What do you mean?" Kathy feared the worst.

"Well, I guess it won't hurt to tell you. As you know, I wanted to be a policeman, so when I was eighteen I purchased a gun, took lessons, and learned how to shoot. I figured if I put the barrel in my mouth and pulled the trigger, I couldn't miss..."

"Oh no!" Kathy put her hand to face and started to cry.

"So I sneaked the gun into my dorm room. After supper when things tend to get rowdy, I pulled my chair into the middle of the room, sat down, and put the gun in my mouth..."

Kathy was now openly crying. "Oh, please, don't say any more; this is too awful!"

Deb persisted. "No, you might as well hear the ending. Look, I'm sitting here, obviously I didn't kill myself."

"I know, but it's so gruesome. One night in emergency they brought in this patient who shot himself; I won't forget that sight for as long as I live." Kathy's face was tinged with horror.

Deb tried to calm her. "Okay, I'm not trying to gross you out; just let me tell you what happened." Kathy nodded; the detective continued. "I put the gun in my mouth, held my finger on the trigger, and paused for a moment. I thought about my life, family, friends, and even my unborn baby. Everyone would be better off without me; I was too stupid to live. I started to pull the trigger, and then something happened."

Kathy's eyes got big. "The gun misfired...it wasn't loaded...what?"

"You'll never believe it—a scream in the hallway."

"A what?" Kathy was curious and puzzled.

"A scream in the hallway; this girl two doors down the hall from me had just gotten back from being gone a day or two. She opened her door and discovered her room was partially ransacked; numerous valuables were missing. She screamed. 'I've been robbed!' At that moment it occurred to me that I wanted to be a policeman, to help people and solve crimes; you know, get the bad guys. I sure as hell couldn't do that if I were dead. I put the gun down, marched down the hall to help her, then thanked her for saving my life. She thought I was crazy; I probably was, but I was alive. I've never looked back."

Kathy observed. "Instead of being saved by the bell, you were saved by the scream."

"Yup."

"What about the baby?"

Deb frowned. "I miscarried about a month later; I cried about it, but I guess it was nature's way of solving my problem; I live with myself hoping the baby was not right, but it saddens me when I'm down. You know, protect and serve." Tears began to flow down Deb's cheeks.

Kathy and Ms. Johnson reached out and hugged one another for a long time. Patti brought each of them tissues. Finally, Kathy released her grip and said, "It sounds like we are couple of kindred souls badly in need of a friend; I want you to know you will always be welcome here. Patti and I love you, not only for what you've done for us, but because you too are a good person. I know it must be tough to go to work and not get the recognition you deserve for all you do. You have our love and trust, and you are not leaving here without making another date; I don't care if you do have a gun!"

The detective grinned. "Oh, so we're dating now?"

"Well, I don't know if I'd go that far; let's just think of ourselves as the 'three musketeers.'"

Patti laughed. "I think the 'three stooges' makes more sense. Group hug!"

Patti decided that many good things can come out of tragedy; it was not necessary to recount them all, but now she and her mother had a new friend, and they were very much in need of friends. Patti knew kids at school, but

Colby was her only real friend. Her mother, of course, had friends at work, but she didn't socialize with any of them, and it was very rare for someone other than the Benders or Mr. Mitchell ever to be in their apartment. Patti loved to be with her mother, but company was nice. Deb promised she would see them again as soon as she checked her schedule and could give them a little more advance notice. Both Patti and Kathy insisted it didn't make any difference how much notice they had, but sometimes they were not at home. Deb was more than gracious and told them if they weren't home, she would just track them down and place then under house arrest...in their house.

❧ Fifteen ❧

The month of April roared along and Patti was looking forward to the end of school and going camp. She had not been away from home for a long period of time and this opportunity excited her. Colby was going on an early vacation with his parents, where they hoped the weather would be cooler. Near the end of April after school, Patti got a call from Deb; she suggested a big bash on Friday and hoped everyone would be available. Patti was certain her mother would be home early due to a schedule shift. Patti suggested Deb come around 4:00 pm, and they would have plenty of time to visit, then fix something special and enjoy the evening.

Friday afternoon, Patti rushed home so she would be there when Deb arrived. The detective was right on time and asked what Patti was planning for dinner; Patti had to admit she had only helped; her mother had prepared it and all Patti had to do was make sure it went in the oven. She wasn't supposed to tell what she was cooking but promised Deb would like it. The detective brought a bottle of wine and two videos. Patti asked what movies she had rented. "Hey, I watch police movies; I'll bet your mom watches hospital shows; and you probably watch fairy tales.

"Hey, this must not be your day; Mom hates hospital movies unless the hospital is burning down, you know, disaster flicks. I bet you don't really like police movies; I figure you get enough of that stuff at work. As for me, well, I like funny movies; my mom needs to laugh more so I always try to have her rent at least one comedy. I think it's good for her."

"You think a lot of your mom, don't you?"

"You bet; she's a good mom, but she's too busy. I worry about her. She's the only real family I have, and I want her to be happy and not work so hard."

"Patti, you are so special; I would kill to have daughter as nice as you; thank you for being a good kid."

"Well, thank you; it means a lot."

A noise at the door told them Kathy was home, just as excited as everyone else. Patti went to the kitchen to make sure everything was cooking and started setting the table for dinner. The two adults exchanged pleasantries in the living room and made the usual comments about another Friday at work. Both were tired and discovered they had worked a long shift today, which made them laugh at how things sometimes work. Deb looked a bit sad. "I hope I can stay awake for all the fun."

Kathy tired to encourage her. "Well, dinner can be ready early so we can start the movies right after we eat; it doesn't matter about the mess. Patti and I can get it tomorrow."

"I don't want to make extra work for you; that's not why I'm here."

"Look, when Patti and I eat, we make a mess; I figure your dishes are not going to make much extra work; don't worry about it. How about a short glass of wine before dinner?"

"You took the words right out of my mouth." The detective smiled.

Patti announced dinner would soon be served if she could get the help out of the living room and into the kitchen. Kathy and Deb laughed as they went to get the food ready.

The tuna casserole was great and the adults noted that wining and dining was a great way to end a busy week. Patti noticed both of them drank a little more wine than usual, or at least, more than her mother usually drank. The first movie was a comedy which made everyone laugh. Kathy and Deb drank a little more wine, and Patti took a break to pop some corn; she preferred soda over wine. The movie ended, and they continued laughing at one of the silly characters. They decided they could handle the second show, which was shorter than the first, a romance story with a couple of sad moments. Patti noticed the adults were crying; they were also drinking more wine. When the movie ended, everyone sat there silently and teary eyed. Kathy finally said, "How about a night cap before you go; the bottle is nearly empty—we might as well finish it."

Deb looked somewhat forlorn. "It would be a shame to let it spoil."

Kathy started to get up but had trouble getting to her feet. "You know, I think I had a little too much to drink; Patti, can you bring the wine here?"

"Sure, Mom."

They split the remaining contents, and Deb looked at Kathy. "It didn't help."

"What didn't help?" Kathy seemed confused.

"The wine; it didn't help."

"What do you mean?"

"We had a bad week...a shooting; I was involved. We broke up a drug deal and the bad guys were not happy about it. I had to shoot someone; it was self defense. I'd like to forget about it...the wine didn't help."

"Hey, I understand; we lost a lady at the hospital...cancer. She had two kids; it was a tough one. The wine didn't help me either."

Deb feigned enthusiasm. "Well, aren't we a couple of jolly old ladies."

Kathy's voice was unsteady. "Yeah, don't let your work get to you; it's just a job."

"Protect and serve; then every once and a while shoot someone to keep things interesting."

"Yeah, the hospital is here to help, but you're going die anyway." Kathy spoke rather loudly.

"I'd better be going home; you guys need your rest." Deb rose to leave but slumped back onto the sofa.

Patti looked at her concerned. "I don't think you should go home like this; maybe you should stay here tonight."

"She's right; drunks don't let their friends drive." Kathy's words were slurred.

"Mom, I think you got that wrong; I need to put both of you to bed before you make fools of yourselves."

"I have such a brilliant child." Kathy smiled; Deb nodded.

Patti put both women to bed; she hoped they didn't mind sleeping in their underwear because as she figured it, a good turn only goes so far. She had enough trouble just getting their clothes off. She put the detective in her bed and her mom in her own bed and tucked them in for the night. She picked up and arranged everyone's clothes but was nervous about handling Deb's service pistol, which she gingerly placed on top of her clothes. After tidying up here and there, she opted for a place to sleep; the choice was simple: the sofa or the floor. She picked the sofa.

Saturday mornings were usually quiet in their apartment; Kathy almost always slept in unless she had to work, and Patti liked to stay up late on Friday night, so it was easy for her to sleep in too. However, she was almost always up before her mother, and they had a tradition of eating a Saturday brunch, which Patti often prepared. When Patti awoke this particular morning, the adults were still asleep. She wasn't sure what to do about eating so she found a book and read quietly.

Deb woke first; she was rather startled waking up in a strange place, and apparently did not normally sleep in her underwear because she seemed shocked when she pulled the covers away. She quickly pulled them back and looked around in a state of panic. She finally saw Patti, who had witnessed the entire process with some amusement. Deb didn't need to be shy around Patti. Her mother ran around in her underwear all the time, so she was used to it. Realizing the situation, Patti went to her. "Hey, it's okay; I put you to bed. You don't need to be embarrassed...we're all girls around here."

Deb tried to smile. "Yeah, but I usually wake up in my bed; this is different."

"I know; it's the same for me, but I gave you my bed and slept on the sofa."

The detective looked at Patti sheepishly and said, "Listen, I want to apologize for my behavior last night; I drank too much and I don't want to give you the wrong impression. I shouldn't drink like that; it's important to show a good example. You can't go around arresting people for drunk driving if you're a drunk yourself."

"Mama doesn't drink like that either; you guys had a bad week and needed to blow off some steam. Mama tells me to stop and calm down when I get angry so I won't do anything stupid. I guess that's what you were doing. You don't need to be ashamed; I won't tell anyone. You were both kind of silly." Patti grinned.

Patti reached to shake Deb's hand. Deb reached out instinctively to respond; the covers slipped a bit and she started to pull them back to cover herself, but extended her arm and shook Patti's hand. A bond had formed, and Patti was the oldest twelve-year old Deb had ever met.

Kathy soon woke and was beside herself, also embarrassed

for drinking too much and apologizing for her behavior. Patti hadn't seen or heard anything these adults should be ashamed of; they had not demonstrated the best example of adult behavior, but they had acted responsibly. No one had done anything stupid or childish, and except for putting them to bed, it had caused her little inconvenience. Perhaps next time they would do better.

They talked Deb into staying for brunch, and enjoyed each other's company the rest of the morning. Deb thanked Kathy and Patti for the good time; she would be back, but could not say when. She did want to take both of them out to celebrate Kathy's birthday in about two weeks, but they would have to talk more about it later; Deb had work to do at home, and Saturday morning was almost gone.

With the case solved, or at least, most likely solved, Patti no longer felt she needed to keep her park experience a secret but did not want to divulge all the details. She first told Raven she had been attacked in the park the night after their big spring party. Raven was dumbfounded; she could not imagine such a thing and admitted walking through the park at night numerous times. She also told Patti she was backing away from the group. Getting sick had made her more cautious; it bothered her that there were always quite a few older kids, people out of high school, at these parties. She began to think some of them wanted to take advantage of the younger kids one way or another, and she didn't like that. Patti told her it looked like many of the younger kids were putting themselves in harm's way by drinking, using drugs, or smoking; you don't realize how vulnerable you are until you get attacked in the park by a giant!

Patti was busy with school as May rolled around, and everyone seemed to be trying to make up time lost earlier in the year. Patti could hardly wait for summer, and if the truth were told, she was really looking forward to seventh grade and being in more classes with Colby. By May Kathy was back in her rut, which often left Patti alone and occasionally resentful. She could not understand why her mother seemed to forget about everything in her life except her work, and Patti had noticed her mother had become less responsible at home and didn't spend much time taking care of herself or trying to look nice. Patti envied her mother's beauty; she had a classic face like those on Greek statues. Patti knew people looked at her mother then did retakes because she was so striking, but she was so preoccupied she paid little or no attention. Patti looked nothing like her mother, and according to this same lady, looked nothing like her father either. Patti looked, well, she looked more like "Peppermint Patti" from the Charlie Brown cartoons. Her short hair and hint of freckles imparted a boyish quality, especially when she wore a hat. She'd heard her mother call her a "late bloomer," but Patti had no idea what that was; she didn't see any blooms, late or otherwise.

Deb took the girls out for Kathy's birthday; it was both sad and amusing that Kathy couldn't remember the last time she had done anything for her birthday since she was a little girl. Deb said it was important to celebrate your thirtieth birthday; it was a sign that you were a real adult. Kathy wasn't so sure being thirty was all it was cracked up to be, but agreed it was better than being forty. The girls had a great time and Patti especially enjoyed her evening. She ordered shrimp; it was her favorite food she never got to eat. She received extra attention when Deb was around because Deb liked Patti. They could visit like adults, and it meant more to Patti than anyone realized. The girls had a great evening and hated for it to end.

School wound down before the teachers knew it. Patti said goodbye to Colby but would call him in the middle of June, and they could get together to discuss his vacation and her camp. Raven told Patti there was a chance her family might move; she just didn't know when. Her dad had been looking for a new job but had no idea if or when he might get it. Patti told Raven to take care and keep her eyes open. Raven had discovered that when she applied herself, she could do fine in school. It seemed to have a positive effect. She thanked Patti for making it happen.

Patti was beside herself waiting for her camp; she had to endure several days home alone waiting for it to start, and they almost drove her crazy. Uncle Bob had volunteered to deliver supplies to the camp and asked Patti if she would like to ride along and help unload. Patti thought that would be better than riding the church bus. When her uncle arrived, she had her things ready; her mother told her to have a great time and not get hurt or hurt anyone else. Patti promised to do her best; she was such a brute! The camp opened officially at 4:00 pm on Sunday afternoon and would end after a farewell lunch on Friday. Patti and her uncle chatted about school and the weather; neither mentioned her park problem, and Patti was happy about that. He also asked her if she would like to ride home with him Friday. There were some chores to take care of for the next group of kids, and the sponsors didn't want to make a special trip back on Saturday or do last minute work Sunday morning, so they stayed and finished everything on Friday. Patti said she would be glad to help, especially, since she was attending without charge.

When they got to camp, they registered in the assembly room next to the cafeteria, which was called the Chow House. Each youngster was assigned to a lettered group of three or four cabins, Patti to Group B. Each cabin held up to four people, so a group consisted of twelve to sixteen kids plus a counselor or adult leader and an older student, usually from high school, to assist. However, Patti's group had no assistant; he had come down with appendicitis and was in the hospital. Patti's leader, Counselor Dave, would have to take care of his kids by himself. They were told to take their luggage and belongings to their cabins, where the counselors would meet them and discuss rules. Then they would get a short tour and return to the assembly room for a welcome and supper.

Patti was surprised to meet Counselor Dave; she had envisioned a young man full of energy and enthusiasm. Counselor Dave was older, probably older than her Grandpa Bender; he didn't seem exciting, but he had the voice of God. He didn't talk much or loudly, but when he spoke, everyone listened. Patti liked him.

One of the kids' responsibilities was to keep a journal of their activities they could share with their parents. Patti must have had the time of her life because she nearly ran out of room writing about all that she had done. One thing Patti did not have to mention was that she felt safe and secure at camp. No monsters hid in the trees during the day, and no ghastly images disturbed her sleep at night.

Thursday was Explore and Discover Day. They would hike into the nearby hills and explore a cave, then head to a backwoods picnic area for lunch. After eating, they would hike again to explore a low area with a stream and small waterfall, then to a rest area for refreshments, and finally, back to camp to go swimming before the big evening barbecue. The groups left at different times and took different trails so they would not be in each other's way; it also allowed them to be fed in shifts. Thursday was an absolutely beautiful day; the weather was warm, but not hot; the sky was clear and the air seemed dry and crisp. Everything was going even better than planned.

Patti's group arrived last for lunch. Starved, they ate heartily. It was nice to sit down for a while; they had been on their feet all morning. Even kids get tired. Counselor Dave explained the last part of the trip involved walking in some wet areas where they needed to watch their step and not fall. Wildlife should be left alone, and everyone stick to the trail. They didn't want anyone to get hurt, lost, or eaten by a bear. Some of the kids pretended to be scared, but Counselor Dave laughed, assuring them there were no bears anywhere near the camping area because the bears knew the hungry kids would eat them...giving a whole new meaning to the expression, "hungry enough to eat a bear."

As they regrouped and headed out from their lunch site, Counselor Dave was probably the only one who noticed the wind was dead still as they headed into the low land. The river area had more trees and shade, but the weather seemed hotter now. The river was a swirl of activity and everyone was absorbed by the wildlife and simple beauty around them. Counselor Dave had to prod the kids or they might have stayed forever. Going to the low land had been all downhill; thus, leaving it took more effort. The youngsters may not have cared about the muggy weather, but Counselor Dave preferred dry and cooler air.

During their first break to stop and rest, their leader noticed a cloud bank had formed in the northwest, and while it looked a long way off, it appeared threatening. He cut their break short by a few minutes so they could continue to higher ground. The trail was much steeper here and there was still no wind. The cloud bank continued to move toward them, more threatening than ever. Counselor Dave persisted, prodding and urging the kids to move forward; they had a tendency to go sideways. When they reached a plateau where the trail leveled off, anyone who looked ahead could see the storm approaching. Several kids hoped it would rain and cool them off; others seemed to sense this was not a late spring shower, but a real storm.

Counselor Dave noted their apprehension and quickly focused them on their objective, namely to keep on the trail. The kids responded with renewed energy and moved ahead. Within moments they all felt a cool, almost cold, breeze which was very refreshing, but their leader knew from experience they were about to face this storm head on...and it could get ugly. He continued to urge everyone forward, reminding them to keep to the trail and not tarry. One of the kids shouted, "Hey, sprinkles," but these drops were not sprinkles; they were large droplets of warm water that splattered on the ground and the hikers. Counselor Dave immediately thought about the possibility of hail and searched for hints of green in the clouds overhead; he knew if it started to hail, they were in big trouble; no protection from that kind of weather existed until they reached the shelter at the rest area.

For a few minutes, the warm droplets continued, and the kids enjoyed this harmless cool down as they moved ahead. Patti noticed the drops getting colder and shivered as her body adjusted to this new temperature. Suddenly, the wind seemed to swirl; the sky boiled above them as big dark clouds surged and rolled. The kids were distracted enough by the rain to not particularly notice the sky, but Counselor Dave was genuinely worried they were in the midst of something much bigger than they could handle. He again prodded them to keep moving and stay on the trail. The rain was no longer a shower but a barrage of large drops, almost cold, and some of the kids began to run forward as if to escape it. Counselor Dave moved quickly to stop them with a warning not to run on the trail; a fall could be nasty, and he reminded them he didn't want anyone to get hurt.

At this point, the rain was no longer what anyone would think of as a shower or even a thunderstorm; it was more like walking through a waterfall. Patti had never seen rain like this; sheets of water poured upon them, making it hard to breathe; everyone was soaked to the bone in less than a minute. Many kids were genuinely scared and even started to cry. Counselor Dave seemed to be everywhere, urging them to keep their heads down and follow the trail; they would soon be at the shelter and out of the rain; he knew, but did not say, that the shelter was still quite a distance away. The kids did their best to follow his directions. The trail became slippery and difficult to see; the rain was so cold it was impossible not to shiver, and wet clothes are heavier than dry ones. Moving became more and more of an effort, but Counselor Dave continued to be there comforting, urging, and encouraging.

Patti was wet and tired; her chest hurt from trying to breathe through the water; she was cold and soaked...and of course, just as scared as the rest of the kids, but she didn't cry; there was already enough water, and she didn't need to add to it by shedding tears. The kids continued walking, and Counselor Dave stayed with them, providing all the encouragement he could. The terrain began to incline upward again; the rain had slowed a little, but water was everywhere. Finally, one of the kids near the front saw a sign along the trail pointing toward a rest area and shouted his discovery. Encouraged, everyone picked up their pace, and in a few minutes they found dry shelter.

The idea of being safe and warm did not exactly fit this situation. Yes, they were now under a roof and safe from the rain, but warm was another thing altogether. Everyone was soaked; the rain was bitter cold, almost icy; considerable wind was blowing; and the current dance craze was the shake and shiver. Patti's teeth rattled. She felt silly standing there with water dripping out of her clothes, running under her clothes, and squishing in her shoes. In addition, somehow she began to think the shaking and shivers were not just the cold; she sensed her fear had returned. Patti was scared; everyone was scared; that is, everyone except Counselor Dave. He didn't seem afraid at all. Patti couldn't understand. Why should she feel this way? They were safe, cold but safe. There was no reason to be scared, but she knew she was; it was the same sensation she had when she got home from the park that night...Patti hated that feeling and was absolutely determined to find a way to never have it again!

Their refreshments had been left at the shelter, and it seemed weird to be drinking cold soda when everyone had nearly drowned in cold water on the trail, but kids have a way of eating under any circumstances. The rain ended before they were through, and just as it did, a rescue party of sorts arrived to make sure everyone was okay. They rested and took it easy for a while, letting the running water subside and allowing things to dry. The trail was messy, but they made it back to camp intact. By the time they arrived, the sun was shining again, and incredibly, many of the kids in Patti's group went swimming; Patti decided she'd had enough water for one day.

Heading for her cabin, she met Counselor Dave, who had changed his clothes and was going to check on his "kids." Patti asked if he would be staying late Friday; he told her he had to get the camp ready for the next group. Patti explained she was going home with her Uncle Bob and would also be there. Would it be okay to talk with him privately during the afternoon after everyone had left? Counselor Dave told her that would be fine. He would meet her in the cafeteria after the buses left. Patti was thrilled and thanked him.

Camp ended; no one had disappeared or died; the kids admitted they had fun. The counselors complimented the young people on their good behavior and making this year's camp a success; they hoped everyone would consider coming back to Exploration Camp next year. Many goodbyes were said and even a few tears shed as the kids boarded the buses and headed home. Patti was more interested in the cafeteria...but not for the food!

As promised, Counselor Dave was in the cafeteria when Patti got there; she sat down at the table by him. "Thank you for meeting with me. I have a really important question, and I know you can answer it."

Dave scratched his head. "Well, Patti, I don't know if I can answer any really important questions, but I'll try."

"Yesterday in the storm, us kids were all scared."

Dave nodded. "You bet; it was scary out there. Most kids are not used to such things."

"Sure, I've never seen it rain so hard, but you weren't scared, were you?"

"Well, I...I mean, I had no reason to be afraid."

"I don't understand. Why weren't you afraid? Was it because you're an adult and we're just kids?"

"Well, Patti, I was doing my job. I do it every summer."

Patti persisted. "Have you ever been caught in a storm like that?"

Dave shook his head. "No, I can't say I have; this was a new experience. I hope it never happens again."

"Then you should have been just as scared as we were, but you weren't. I want to know why."

"Look, Patti, how did you feel out on the trail when the heavy rain began?"

"Well, I was wet and cold and sloshing in the mud..."

"And helpless...all alone...with no one to help you."

"Yeah, kind of like that; like when Mom's gone and there's no one home."

"Okay, I didn't feel that way; I wasn't alone."

"Whoa, that's not so; it was just you and us kids. There was no one else."

"Patti, you're wrong; I was not alone. Jesus was with me...the whole time."

"Well, I didn't see Him. Are you sure?" Patti felt confused.

"I'm positive; He's with me right here in my heart." Dave brought his hand to his chest.

"Gosh, I'm confused; I guess I don't understand." Patti was getting frustrated.

"Patti, you love your mother, right?" Patti nodded. "Okay, she isn't here is she?"

"No."

"All right, even though she isn't here, you still remember and care about her, don't you?"

"Yes, sir."

"Then isn't she with you..."

A flashbulb went off in Patti's head and she interrupted. "I've got her in my heart! Now I understand what you mean; she's in my heart, and you have Jesus in your heart; He takes care of you just like my mom takes care of me!"

"Well yes, it's something like that; you're catching on."

"Okay, then I want Jesus in my heart...right now; I don't want to ever feel alone again. What do I have to do?" Patti was trying hard not to explode.

"Do you know who Jesus is?"

Patti stopped, paused then stuttered. "Uh, well...I mean, He's in the Bible; I know a little bit about Him, but I've just got to have Him in my heart!"

Counselor Dave leaned back in his chair and eyed this remarkable girl who had now touched his soul. He tried to collect himself as a tear formed in each eye. He looked at her and smiled. "Patti, what you want is easier than you can ever imagine, but you're not ready for Jesus." Patti looked a bit crushed. "But I can help you and you can find Him all by yourself." Patti sighed with relief. "I have a copy of the New Testament in my cabin that we give our seventh graders; I would like for you to start reading it. Don't read the last book; it needs to be read in a group where it can be discussed and better understood. Our church has a youth group that meets on Friday evenings during the school year and on Sunday evenings in the summer; we try to answer questions there to help young people get to know and love Jesus. I'd like for you to come. And finally, I want to ask you...a big favor. Would you consider being my assistant next year at Fun Camp? It won't cost you anything, and you would be a big help to me."

Patti looked at Counselor Dave. Her eyes sparkled and she nearly jumped on the table. "Oh, Counselor Dave...oh, that would be wonderful; I would love to help...thank you, thank you, thank you." She leaned across the table and kissed Counselor Dave on the cheek.

Her new friend was taken by surprise; he looked at her and blushed. He reached for and shook her hand; he didn't need to say any more. The fireworks going off in Patti's head made it impossible for her to hear anything.

⤙ Sixteen ⤚

Counselor Dave and Patti went back to the leader's cabin where he found and gave her the promised testament. They discussed a little more about how they could get together later during the summer and when the youth group met. Patti clutched her testament as if it were her only possession until she finally got it safely in her bag to take home. They found Uncle Bob. Patti had agreed to help, so they found numerous chores for her, and time flew by quickly. She said good bye to Counselor Dave, then she and her uncle headed home. Patti told him that

Dave had asked her to help next year at Fun Camp; she was really excited about the offer. Her uncle asked if she would like to stay on and attend the Exploration Camp for seventh graders. Patti did not hesitate for one second; she would love to go. She told Bob she'd had more fun than any other time she could remember; camp was great, and looking back, even the storm was fun...in a scary way, and while she didn't tell her uncle, she knew that if the storm had not happened, she probably would not be Counselor Dave's assistant next summer and more importantly, she might not be getting an opportunity to know Jesus.

Patti's life in the church was generally nonexistent. Her mother and the Benders had always been regular church attenders. Kathy had been raised in a Christian home and had spent many hours at church services and activities. In fact, the church was where Kathy had learned to love music; she enjoyed the majesty and joy of the hymns and anthems sung by the choir. She had joined the youth choir and had participated in many church programs and specials; she loved to perform in these group events. However, about the time she started to high school, her father became increasingly discouraged and disgruntled with their church and its ideology.

He would come home, complaining bitterly that many in the church, including their pastor at the time, either believed in everything or believed in nothing. He became more and more offended by this a "lack of faith." He would rant. "How can you call yourself a Christian if you don't believe in anything?" or "Folks know more about *Gone with the Wind* than they do about the *Bible*...and 'frankly, my dear, they don't give a damn'!" Kathy had felt bad they drifted away from the church, and by the time she had Patti, stopped attending altogether. Kathy had always been so busy, working two jobs, going to school, trying to raise Patti, she never had time to reestablish her Christian roots. Patti had not been baptized, and no one even bothered to bring up the subject. Patti, of course, had heard of Jesus and had seen a few Christian movies but was unfamiliar with the church or anything resembling real Christianity.

Patti rode quietly with her uncle; she wanted to get home quickly so she could look at her testament. Her uncle did ask if she had written a lot in her journal, and Patti admitted she had run out of room, but she could still share what had happened with her mother since her last entry. Patti realized that even though she was writing her journal for her mother or grandparents, she had not really thought about her family very much while she was at camp; everyone had been so busy, and there was so much to do there wasn't time to think about anything else. Patti could understand perhaps why her mother seemed to forget about her with all the things she had to do, but that didn't make it easier to accept.

When they got home Patti thanked her uncle again for this wonderful opportunity and told him she looked forward to next year. Her uncle was pleased and said he would make sure Patti got a chance to go again. They arrived a little later than supper time, but Kathy had fixed a special meal for her "happy camper." They spent their evening reviewing Patti's week and talking about her plans for next summer. Kathy was thrilled Patti had enjoyed camp. Patti did not say anything about Jesus or the New Testament she had received; she wanted to save that for later. She knew she would need her mother's support to get back and forth to youth group, so she decided to study this book before seeking her mother's approval.

Instead of sleeping in on Saturday, Patti got up and began reading her New Testament. She was familiar with parts of the story; it was hard not to know the Christmas story, but she knew very little else about this man that she now wanted in her heart. Patti found the reading slow, but she was also intrigued by what she read. It seemed the more she studied, the more she wanted to learn. And yes, Counselor Dave was right; she did need to know more about Jesus. Patti thought you don't call someone a friend the first time you meet him; you had to know where you stood with him. The more she thought about it, the more sense it made.

When her mother got up and seemed more alert, Patti approached her. "Mom, can we talk a little more about camp?"

Kathy was curious. "I guess so; I thought we covered that yesterday. What else is there?"

Patti briefly reviewed her experience in the storm but this time told how Counselor Dave had "fearlessly" led them to safety. Kathy was intrigued, immediately grateful he had been there and acted so heroically to help the children. Patti then told her how she had asked to meet with him and find out why he was not afraid. She then looked intently at her mother. "Mom, Counselor Dave told me he was not afraid because Jesus was with him, the whole time, in his heart—that way he's never alone." Patti paused. "He gave me this New Testament so I can read about Jesus; he also invited me to come to Uncle Bob's church and join their youth group. I can learn more about Jesus there."

Kathy's reaction was not what Patti had expected. She sat quietly for what seemed like a long time. "Patti, I'm ashamed to admit this, but once again I have failed you. When you were little, I never had time to take you to church or anywhere else for that matter. I realize I have cheated you out of something very precious. It never occurred to me until now that you don't have the same background I do, so you've missed out on the story of Jesus and Christianity all these years. Counselor Dave is right, and he has provided you with the only tool you'll need." Kathy pointed to the book in Patti's hand. "I will do everything I can to see you get to youth group; it will be good to be around kids your own age who are struggling in the Word. I support you, and we will make this work."

Patti thanked her mother and assured her she didn't feel her mother had failed her; she only wished they had more time together and that her mother would pay more attention to her. Kathy did not reply, but she knew Patti was right; sometimes it was hard to raise a child, especially one as smart as Patti.

Patti continued to read her testament; she thought it was neat how Jesus told little stories to get people to learn. She didn't understand all of them, but then she was new to this.

Patti was also fascinated by the disciples, but she was angry at the one named Judas for betraying his Master. Patti cried when she read about how they killed Jesus; she couldn't understand why He needed to die when He had done so much good. Patti had heard adults say that sometimes life isn't fair, and she figured Jesus got a bum rap. Of course, she was surprised to discover Jesus came back after He died. She sure didn't know anyone who had ever done that! Then it hit her, almost like the giant in the park...Jesus came back from the dead! He wasn't some corpse rotting in a grave. He came back; He was alive, and that was why Counselor Dave could have Jesus in his heart and she could have Him too...and never be alone or afraid again.

When Patti had finished the first book in her testament, she discovered the second one was much like the first; it seemed odd the story was repeating itself. She decided she would keep a journal of her reading and write down questions; she could then ask Counselor Dave about them. However, as she continued to read and think about it, she remembered her mother had been active in the church and maybe she could help. So Patti went into the kitchen. "Mom, I know you're trying to get supper ready, but if it's okay, I have a question about my reading; I was wondering if you could help."

"Why, Patti, I can try; I guess it depends on the question."

"Well, I finished reading the first book in my testament, Matthew, and now I'm starting the next book, Mark. It seems like they're both telling the same story and I was wondering why there are two books that are...well, kind of the same. Do you know?"

"I don't want to confuse you because the Bible can be mysterious, but I'll try to help. Be sure to tell me if you don't understand. Okay?"

"Sure, I just want to make some sense of this."

"All right, the first four books of the Bible are called the Gospels, which means "good news"; Jesus was the Good News. The first three books tell about Jesus the man. Some people believe Matthew was a teacher so he wrote about Jesus, the Teacher; his book emphasizes the stories, called parables, that Jesus told. They think Luke was a doctor so he wrote about Jesus, the Physician; he writes about the healings Jesus performed. No one seems to know what Mark did, but he must have been a man of action because he writes how Jesus acted quickly and decisively to deal with situations. In other words each of these men wrote about Jesus the way they saw Him...so they all tell the same story, only differently because they each saw Him in their own way. Does that make sense?"

"I think so; I haven't read any of Luke yet."

"The last gospel, written by John, one of the disciples, is about Jesus, the Son of God. This book will be different from the others, and you may find it a little confusing. The next Book, Acts, was probably written by Luke, and it's about the good things the disciples did after Jesus was crucified. The rest of your testament was written by the disciples or by apostles, followers of Jesus. The Apostle Paul wrote most of them; I think you'll like him. He is very interesting; he was caught in a bad storm too and blinded by lightning..."

Patti interrupted. "Wow, I want to read about him."

"Well, you and Paul have something in common. I hope this makes sense."

"It does, I get it. Sometimes in school we have to watch a video or do an experiment and then write about what we saw; we don't all say the same thing because we don't all see things the same way. By telling four stories about Jesus, we are getting to see the many sides of Him. That's cool; thank you." Patti figured this Jesus must have been pretty important to merit four stories in the same book.

Kathy was pleased Patti had taken an interest in Jesus; she believed the Bible teachings had been helpful in her life. She also knew she had neglected to share this experience with her daughter and felt a swell of shame and grief engulf her. How could any mother be so busy and self-absorbed to deprive her child of the knowledge of Jesus and His teaching? Supper tonight might be a little saltier than usual as tears began to flow down Kathy's cheeks and drip on her blouse.

Patti continued to read off and on the rest of the evening. Kathy had the usual chores to do; things done today had to be done again a few days later, then over and over ad nauseum. By bedtime she was tired; she worked hard and did not get enough rest—at work they called it exhaustion; to her it was normal. As a rule, when she went to bed, blessed sleep came quickly, but tonight was different. She couldn't help thinking she was a failure as a mother. In the last three months, Patti had physically become a woman. She had nearly been raped and/or killed in the park, rebelling due to Kathy's lack of attention. Someone at camp had introduced Patti to Jesus. Kathy wondered just how much better off everyone would be if she could just fall asleep and pass during the night; she could never kill herself, but it would sure be nice if she could die. These were foolish, selfish thoughts, but Kathy couldn't get them out of her head, and the tears flowing down her cheeks failed to wash away her guilt as she dealt with the shame.

June flew by quickly; Patti read her whole testament except for The Revelation, as Counselor Dave had said. Then she started to read it again. She figured if she had time, she might as well keep reading; she also discovered that as she reread, she was able to answer some of the questions she had written down for either Dave or her mother. There was a lot to learn and she wanted more than anything to have Jesus in her heart. She believed if she could do that, she would never again be alone or afraid.

Kathy took Patti to the first youth group meeting after the camps ended and picked her up. Patti enjoyed herself and learned more things she did not know. She liked the kids there, and the adults in charge seemed so patient and kind. Counselor Dave had been there but had to leave early. He asked Patti if he could talk to both her and her mother either before or after their next meeting. He wanted to introduce himself and explain a few things to them. Patti waited anxiously; she wanted her mother to meet Dave.

It worked out best for Kathy to meet with Counselor Dave after their meeting, so Patti told Dave her mother would be there when they were finished. When the meeting ended, Patti found Dave, and they waited for her mother to arrive. When Kathy came inside, they all went to one of empty classrooms to visit. Counselor Dave spoke first. "I want to tell you, Ms. Bender, you have a wonderful daughter; Patti is such a delight, and we are so pleased to have her with us. She asks a lot of good questions and keeps us on our toes. Thank you for letting her be a part of our group."

"Well, thank you; I have always believed Patti was special, and of course, every parent likes to hear good things about her child...and please, call me Kathy."

"Well, Kathy, I just wanted to share a few things with you so we will all be on the same page. None of the leaders of our group are clergymen or educated in religion; we are merely a group of lay people who want very much to help children reach their Christian potential and provide a positive, godly alternative to our pop culture. We don't have the answers to all their questions, but we all want to grow in our understanding. As you know, children often ask tough questions and surprisingly, when you get a group of them together, they come up with great answers. We simply provide an opportunity for this to happen and challenge each other to grow in the Lord." Dave paused. "Many people ask me why I want to spend my "silver" or "golden" years working with a bunch of crazy kids. Well, I can tell you I didn't plan it that way; God had other ideas."

Kathy was curious. "I don't understand. How did God change your plans?"

"Well, the wife and I couldn't have children so we took a stab at foster care for a while; quite honestly, I didn't think we were cut out for it, and after a few tries, we decided we just needed each other and not the headaches and heartaches of trying to raise other people's kids. I had been in construction for a long time and was working out of town. It was late March and the weather had been lousy all day; you know, heavy, wet snow...really messy. They let us off work early due to the road conditions. I headed home not all that concerned; I'd lived around here long enough to be familiar with whatever Mother Nature threw at me. What I hadn't counted on was other people were not so fortunate.

"Someone from out of state...I saw their license tag...lost control of his car, crossed into my lane, and forced me off the road. I was driving fast enough that my car slid down an embankment and hit a cement culvert. I was knocked unconscious; I don't know how long I was out, but when I came to, I discovered my leg was pinned between the seat and firewall of my car. I could move but couldn't get free. To make matters worse, the road crews had plowed the snow and thrown it all over my side of the car until it was barely visible. My wife was out of town visiting her mother, and no one knew anything about my situation. I had a little food, and there was plenty of snow for water, but it was hard to keep warm. I kept thinking help would arrive, but no one had any idea where I was.

"During the second day it dawned on me I had failed to utilize my greatest resource, my Lord and Savior, Jesus Christ. I prayed He would get me out of this mess; I explained I wasn't a beaver and I couldn't have reached my leg to chew it off even if I were. I admitted I was in a bad spot and began to realize maybe He'd put me there to get my attention. Well, it worked; He had my full attention. The only problem was I had no idea what He wanted, but I had plenty of time to think about it. Finally, I told Him if He could get me rescued, He could certainly reveal what He wanted me to do, so I said, 'Lord, You make it happen, then I'll do whatever You show me.' Well, about an hour later I heard voices outside and then digging. In no time at all they got me out of the car and took me to the hospital.

"I found out later the sun had come out and melted the snow on my tail light. A trooper came by, saw the red reflection, and came down to check it out. God works in mysterious ways: He knocked me down, then picked me right up. Anyway, when I got home from the hospital, my wife called and told me an old friend of hers was working with troubled kids; she had it in her head we should get back in that business. I told her we could talk about it when she got home. In the meantime your uncle Bob got a chance to purchase the land for our camps and asked me if I could help get the place ready. When I told my wife about this, she said this must be the reason my accident happened; God wanted me to help and make it a success; I could also work with kids. I prayed about it and began to feel more and more like this was what He wanted me to do...so here I am."

Kathy sat amazed at his story. "God does do wondrous things. We just don't always understand them."

Patti looked up at Counselor Dave in awe. "Wow, just like Paul."

Kathy looked at her curiously. "Patti, what are you talking about?"

"Paul in the Bible, when his name was Saul, God knocked him down with lightning and got his attention too; he was blind for a while, but when God fixed him, he saw things differently and changed his ways."

"Why Patti, you're absolutely right; that is what happened. You're quite the Bible student!"

"That she is." Dave smiled and nodded, repeating softly. "That she is." Patti beamed.

"Anyway, Kathy, I guess the main reason I wanted to visit with you is to ask for your help. We have determined that parental support is vital as we work with kids; we need to know you will encourage Patti to attend our meetings and be active in our group. It really makes a big difference when we know parents will bring the younger kids and pick them up...even remind them we are having a meeting. The longer we can keep the kids involved, the more likely they will stay that way. We've had enough experience to know what works and what doesn't. I know Patti will benefit from this environment, and we have some kids here who will be good role models for her as she continues through school."

Kathy listened and replied, "I know how important faith is as you go through life, and I want Patti to have an opportunity to find and develop hers. I will do everything I can to encourage and support her...although right now it appears she is doing quite well all by herself."

Between youth group, several visits to Colby's house, occasional walks in the park with her mother, and visits from Detective Johnson, Patti's summer flew by quickly. She often wished summer vacation would last a few weeks longer, but it never did. Patti had learned long ago the pleasures of being alone and entertaining herself, but she also enjoyed the company of other people and had discovered she would really rather be around adults than kids her own age. While it may have been true that Colby was the "perfect" little gentleman, Patti never thought of herself as a little lady, but she was well behaved and polite; adults seemed to like those qualities. She often thought this was the reason kids her own age wanted nothing to do with her...she was too grown up for them. On the other hand, Patti was well aware of her deficiencies. She was just a kid and there was a lot more to life than riding bicycles or being in middle school. She loved to learn new things and had trouble understanding why others her age did not. They only wanted to have "fun"...but learning was fun, and it was hard to feel sorry for those who made little or no effort. What future could anyone have without a decent education and a positive work attitude? Patti figured she had inherited these qualities from her mother's side of the family; hard work meant a lot, perhaps too much, to them.

At the end of July during the last youth group meeting of the month, Counselor Dave asked to conference with Patti. They found an empty classroom. "Patti, I have a couple of questions, then decide what to do. Is that okay?"

"Sure."

"Okay, I know you've been reading the New Testament I gave you, right?"

"Yes, sir, I have read it twice, some parts three times."

"Good. Okay, what do you think about sin?"

"Well, sin is a little word, but it causes lots of grief. I see it like being bad, you know, when you don't do what your mother says...only it means you don't do what Jesus says."

"Okay, in Romans 3:23 it says we have all sinned and fallen short of God's glory. What do think about that?"

"I think that's true; no one is perfect...everyone goofs up..."

"Are you a sinner?"

Patti was blunt. "Yes, sir, I am."

"How do you feel about that, Patti?"

"Well, I feel bad, but I think it can be fixed."

"What do mean?"

"Well, somewhere in Acts one of the disciples explains this; it was pretty simple; I read it over several times and wondered about it."

"Okay let's see if we can find that passage in my Bible...I think...oh, here it is, Acts 2:38. Peter responds to the question, 'Brothers, what shall we do?' and he says 'Repent and be baptized, every one of you, in the name of Jesus Christ so that your sins may be forgiven and you will receive the gift of the Holy Spirit.' Is that the passage?"

"Yes, it's the one I remember."

"Do you understand what it means?"

Patti hesitated. "No, not exactly, but I kind of get it."

"Okay, let's review it. *Repent* means to deeply regret our sins. When we confess to God that we have sinned, we are repenting. Some people confuse this next word, *baptize*. It has multiple meanings. In this case Peter is telling his audience their souls need to be made alive to

God...touched by the Holy Spirit. To do this they must renew their belief in Jesus Christ and accept Him as their Lord and Savior. Does this makes sense?"

"Uh, I think so."

"Good. Okay, let's go through this and see what happens. Patti Linder are you a sinner?"

"Yes, I am."

"Do you believe in Jesus Christ, that He's the Son of God?"

"Yes, sir, I do."

"Will you accept Him as your Lord and Savior?"

Patti responded confidently. "Yes, I will."

"Now if you have done these things, what will happen?"

"The passage says my sins will be forgiven and I will receive the gift of the Holy Spirit, but I'm not sure what that last part means."

"Patti, it means you will get what you most want...you will have Jesus in your heart." Dave tried to hold back his tears.

Patti looked at Counselor Dave as if he had just given her all the money in the world. "Is this what you meant when we talked at camp; it's really this easy?"

"Yes, Patti, but I said you have to be ready. Are you ready to do that right now?"

"Oh, yes! I want more than anything to have Jesus in my heart."

"Okay, let's get down on our knees and you can pray the ABC's backwards to God."

"What?" Patti looked confused.

"C stands for confess, B means believe, and A is accept. Confess you are a sinner. Believe Jesus is the Son of God. Accept Him as your Lord and Savior."

Patti bowed her head. Dave placed his hand on her shoulder; she began. "Dear God..."

Dave interrupted. "You don't have to pray out loud; this is between you and God."

Patti nodded and continued silently. Dave felt a slight tremor in her shoulder and could see that Patti was crying, tears rolling down her cheeks. She remained very quiet for a long time; she finally looked up at Dave with a warm smile. "I can feel Him, Counselor Dave; I can feel Him in my heart. I'll never be alone again!"

Dave thought, but did not say, "And you'll never be the same, praise God!"

Patti's mother came to pick her up. When they started home in the car, her mother asked, "Well, what did you do at your meeting tonight?" Patti beamed at her mother. "Mama, tonight I got Jesus in my heart; I'll never be afraid again."

Kathy was not prepared for this; she understood what Patti was saying but its impact remained unclear. She was silent for a moment. "Why Honey, that's wonderful; I'm so happy for you."

Patti smiled confidently. "I'm happy too; this means everything to me."

ᴙᴙ Seventeen ᴙᴙ

With July out of the way and her newfound companion, Patti decided to focus on school. She really hadn't given it much thought since early in the summer when she had just wanted to be with Colby in as many classes as possible. Older kids did not have to go to orientation unless they were new to the district, but they could come pick up their schedules and report possible errors. Patti called Colby and asked if he might want to go to school and get his schedule. Colby told her he was about to call and ask same thing. Geoff wanted to find out about a class he had enrolled in that might not be offered. They agreed to meet and headed for the middle school. On the way, they visited about the start of school and what seventh grade might be like. They were rather anxious for it to start, but were still enjoying their vacation. Patti did not mention anything about her spiritual renaissance. It had been private, and she decided to keep it that way.

When they arrived at school and got their schedules, they were genuinely surprised. Patti and Colby were together in every class—that is, except for PE. That would have been difficult, and they laughed. Geoff was also in most of their classes so these three musketeers would be together every day. Patti told Colby she was really happy it had worked out that way and was surprised when Colby came right out and said the same thing. He was often rather quiet about their relationship even though Patti was certain he had feelings for her. Sometimes she believed they were meant for each other even though that sounded silly, and she had never told a soul how she felt; there was just a connection to him she couldn't explain. She knew this school year would be great. Many things in her life seemed to be coming together. If only she could find a way to help her mother, everything would be perfect.

Seventh grade was truly a breath of fresh air. All the kids Patti and Colby knew were excited about their new classes. Patti was enjoying science; Colby was interested in math because his book included the word *algebra* in its title and algebra was taught in high school...it made him feel older; Geoff claimed he didn't like anything, but Colby knew he loved social studies. In addition, Patti continued attending youth group, and it had become the highlight of her week. She was looking forward to September when youth group returned to its normal structure and met on Friday evenings. Patti found herself looking forward to so many positive things that her attitude was changing; she even managed to stop worrying so much about her mother.

Patti's Christian conversion had not changed her basic attitudes or feelings about life, her family, or the way she lived, but she realized she did have some responsibility to care for those around her, other than just her mother, and this new burden was about to raise its head. When teachers seated the students alphabetically, Patti and Colby were usually near the front of the classroom because their last names were in the first half of the alphabet. Their first class in the morning was English and one day when their teacher arrived late, Patti scanned the room, "checking out" her fellow classmates. She noticed a girl behind her who looked very familiar; she puzzled over it for the rest of the morning. She knew she had seen her before, but just could not remember. She asked Colby and he didn't know her at all. Later in the day, she realized this same girl was also in their social studies class so she asked Geoff if he knew her.

When it came to knowing people, Geoff knew just about everything about everyone; it was almost scary. Yes, Geoff knew her name was Sarah and all the kids made fun of her and called her "stinky" because, well, she didn't smell good. Patti thought and thought about her and the name Sarah rang a few bells; it seemed like Patti had been in school with her before but couldn't quite place her. Patti felt bad kids made fun of her; it seemed mean and unfair. Kids can't control the way they lived; you can't always pick the parents or the environment you want—you get what you're born into. Patti decided to help her.

Patti kept an eye on Sarah and watched where she went after school; she didn't ride the bus and she didn't always walk in the same direction. Patti planned to follow her and they could talk. The afternoon Patti chose was rather hot, and she began to wonder if tracking down Sarah and then having to walk home was such a great idea. This day Sarah left and headed along the sidewalk by the playground. Patti hoped they could stop to sit on a bench under one of the trees and visit. Sarah was nearly a twin to Patti. They were about the same size; both had cropped hair except Patti's was dark and Sarah's was a sandy blonde; they were freckled, and both had a rather boyish look. Sarah had gotten ahead of Patti, so Patti hurried to catch her; Sarah walked really fast and finally Patti yelled, "Sarah! Sarah,

198

wait up." Sarah jumped, as if startled, then walked even faster. "Sarah, please, wait; I'd like to talk to you."

This time Sarah stopped and looked back to see who was speaking. "What do you want?"

"I'd like to talk to you."

"Why? About what?" Sarah's tone was curt and cold.

"Look, I'm not going to hurt you or make any trouble; I'd like to ask you a couple of questions. How about we just sit down and visit?" Patti motioned toward a shaded bench.

"Well, I guess it's okay; I've no place to go anyway. You wouldn't happen to have something to eat would you? I didn't have any lunch."

"Yeah, I think I've got a granola bar in my backpack; you are welcome to it." Patti figured Sarah was really hungry.

"Thank you. What do you want to know?" Sarah took the granola bar and removed its wrapper.

"Well, I saw you in English class the other day and you looked so familiar; I've been trying to figure out why."

"Oh, that's easy. We've been in school together several times. Let's see, we were in third grade for a while, then in fourth grade—same school, different classes; then, I think, we were in fifth grade too. I didn't live here last year. My folks, well...we move around a lot so I'm never in the same place very long."

"Gosh, I'd think I would remember you better; I'm sorry."

"Hey, it's okay. I'm not much to remember; I'm a nobody, and nobodies are very forgettable." Sarah was quite blunt as she tried to eat her "lunch."

Patti was offended by her remarks. "Now wait a minute; I don't think you're a nobody. What makes you say that?"

Sarah obviously doubted her. "You don't?"

"No, I don't."

"But you don't even know me; remember how this conversation began?"

"Look, here's the deal; I don't have to know everything about you or anyone else to care about them. The way I see it, I can make friends or care about anyone I choose...and right this moment I care about you. I don't know when you last looked at yourself, but it seems to me you could use a friend."

Sarah sat looking at her for a long time, finishing the granola bar. "You're not kidding are you?"

"No, I'm not spending time with you on a hot afternoon just to get fresh air."

Sarah looked again at Patti. Her demeanor seemed to change; she then spoke in a hushed tone. "All right, I'm going to trust you; you seem pretty straight to me, but understand what I have to tell you is between you and me. You can't tell anyone or I could get into trouble."

Patti's interest in Sarah was immediately piqued; she looked at her. "If you have secrets, they're safe with me. I don't rat on my friends."

Thus, Sarah began her tale. If it were true, it was the most incredible story Patti had ever heard.

Sarah sort of lived with her mother and her mother's live-in boyfriend; her real father was long gone, and she had not seen nor heard from him in years. Her mother had a serious drug problem and had spent time off and on in jail for just about every drug offense possible. In fact, the last judge had told her the next time she ended up in court, she could say good bye to the "free" world for a long time. Sarah absolutely hated her home and everyone in it; the house smelled of marijuana, alcohol, and vomit, and the people there didn't smell much better. Sarah had hoped they would all just die.

Life away from home was no improvement. She had been in temporary foster care on two or three occasions and did not have good experiences. In one place she was badly beaten by a foster sibling and in another nearly molested by a friend of the family. She had tried to kill herself on two occasions, but was unable to carry through with her plans. She had finally resigned herself to dying from either exposure or starvation, and it was obvious she did not eat regularly or well. Interestingly, she was apparently quite bright, despite her environment, and was a lot tougher than her small frame and appearance suggested. She had not been home for about a week, and was living in a damaged dumpster. She had eaten only sparsely from trash, but had managed a few handouts. She had not bathed or cleaned except to wash her hands.

When Sarah finished her story, Patti was appalled; she could not even imagine living like Sarah did; she couldn't believe it, but the evidence was right in front of her. She reached for Sarah's dirty hand. "Sarah, I can't imagine the life you've described, but we are going to get up right now and you are coming home with me. You are going to take a bath, put on some clean clothes, and eat supper with my mother and me; if you will, I'd like for you to stay with us and get a good night's rest...in a clean bed."

Sarah looked at Patti; her face was so sad...a few tears had formed at the corner of each eye. She squeezed Patti's hand. "Do you really mean it?"

"As God is my witness, I mean every word."

The girls got up. Patti asked if there was anything Sarah needed to pick up and she could think of nothing. They headed toward Patti's apartment. When they arrived, Sarah was surprised Patti lived in an old warehouse, noting it was very big; Patti laughed and agreed. Once inside, and just as promised, Patti led Sarah to the bathroom. Sarah quickly undressed and jumped in the tub. There was no hint of modesty; Sarah was so happy at the prospect of being clean she didn't care who saw her naked, and Patti was not embarrassed to help her new friend. As the tub filled, Patti asked if Sarah would like some bubble bath; Sarah decided to give it a try and was amazed at all the bubbles. Patti felt so good about helping Sarah that she was beside herself with joy. She gave Sarah soap and a sponge and told her to enjoy every moment; Sarah was in heaven.

At about this time Kathy came home from work, and Patti rushed to her. "Shhh, Mom, you can't go in the bathroom; a naked stranger is in there."

Kathy looked at Patti curiously. "Young lady, what are you doing with a naked stranger in our bathroom?"

"Why, Mom, I'm getting her clean!" Patti then explained the situation.

"Oh, my goodness." Kathy was shocked, softly repeating, "Oh, my goodness."

Patti gathered some of her old clothes which she figured would fit Sarah, and Kathy tried to think about what they might have for supper. It wasn't long before Sarah said she could really use a towel; she'd managed to get all wet in the tub and didn't want to track water all over the place. Patti got her a towel and gave her clean clothes. "Hey, do you need a checkup? My mom's a nurse."

Sarah was unsure. "Why would I need a checkup?"

"I don't know; I thought since Mom does that kind of work...you might need the once over."

"Well, if she wants to, I guess it's all right, but I'm all wet right now."

"Yeah, but you're a lot cleaner!" Patti then asked her mother to check and make sure Sarah was okay.

Kathy went into the bathroom and examined Sarah as best she could; she was surprised to discover Sarah appeared to be in good shape...no lice or bugs. However, she did seem to be underweight, and Kathy thought a toothbrush would be helpful, but generally, Sarah had cared for herself better than most street kids.

Patti and Sarah talked while Kathy prepared supper. Patti promised Sarah a warm meal plus a safe night with them. She could go to school with Patti the next morning if she wanted; it would not be problem. Patti was surprised at what happened next. Sarah looked straight at her. "Look, it's okay if I stay with you tonight, but I've got to be really careful; it's complicated. You see, I've got to stay with my mother, or I have an aunt; I can stay with her. She doesn't like having me around, but she'll let me stay with her sometimes when things get bad. If I don't stay with a relative, I can be declared a runaway; if the police or social welfare catch me, I'll end up in foster care permanently. I can't let that happen. I have to go to school or they will turn me in; I know I'm in a bad way, and I know you want to help me, but I've got to be careful."

"Okay, I get the picture, but you can't go around living in a dumpster; you're welcome to stay with us anytime you need a place to crash. I just want you to know this is a safe place—warm bath, good food, and a clean bed with no bugs. You will always be welcome if we are home and if we're not, I can show you where you can hide until we get here. How does that sound?"

"That's good...real good; I can find this place easy. Hey, thanks for caring, and remember." Sarah put her finger to her lips, lowering her voice. "Don't tell anyone about me."

Supper was good. Sarah seemed more relaxed and less nervous. She and Patti chatted about school and finished some homework. Patti enjoyed the company and Sarah seemed content with the situation. Near bedtime Patti said, "Look, you can sleep in my bed tonight; you deserve a good night's rest. I'll be fine on the sofa."

Sarah looked at Patti with an odd expression, sad and disappointed. "What's the matter?"

"Well, I don't want to take your bed; I mean, you don't have to give it up for me."

Patti persisted. "But I want to."

Sarah appeared uncertain and stammered. "Of course, I understand...I just wondered...I was wondering if maybe...maybe, I could sleep with you; I don't like to be alone all the time. That's the big drawback in my life; I'm by myself most of the time, and it's nice to be around people that don't want to hurt you."

"Believe me; I understand. You're looking at someone who's been there; done that. You can sleep with me, and if you will give me a chance, I can tell you how to never be alone again, but I think we had better let that go until later. You know what they say, 'us girls gots to get our beauty sleep.' We don't want to scare anyone at school tomorrow; it's scary enough as it is." Sarah nodded and laughed. The bed felt wonderful to both of them, but for different reasons. Patti was beginning to like helping people; it made her feel good, and it sure wasn't hurting Sarah.

The girls went to school the next day and nothing was said of their recent encounter. Sarah promised to keep in touch; they could continue to meet after school. Patti just needed to let Sarah "do her thing" and everything would be okay. Over a week passed before they really talked again. Patti noticed she seemed cleaner, a definite plus. Sarah had been home for a bit and had also stayed with her aunt. Patti asked if they could meet again in about a week; she wanted to visit with Sarah about something and it might take a while; maybe they could walk to Patti's apartment, have supper and spend an evening together. Sarah appeared pleased at the offer and thought she could make it happen; she told Patti her busy schedule and active social life made it difficult to arrange such meetings. Patti's jaw dropped as she looked at Sarah; both girls were quite amused—Sarah trying to be serious about her remarks and Patti surprised at Sarah's dark and dry humor.

The following week the girls met again; Sarah told Patti they could have the entire evening, and she could even spend the night. She wondered if they still had some of that bubble bath, and she had a clean set of clothes in her backpack. Patti told her the bathtub still worked and they would get her all the bubble bath she needed. As they walked, Patti asked, "Do you remember the last time you stayed with me? You said you didn't like being alone."

"Sure, I remember; you told me you knew how to solve my problem...I've been meaning to ask about that."

"Okay, well, I want to tell you, but I also have a question. I was wondering what you do on Friday evenings; I mean what's your schedule like?"

"Patti, I don't have any schedule...mostly I just try to stay alive. Friday nights are a bad time at home; my mom likes to start partying then, and it pretty much goes on through Sunday. I try to stay away; it isn't safe. I figure there's no sense inviting trouble."

"Well, what do you do...I mean, for the whole weekend?"

Sarah shrugged. "It depends. Sometimes I spend time with my aunt; I can watch her kids and she will pay me a little for it; sometimes I go out...you know, like to a movie or just hang out on the street."

Patti was worried. "Isn't that a little dangerous? There are crazy people out there."

"Tell me about it...you've got to stay in the shadows and keep your eyes open; you can't trust anybody."

"But you trust me."

Sarah replied quickly. "Yeah, but you're not on the street!"

"Well, here's the deal. I go to a church youth group and they meet every Friday evening throughout the school year. We have refreshments, talk about stuff, play some games, and just hang out. I've been going all summer, and I'd like you to come with me. We could come home from school together, grab a bite to eat, then go to youth group. When my mom comes to pick me up, she could drop you off wherever you want, or maybe you could spend the night with me. I just thought you might enjoy the company; there are some nice kids in our group and we have a lot of fun."

"I don't know; I guess I could give it a try. Do I need anything?"

"Nope, you will be my guest, and that's all, but there is one more thing I need to ask. What do you know about Jesus?"

Sarah looked at Patti somewhat puzzled but not really surprised. "Jesus? What does He have to do with me?"

Patti pressed her. "Come on; help me out. What do you know about Jesus?"

"Well, I...well, I don't know; that is, I don't know too much...but I like His music."

"What!? His music?" Patti looked almost as confused as Sarah.

"Look, you know I don't live at home; I live around. I don't want to tell you everything because my secrets are important. Okay? One of the places I used to crash was down by the Salvation Army shelter; the people there would help me out sometimes; you know, get me food and bring me out of the cold. They have services there; I guess like church or something, and if I was around, I could hear them inside. They talked about Jesus, but I didn't pay much attention; I liked the music...it made me feel good, kind of warm inside. That's about all I know about Him. I mean, He's in the Bible and all, but I don't know Him."

"No problem, you know enough to understand what I need to tell you. If I can get you a certain book, just like one I have, will you read it for me; and then come to youth group for the next few weeks? If you will do these things, I can show you how to never be alone, afraid or scared again, and Sarah, I promise you I'm not trying to fool you or be funny; I mean every word."

Sarah looked at Patti with a glimmer of hope. "Yes, if you can do that for me, it's a small price to pay; I'll do anything I can. It's a deal."

Patti stopped, got her New Testament from her backpack, and showed it to Sarah, who thought it was pretty small to be so important. Patti reminded her good things can come in small packages, and if she didn't believe it, they could stand in front of a mirror when they to got to the apartment; after all, they were small packages and a couple of good kids. Sarah was amused and Patti started to laugh. Friends are good.

The girls had pleasant evening: the bubble bath smelled great, the food was good, the apartment was comfortable, and the bed was clean and soft. Sarah was indeed blessed to be with Patti and her mother, but it did make it difficult to resume her "normal" life when she left. Sarah hoped more than anything that someday she might have a good life, but right now it simply was not possible; however, if Patti could open new doors, it would not hurt to look inside—Sarah would give the youth group and Jesus a try.

⤜ Eighteen ⤛

Just before Labor Day weekend, Detective Johnson showed up to visit with Kathy, who was not home from work. Patti was working around the apartment picking up and putting things away that should have been taken care of days before. Deb was disappointed Kathy was not home, but decided to wait and pass time with Patti. They sat down in the living area; Patti spoke first. "You know, I've been thinking about that time you were in your dorm room with the gun in your mouth. I mean...what I mean is...I wonder what would have happened if that girl across the hall had fumbled with her keys or arrived later. Where would you be now? I mean, do you ever think about it?"

"Patti, it's something I'd like to forget. You know, it brings back bad memories; I made a mistake and quite frankly, I don't like to think about it."

"Well, sure. No one likes to think about their mistakes, but it's kind of hard to escape them. I just wondered what you think about it."

"What do you want me to say? I figure a few seconds later, and let's just say we wouldn't be having this conversation." Deb was rather emphatic.

"Yeah, that's what I think too; I guess what I'm wondering is why she screamed when she did?"

Deb tried to put a good spin on it. "I don't know. I guess you could say I was lucky."

"You bet; you were lucky, but have you ever thought it might be more than that."

Deb was becoming annoyed. "What are you getting at?"

"Well, do you think your life has been worthwhile?"

"Sure, I'd say so."

"So you've done your share of good things and are proud of it."

Deb thought a moment. "Yes, I could say that."

"That gun would have ended your life and your good work would have never happened. Maybe God intended for you to live...maybe, He timed that scream to save you."

Deb snapped back. "Now listen, young lady, you leave God out of this; I have no use for Him."

"But He has a use for you. You've helped my Aunt Sherry; you've helped me; and I know you've helped a lot of other people. You do God's work everyday; you should be proud of it."

Deb became almost nasty. "Patti, I don't know what's got into your head, but you keep your ideas about God to yourself. I didn't come over here to be preached to, and I don't want to discuss it any further. Do you understand?"

"Yes, I do; I understand, but I'm not preaching at you. I'm asking you to consider it might be more than just luck that

208

we are having this conversation. I'm sorry if I made you mad; I won't bring it up again. Just remember my question and if you ever want to talk about it, fine...if not, well that's fine too." Patti almost regretted discussing the matter.

Kathy arrived and no other words were spoken; Patti resumed her chores and the detective and Kathy had their tête-à-tête.

Patti was really looking forward to their first "formal" youth group meeting. The summer meetings were informal. Patti had enjoyed that format but was curious how the school-year meetings would work; she was excited because Sarah would be coming too and hoped she would stay involved, so Patti would have a friend there. The kids had voted to begin their Friday meetings at the beginning of Labor Day weekend. Normally, the meetings began at 7:00 pm, but this time the first meeting started at 6:00; they were having a cookout and needed to discuss things for the upcoming year. They especially wanted to give the group a name to help identify who and what they were. Patti had been thinking about some possibilities but was not happy with any of them; she finally decided someone else could have that honor.

When the last bell rang at school, Patti met Sarah at her locker and they packed for the long weekend. Patti didn't mind walking home when someone went with her; it reminded her of the times she and Colby had walked together. Patti was pleased to know Sarah was looking forward to their evening; she thought it was better to be doing something worthwhile than just hiding from her family or "hanging out" downtown. When they reached Patti's apartment, they freshened up and changed clothes. Patti was really anxious to get there, and Sarah told her to calm down and be patient; they only had to wait about an hour. Sure enough Kathy got home; they chatted and were soon on their way.

As the kids gathered to eat, the group leader asked everyone to introduce their guests; Patti was pleased to see many new faces; she wanted the group to grow and believed they had much to offer everyone. As they finished eating, the leaders asked their regular members if anyone had come up with a name for the group. Several kids stepped up and made suggestions, but Patti liked the idea one of the boys suggested; he did crossword puzzles and had needed to respond to the clue, "on fire, burning." As he worked around that response, he finally realized that the correct answer was the word *aflame*; for some reason, he was taken with this word. He then thought that *AFLAME* could stand for "a faithful life assures my eternity." The idea was so popular the kids decided, without voting, they would henceforth be known as AFLAME. Patti observed that if wisecracking Geoff was there, he would have said something like, "Aha, AFLAME...on fire for Jesus!" amused, she started to laugh. Sarah wanted to know what Patti was thinking; she didn't see or hear anything funny. Patti promised to tell her later; it was just a thought about one of her friends.

Remarkably, their meeting started right on time and Patti liked the way it began. The regular members all sat, or stood when there were no chairs, and going around a circle, each would say his name followed by the statement, "I am a sinner." When everyone had finished, they would raise their hands and shout, "but Jesus saved me! Amen." Patti loved that opening; she sure knew she had sinned and was mighty happy Jesus had saved her...because now she could have Him in her heart, all day, everyday.

After the opening ceremony, they had group singing: hymns, gospel songs, gospel rock, whatever they wanted. Some of the kids might sing solos or small-group numbers. The singing was a big deal and it was hard for some of them to keep from dancing. Sarah told Patti later she had never seen kids having so much fun and not breaking the law; Patti told her they were all celebrating their love for Jesus, and it was a joy to be there and participate. The singing could last an hour, but on this particular evening it was cut short because their sponsors wanted them to elect officers and go over rules. Items of business were next on the agenda, but nothing was planned that demanded immediate attention. They always had some lesson or presentation set up by the leaders which often involved the kids. There were also discussions about issues of the day and how they should deal with them as Christians.

The last part of every meeting was a time for kids to present questions from their study of the Bible or follow up issues from previous discussions. The time always flew by, and Patti hated for the meeting to end. When they had finished, Patti asked Sarah if she thought she would like to come back and become a member. Counselor Dave had given Patti a New Testament to give to Sarah, and she had been very grateful, promising to read it every day. As for coming back, Sarah's response was, "Yes, I'd like that very much." Patti was thrilled; she wanted to share the gift of Jesus. It made her feel even better than the singing.

On Labor Day, Detective Johnson came by to spend the afternoon with Kathy, who had arranged to take the day off; she had some flexibility when she gave the hospital advance notice. It was a good deal that Kathy rarely used and Patti probably needed. The detective went out of her way to avoid Patti, making Patti think she had certainly hit a nerve with Deb, but it was none of her business, and if adults don't want to talk about things, you might as well shut up. Patti didn't pay much attention to Deb's and her mother's conversation, but she did pick up the juicy part.

Word had gotten out that Deb and her mother were friends; both were young; both were single and unattached; and they were seeing each other often. Therefore, they must be lesbians. Kathy was both amused and angered by the news. She found this conclusion sorely deficient, and whose business was it that two people, who happened to be friends and both female, were more than just friends? On the other hand, she had been sleeping alone all these years except for an occasional all nighter with Patti. Did this mean that she and Patti were lesbians? People were sick, and obviously many of them weren't very smart.

Deb had found it amusing because she had been out with several men, most of them local; she hadn't found one she wanted, but she hadn't given up looking...of course, if she were going to look for a "girl" friend, Kathy would be a good choice. She could cook and take care of her when she got sick, and since Deb was good with a gun, she could protect Kathy from all the evil men who stalked and annoyed her. The girls had it all figured out; well, that is, all but Patti...she was mostly confused. Adults can be weird at times; no, make that most of the time. Regardless, Kathy and Deb were still laughing about this nonsense when Deb left a short time later.

It wasn't until after Labor Day that Patti finally discovered Raven no longer attended their school; she had apparently moved. Patti thought about Raven every time she had a youth group meeting. She noticed that so far no one had said anything about hot wax, whipping, or blood sucking, and that was for the best. Raven had dabbled in darkness; Patti had shared her lifestyle and could have died there. Interestingly, it was the light in the darkness that saved Patti, and she now had found an even brighter Light. Fortunately, at he end of the school year, Raven had begun to turn away from darkness, and Patti hoped she also found the true Light some day. Patti decided to pray for Raven; she had been a friend.

Patti and Sarah continued attending the weekly AFLAME meetings, which were attracting a few more kids all the time. By the end of the month the weather had cooled slightly so it was more fun to walk home from school. On the last Friday in September as they walked to Patti's apartment, Sarah began the conversation. "Patti, I was wondering about something. Do you think I am ready to have Jesus in my heart?"

"Well, how many times have you read your testament?"

"Almost twice; I should have it finished by Sunday."

"Do you know what sin is?"

"Yes, I do; sin is when you do wrong in the eyes of the Lord."

"Are you a sinner?"

"I surely am; we are all sinners, according to the Bible."

"Okay, do you know and love Jesus?"

"I do; I know He was the Son of God; I truly love Him."

"I have an idea. Let's go to the park by my apartment and do the ABC's backwards; then tonight you can join our opening circle at AFLAME. Would you like that?"

"Absolutely, but what's this ABC's backwards business." Sarah seemed confused.

"It's simple. C stands for confess, B means believe, and A is accept. You have to confess you're a sinner, then believe Jesus is the Son of God; finally you must accept Him as your Lord and Savior. If you do these things, God will forgive your sins and you will have Jesus in your heart forever."

Sarah stopped and looked straight at Patti. "Is that all I have to do?"

"That's it; let's hurry to the park."

The girls picked up their pace. They located a big tree whose leaves were turning into yellows and reds, then sat down on the bench beneath it. Patti said to Sarah, "It might be better if you got down on your knees; you need to pray the prayer we just talked about to God, the backwards ABC's. You can just pray it to yourself because God will hear you, and I'll stay right by you."

Sarah bowed her head and Patti placed a hand on her shoulder just like Counselor Dave had done for her. Sarah was very still, but Patti could feel her small body shake. When she finally looked at Patti, tears were rolling down her cheeks; she started to speak, but the words simply would not come out. Patti reached around and pulled her close with a gentle hug; Sarah sobbed in her arms. Patti held her, then realized she was crying too. Sarah looked up and kissed Patti on her cheek; Patti kissed her back.

They continued to hold each other and finally Sarah spoke, her voice quivered. "Patti, I do...I think...no, I can feel Jesus inside me just like you promised."

"I know, but God made that promise...not me."

Patti now knew she loved Sarah and suspected Sarah loved her. In case any rumors got started, they were...just friends!

Patti figured her life was back in balance. She had made Detective Johnson mad at her and lost that friendship, but she had gained a mighty ally in Sarah. She couldn't win them all, but she couldn't stand by and say nothing when in her heart, she knew she had found something special and precious. Sharing something special meant a lot more than sharing a soda or even a banana split; it was like giving up a part of yourself.

When the AFLAME meeting began that night, a new member stepped into the circle to declare she was a sinner...but now was saved. Patti was so proud, and she knew Sarah felt a new belonging. Her family at home was lousy or worse, but now she had a new family, one on which she could trust and depend. Kids need to be safe and a home should be more than just a shelter.

Later into fall, Detective Johnson had come by after supper to visit; Kathy was in the shower and this left Patti and Deb with an awkward moment. Patti chose to speak first, "Deb, I know you don't want to visit with me, but I have a question that relates to what you do, and I was hoping you might have an answer."

"Why, Patti, I don't know what gets into you. I'm glad to visit; we're old friends." Deb acted puzzled.

"I don't want to have any trouble, but you have not treated me the same since we talked about your situation at school. I told you then I would not bring up the subject again; I only wanted you to think about it. You will have to make the first move to get anymore out of me. You can say we are friends, but I know I'm just a kid and you're an adult like my mom. I know you have much more in common with her, but you've changed your feelings for me, and that's okay. I just have a question about one of my friends."

"Sure, I'll try to help, but I think you're wrong about me."

"Do you remember how when I got attacked in the park, you said you would like to hire me as your assistant, then told me you would like to have me live with you?"

"Yes, I remember."

"Okay, did you really mean it; I mean, would you like to have a kid my age live with you and be a mom to her?"

"You mean like a foster parent or guardian?"

"Yeah, that's what I mean."

"Well, a few years ago I gave some thought to it, but I'm not so sure I'm cut out to be a mom to anybody; I don't even take good care of myself."

"I was just wondering. I have this friend at school; she needs a good home really bad. I worry about her and I thought maybe you'd consider, like, adopting her; she's a good kid and deserves better." Patti looked rather sad.

Deb seemed a bit frustrated. "Look, Patti, like I said, I'm probably not the one you should be talking to about this; I don't think I would make a very good parent, but let's say I'm not totally against it and leave it at that."

"Okay. If you know any good people who would like to have a girl my age, I would like to know. My friend needs a family and I'd like to help. You can think about it. Thank you for answering my question."

"You're always welcome, Patti; I'm sorry you think I'm mad at you. It's not true; I hope we can always be friends."

Patti didn't believe the detective; she knew she had struck a nerve, making Deb angry. She also knew Deb avoided her when she came to visit. Patti wasn't going to cry about it, but she wished Deb would get her head straight about why that girl screamed at exactly the right time. Accidents happen all the time, but this was no accident; it was planned and Deb should be thankful—it had saved her life!

Patti tried to maintain contact with Sarah as much as possible. Sarah still didn't have any real friends although most of the kids had stopped teasing her about not smelling good after Patti made her bathroom available. They almost always walked home together on Fridays so Sarah would have a ride to youth group. Other days Patti tried to get Sarah to come home and eat with them; Patti worried about her.

Near the end of October, the youth group joined with other organizations to do volunteer service for the elderly or disabled. The community sponsored two such events, one in the fall and another in the spring. The fall event mostly involved raking leaves and picking up trash in preparation for winter; the spring event was more window washing or garage cleaning. AFLAME skipped their Friday meeting. Saturday was reserved for service work which ended with a cookout and fun night. Patti and Sarah asked to work together.

The leaders drove each work crew to their respective locations and made periodic stops to bring something to snack on or drink and make sure everything was okay. Patti and Sarah were taken to an elderly couple's house; they had a small yard, but it was surrounded by big trees with leaves everywhere. When they checked in with the couple, they discovered the husband was confined to a wheel chair and his wife used a cane; they were in no condition to be working in their yard. The lady told them where the rakes were and gave them a big box of trash bags. After gathering these items, Patti realized she had never raked before. She asked Sarah if she knew anything about raking. Sarah had no experience either but had watched a neighbor and it looked a lot like sweeping with a broom. The girls decided they would give it a try and soon discovered raking wasn't very hard, but they had a lot of leaves to rake and bag. They worked really hard for about an hour; their hands were sore, and they were itchy from the leaves.

When they sat down on the front porch to rest, the lady came to the door and asked if they were thirsty. Yes, a

drink would be great. The lady returned with two big
glasses of cold lemonade, which Patti and Sarah wasted no
time drinking. Patti later told her mother it was the best
lemonade she had ever drunk, and she could not believe
how much better she felt afterwards. Now much refreshed,
the girls tackled the leaves with renewed determination.
About an hour later, one of their leaders came by to check
on them and bring a sandwich; the lady brought more
lemonade and they ate, drank, and rested. While they were
eating, Patti admitted she had never done any work like this
and Sarah said the same thing. They had played in leaves
but never cleaned them up. Both decided this was hard
work, especially in a big yard.

After their break, the girls tore into the job again and were
piling up quite a stack of bags. They found it interesting
that while leaves are generally light enough to blow in the
wind, a big bag of them was heavy. Apparently, the lady
inside enjoyed watching the girls work; she told someone it
was like a couple of ants trying to move an elephant. They
worked for another hour or so and drank more lemonade
they were discouraged because it seemed like a lot of the
yard remained untouched. Right after they started again,
another leader came by and asked if they could use some
help; one of the crews had finished early and was available.
Patti spoke right up and told him it would be great then
told Sarah her prayers had been answered; Sarah said she
was just about ready to ask for God's help too, but was
almost too tired to pray.

The girls laughed, the extra help soon arrived, and they got
the last leaves picked up just in time for their trip back to
the church and the evening festivities. Sarah had agreed to
spend the night with Patti, so when Kathy picked them up,
they admitted it had been a long, tough day. Kathy kidded
them about being a couple of softies because they weren't
used to hard work. Both girls had several blisters and
Kathy could tell they were worn out. She asked them what
they thought about helping the lady and her husband.
They agreed that even though they were tired and sore, it
still felt good to help other people. Kathy reminded them
that even though she didn't have to rake leaves, she helped
people all day long every day; it made her feel good...that's

why she was a nurse.

Near the end of the month Patti discovered she and Sarah had another thing in common; neither of them celebrated Halloween. Kathy almost always had to work because the hospital hired extra help to take care of emergencies; over the years Halloween seemed to bring out worst in some people, and the emergency room did extra business. In addition, Patti did not live in a residential neighborhood so she had no real neighbors. Except when she was little and had stayed with her grandparents, Patti had never trick or treated. Sarah noted no one in her family even suggested taking her out for Halloween activities. So Patti decided they would have their own Halloween party at the apartment. They could have a good supper, watch a scary movie, and have a few treats. Sarah didn't much like scary movies, but decided it would be fun to be with Patti; being on the street at Halloween was not safe, and Sarah would have to remain in hiding if she didn't go home.

On Halloween everything went exactly as planned. Kathy had left them food for supper and bought a few wrapped candies for treats; they had rented a movie. Kathy told Patti she didn't want her staying up late on a school night, so the girls started the movie right after supper. Sarah kept getting scared and asked to hold Patti's hand; then she wanted Patti to put her arms around her to protect her from the "monster" in the film. Patti was surprised the movie bothered her. "Why are you so scared? It's only a movie."

"I don't like to talk about it, but my life is a horror show. I've seen things that scared me and I've been around a lot of people that are monsters in their own right. These movies bring it back; I'm not so much scared by them, only by the things in them—they remind me of things that really happened."

Patti began to feel bad. "I'm sorry they bother you; we don't have to watch any more."

"No, I enjoy the movie ; I don't mind being scared when I'm with someone, besides, I've got Jesus now. I'm never alone." Sarah paused. "Could I ask a favor?"

"Sure."

"Could I sleep with you tonight? I would like that."

"I'd like that too." Patti was more convinced than ever that Sarah needed a good home.

AFLAME did not meet on the Friday after Thanksgiving. So the week before Thanksgiving, they had a special "I'm thankful" activity. The kids would sit in a circle, and name one or two things. Patti and Sarah were near the end and Patti was having a hard time deciding what to say. When her turn came, she looked up. "This is a lot harder for me than it should be; I can think of so many things for which I'm thankful it's hard to pick just two, but for sure I'm thankful for Jesus, my Savior; I have nothing to fear since He is with me. I guess the next thing I'm thankful for is my mom. She has worked very hard to take care of me and without a dad, she's all I've got."

Sarah looked at Patti. "Of course I'm thankful for Jesus, but I've got to say that I'm thankful for Patti; she's been a good friend, and even though we aren't related, she's the only family I have. I'm glad she tries to take care of me."

Patti reached for and held Sarah's hand; both girls looked a bit teary-eyed.

The Friday after Thanksgiving Deb came by late in the afternoon to see Kathy, who had just stepped into the bathroom so Patti had to welcome the detective. She asked her if she survived all the turkey, stuffing, and other holiday fare. Deb told her she had not gone anywhere special for Thanksgiving so she was not suffering from turkey hangover like most of the guys at work. She and Patti both agreed that too much turkey can be hazardous to your health! Patti asked. "Deb, have you been thinking about our conversation a while back? I asked you about a friend who really needs a home. Do you remember?"

"Yes, I remember; I told you I would think about it...and Patti, I have, but I haven't. It's complicated. I don't want you to think I don't care because I do; I know there are kids who only make it one day at a time. We don't have a lot of them here, but they are out there. Our patrols watch out for them as best they can, but it's tough; you and I both know it. I have thought about helping a kid, but I feel I'm little better than no one at all. My life's a mess, and I have no one to blame but myself. I do care; I hope you believe that. I hope your friend is okay...and Patti, just between you and me, I want you to keep reminding me. Maybe I'll come to my senses and do something good for her one of these days." Deb felt a little guilty.

"Look, Deb, it would not be fair to blame you for not wanting to help; I know you're really busy. I just want her to be safe, and the street isn't." The detective nodded.

Whenever Thanksgiving is over, the end of the year is not far behind. Patti looked forward to Christmas break; she hoped it would snow. Somehow Christmas was better with snow. Sarah would be with her aunt for most of the holidays but thought they could get together sometime during vacation. Patti's schedule was full with family events and the youth group's New Year's Eve dinner and party.

The snow came after the holiday, just enough to be messy, but not enough to cancel school; there was much weeping and wailing when school closing reports failed to materialize. The weather was cold, but not bitter. Patti always wondered about Sarah when it was cold, and Sarah did not like to talk about her specific circumstances because she felt safer if no one knew where she was. Patti did ask if she could use one of her old coats, and Sarah accepted it without argument; Patti was glad she took it. School was busy. The seventh graders were preparing for state exams. There had been more homework, but nothing that could not be handled with extra effort. Patti figured the teachers were just getting kids better prepared for high school; her mother had warned her it would be different from middle school. Patti wanted to be ready, and even Geoff was working harder. Apparently the word was out.

Winter tried to hang on, but by the end of February, the weather warmed and spring was on its way. Patti was thinking about her birthday. Her mother had noted she would soon be a teenager; Patti thought that was funny since she didn't feel any different. On the other hand, she knew she was growing up; she'd had a bit of a growth spurt and was two or three inches taller, but it seemed all of the other kids were growing even faster. In addition, some of the girls were filling out and Patti couldn't help noticing in the PE dressing room that she was pretty flat compared to the rest; at least Sarah wasn't busty, so Patti didn't have to be the Lone Ranger in that department. She talked to her mother about it, and Kathy was puzzled too. She had always had a nice figure, and her mother was well shaped. Kathy had only seen Brandon's mother once, and while she hadn't been attracted to her chest, she did remember she was not a rail. Kathy insisted Patti was just a "late bloomer" and that one of these days, she would "pop" out and become a woman. In the meantime, she should be thankful she didn't have to wear any extra underwear. A bra was a lot of things, but comfortable was not one of them. Patti decided her shape was not a big deal, and since no one seemed to care or give her a bad time; maybe being a teenager would take care of the problem.

Nineteen

March was a difficult month for Patti and her mother; it brought many bad memories. In addition, March weather was so confusing that no one knew how to dress. One day would be fairly warm, the next snowy. It was almost always windy, and, of course, the beginning of tornado season. Patti could not help thinking about Sarah and the nights she spent outside in a dumpster or trying to find someplace to stay out of the weather. Patti was really looking forward to spring break. She hoped to spend some time with both Sarah and Colby. In school, it was hard to find a good block of time to be with her friends, the weekends were always busy, and Patti hated to miss what little time she had with her mother.

This had been a particularly difficult time. One of the

221

regular nurses was pregnant and really sick, so the rest of the nursing staff was trying to cover her hours. Kathy had volunteered to fill in this week, so Patti did not get to see her until late in the evening. Patti hated when her mother worked late; it didn't fit with her schedule, but it was Wednesday night and the week was half over. Patti figured she could hang on for a couple more days. Then it would not only be the weekend, but spring break as well.

Patti had gone to bed a little early; she liked to read with the covers all wrapped around her. She had been reading a library book she wanted to finish and had just snuggled into bed, ready to sleep. As she lay there; she was thinking about Sarah and feeling very tired. Suddenly, the phone rang. Patti was startled—no one ever called at this time of night except the hospital to see if Kathy could come in for some emergency, but her mother was already there. Who could be calling? Patti rolled out of bed and ran to the phone. She picked up the receiver. "Hello?"

The phone voice responded. "Patti, this is your mother; something terrible has happened. Someone has tried to kill your friend Sarah; she's here in the ICU and we're not sure she's going to make it. I thought maybe you'd like to be here; we can't locate her family, and I guess you're about the only friend she has."

Patti was incredulous. "Is Sarah going to die?"

"Well, we don't know; she's unconscious with serious head trauma. Right now she's stable, but earlier we didn't think she'd make it. Look, I can't stay on the phone. Why don't you get dressed and come here? Do you think you'll be okay; it's late and, well, you already know...things happen."

"It's okay Mom; I'll be fine. I'll be right there." Patti was now wide awake and thinking clearly.

"I'll meet you at the front desk."

Patti hung up the phone and dressed in record time; she ran out of the building and all the way to the hospital at full speed. She burst through the front entrance into her mother's waiting arms. "Oh, Patti, I'm so sorry about this. Normally you would not be allowed in ICU, but the doctor thought someone should be with Sarah so she can hold on to what life she has left. Do you think you can do that?"

"Yes, I can."

Kathy led Patti to ICU. Looking at Sarah, Patti tried to suppress her gag reflex. There were tubes in her nose and right arm. Her head and left shoulder were bandaged. Her left eye was swollen shut, the left side of her face discolored and bruised. The rest of her appeared virtually lifeless; her skin had that pale ashen look associated with those who sleep in caskets. Sarah looked dead. Patti walked over to the bed and reached for Sarah's right hand; it was cool and lifeless. As Patti stood there, tears began to flow down her cheeks. How could anyone have done this? Kathy watched Patti, and she too was crying, perhaps thinking about that morning only one year ago when her own daughter could just as easily have been a victim of senseless violence. "Patti, will you be okay?"

"Yes, I'll just sit here and hold Sarah's hand; we can talk." Patti wiped her tears and tried to regain her composure.

When Kathy left, Patti looked intently at her friend, then bowed her head and prayed, "Lord, this is my friend Sarah; you already know her. She can't talk right now, but she needs your help. You know what's best for her, and she will be with You whether she lives or dies, but Lord, she's my friend; I love her. I think Sarah can do a lot of good in the world. I would like for You to heal her and make her well; then Lord, I'd like for you to find her a good home with a new mom and dad. You won't be sorry; I'll make sure she stays on the right path. I love You, Jesus. Amen."

Patti raised her head and looked at her friend and then felt the strangest sensation; it felt to Patti like Sarah's hand had gotten a bit warmer. A few minutes later when her mother came to check on Sarah, Patti confidently announced, "Sarah is going to be okay." Kathy was dumbstruck.

Patti sat with Sarah all night, holding her hand and

223

chatting. Sarah didn't say much, so Patti did all the talking. They talked about youth group, plans for spring break, finding a new family, things at school, and even the stupid weather. Patti was especially pleased that Sarah was so agreeable, but friends are supposed to get along...and Sarah was a good friend. Sarah even told Patti to take a nap, so she was surprised when her mother woke her. "I'll be off pretty soon. What do you want to do? I'll call the school and tell them you won't be there today; I probably shouldn't tell them about Sarah, but I think I will anyway. They need to know about her, and maybe let the kids know she's in the hospital."

"Mom, I'd like to stay here; Sarah needs me. I'll be okay. You can check on me this afternoon."

"Okay, I'll have someone in the cafeteria bring you something to eat; if you need anything else, give me a call. I need to get home and get some rest. I love you, Patti."

"I love you too."

A little later a cafeteria worker brought Patti some food; she was hungrier than usual after being up all night. She visited with Sarah, who continued to be most agreeable. When the nurse came in a few minutes later, she told Patti that Sarah's vital signs were much improved; she was fairly certain the doctor would upgrade her status as soon as he arrived. Patti didn't know much about vital signs, but she knew Sarah was going to be okay; God had plans for her.

Around 8:00 am, Patti was shocked to see Detective Johnson; she had come to check on Sarah. Apparently, the detective was also surprised. "Patti, what are you doing here?"

"I'm here with my friend Sarah; she doesn't have anyone to care for her, so I guess it's up to me."

Deb seemed quite concerned. "Is this the little friend you've talked about?"

"Yes, ma'am; no one in her family cares about her; they

only care about drugs and alcohol."

"Yes, I know; we've been checking them out, and I can't say they're worth much." Patti nodded her agreement. "Do you know what Sarah was doing last night?"

"No, she just told me she had to be out for a while. I don't think anyone was home. What happened anyway? Who did this?"

"Well, Patti, we don't have a lot to go on; we are hoping Sarah can help us when she regains consciousness, but we do know this much. Last night in an alley uptown there was a stabbing. We think it was drug related; the guy who got stabbed is not talking. We think Sarah must have witnessed the crime; she may have been hiding among some boxes and other trash. Our stabber probably discovered her, and she was cornered with no place to run. He hit her with a board we found in the alley; the board glanced off her shoulder, then caught the top of her head. I guess she was pretty lucky it was dark; if that blow had struck her head full force, it would have killed her. She's lucky to be alive."

"You already know what I think about luck. Sarah is meant to do good—God saved her. I know you don't want to talk about it, but it's a fact."

"No, Patti, this time you're wrong; I do want to talk about it, but I can't right now. How about I pick you up later. We'll talk one on one; we need to settle this."

"I'd like that; I'd like that a lot." Patti reached for and shook the detective's hand.

"I'll see you later then, okay?"

"Yeah, later...I'll be here."

Patti was pleased she might finally be able to end the rift she had with Deb. She liked Deb, and it hurt her they did not agree upon something so important. When the doctor arrived, he was surprised at Sarah's improved condition; he told Patti he thought Sarah was going to survive. Their

225

major concern was whether or not she might have any brain damage, only time would tell. As he put it, she looked a lot worse than she really was. Patti was pleased to hear the good news officially but was not surprised. She kept holding Sarah's hand, comforting her, and they continued their one-sided discussion. Two or three times she felt Sarah twitch; she hoped that was a good sign.

The detective left a message she would pick Patti up for lunch, and she could decide what she wanted to do about Sarah when they finished. Patti waited for her near the entrance and jumped into her squad car when she stopped. Deb smiled. "Say, I was going to ask you where you wanted to eat, but I have already decided, so don't argue with me when they bring you a dog bone."

"Well, I'm pretty hungry; a dog bone might taste pretty good." Patti was not fooled by Deb's nonsense.

In the meantime the squad car pulled up in front of the ice cream shop, and Patti did not have to ask, "What's for lunch?" They ordered their food and the detective told the waitress not to hurry with it because she needed to talk with this runaway before she ate her last meal. The young girl at the counter was surprised, so the detective explained they had finally captured this repeat offender and were tired of tracking her down, so this was it...an ice cream treat, then the firing squad. The girl gasped, and Patti, trying not to laugh, was about to explode as she headed for a booth.

When they sat down, Patti said, "You've got to stop being so honest; you nearly gave that poor girl a heart attack."

"Yeah, but you're the repeat offender. If you'd stop running away, it wouldn't have come to this."

"Okay, I confess; do your worst, anything you want...just don't make me go home; I just can't take it any longer!" Patti expected an Academy Award for this performance.

Now she had the detective laughing, but Deb finally said, "Listen, I want to apologize to you. I've not been completely honest, and I figure I need to square it with you before the firing squad arrives. First of all, I'm awfully sorry about your friend, and I'm going to make it right with you, but I can't tell you everything right now; just trust me on this...I'm going to make it right. The second thing is more complicated, but I want to tell you the truth. Patti, I have asked myself over and over a thousand times why that scream came when it did; you can't ignore something like that. It was my life, and it would have been over then and there. I don't feel the same way about God you do; I've seen a lot of ugly things in my years on the force...bad things, evil things; I figure if I give Him credit for saving my life, then He must be responsible for these bad things...because if He could save me, He could prevent them. Do you understand?"

"Sure, but I don't think it works that way. I think God hates evil, but He doesn't stop it because otherwise we would never recognize good; you know, like food...you can't appreciate good food until you've eaten bad food. I'm kind of new at this stuff, but I can tell you this morning when I prayed for Sarah, I could feel God healing her; I can't explain it, but I felt it. Now you'll say, 'Why did God allow someone to hurt this girl?' I don't know. It was awful, but something good is going to come of it. I can't explain it. I can tell you when I was attacked in the park, it was a terrible thing I would never want to happen again, but because of it, I met you, I went to summer camp, I met my friend Counselor Dave, I now have Jesus in my heart, and I helped bring Sarah to the Lord...all because something bad happened. God evens things out. I hope you will change your mind and try to see it differently. I will pray for you."

Deb sat there, reflecting on what she had heard. Here was a thirteen-year-old kid trying to explain something, making just as much or more sense than she did. Deb didn't understand either, but it didn't stop her from saying, "Patti, I'd like for you to do that; I really would."

Their treats arrived and no conversation is more important than enjoying ice cream, so these two "ladies" jumped into lunch, dessert, or maybe both. When they started to leave, Patti walked over to the girl at the counter. "Thank you for serving me my last meal; it was delicious. I'd like to come back some time and do it again, but I have to pay for my crimes, so this is it. Good bye." As they headed for the car, Detective Johnson hoped that girl found her chin in her bra and put it back soon; she sure looked silly without it.

Patti decided she would like to go home; she could go back to the hospital and check on Sarah later. She had not slept, her stomach was full, and she was tired. Deb pulled the car in front of the warehouse. "Now you remember what I said about Sarah, and I'm going to give some thought to what you said about God; I would like to resolve that issue for myself. Patti, I want to thank you for wanting to help me and Sarah; you are truly special. I'm not sure your own mother even realizes it. I haven't said this to very many people in my life, but I love you, you little scamp."

The detective leaned over and kissed Patti on her cheek; surprised by the action, Patti looked warmly at Deb and returned her kiss. It appeared Deb's eyes were watering. Patti reached for the door handle, then turned with a smile and started to laugh. "I guess this makes me a lesbian too?"

"Ha! Yeah, you, me, and your mom." Deb swatted at her as she exited the car with a final comment, "Now you get up to your apartment; no more skipping school. You hear?"

"Okay, I've learned my lesson. Besides, your handcuffs pinch." Patti was still laughing as she started up the stairs.

As Patti approached the apartment, she could not help thinking how different her mother and Deb were. Kathy was soft and tender; she could cry at the drop of a hat. She truly loved her work at the hospital; helping others was who she was. On the other hand, Deb was "tough as nails." Even in her most unguarded moments, she was rough and ready. Patti could imagine Deb in a fist fight; her mom would probably faint. It was hard to see any mother in Deb, and yet today Patti had seen something long suppressed. The detective did have compassion lurking within her. It appeared she too was so consumed by her work that the real woman in her never really showed. If only Patti could get these two women to see their real beauty, everyone around them would be blessed. It was a puzzle way bigger than Patti could solve; she would expand her prayer circle to include all of her "girlfriends," and yes, maybe she'd better throw in Colby. There was always a chance he might do away with his sister, Caitlyn, and if he got caught, she would only get to see him in jail.

Patti went in the apartment quietly to not wake her mother, but Kathy was already up and dressed. Kathy immediately wanted to know how Sarah was doing, and Patti shared what the doctor had said. Kathy was relieved; she had been worried about Sarah. Patti told her again that Sarah would be fine and not to worry; God had plans for her. Patti asked if her mother would wake her up between 4:00 and 5:00; she wanted to call Colby and tell him about Sarah. She also wondered if Kathy would take her to the hospital later to see Sarah again before she went to school Friday. Kathy said they would work out something after supper. Patti went to bed and was soon sleeping soundly. Kathy stood by her bed and stared at her for the longest time, marveling at how she could have produced such a child. All her life, people had called her pretty, commented on her good grades and hard work, given her credit for her ideas and extra effort; but she felt small as she gazed upon Patti. She knew that in many ways she didn't hold a candle to the dazzling light abed before her.

When her mother woke her around 4:30, Patti immediately phoned Colby, who was about to call her. He was worried she had not been in school. Patti shared her day. When she attempted to describe Sarah, Colby asked her to stop. The description was too gruesome, and he could not comprehend how anyone could do such a thing. Patti asked if he would like to go see Sarah later; she and her mom could pick him up and even take him home. Colby stuttered and stammered but finally agreed to go; it seemed important to Patti. She then asked him to spread the word that Sarah was in the hospital; maybe some of the kids could send a card or do something nice for her. Colby said he'd contact Geoff and put him on the case; this was just the thing Geoff was good at...either spreading news or finding it. Patti thanked Colby for being concerned and helping; she would see him later.

When Patti finished, she reported. "Mom, Colby says he will go with me to see Sarah. Would you be willing to pick him up?"

"Listen, I have to do a little shopping; I can do that after supper and pick Colby up then. One thing though, Colby's a lot bigger than he used to be, and I don't know how much longer I can keep picking him up; I don't want to hurt my back."

"Mom, you've got a serious problem." Patti acted annoyed.

"I know, and you're it."

"Speaking of problems, I had lunch with Deb today; I guess we're in a relationship now."

"Oh, Patti, how dare you steal my one and only friend! How can you be so cruel?"

"Well, it's not my fault she fell for me. Why can't we share her? That would be fair."

Kathy opined. "I guess we could cut her in half. Which half do you want? The left or right?"

"Gosh, Mom, that would be so messy; you know, blood and intestines spilling out everywhere. Why don't we split her differently. You can have her Monday, Wednesday, Friday, and every other Saturday. I get her the rest of the time."

Kathy shook her head. "That's kind of confusing. It might be better to just leave things the way are."

Maintaining a tradition, the fiddler would be proud.

They picked up Colby and headed for the hospital. Kathy would shop and then come back for them; she wanted to see Sarah too. Colby was not very excited about this trip; he didn't much care about hospitals, and he didn't really want to see a real victim of a crime. TV was one thing; real life was something else. When they got to the ICU, Patti could see that Sarah's color had improved, and it appeared she was trying to wake up; Patti also knew as long as Sarah was unconscious, she was not suffering. She had to be in pain, so maybe it was just as well she continued sleeping. Colby said nothing, but Patti could tell he was crying, and he hardly knew Sarah. Patti held Sarah's hand, and it felt warmer; she also thought Sarah seemed to respond. She didn't care what anyone else thought; "doctor" Patti knew Sarah was going to be fine. End of discussion. Patti finally coaxed Colby into holding Sarah's hand and she seemed to respond to him also. When Kathy arrived, she was amazed at how much better Sarah looked; she agreed with "doctor" Patti. Colby hadn't seen Sarah to compare her condition; it just appeared to him she had been run over by a truck, and he felt very sorry for her.

⤞ Twenty ⤝

The Friday before spring break is no time to start anything, but the school was abuzz about Sarah. Kids seem to band together when one of their own is in trouble, and everyone was angry or concerned about what had happened. The kids decided they were going to send Sarah a card. They knew they would not be allowed to see her in the ICU, but they could be thinking about her and let her know they cared. Patti overheard teachers talking in the hallway; they had never seen kids so riled up, wanting to support one of their own. Patti was pleased, but she didn't know how the mailman would feel when he had to deliver a ton of mail to the hospital...and all of it for Sarah!

After school on Friday, Patti went to get Sarah a card and then stopped by the hospital to see how she was doing. The nurses at the desk gave her a thumbs up as she walked by. Sarah looked about the same, but it was obvious she was trying to regain consciousness. Patti noticed her twitch, and she actually gripped Patti's hand; her feet moved under the covers and she seemed to be trying to move her head, but she was so wrapped up movement was almost impossible. All the signs looked good to Patti, who would have loved to stay, but she wanted to go to youth group to encourage prayers for her friend. Right now, Patti figured

Sarah needed God more than her, and Patti was determined to do whatever it took to bring her back into the fold. As Patti started to leave, a nurse came to check on Sarah, and Patti asked if her activity suggested she might be about to regain consciousness. The nurse told her these were positive signs, but it was hard to tell when she might come around. It was all a matter of time.

The youth group held a special prayer for Sarah right after the meeting began. Everyone was upbeat, and most agreed to send her a card or note of encouragement. The concern was real and so was the love. Patti just knew with God on their side, things would work out fine, but she was impatient, and like so many other things in life that can't be hurried, this would happen in due time.

Weekends were always special and weekends before holidays or breaks were even better. However, this time was different. Sarah was in the hospital, and Kathy had to work a half shift on Saturday afternoon. Patti slept in then went to see Sarah before lunch; it was hard to tell, but she looked a little better. Her color had improved and her face wasn't so swollen. It was obvious she wanted to regain consciousness but was not quite ready. Patti stayed with her for about an hour, holding her hand and talking to her; Sarah responded to their one-sided conversation by making slight expressions and squeezing Patti's hand.

Patti decided to go back to the apartment, put things in order, then return to the hospital, and ride home with her mom. Patti also wanted to get away from the hospital for a while; it was not very pleasant being in a room with strange machines and her broken friend. Home just felt better.

Patti went back to see Sarah several hours later; she had still not come to and looked much the same. This time Patti prayed and asked God to heal and protect her. Her mother stopped at the end of her shift and thought Sarah looked much better; it was encouraging.

On the way home, Patti asked if they could go to church in the morning; the church had an early informal service well attended by people who either did not want to dress up or had other plans for later in the morning. Patti wanted to announce at prayer time that she had a friend who needed everyone's prayers. Kathy was not excited about going but realized it meant a lot to Patti; it would not kill her to make this sacrifice Sunday morning.

Just as they got home, the phone rang and Patti ran to answer it. Deb was calling to ask about Sarah; she hated to bother the hospital and knew someone in the apartment probably knew her condition. Patti told her what she knew, and the detective seemed pleased the news was generally good. Patti then dropped a bomb on the detective; she and her mother were going to go to early church in the morning to pray for Sarah and solicit prayers from the congregation. "Would you like to come too?"

After a long pause, Patti was rather surprised when Deb responded, "I should probably do that; yes, I'll go with you. Could I please speak with your mother?"

Patti was overjoyed as she gave the phone to Kathy, who visited with Deb for several minutes. When the conversation ended, Kathy turned to Patti. "You know, you are an ornery little scamp; at least, that's what Deb said."

Patti looked up and grinned. "I know."

"Deb says you invited her to church in the morning, and she is going with us; then I invited her to come back for brunch. What do you think about that?"

"You know, Mom, I think it's great when the three of us...well, uh, you know, get together." Patti tried hard not to laugh.

"Well, one thing for sure, Detective Johnson is a mighty good judge of character; she knows an ornery little scamp when she sees one!" Patti looked sheepish and nodded. Some policemen are really smart!

The next morning, much earlier than usual, Patti and Kathy got dressed, and went out front to meet Deb, who managed to arrive right on time. They climbed into

Kathy's car and drove to church. Neither Kathy nor Deb had ever attended a service there, but Patti had gone with her Uncle Bob two or three times when she had stayed with his family during summer vacation. When they arrived, Uncle Bob was one of the greeters and very pleased to see them; he did not know the detective, but if she was with Kathy and Patti, she must be "good people." Deb was impressed with his family loyalty and friendly manner. Early in the service, the worship leader called for prayer requests. When her turn arrived, Patti stood up. "I'd sure like everyone to pray for my friend Sarah; she is in the seventh grade just like me; she was hurt really bad and is in the hospital. She needs our support."

Patti enjoyed going to the early church service, even Kathy mentioned it was nice to be there. The liturgy was simple and friendly, and everyone seemed genuinely concerned about each other. Deb had not been to church since she was a little girl, so the service was rather foreign to her, but she acknowledged a peace there she found comforting, nothing like the chaos at the police station. Patti hoped they could return soon but knew it was not her decision.

On the way home the detective shared more about Sarah. Obviously, the police wanted her to regain consciousness to identify her attacker, but whether she knew anything or not, she was a material witness to the commission of a felony and could be in potential danger from her attacker. Thus, Deb was going to see she was placed in protective custody until the investigation concluded. They had the hospital under surveillance and plain clothes officers inside the building checking on Sarah. The detective assured them she would be safe, and everyone in her department hoped they could bring this criminal to justice; he deserved nothing less for this awful crime.

The girls had a wonderful breakfast of blueberry pancakes topped with creamy butter and syrup, served with fried eggs and link sausage. While Deb had little in common with Patti and Kathy, she provided a positive social contact outside of work which benefited everyone. Kathy felt comfortable talking about private issues with Deb, and Deb seemed more open about herself around Kathy. Patti was pleased her mother was happy and relaxed when Deb was around, but Patti liked Deb too; she was a straight shooter who did not play games. She could be funny too, and Patti liked that. After breakfast, Patti suggested they could all go check on Sarah's progress, and everyone agreed. In Sarah's current state, activity in her room was welcome and helpful to reconnect her with reality.

On the way to the hospital, Deb asked if Kathy and Patti planned to attend church next Sunday. Patti quickly stated she would like to go again; Kathy was not scheduled to work but hated to commit herself to early church. Deb said she thought she would like to go back; she had enjoyed the service and somehow felt she the need to return. When Kathy realized she was serious, she agreed to go too. Patti didn't say anymore about it, but inside she was thrilled her "big girlfriends" would be attending church with her. They also decided to let Deb take them out for breakfast. Patti asked, "You mean, you're not taking us to your place and fixing a delicious meal?"

Deb started to laugh. "I love you guys too much to make you eat anything I'd fix; we'd better stick with the diner."

"Are you trying to tell us you can't cook?"

"Patti, you're probably looking at the only person in the world who can burn water...so I don't think you should ever trust me fixing food for you."

Patti looked at her mother with one of those "are you kidding" expressions. "Mama, how do you burn water?"

Kathy was having a terrible time suppressing an urge to roll on the floor...not a good strategy while driving...but finally managed. "Patti, it ain't easy!"

At the hospital, while Sarah looked better, she was still unconscious. Kathy talked to a nurse and found out everyone felt positive about her but had no idea when she might rouse. Deb gave the hospital her home phone number and asked if they could call her whenever Sarah regained consciousness. Kathy asked Deb to call her so she and Patti could come be with Sarah; she knew them and it's more comforting waking up with friends than complete strangers. Everyone agreed. They stayed with Sarah for about thirty minutes and decided to go home and make the best of their day. Patti planned to come back later one way or another; she wanted to be with her friend; they had plans to make for spring break.

Later in the afternoon, before dinner, Patti asked her mother if it would be okay for her to go check on Sarah. Kathy agreed, but asked her to please be back for dinner; that would give Patti maybe an hour and a half. Patti grabbed her jacket and headed for the door, but just as she reached for the door knob, the phone rang. She stopped. Kathy answered the phone. It was Deb; the hospital had called...it appeared Sarah was waking up. Kathy told Patti she could go be with Sarah but not get in anyone's way; it might be pretty hectic in Sarah's room for a while.

When Patti got there, she discovered her mother was right; Sarah was attracting much attention. A doctor and at least two nurses bustled in and out. Patti stood back and waited for them to do their business; she just wanted to see Sarah...not poke and prod her. When things quieted down, Patti moved closer to Sarah's bed and reached for her hand. Sarah was awake but seemed out of it. One of the nurses told Patti it might be a while before Sarah was able to make any sense or communicate; she was medicated for both pain and possible infection. Patti figured she had plenty of time, so she held Sarah's hand and stood by her. Sarah gripped Patti tightly; she knew Patti was there. She would stare at Patti with her good eye, the expression on her face rather blank and unchanging. In some ways, she had looked better when was she was unconscious. Patti began to talk to Sarah; they had a lot of catching up to do. Sarah responded to her voice by looking right at her. In a few moments she smiled. Patti started to cry; she felt so bad her friend was lying there all bruised and battered. As Patti looked at Sarah, she could tell she was crying too; Patti leaned over and kissed her cheek, whispering, "I love you."

When Patti regained her composure, she started talking to Sarah again; the more Patti talked, the more she could tell

Sarah was trying to talk back...but the words were not coming. Maybe that knock in the head had affected Sarah's speech; maybe it was the medication; Patti was frustrated they couldn't visit. She decided to keep talking because she was certain Sarah heard her. After several interruptions from the nurses, Patti ran out of words. Sarah wasn't talking, and their conversation was going nowhere. She pulled a chair to the side of the bed and sat down; she looked at Sarah and noticed her lips trying to move. In a moment she thought she heard...no, she definitely heard Sarah speak. The word sounded familiar, but garbled; Sarah seemed to understand and tried again. It sounded like she said, "a tee," then repeated, "pa a tee," then finally hit a home run, "Patti."

Patti jumped out of her chair and leaned over her. "Yes, Sarah it's me, Patti!"

Patti buzzed for the nurse, who quickly arrived. "Sarah knows me...she said my name."

The nurse seemed thrilled, and Patti almost ran to give her a hug but didn't want Sarah to think she was leaving. Sarah was going to be fine, but Patti had already known that.

The nurse had no sooner gone when Deb arrived to see Sarah. Patti was still excited and told the detective Sarah had spoken her name. Deb was pleased Sarah could talk, but it was obvious they wouldn't be having a conversation anytime soon. However, the fact she was able to speak and recognize a friend was certainly a plus. Deb hoped she might shine some light on this dark event. Deb motioned for Patti to step away from Sarah. "I just want you to know that as soon as Sarah is released, she will be in my custody. We are in the process of getting a court order to have her taken away from her mother, and she will be staying with me; I wanted you to know."

Patti reacted with complete joy. "Oh, Deb that's wonderful; you will make a good mom...I just know you will."

Deb held up her hand. "Now Patti, hold your horses; I'm not going to adopt her or anything; she will just be staying with me until we settle this case."

Patti became concerned. "Listen, this is really important; you can't put Sarah in foster care. You just can't. Okay? We have to take care of Sarah; we owe her that much."

"Patti, I promise we will work things out; you've got to trust me. I won't put Sarah at risk."

"Thank you." Patti gave Deb a big hug.

Patti went back to Sarah, and Deb left, but she must have met Kathy in the hall because Patti could hear them talking. In a few moments her mother came into the room and observed. "Our patient is looking a lot better."

Patti was thrilled. "Yes, she's talking and said my name."

As Kathy got closer, she could see Sarah appeared to recognize her and was trying to smile; she then tried to say "hi," but it came out "i." Kathy asked Patti what she wanted to do; it was okay to stay for awhile, but Sarah needed rest, and perhaps it would be better if Patti came back in the morning. Patti thought about it and decided her mother was probably right; she would come back tomorrow and stay as long as Sarah wanted. Patti went over to Sarah's bed and summarized her plans, then asked if that was okay. Sarah tried to nod with little luck and say something which Patti interpreted as an okay. Patti told her to sleep tight and keep getting better. They had a lot of catching up to do.

Most kids would not put staying in a hospital with a friend at the top of their "fun things to do during spring break" list, but most people are not Patti Linder. She was determined to be with her friend, and she hoped she could convince other friends to visit Sarah. Patti could not imagine being in the hospital with no visitors or family, and when she went to bed that Sunday night and prayed for Sarah, her mother, grandparents, and other friends, she couldn't keep a few tears from rolling down her cheeks. Patti felt so bad for Sarah, lying there in bed, not really able to move, all alone. Patti also hoped no one gave Sarah a mirror; she did not look very good right now.

Kathy finally decided Patti would go to work with her the next day and stay at the hospital as long as she wanted; there was no school, and Patti had made no other plans, so she had the next few days to do whatever she wanted, and that was to be with Sarah. The next morning Nurse Kathy and "doctor" Patti went to work. Sarah was sleeping when Patti arrived in her room, and when the nurse came in to check on her, she told Patti that Sarah had a good night and was talking better. They thought the pain medicine might be causing her slurred speech. Patti sat by the bed and held Sarah's hand; it felt warm and strong. Shortly thereafter, Sarah began to stir, seemed to wake up, suddenly opened her eyes, looked right at Patti, and said her name rather plainly. Patti jumped; she was surprised by Sarah's sudden activity and clear speech. Regaining her composure, she spoke Sarah's name; Sarah responded with an attempt at a smile...and Patti sensed Sarah had tried to scare her on purpose.

Patti faced her. "Were you trying to scare me?"

Sarah smiled again and attempted to nod.

"You are a rascal, and I've heard of the 'little rascals;' you must be related to them."

Sarah was almost grinning now and trying not laugh, but she was having a hard time. "You're a rascal too."

"Oh, I know; That's how I figured you out!" Patti knew it was difficult for Sarah to talk, but had to ask, "Are you okay? Are you in any pain?"

"No, I don't feel any pain...I don't feel much of anything."

"Well, you rest and I'll go tell the nurses you're awake. Are you hungry?"

"It feels like I haven't eaten in a long time. Eating sounds good."

"Okay, I'll tell them and maybe they can get you something to eat." Patti scurried away.

Very soon Patti came back with two nurses, who gave Sarah the once over then maybe the twice over. They asked her a few questions, and Sarah did her best to respond; the nurses seemed pleased and left. Shortly, a doctor entered and looked carefully at Sarah. He also asked a couple of questions, and as he turned to leave, he gave Patti a thumbs up; Sarah was doing just fine. Patti looked up and said quietly, "Thank You, God, for helping Sarah."

The room was soon a beehive of activity; nurses brought carts and trays. They buzzed around Sarah; one raised the back of her bed; another put an extra pillow behind her back. Soon they brought in some food, and Sarah was getting a chance to eat for the first time in several days. It hurt her to chew, so they replaced part of her food with softer fare. When she finished, they left her bed up, and Patti could see Sarah was looking much better. The swelling in her eye had subsided, and her bruises were fading substantially. All in all, she was beginning to look more like herself. Patti moved toward the bed and asked her how the food was; her response amused Patti. "It all tasted pretty much the same, but nothing like chicken."

Patti wanted to talk but knew Sarah needed to regain her strength. She decided to continue a one-sided conversation; they could really visit later. After all, Sarah was going to be there quite a while. Kathy came to tell Patti that Deb wanted to talk with Sarah as soon as possible; she had advised her to wait until tomorrow when Sarah was more alert. Patti also wanted to ask Sarah questions but knew it was best to wait for Deb and just listen.

The morning went well. Sarah napped, then awakened but was fairly groggy. Patti managed to coax a few words out of her each time she roused. Patti was convinced Sarah was aware of her situation and fairly alert considering her trauma. Kathy came at lunch time and took Patti to eat; it was special to have lunch with her mother; she only wished it were under different circumstances. After lunch, Patti decided to go home and make a few calls; she wanted to let Colby, Geoff and a few others know Sarah was going to be okay, and it would be nice if they could visit her but probably not before Wednesday.

By afternoon Sarah had eaten another meal and was feeling much better; she complained her head ached. The doctor had reduced her medication in order to check her level of pain. They wanted to be able to ask her how she felt and get an honest answer. Patti stayed until her mother came. When she was ready to leave, Patti told Sarah she would be back the next day, and her assignment for the evening was to try to remember as much about what had happened as possible. Sarah gave her a really sad look. "I didn't think we were supposed to have any assignments over spring break." Patti stuck her tongue out and waved good bye.

The next morning, Patti had not been there long when Deb showed up. Sarah was still sleeping, so Patti and the detective went into the hall and spoke quietly. When Deb asked how Sarah was doing, Patti could only say she hoped Sarah would be able to share information. Back in the room, Sarah roused. Patti went to her bedside. "Sarah, this is my friend Deb; she's a policewoman and would like to talk with you. Do you think you can answer her questions?"

Sarah nodded.

The detective moved closer. "Sarah, do you know the person who did this to you?"

"No, I don't know his name, but I've seen him before."

Deb perked up. "You mean you could identify him."

"Yes, I'm sure I could."

"What exactly happened?"

"Well, these two men were yelling...something about money, then the man that hit me hurt the other man because he cried out. I was hiding by a trash bin, and when the one man yelled, something fell behind me. The other man came my way; I tried to hide, but I had nowhere to go. He swore at me and said something. Then he picked up a board and hit me. That was it...I died."

Deb looked shocked. "You what?"

"I died; everything went black. There was nothing; I can't explain it. I looked up and saw a light. It was really bright, and it scared me. As I looked at it, I could see a shape. I moved forward to see better, and it seemed to move toward me. I stopped and could see it was a human form...you know, a man or a woman. It called my name; I was scared because I didn't know what was going on. Suddenly, the light began to fade and the figure stopped; it kind of leaned forward, put out an arm, and said, 'Come no farther; it's not your time. There is much for you to do.' Then it disappeared and the light went out. It was dark again, pitch black, but this time I could hear voices, two or three talking about not breathing, low or maybe no pulse. I saw some flashes; the next thing I knew, I woke up here. I was having a dream about Patti. That's all I can remember."

Deb sat, stunned; Patti was confused. Finally, Deb inquired, "If I send a sketch artist, do you think you could help him draw a picture of the man who hit you?"

Sarah nodded. "I could try."

"Sarah, you are a brave girl and you've been a big help; I'll try to have someone over this afternoon, and you guys can draw pictures, okay?"

"I guess so." Sarah sighed. "I'm sure getting an awful lot of work to do over spring break."

Deb didn't stay long; there was much to do. Patti sat quite a while without speaking; she was trying to make sense of what Sarah had said. It made her uneasy. She'd heard a little bit about how when you die, you are to go into the light; this had to be what Sarah was talking about, but what did the voice mean? How could she find out what God had planned for her? How did anyone know? It was weird, and Patti was curious.

Patti looked at Sarah. "Wow, that was quite a story. Do you really think you were dead?

"Yes, I do; I'm sure of it, but I didn't tell the detective everything."

Patti perked up. "What do you mean?"

"Well, I didn't think it would make any difference, so I didn't tell her about you."

"About me? What do mean about me?" Patti was puzzled.

"I don't know if I can explain it. You were here with me, weren't you, and someone else? You held my hand...I felt you. It felt good."

"Yes, I was here, and Colby came one night; he held your hand. He was uncomfortable; it bothered him. I think he only came to please me; Colby's nice that way."

"Patti, thank you for being a good friend; I love you."

Patti gazed at Sarah, her eyes starting to tear. "Sarah, when I first saw you, I was afraid you were going to die; Mom called me late at night to come and be with you. Everyone seemed to think you weren't going to make it, and Sarah, you looked bad...real bad. I was scared; I didn't know what to do so I asked God to help. I guess He did; He must have things for you to do. I'm sure glad He saved you; I love you too."

That afternoon, the sketch artist sat with Sarah while she tried to describe the man who hit her. She got frustrated because she could see him in her mind but could not describe him. However, after a while, the sketch began to look more and more like the "perp," as Deb called him. Sarah was finally satisfied with the picture, and the artist thanked her for her help and left. About an hour later, Deb came by to report that one of the patrolmen at the station recognized the man in the sketch; he had seen him while on patrol and even remembered the car he drove. Deb told Sarah it was just a matter of time before they nailed this bast...bad guy, and it was her evidence that would convict him. As good as this information was, it was what Deb said next that echoed in Patti's head for the next several days,

"Sarah, you are a hero; we are so proud of you!"

Could this have been why Sarah was spared...so she could help put away this very bad man? Patti didn't know, but it was something to think about.

Patti waited and went home with her mother. Just before they sat down to eat, the phone rang; it was the detective. She asked to talk to Patti. Deb had talked to the EMTs sent to help Sarah when she was attacked; one of them admitted Sarah was dead when they got there, but they had brought her back; she wanted Patti to know. Patti told her mother the whole story and then Deb's followup information. Kathy sat down and began to cry; Patti tried to comfort her but was crying too. They had come so close to losing Sarah, but if Deb was right, she might get a new family, and that had to be a big improvement.

Wednesday proved another day filled with new information and surprises. First of all, the extent of Sarah's injuries was revealed. Her shoulder bone was chipped just above her left arm, she had a hairline fracture in her scull above her left ear, her left eye was partially detached in its socket, and she had minor lacerations on her shoulder with a major laceration on her skull. She was healing well, and it appeared she might need minor surgery on her eye. She had suffered a moderately severe concussion, but there appeared to be no complications. One of her doctors noted she had been very lucky and was rather amazed at her recovery. Her prognosis was excellent; there should be virtually no permanent damage except that the vision in her left eye might be impaired.

The second good thing was that Sarah could now have visitors; she had no family that cared about her, but several classmates took time out of their vacations to come say hi. Colby showed up and remarked how much better Sarah looked, and Sarah was thrilled to have the company. Even though Sarah was far from popular, kids rallied around her, and the nurses let them present Sarah with her huge box of mail. Sarah cried and could not believe so many people would go out of their way to wish her well. Patti opened cards and Sarah read them. The kids wanted to see her back on her feet and "normal" again; Sarah was just thankful to be alive.

The final bit of excitement came later in the day when Deb came back to see Sarah. Deb wanted to know where all the mail came from, and Patti shot back, "Everywhere!"

The detective needed to talk. "Sarah, no one knows exactly when you will be released from the hospital, but I need to ask you something important. Would you be willing to live with me for a while when you get out of here?"

Sarah looked at her. "Sure, if you're a friend of Patti's, you're my friend too; I would be glad to stay with you. I don't have anywhere else to go."

"Good, that's what I wanted to hear. Listen, we are in the process of having you removed from your mother's custody. Now, before you get the wrong idea, we are not having you placed in just any foster care situation. We want to find you a good family; one that will take care of you and love you as their own. It may take some time, but you can stay with me, and we'll put Patti in charge of your welfare." Deb ended with an ornery smile.

Patti was shocked. "Wait a minute...put me in charge? I don't think so. I have enough trouble taking care of my mom; you of all people should know that."

Sarah laughed. "I don't know if Patti should be in charge either; she's pretty goofy sometimes. Why, she might have me washing with my towel and drying off in the water."

Patti started nodding and Deb continued. "Okay, maybe we'd better not put Patti in charge of you. We'll put her in charge of taking care of me; she'll get a really tough job!"

Patti's mouth dropped open. "Why do I get the feeling everyone is picking on me?"

Sarah looked back at Patti. "Hey, that's easy; we love you, Patti."

Patti sighed. "Yeah, well, all this love is killing me."

Too much love might be hazardous for your health, but just the right amount could mean a new life and a new home for Sarah.

⤝ Twenty-One ⤞

On Thursday, Patti decided Sarah could do without her for one day; they had talked, and Sarah understood spring break was more than just sitting with her although she told Patti how much she appreciated her company. When Patti had seen Colby Wednesday, she asked if it would be all right to visit him the next day. Colby admitted he had been a bit lonesome; Geoff was out of town with his family, and Patti was busy with Sarah, so he was trying to tough it out and stay away from his sister. It would be great to see Patti.

Kathy dropped Patti off at the Duncans' on her way to work, and she would be on her own unless something out of the ordinary happened. Kathy would keep an eye on Sarah and report any news when she got home. When Patti arrived, Mrs. Duncan offered to get her breakfast, but Patti had already eaten, so they just visited until Colby came down to eat. Mrs. Duncan said how proud she was of all the ways Patti had helped Sarah and her willingness to make so many sacrifices. Patti told Mrs. Duncan she was really the only friend Sarah had; she just couldn't leave her in the hospital all alone. Mrs. Duncan's opinion of Patti had changed considerably over the years. Patti might not be an American Beauty, but she had a good heart and was faithful to her friends. Colby had never expressed any romantic interest in Patti, but Mrs. Duncan had decided if that should ever happen, he could do a lot worse. She was thankful these children were still having fun being kids. Childhood is fleeting, and once over, it's gone forever.

Colby was eager for school to start again; the sooner it started, the sooner it would end. He enjoyed his summer vacation; he seemed to need time to just be silly and have fun. Patti asked him if his family had any specific plans after school ended. Colby was disappointed to tell her they had a lot of work to do on the house, but his dad had said if everyone chipped in, they could get it finished. Then next summer he would reward the family with a big vacation. When Patti heard this, a flashbulb went off. "Hey, Colby, do you suppose you could get a week off in mid June?"

"What do you mean?"

"Well, look, our youth group and church sponsor a summer camp. You know, I went last summer and nearly drowned on the trail."

Colby grinned. "Oh yeah, I remember. That's when you went swimming standing up!"

Patti pressed ahead. "Something like that. Anyway, they have a different camp this year..."

Colby quickly injected. "You mean a dry camp."

"Colby, I worry about you." Patti shook her head.

"Yeah, my mom says the same thing about me...and my dad."

"Well, your mom's no dummy; you guys both need a lot of supervision." Patti laughed. "Anyway, they have this great camp, and I'll bet you would have a lot of fun. My Uncle Bob said he was going to send me again this summer, and I am going to be working at the Fun Camp for sixth graders a week earlier. It would be great if you could be there. I guess you'd have to come up with some money, but maybe your folks would be willing to do that since you're helping them...you know, like a reward. You should talk to your mom."

"It would be nice to get away from my crazy sister. Would you talk to my mom too? You know, she kind of likes you. She thinks you have a good head on your shoulders; she doesn't know you like I do."

"Colby, I should bop you on the head, but after what

247

happened to Sarah I guess that would be inappropriate...so if you aren't going to be nice to me, I'll just have to give you a big kiss." Patti leaned toward Colby with her lips puckered.

"Oh no, not that...I'll be good, I promise...torture is a violation of the Geneva convention...I know my rights; I read it somewhere." Colby drew quickly away.

"I think it only applies when we're at war." Patti remained armed and puckered.

"Okay, I surrender; I'm sorry. Please don't slobber on me."

Patti made a face. "Ah, Colby, I'll bet you'd look nice with some slobbers, right there." She pointed to his cheek.

Colby said no more, but his "yuck" expression spoke volumes...no kissy face for him! On the other hand, Patti would very much have liked to kiss Colby...but even more importantly, she would have liked him to kiss her back.

Patti and Colby continued their talking and playing games. They were excited about eighth grade next year and being the "big dogs" on campus. Of course, that might require both of them to get taller and gain some weight; they were no more than average size for their age, and most of their friends were bigger than they were. Patti reminded Colby they would soon be in high school. Then they would really be grown up...maybe.

Colby liked the idea of going to camp; it would be fun to be with Patti. They always had fun together. Even though Colby was not really interested in girls, he still thought Patti was special, and he had never viewed her as pretty or plain, lovely or ugly. She was just "one of the guys." Patti had similar thoughts regarding Colby; he too was special, and since he was a boy, he hardly qualified as "one of the girls," but rather held the unique position of being the only "man" in her life, although she couldn't say anything about it to Grandpa Bender because it might hurt his feelings.

At lunch Patti asked Mrs. Duncan if they might let Colby

attend summer camp; Colby added he would like to go, but omitted the real reason. Mrs. Duncan knew nothing about the camp or any other particulars but said she would investigate then visit with Mr. Duncan. She was pleased to hear Patti's uncle was involved, and she liked the fact the camp would have a Christian influence. Kathy had made a good impression on Mrs. Duncan; she was one of those people who believe your family is largely responsible for the kind of person you are. Uncle Bob was family; he was a good man. Colby and Patti were pleased Mrs. Duncan was not opposed to their request. After lunch, both admitted it would be fun to go to camp; there was a chance they could be in the same group. Patti had a little bit of "pull," and it wouldn't hurt to ask.

Kathy came to pick up Patti after work and wanted to know what she'd been doing; it appeared she'd been involved in a mine rescue exercise and all the dirt was dumped on her; Colby didn't look much better, and his mother scolded him for looking like a pig. Colby winked at Patti. "Well, if Mom hadn't locked us out of the house, we could have played inside where it was nice and clean!"

Mrs. Duncan was not amused. "Young man, perhaps what you need, even more than a bath, is to have your mouth washed out with soap for telling such tales and trying to embarrass me."

Patti jumped to the rescue. "Look, sometimes you have to get dirty to have fun!'

Her mother smiled and laughed. "You and Colby must have really had fun!" Vigorously nodding her head, Mrs. Duncan fully agreed.

Mrs. Duncan then asked Kathy about the summer camp, and Kathy admitted she didn't know very many details but if Uncle Bob was involved, it was a worthy cause. He was the crusader in the family and had done a lot to establish his church and to do good things for kids. Everyone would be in good hands; Kathy also knew one of the camp counselors named Dave, and she had been very impressed with him—he was a friend of Patti's. Mrs. Duncan liked the idea, and in the Duncan family if Mrs. Duncan liked something, everyone else in the family did too...or things could get ugly.

><•~   ~•<

Kathy reported Sarah had another good day, a few visitors, more mail, and good reports from the doctors. Even though she had been badly banged up, she was healing fast. There was a faint possibility she could go to school by Monday although it might be a few more days; she might have to wear an eye patch, but being a pirate would only be temporary. Patti was thrilled to hear the news, and despite the fact her spring break was not what she had planned, it was quickly becoming one of her best.

Kathy's work shift began a couple of hours later on Friday, so Patti arrived later than usual to see Sarah. When she walked into the room, she was shocked to find it empty; Sarah was gone. For a fleeting moment it occurred to Patti that something might be wrong; maybe Sarah had relapsed. No, she was okay...Patti was certain everything was all right; God was taking good care of Sarah. Patti went to the nurse's station to inquire and discovered that on Thursday the nurses got Sarah out of bed and down to physical therapy. Head injuries often leave people with problems far worse than headaches; they wanted to make sure she could function normally, and if there were problems, take corrective action. Patti went back to Sarah's room.

Patti had just settled in a chair when a nurse wheeled Sarah into the room. Sarah looked really good compared to the first time Patti had seen her; she was smiling and happy. As it turned out, she was walking fairly well; she had a limp in her right leg and was stiff and sore. Not being on her feet for nearly a week while bedridden had not done much for her muscles, but she said her session had gone well. Her therapist joked she would be running around in no time. The nurse helped her back into bed and told her to rest; they were going to get her up again during the afternoon.

Patti could tell Sarah was her old self. The doctor told her she should be able to leave the hospital in just a few more days. In addition, Detective Johnson had come by on Thursday and told Sarah she would be going home with the detective to live for a while; Sarah felt good about that...she was excited to have a new home and knew Ms. Johnson would be good to her. She thanked Patti again for being there and praying for her recovery; Patti told her it was the least she could do and knew Sarah would have done the same for her.

Shortly after Sarah had lunch, Kathy came by to take Patti to eat in the hospital cafeteria. Kathy had found out a little more about Sarah. The doctors had scheduled an operation on her left eye early Monday morning. Sarah would likely be released Tuesday morning and probably go to school on Wednesday. She would have to wear an eye patch for a while, but everyone felt good about her prospects for a full recovery. Kathy also told her that Detective Johnson was coming over for a later supper with them; she wanted to talk about Sarah and just say hi. Patti figured she also wanted a good meal; she wondered who would be doing the cooking for Deb and Sarah when they finally became a "family." Kathy laughed and said it was a good thing Sarah knew how to look after herself...because now she would likely have to look out for herself and the detective!

The afternoon went quickly. Technicians took Sarah for another physical therapy session, and Patti tagged along; they even let her walk with Sarah. Patti thought later it might be fun to work in physical therapy and help people regain or maintain their motor functions. Sarah was getting along better; her limp had improved, and she had a good sense of balance. The therapist was impressed with her progress and commented she was probably fit enough to get around by herself if she were careful. When they got her back to her room and out of the wheelchair, Sarah asked to sit in one of the chairs for a while; she wearied of lying down. The nurse thought it would be okay, but she would have to get back in bed later. Sarah thought it was funny that she was supposed to be walking in therapy but they made her ride in a wheel chair to get there and back...then lie in bed. Patti thought maybe they ought to let kids run more things so they made better sense.

The girls visited until Sarah had to go back to bed, then

they took a reading break, and Sarah fell asleep. Patti could not help feeling sorry for her but somehow thought Sarah's eye patch would be a hoot. She could become Black Beard's daughter, the toast of the Barbary Coast. "Arrgh, if you cross me, matey, you'll be walkin' the plank and checkin' into Davy Jones's locker." Sarah could have a lot of fun with that...and if anyone deserved some fun, it was Sarah.

Patti was anxious for her mother to pick her up and get home; she wondered what Detective Johnson really wanted. If she had known, she might have stayed longer.

➤➤   ➤➤

They had been home for about half an hour when Deb arrived; she seemed distracted and not her usual self. Kathy saw immediately that something was wrong. "Hey, what's up? You look like you've lost your best friend or your goldfish died."

"Kathy, I'll admit it; I'm a wreck."

"What's the matter?" Kathy showed concern.

"Well, it's kind of embarrassing, and to be honest, I'd rather not talk about it, but you are probably the only person I know who can help me. I've got myself in a mess. I don't like to ask people for help; I see it as a sign of weakness. I have this persona of being a 'tough girl,' so I don't cry, and I don't ask for help, but I guess what I am trying to say is, 'I really need your help...and Patti's too.'"

"What exactly do you need?" Kathy felt sorry for Deb.

"Well, I took on the responsibility of taking Sarah into protective custody when she leaves the hospital next week; we still have not caught the man who tried to kill her...we do have several good leads. Kathy, what in the hell was I thinking? I felt guilty because Patti had been after me to help find a safe place for her friend...and I wanted to help. I really did." Deb began to tear. "But I put it off and let other things get in the way, and it didn't happen. Then Sarah was nearly killed, and I felt terrible about it; I figured the least I could do was get her out of her mother's custody and find a good place for her to stay. I'm a mess; I don't know the first thing about being a mother...I don't even take good care of myself. What am I going to do?" Deb was crying now, her face in her hands.

Kathy's heart was immediately touched; she moved close to Deb and put her hand on Deb's shoulder. Deb began to collect herself. "Look, may I be frank?"

"Sure, I didn't come here to be lied to."

"Okay, I'm not going to judge your motherly qualities or lack thereof; I'm no expert in that department, and I'm not sure anyone is. I guess you could say some people mother better than others. For example, everyone here would agree that Sarah's real mother did a lousy job. Don't you think you can do better?"

Deb half smiled. "Sure, that won't be hard."

"Of course not. You are a responsible adult, and you will do your best to take care of Sarah; I already know what your problem is, and excuse me if I'm too blunt, but you already said it. You can't take care of yourself. My guess is you have trouble boiling water and you have to eat cereal dry because pouring milk is too complicated. Patti and I both know why you like to come here...you like the food...so do we! Have you ever thought that maybe Sarah can help you...that she would love to help her new mommy in the kitchen. She is not going to be ashamed of you because you can't cook; she'll more likely be ashamed if you don't try. Most kids understand adults aren't perfect, and all Sarah really wants is love. Can you give her that?"

"How could anyone not love Sarah; she's delightful. You're right about me; I just don't like to admit it. I'm ashamed I can't do certain things..."

Kathy interrupted. "But Deb, everyone feels that way about something. Being a woman doesn't automatically make you a cook anymore than it makes you a good mother; we all have to work at these things...and believe me, it takes time. Patti and I can help, but you have to make an effort."

"I'll give it my best shot, but I need a lot of help. That's the reason I'm here. Do you think you and Patti could help me get my place ready for Sarah. I don't even know where to start!" Deb threw up her hands.

"You know, you have a way of pushing our friendship right over a cliff. This is going to take more than just a trip to the ice cream shop; I'm thinking maybe a nice cruise in the Bahamas this winter . What do you think, Patti?"

"I'd say at least a week...maybe eight days." Patti did her best to seem annoyed. "Plus, two or three trips to the ice cream shop."

Deb began to moan. "You guys drive a hard bargain."

Thankfully, the conversation turned to other things, and its tone and mood, which had started off so grim, now approached normal. Deb felt good about the progress they had made in Sarah's case; she was also excited that Sarah was recovering so well, although concerned about her forthcoming surgery. The detective went out of her way to thank Patti for the support and love she had given Sarah, and when Kathy started supper, Deb spoke quietly to Patti. "I hope you can forgive me for not acting sooner. I know you probably had other things to do on your vacation than spend it in a hospital. Patti, you know you mean a lot to me; you have helped me rethink my position on God, and in your own way you have helped me find the woman in me. It scares the heck out of me. I have denied who I am for so long that the notion of being something else is really weird. Can I continue to count on your support?"

"Deb, I know you've got 'issues.' It's hard to admit you're wrong. We've had our differences, but I still love you; more importantly, God loves you. You need to trust Him."

Deb looked into Patti's eyes, and Patti could see her tears; Deb reached for her hand, grasped it, and pulled Patti closer, kissing her on the cheek. Patti smiled, and Deb whispered, "Thank you."

"Hey, what's going on? I hear you guys gossiping like a

couple of old ladies."

Deb looked up quickly. "Uh, well...we were trying to figure out who's buried in Grant's tomb, and we didn't want you to hear the answer."

"Yeah, Mom, this is a tough one." Patti was trying to keep a straight face.

Kathy's face brightened. "Oh guys, that's easy...it's Abraham Lincoln!"

"Very good, Mom, I guess history must have been your best subject."

"Only on Wednesdays!" Kathy giggled. "Only on Wednesdays." Deb and Patti shook their heads.

After supper, arrangements were made to see what Kathy and Patti could do to help the detective get ready for her new charge. At one point, Kathy asked to borrow her service revolver so they could put her out of her misery; surprisingly, Deb was more than willing to oblige...but she would keep all the bullets. Sometimes it's harder to fool people than it ought to be. After some wrangling, they decided to help her the next morning, Saturday. Kathy would take Patti by the hospital to say hi to Sarah and let her know she would be back after lunch; she was not to inform Sarah she was about to assist her "new mom" clean up their home.

Sometimes things work out just like they were planned. Sarah was to have another physical therapy session, and then a lady would be there to conduct some kind of psychological evaluation, so Sarah was going to be busy most of the morning. Patti told her to be careful and not act like her usual crazy self, or they might lock her up and throw away the key; Sarah promised she would fool everyone so she could escape as scheduled.

When Kathy and Patti arrived at the detective's house, they were impressed that the lawn and other plantings were well maintained and trimmed. However, upon entering, Kathy gasped. "On my God, I knew they called cops 'pigs,' but I never dreamed you lived in a sty!"

Deb tried to ease the shock. "Hey, be kind...it's my sty!"

Kathy held her nose. "Deb, this is disgusting; How do you live here?"

"I don't really live here; I just sleep and use the toilet."

Patti, surveying the scene in silence, muttered. "Deb, this is awful."

The detective looked at her and then at Kathy. Tears were beginning to swell around her eyes. "I told you I was a mess, and I am ashamed...but I still need your help."

"No, what you really need is a good spanking. At least you keep the outside looking nice."

"Oh, I hire that done." Deb began to cry.

"If I didn't care for you, Patti and I would leave right now and make you do this yourself; it's your mess...not ours! I suppose when you go out with a male friend you don't have to ask, 'my place or yours,' because the yard is the only place that looks nice, and it might disturb the neighbors if you guys were doing a 'love dance' on the front lawn!"

Patti covered her mouth to hide a grin.

Deb pouted. "You're being unfair."

Kathy was very blunt. "No, you're the one who is unfair, but I can speak for both of us; we'll do it for Sarah...and so help me, if I ever find a mess like this when Sarah is here, I will turn you over to county health authorities."

The detective looked at her shocked. "You're serious, aren't you?"

Kathy nailed it. "As a heart attack!" Patti nodded beside her.

Deb looked like a kid with her hand stuck in a cookie jar; tears lingered in her eyes. "You are right; I am a pig. I am ashamed to call this place my home. I don't want to forget what I am about to say. I promise you in front of God and everybody that when we get this place cleaned up, it will stay that way...and it won't be because I make Sarah do it. Let's get to work!"

Patti sorted the clothes scattered everywhere; Deb determined clean from dirty. Kathy started the laundry and began filling trash bags with anything looking worthless. Patti and Deb transferred clean clothes to her bedroom, which looked better than the living area, but Patti wondered when the last time her sheets had been washed. The kitchen was the only room showing any semblance of order...because Deb spent no time there to mess it up. They vacuumed and straightened up the front room. Deb had arranged to get the carpets steam cleaned; they had not been nice when she moved in five years ago. As the front room began to take shape, the girls turned their attention to Deb's bedroom. They put away clothes, picked up trash, stripped the bed, flipped the mattress, and changed the bedding. The bedroom took shape quickly, but the laundry generated more and more things to store.

The next room to restore was for Sarah; it was used for storage. Once they got some of the stored items put away, the room began to look like a bedroom. Deb had ordered a new bed with mattress and springs to be delivered on Monday; she also had a nice dresser, a plush chair, an end table and a storage chest for Sarah to use. A closet offered plenty of room for Sarah's hanging clothes. Kathy dreaded the thought of even going into the bathroom; they had saved it and the kitchen for last.

Patti volunteered to work in the kitchen. Kathy finally worked up the courage to go in the bathroom and was surprised to find it was in fairly good order. Deb admitted she could not tolerate a filthy bathroom and made an effort to keep it presentable. Kathy observed that Deb did have some cleaning talent. By lunch time everyone was exhausted, but the house was reborn. Deb insisted she take them out for lunch. They could take Patti by the hospital on the way back to Deb's house. The laundry room and kitchen appliances needed cleaning, so Kathy agreed to help Deb finish during the afternoon.

Deb changed her clothes, Kathy and Patti spruced up as best they could, and everyone went to lunch. Deb thanked them repeatedly for their help. Kathy reminded her of her promise; if she lived up to it, that would be thanks enough. They dropped Patti off at the hospital, and Kathy told her she would be back later to pick her up.

Once at Deb's house, Kathy was shocked by the contrast. It was a completely different house than the one she had stepped into early that morning. Even Deb was shocked. Deb went to the utility room and worked there while Kathy tackled the kitchen stove and oven. When Deb returned and asked for an inspection, Kathy told her they were going to get the microwave cleaned up before she went anywhere. It looked like someone had been using it for a barf bag; it nearly made Kathy gag. They worked on it for nearly a half hour. The utility room inspection went fairly well; the air filter in the dryer had not been cleaned in ages. Deb admitted she had forgotten about it for "a while." The refrigerator was better than Kathy had imagined; she found nothing unusual growing there. Deb had a thing about mold, so she made an effort to check the contents of the refrigerator on a regular basis. Kathy put the final touches on the kitchen floor, then with a grand flourish announced, "By jove, I think we've got it!"

Deb was elated, rushing to her with open arms, ending in a big hug. "Oh Kathy, thank you...thank you so much, and Patti too; you guys are so wonderful."

Caught up in the excitement, Deb did something totally unexpected, she pecked Kathy lightly on the lips. Startled, Kathy raised her hand between their faces and shook her head. "No, Deb, I'm not like that." Kathy's face flashed a hint of embarrassment.

"Neither am I, silly, but it doesn't mean I don't love you." Deb pulled Kathy's hand away and kissed her again, this time lightly on the cheek.

The girls stood there with their heads on each other's shoulders for a long time. Kathy sensed the joy flowing from Deb and how much more relaxed and comfortable she seemed. This house and its mess had been eating at her for a long time, and that burden had now been lifted. Kathy pulled away slightly. "Deb, I'm sorry we had to put you through this; I have always thought you were special; I love you too." Kathy kissed her lightly on the cheek.

The detective responded, "You know, ever since I got dumped on by that SOB when I was in college, I think I have tried to be a man...you know, one of the guys. You and Patti have made me realize I'm better than that. I'm a woman, soon to be a mother, and you guys have shown me it's the most important job in the world. Thank you so much for helping me discover who I am!"

Both girls were crying; they held each other for the longest time. Kathy finally spoke. "The place looks so much better. How do you feel about it?"

Deb quickly nodded. "It's almost like a new home."

"Be sure to keep it that way!" With that Kathy swatted her on the butt.

"Ow! Take it easy with those love pats!"

While her mother worked with Deb, Patti enjoyed her time with Sarah and heard wonderful news. The physical therapist had released Sarah; she could now walk about as needed and would require no more sessions. He simply told her to take it easy and not run any races; skydiving was also out of the question. Her psychological evaluation had also gone well. Sarah was cognitive and mentally alert, capable of reasoning and making decisions. They didn't figure out she was crazy, so she was released with the same warning: not to overdo or push herself too hard for a few days. Sarah was thrilled because this meant she would soon be able to leave the hospital and return to school.

She and Patti discussed school and Patti agreed to help her catch up if needed. They hoped she could return Wednesday. Sarah had a good attitude, and Patti thought she seemed happy...considering her condition. When Kathy came by, they shared the morning's information. Patti decided she would like to go home; she was tired but would be back tomorrow.

Patti reminded her mother that Deb had suggested they go to early church again this week; it would be nice to go back and thank God for Sarah's recovery. In addition Deb had other things to be thankful for, especially after today. Patti called to confirm their plans, and Deb seemed pleased by the reminder. Patti and Kathy went to bed early. It had been a long day.

Deb picked them up, and they headed to church; the service was uplifting. The detective commented on the way home she would like to take them out for a late breakfast or brunch; she also assured them she had not made a mess at home and was practicing better homemaking. Kathy told her she needed to work at it every day. Deb admitted she felt better about where she lived; she now enjoyed coming home instead of dreading it.

The rest of Sunday flew by. Patti and Kathy went to see Sarah, and Deb dropped in to discuss plans with her. Patti called Colby and asked if he was ready for school the next day. Colby said it didn't matter because it would start whether he was ready or not and figured they might as well get back to school and finish the last quarter. He was excited about the possibility of going to camp with Patti.

While many consider Monday a day to begin new things, go back to school, and start over; others view this opportunity with dread and remorse. This Monday was just one of those days...except it was more like a runaway train or a stampede of buffalo...go along for the ride or get the heck out of the way!

Sarah's Monday began in surgery. The damage to her eye

was minimal, but it had to be repaired. The doctors felt they could make her as good as new, and the operation went as expected. Sarah would need to wear an eye patch and avoid overactivity—no jumping, fast running, or being jostled. They wanted to keep her under observation for about twenty-four hours to make sure there were no complications. Her prognosis was excellent; she could probably be released Tuesday morning following her doctor's examination.

By mid morning, Detective Johnson's day brought both joy and dread. The judge hearing Sarah's custody case issued his order. Sarah's mother would release all rights to Sarah in exchange for having no criminal charges filed against her. She was also ordered to leave town and have no contact with Sarah until she was eighteen. The judge ordered Sarah be placed in Detective Johnson's custody until the criminal case had been resolved and she was placed in an appropriate adoptive family. The joy the detective shared was overshadowed by the reality she was now going to be responsible for someone other than herself. She was genuinely apprehensive about her "family" obligations; her past record in that regard did nothing for her confidence. Deb's Monday began rather blue.

However, Monday was not all bad. Good news arrived after lunch. At the police station, a standing joke went something like this: You've had a good morning when the pot of coffee and the dozen doughnuts you consumed haven't killed you. No one had died, but someone had been picked up in a nearby city late Sunday evening. The "fine, community-minded" drug dealer who tried to kill Sarah had been arrested. The good news brought a roar of approval from the officers at the station, and they even broadcast it to the squad cars. There were "atta boys" and "way to goes" all over the place. The scumbag in question would be arriving in time to be charged and brought before a judge; it would all be over by dinner. The detective was eager to share this good news with Sarah.

Meanwhile, while Sarah relaxed in her posh hospital room where servants attended to her every whim and desire, the rest of her classmates headed back to school. Many students inquired about Sarah, excited she might be returning soon; everyone wished her well, and in one class the students wanted to make a welcome back sign for her. Patti almost cried when she witnessed this genuine concern for her friend. By the end of the day, the idea had spread to other classes, and Sarah was becoming the school celebrity. Patti thought it was awesome, and Colby noted he had never seen everyone so involved. By the end of the day, Patti told Colby that a class of students was like a family; when one member is attacked, the rest of the family is there to defend them. Colby said it must be something like that because kids who didn't even know Sarah were going out of their way to support her.

Patti planned to walk by the hospital on the way home; she asked Colby if he would like to come along. After some thought, he decided he would. When they got there, Sarah, eye patch and all, was in her room and back in bed. She was pleased to see them and reported her operation had gone well. It appeared she would be released in the morning. She had no sooner finished her good news when Detective Johnson burst into the room with even better news; the dirty so-and-so that tried to kill Sarah was under arrest, and they planned a long vacation for him in some remote prison. All of the kids shouted for joy, which produced the arrival of a nurse, who was not amused by their rowdy behavior. "This is a hospital, not a playground!" However, upon hearing the same good news, this nurse actually jumped up and shouted, "All right!" Patti "shhed," reminding her this was a hospital. The nurse was embarrassed and left, but everyone soon heard cheers at the nurse's station.

As soon as things calmed down, Detective Johnson went to Sarah's bedside. "Sarah, do you feel like you could come down to the station with me tomorrow and identify this man for us? Maybe we could do it on the way home from the hospital. What do you think?"

Sarah looked at her. "Sure, let's get the bad stuff out of the way...before my new life begins."

The detective was taken back by Sarah's honest reply, and

Patti thought she could see a tear or two in Deb's eyes as she hurried to leave. Patti figured she didn't want to spoil the "tough cops don't cry" image she tried to maintain. Patti had seen right through that facade. The detective might be hard on the outside but was much softer inside.

Patti decided she would stay at the hospital and go home with her mother; if Colby wanted to hang around they could take him home too. He thought that was okay but decided to call his mother so she wouldn't have a coronary wondering where he was. The three friends talked about school and Sarah's release from the hospital. She was excited to be living with the detective but would have been less so if she had seen what Patti and her mother did only a couple of days before. Patti did tell Sarah that Deb had fixed up a bedroom just for her, but the doors were too small to get a new dumpster inside, so Sarah would have to sleep in a bed. Sarah was crushed, but admitted sacrifices have to be made. Colby thought both girls were slipping fast and opined that maybe they should be roommates in a "different" kind of hospital. Patti agreed. "Yeah, they need to keep us 'nut cases' together, but that means you'll be there too!"

Colby was not one to disagree when great truths were spoken, so he just nodded.

When Kathy came by, everyone was excited to tell the good news, and Kathy rejoiced just like they had. She could tell Sarah was happy and eager to be out of the hospital; she only hoped Sarah would not have to take care of Detective Johnson instead of the other way around! Kathy was glad to take Colby home, and she and Patti shared their joy about Sarah on the way. Monday doesn't have to be a bad day.

Tuesday morning found Detective Johnson nervously awaiting Sarah's release; she had arrived early to talk to her. She related that Sarah's mother was out of the picture; Sarah showed no remorse or sorrow at the news. Detective Johnson thought it sad someone could lose a mother and not feel bad about it; she could do better than that. The doctor finally arrived and gave Sarah the once over, checking her vitals. "Well, young lady, I think you are ready to be released. What do you think?"

Sarah beamed. "I think it sounds great!"

"Okay, now I want you to take it easy today; you can't do the things other crazy seventh graders like to do...you know, jumping out of trees, scaling cliffs or roller blading, right away. Your eye needs to heal, and the rest of your body needs rest too. However, it is okay to be active, and I've made arrangements with the school to keep you out of the hallways during passing periods and not be run over by your classmates. You can go back to school Wednesday, but think of yourself as fragile and be careful; I think you'll be fine. Everyone is eager to see you, and I know you miss them. I hope the rest of the year goes great."

Sarah thanked the doctor, who told her the nurses would come get her in a few minutes. Deb helped Sarah gather everything. The nurses soon delivered a wheelchair and rolled her to the waiting squad car. After they got Sarah inside the vehicle, the detective told the nurses, "Thank you for your help; you've been great. I'll make sure we get this runaway back in jail and off the streets. You know, some kids will do anything to avoid school. Why they'll even let someone hit them in the head as an excuse to get away. What's this world is coming to?"

The detective was shaking her head, and the nurses looked like she had lost her mind. Police work will do that to you!

✎ Twenty-Two ✎

As Sarah and the detective pulled away from the hospital entrance, Deb asked quietly, "Hey, do you know anything about cooking?"

"What do you mean? I know a little bit and Patti has shown me a few things. I can make macaroni and cheese and a wicked bologna sandwich."

Deb grinned. "Good, at least we won't starve."

"I assume this means I'm taking care of you instead of you taking care of me." Sarah flashed a smile.

"You've got it...something like that."

"Maybe we can learn together; I like to cook."

"Yeah, maybe we can. That would be great."

When they arrived at the police station, Detective Johnson took Sarah inside where she received lots of thumbs up from the officers. They led her toward the back of the building into a small room with a big window. Pretty soon a light came on in the room across from the window and several men marched in, turned and faced her. She counted five, and gave each a hard look. Detective Johnson asked, "Have you ever seen any of these gentlemen?"

"No, ma'am, I've never seen any of them except the one in the middle; he's holding the number three."

"So you've seen the man in the middle, the one with the three." Sarah nodded. "How is it that you know him?"

Sarah spoke without hesitation. "He's the man that killed me."

Detective Johnson was astonished by her remarks, as was the other officer in the room. Trying to compose herself, her voice broke. "Don't you mean the man that tried to kill you?"

"No, ma'am, he killed me, but an angel sent me back; that's why I'm here identifying him right now. He's a bad man. He hurt another man in the alley before he killed me. I hope you send him away for a long time. I don't know the other men."

For a long time, the room was silent as a tomb. Detective Johnson was still unnerved. "Sarah, thank you for helping us; I think I speak for everyone here when I say we are mighty glad that angel sent you back so we can get this debris off the street. We need you to sign a statement acknowledging you made this identification, and we'll go home, but I want you to know you are our hero."

The other officer shook Sarah's hand. When they went back to the front of the station, Detective Johnson gave all the officers a thumbs up. A great cheer arose from the office. Many of the officers shook Sarah's hand. Sarah beamed with pride; she'd never gotten this kind of attention until she'd been killed. One officer noted. "I always thought pirates were a bad lot, but now that I've met you, I see the whole thing differently."

"Thanks, matey." One good pirate smiled at one good policeman.

From the police station, Deb and Sarah went directly home. The detective had taken the day off to be with Sarah and help her adjust to her new home. When they pulled up in the car, Sarah commented on how nice the house looked; she thought the inside was also in good order. The detective refrained from admitting it was very much improved from only a few days ago. Sarah was pleased with her room. "Patti told me you couldn't get a dumpster to fit in here, so I would have to sleep on this old bed instead. I guess it's okay; I'll have to get used to something soft."

"Well, Patti is right; we tried to give you all the comforts of the streets, but I couldn't afford to rebuild the house and enlarge the doors. This place has heating and air conditioning too; I've even got indoor plumbing. I hope you can manage."

"Hey, sometimes us pirates have to tough it out; I'll do what I can...and hey, the indoor plumbing is nice, especially in the winter!" Sarah grinned.

Deb thought Sarah looked tired and asked if she would like to rest before lunch; she could try out that new bed. Sarah was asleep in no time. Deb sat down in the living room to think about her day. How in the world had she ended up with this delightful child? They say life changes when you have kids. If that was so, the changes were lying in the next room. It might be easier to face down a gangster in the street than take care of a thirteen-year-old, but macaroni and cheese sounded pretty good right now.

Deb decided to let Sarah sleep as long as she could; tomorrow would be a big day, and she could use the rest. As lunch time approached, macaroni and cheese sounded even more delicious; on the other hand, in about an hour, even a wicked bologna sandwich would be scrumptious. A hungry belly is not picky! It occurred to Deb she might want to check out the pantry and see exactly what was available for lunch. Oops, like old Mother Hubbard's, the cupboard was bare...and the empty pantry had seemed like the ideal place to store some of the items from Sarah's bedroom, but none of them was edible!

Deb began to realize when you don't do any cooking, you don't need any food; she did find some salt, but eating that would make everyone thirsty, and there wasn't really anything to drink unless Sarah liked coffee...the beer in the refrigerator might wash down the salt, but it did not seem appropriate for an officer of the law to be giving a thirteen-year-old beer. This was more complicated than it should be, but if they were going to eat lunch, a fast trip to the market was in order. Deb figured Sarah knew as much about shopping as she did, so if they needed to get groceries, Sarah had better come along. Deb poked her head into Sarah's bedroom and asked her if she knew anything about shopping; Sarah admitted she had little experience in that regard but would go along and help.

Few things excite the female psyche more than shopping, so off they went to buy a few groceries...especially something for lunch. However, everyone, except for Deb, knows that it is impossible to buy only a few groceries; if your cart is not completely full at the checkout counter, you may be laughed out of the building. Then if filling their cart wasn't bad enough; its contents cost a fortune. The learning curve was catching up fast. Being a mom was expensive!

Sarah was smart enough to get some cereal for breakfast the next day and admitted it was better with milk. They found macaroni and got plenty of cheese; Sarah suggested a little ham would be good with the mac and cheese. Frozen entrees would probably work for supper and get them through the day. Sarah would be eating at school so with breakfasts and lunch out of the way, they only needed to worry about an evening meal. Maybe Deb could do this after all. On the other hand, maybe not.

Sarah worked on their lunch and Deb assisted as best she could; it was a bit late but not bad at all. Sarah just needed to expand her cooking expertise and they would be eating like royalty. There was even a chance Deb might pick up a few tips and learn how to do her own cooking; it would certainly be a switch...probably in the right direction.

After lunch, the girls decided to move Sarah into her room. Her few things needed to be put away. When they finished, they sat down in the front room to get better acquainted. Sarah had little to report; her life in recent years was primarily an effort to stay alive. With her mother gone, the detective was all the family she had, and even that was temporary. On the other hand, she was happy to be alive, and the prospect of having a new family was exciting. The detective could report she was not close to her family, partly because she was so busy doing her job and there had been hard feelings when she was younger; no one was willing to forgive and forget. Deb omitted the more seedy details of her life, but it was obvious she and Sarah had much in common.

Later in the afternoon, Deb took Sarah shopping again; Sarah needed a hat to cover as much of the left side of her head as possible. Some of her hair had been shaved, and she still had a bandage over the wound in her scalp. She looked rather woebegone in her present state. They found a hat she liked and a few other items to wear; it turned out Sarah rather enjoyed shopping, so Deb figured she must be normal, and they joked about getting lost in a mall. When they finished, Deb suggested they get right home and work on something for supper. Sarah needed little convincing; she liked to eat.

268

If their timing had been better, they might have picked up the evening paper that arrived after they got home and discovered the same headlines Kathy noted as she left the hospital. Normally, she didn't bother with the paper because she didn't have time to read it. This afternoon, because someone had placed at least one copy in backwards, a headline in the lower right hand corner caught her eye. "Little Hero Identifies Suspect; Murder Charges Filed." Kathy fed the machine and retrieved a copy to take home. The article noted that middle school student, Sarah Matthews, had identified her attacker in a line up, and the district attorney had filed first degree murder charges and additional charges stemming from a stabbing on the same evening. The article went on to say Sarah Matthews had survived a severe blow to the head and was the hospital's celebrated "miracle" child, as well as quite a hero at the police station. Kathy immediately thought, "Wait until Patti sees this!"

When Kathy got home, she shared the paper with Patti, who nearly jumped through the roof...no easy task when the roof is nearly twelve feet above the floor. "Mom, this is fantastic; Sarah's a hero!"

"She really deserves this. If she had died, they might never have caught this piece of garbage." Kathy was emphatic.

Patti's voice also had a serious tone. "That's right. She went through a lot for this moment of fame."

Patti called Colby and told him to look at the paper and read about Sarah, then pass the word. Colby had not heard the news but promised to read the article and call Geoff. Then everyone would know!

Meanwhile, Deb and Sarah picked out a frozen entree and warmed it for supper. Sarah suggested a salad would be good, as well as nutritious. Deb did not argue; she figured Sarah was probably right, and sadly, knew more about food than she did. Their supper was fine, and after cleaning up what little mess they made, they watched a couple of television shows and gave serious consideration to going to bed. However, it seemed unladylike to go to bed dirty, so a bath was in order; Sarah had to keep her head dry for a few more days, so she could only sit in the tub. While she was bathing, Deb talked to her through the door, left slightly ajar. "Sarah, I know this is a new place and a completely different environment for you. Are you okay? Do you feel comfortable here?"

"Yes, it feels like home to me."

This comment brought a sense of comfort and relief to Deb. "I just want you to feel good here. I've not had any experience with children, or even adults for that matter, living with me; it's really important for you to talk to me and let me know what's on your mind. We need to operate like a team; we can't do it without good communication."

"That will be fine; I haven't had much practice living with people either...we'll just have to work on it together. I guess there is one thing I'd like, but I don't know how to say it."

"Look, Sarah, you don't have to be embarrassed around me; just say what's on your mind."

"Yes, ma'am, if it's all right with you, I was wondering if, maybe, you'd sleep with me tonight; I would like that...if it's okay. I think I'd feel safer...you know, not being alone. You don't have to if it makes you uncomfortable, but I would like that."

Sarah could not see Deb crying outside the door, and may have felt uneasy about the long pause that followed. "Sure honey, I can sleep with you; you'll be safe...I promise."

While Sarah finished her bath, it occurred to Deb she had been doing a lot of crying lately; motherhood was emotional, especially for someone who never cried.

When Sarah finished her bath, Deb took a quick shower; she always marveled at how good it felt to be clean. Maybe it was being around the less savory folks that frequent the police station, but it was always good to wash off the "dirt" of the day when she got home. She slipped into her idea of pajamas, tee shirt and cutoff sweat pants, and quietly walked into Sarah's bedroom. Sarah was already lying down. Deb walked to the bed, pulled the covers back, and slipped next to her. Sarah waited for Deb to situate herself, then turned off the lamp beside her. They both lay quietly for several minutes, then Deb felt Sarah's hand reaching toward her under the covers finally resting on her hand. Soon Sarah grasped it more firmly and with tearful eyes said very quietly, "Thank you, for taking care of me; sometimes I think no one wants to be with me. I know it's not true, but I still feel that way."

Deb scooted a little closer. "There's no need for you to feel that way anymore, Sarah. I'm here, and I'm not going anywhere. I love you."

Sarah moved to lay her head on Deb's shoulder. "And I love you; you've been good to me."

They lay there until Deb could actually feel Sarah go to asleep; Deb turned slightly so she could roll on her side. Yuck, her pillow case was wet; some fool had been crying on her pillow. Could it be the same fool who found herself in bed with this incredibly tough but tender child, who had no greater wish in the world than to have a real family? Yup, it probably was.

Wednesday morning was a hassle. Deb needed to get Sarah to school early; they had to check in with the school nurse and counselor to make arrangements for her. They were shocked to actually see Sarah, who though in much better condition than she had previously been, was still a long way from looking normal. They had arranged student escorts to carry Sarah's books and assist her any way they could; she would come to class either right before or right after the bell rang. She was to be given every possible consideration and was to go to the nurse's office if she felt strange. Sarah was uneasy about some of these plans because they caused her undue attention; she was, by nature, quiet and shy and had spent most of her life trying to avoid people rather than be close to them. In addition, she looked more like Rocky after his boxing match than Barbie in her box. In all honesty, she was getting nervous and felt like crying...although that would not help. It was indeed getting very dark before the dawn; that is, until her first morning escort arrived—none other than her old friend, Patti Linder!

Sarah had just received the magic pill that cures everything from flat feet to bad breath. "Patti!"

"Good morning, Sarah; you look chipper today...and say, I like your hat!" Sarah grinned. "Are you ready for another big day at middle school?"

Sarah's spirits soared. "I wasn't, but I am now."

The girls moved aside to visit while the adults continued their discussion. "Oh, Patti, I was really nervous about this, but seeing you has given me courage; thank you for being here this morning."

"Hey, it's okay; I'm glad to be here...and don't forget, you're not alone."

"Oh, I know, but it's still nice to have a friend I can see." Patti grinned and nodded.

Patti reached for Sarah's hand. "Sarah, everything is going to be all right. Paul told the Romans, 'All things work together for good to those who love God,' and I have to believe that. I just know you are going to have a good day; I think some of the kids really missed you...and, by the way, I have something for you. Don't let me forget, okay?"

Just then the first bell rang and barbarian hordes surged through the halls; if anyone had the misfortune of falling to the floor, his only legacy would be a grease spot on the carpet, and tragically, if it didn't match, this memorial could easily be cut out and spliced with a new piece, leaving no trace of his existence. Sarah was lucky to have both God and Patti on her side; she needed all the help she could get! As the halls began to clear, Patti gathered her books with Sarah's so they could go to their first class. Deb wished everyone well and Sarah replied, "Everything will be all right," as they headed out the door. Sarah and Patti didn't know it, but it was going to be even better than that!

Quiet halls are so much more fun than the chaos and insanity usually there, so Patti and Sarah enjoyed their walk to class. When they arrived, it seemed unusually quiet, but quiet does happen once in a while. Patti opened the door, Sarah stepped into the room, and a great cheer arose from her classmates, followed by the chant, "Sarah, Sarah, Sarah...." Above the blackboard at the front of the room was a huge sign, clearly stating, "Welcome back, Sarah," and under it, written in a different color by a different hand, was added, "Our Hero." Sarah stood aghast, gazing in amazement at her classmates and the room...and began to cry. Patti was just as surprised; she knew about the sign. They had made it Monday, but the bottom line was new as of this morning. Sarah wanted to leave; she never dreamed she would receive this kind of attention, but Patti was right behind her blocking any escape. The class finally quieted before the riot squad was called, and someone yelled, "Speech," soon followed by another, then by a chorus of fans wanting to hear from their "famous" friend. Sarah hesitated then inched forward toward the front of the room; her voice broke. "I'm no hero, but you have made me feel really special; thank you for this grand welcome; you're the greatest." Everyone cheered again. Sarah found her seat, then she and Patti sat down. The teacher started class, but little of her lesson was learned that day. Instead, one of life's big lessons was.

At the end of class one of the boys handed Sarah a copy of the article from the newspaper, which partly explained the morning's celebration. Another boy hesitantly approached her, pointing to her white eye patch. "I thought pirates wore black patches."

Sarah looked at him, smiling. "That's right, but only bad pirates; I'm a good pirate!"

The boy laughed. "Gosh, you're right." He paused. "You must be a good pirate!"

Right, no more walking the plank or lashings with the cat of nine tails; good pirates are more into group hugs, "thumbs up," and "way to go's". When the bell rang, Sarah asked

Patti what she had for her. Patti opened her notebook and showed her a copy of the article from the paper. She seemed disappointed. "I guess you already have one of these."

"Yeah, I probably don't need anymore; Deb will probably get one too; you keep it so you can say you once met a real hero." Sarah grinned.

"Okay, but you were a hero in my book even before this happened."

"Thank you, Patti; you're a good pirate too!

No one could have ordered from Sears and Roebuck a better day than Sarah got. She ended up with multiple copies of her article; there were cheers in every classroom; and Sarah discovered her feet didn't get tired when they never touched the floor. When Deb appeared after school to pick her up, Sarah wanted so much to run into her arms and share the delights of the day, but she knew she was not to overdo or might not be back tomorrow. It was strange; all of a sudden school was a lot more fun...maybe kids ought to get hit in the head more often. Well, maybe not.

Deb really didn't believe her when Sarah told what had happened; it was simply too good to be true. However, it was later confirmed by Patti. They visited about school and how she felt after her first day back. Sarah was tired, but that was to be expected; otherwise everything worked out well; she was excited to return tomorrow. She did have some extra homework to finish, so she worked on it before she got too tired. At one point she called to Deb. "Say, do you know anything about math? I've got a couple of problems I don't understand."

Deb was not accustomed to doing homework or helping anyone with it. "Well, I can count to twenty if you're in no hurry, and I know all the even numbers are even."

Sarah paused, then laughed. "You can't cook, and it would appear you can't do math. What are you good for?"

"Hey, I could give you a swift kick in the butt."

Sarah laughed. "No, you can't; I'm sitting on it right now."

Deb stuck out her tongue. "Oh, little miss smarty pants, are we?"

"Yup, that's me!"

Everything appeared to be "clicking" for Sarah. She and Deb were a good match; school had been great, and life was looking up. Sarah began to understand happiness, and it was good. She and the detective enjoyed their evening meal and even managed to get one of those math problems solved. As bed time neared, it was time to clean up. Sarah never tired of bathing, and Deb always looked forward to her shower; these girls definitely knew the meaning of clean, but Deb began to wonder if she needed to add another bathroom to speed things up. She was used to having the whole house to herself, and this new boarder was cramping her style. On the other hand, sacrifices have to be made, and this one seemed worth it. When they were ready for bed, Deb asked Sarah if she was going to be okay tonight. Sarah was tentative in her response; after a short pause, she surprised Deb. "Are you going to be all right?"

Deb stood there unable to respond, but finally looked down at Sarah. "You know, how about you sleep with me tonight, and we'll be even? What do you say?"

"I think I'd like that. I don't want you to get scared if we have a storm or something."

"That's right. You never know when bad weather might pop up; we need our rest."

"Thank you for being my new mom; I love you, Deb."

"And I love you, Sarah; you're a good kid."

Sarah had never disliked school, but it had not exactly been her favorite pastime. School had been a safe haven for her and in many ways more of a home than any other place. She had never done great in her studies, but she never thought of herself as dumb; she also knew she could do a lot better if she only had a place to work, to focus on assignments and projects. These things had been impossible around her real mother. Sarah didn't even like to think about it; she had seen, heard, and even smelled things that made her sick to her stomach. She felt no remorse leaving her past behind and knew she would never miss her mother. Somehow that made her feel bad inside, and yet, it was almost as if she had been reborn. For her, being almost killed had turned out to be a good thing, and Sarah wondered if it was worth the terror and pain, and strangely enough...in her case, it was. Sarah tried to imagine herself as a famous counselor giving advice to the lonely and suffering. They would ask, "What can we do to turn our lives around and become the persons God intended?" Sarah could confidently reply, "Oh, that's easy; have someone, preferably a stranger, give you a whack on the head with a board!" On the other hand, maybe Sarah shouldn't be a counselor.

⤛ Twenty-Three ⤜

This Thursday morning Sarah was really excited, for the first time in years, to go to school. Deb even sensed her enthusiasm. "Wow, a kid who likes to go to school! If I tell this to the guys at the station, I'll be drawn and quartered. I'm only on the job for a couple of days, and my kid is perfect...well, except for a wound on the side of her head, an eye patch, and she is...kind of short. Like I said, 'My kid is perfect'...enough." Deb had never dreamed she could feel this way; it made her think about the baby she had lost. That had been for the best, but to have her own child and be its mother was finally making sense. She had a few soft spots and they seemed to be growing; it felt pretty good.

School was fabulous. The kids had settled down but were still excited about Sarah, who glowed in their glory. Patti was happy for Sarah too. Together they made an ornery pair, and it was wonderful to have Sarah back. Even Colby noticed she was walking on air and was glad Patti had "encouraged" him to visit Sarah in the hospital.

After school on Friday, Sarah caught up with Patti. "What are you doing this weekend?"

Patti was curious. "Nothing special, why do you ask?"

"Well, I told Deb I wanted to go to church Sunday; I need to thank God for saving me and giving me a new life. I was hoping you'd come too...and bring your mother."

"Yeah, I'd like that; I'll talk to Mom. I can fire her up."

"Hey, you want a ride home; I've got a chauffeur. Our limo's in the shop, so you'll have to settle for a squad car." Sarah grinned.

Patti flashed a big smile. "Oh boy, it's every girl's dream to be escorted home by the police; I can hardly wait!"

Sunday morning Deb and Sarah came by the warehouse, and they all went to church together. Deb wanted to take everyone to breakfast or brunch and got little argument. When they arrived, Patti saw her Uncle Bob, who motioned for her to come to him. "Patti, you're just the person I wanted to see; I have to make an important announcement this morning, and it will affect you. I don't want you to worry about it until we can talk after church; I've got some good news for you."

Patti groaned. "Oh, Uncle Bob, now I've got to wait almost an hour to find out what's going on; you're killing me."

He smiled. "You'll live."

At the end of each service, a little time was set aside to make announcements and update everyone. Patti waited anxiously. Her uncle stepped forward. "As you know, we try to award a special gift to a deserving youngster in our community to attend our summer camp at no cost. Last year that award went to my favorite niece, Miss Patti Linder. She attended our Fun Camp and is returning this year as one of our youth counselors. Patti, why don't you stand and be recognized." Patti stood and everyone applauded; she blushed. "This year we are proud to announce our award will be given to another special girl, Miss Sarah Matthews. Would she please stand?"

Sarah was shocked, nearly jumping out of her seat. "Oh, thank you; thank you so much. I'll be all healed by then!"

Everyone clapped and stood to offer congratulations. Her companions of the morning were crying for joy.

When the service was dismissed, and the crowd settled, Uncle Bob came to Patti. "Now don't worry about not going to the Exploration Camp. Your mother is going to pay your fees so you can attend; she wanted to surprise you. We gave your award to Sarah. I knew you wouldn't mind."

"Uncle Bob, that's neat; thank you for thinking about Sarah. It didn't even cross my mind about my award; thank you again. I guess I need to thank Mother too. Don't tell anybody, but you're my favorite uncle."

Uncle Bob winked at her and smiled.

As agreed, Deb took everyone to eat, and all the talk was about Sarah and how her life had changed...for the better. Kathy and Patti could see a change in Deb as well; the responsibility of her new charge had made an impact. She seemed more at ease and comfortable with herself and in this short time had grown to love Sarah as her own child. Sarah had strong feelings for Deb as well. It was almost as if they had known each other for years. Their meal was enjoyable, but the day was young and there was much to do. Deb took Patti and Kathy home; she and Sarah went shopping. Someone was eating up all their food!

Once inside their apartment, Patti said, "Mama, I want to thank you for paying for camp this summer. I'm glad my award went to Sarah. I know she will enjoy camp; I'm sure she has never done anything like it. Thank you so much."

"Look, honey, we all feel sorry for Sarah; I know we can't change what happened, but at least we have a chance to do some nice things now. I asked Uncle Bob if there was anything I could do, and we came up with this plan to make it more special. I didn't say anything because I wanted it to be a surprise. I think it worked out quite well. Sarah now has something to look forward to...and I don't think she's felt that way in a long time."

"Sarah's had a tough life; she's had an address but no home, adults around her but no parents, and nothing to live for. Now she has all those things, and her life is going to be really different. I'm really happy for her."

The next week at school was just as good as the previous one. Sarah had a doctor's appointment on Wednesday to check her injuries and dressings. The doctor's report was very good; he removed the bandage from her head and told her she could wash her hair normally, but it was important to keep her eye dry. Her eye was healing, but he wanted to keep the patch on it until the end of the week. Sarah would no longer need to wear her hat to school, but her hair looked strange where her scalp had been shaved around the wound. Deb suggested they go to a salon and see if they had any ideas for a "new do."

The lady at the salon joked that Sarah must have been attacked by Indians hunting for scalps. Sarah said she could not confirm it one way or another; she had gone to sleep...and when she awoke, part of her hair was gone. She blamed it on an angry tooth fairy...but it could have been Indians. The lady had several ideas, so Sarah got her head washed and a brand new haircut at the same time; she thought it was neat to have someone else take care of her. The folks who owned the salon only charged half price for their work; they thought Sarah was "pretty" special.

The next day at school several kids claimed to not know her except for the eye patch; Sarah laughed and told them that next week her pirating days would be over, and no one would even know she was there. With her new haircut, she didn't look like a pirate anymore; she looked more like a girl, and she admitted the first time she saw herself in the mirror at the hair salon, she thought she was looking at someone else. Those extreme makeovers can be pretty scary when some stranger looks back at you!

The week ended, and the good pirate Sarah disappeared, hopefully forever. Her doctor gave her a pair of dark glasses to wear for couple of days, knowing that her eye would be sensitive to the light, so for the weekend at least, the local celebrity was incognito. Sarah was happy to get rid of her bandages and other gear; she had felt like she stuck out more than she wanted, and it had nothing to do with her bust line. Shy and reserved people tend to want to stay that way; Sarah was no exception. She enjoyed being by herself because she had learned her safety and security depended on it. On the other hand, people were okay; she just didn't want to fill the house with them. Interestingly, her new mother was much the same way, which perhaps explained why they got along so well. Sarah liked her new haircut, and without her eye patch, she liked what she saw in the mirror. It was nice to look like a girl and not an unkempt orphan. It didn't hurt when Deb saw the new Sarah. "Say, you're a pretty good looking chick." Mother hen had noticed.

Even though Sarah was excited about school and blossoming as a student, the announcement in church that she would get to go to camp was driving her crazy. She was agog and talked to everyone about it. Patti got frustrated with her. "Sarah, you need to calm down and take one day at a time."

Sarah was very distracted. "Patti, I just can't help it. I know camp is going to really be special."

Like Patti, Deb had never seen anyone so worked up over a forthcoming event unless it was a kid waiting for Christmas. One night Deb even talked to her about it. "Hey, what's the big deal about going to camp? You're not going anywhere special; I don't get it."

Sarah was somewhat taken back by the question and thought about it for quite a while. "You know, this is kind of embarrassing; I don't know why. In some ways I really like the outdoors, the fresh air, the sounds of nature, and warmth of the sun, but I don't know how to swim; I've never gone hiking or boating; I've not even been around any animals except for dogs and cats. I guess I'm excited because this will be a new adventure for me, and as a former pirate, who sailed the seas, it's time to discover what you land lovers enjoy."

Perhaps another factor in this excitement came from Patti, who told her Colby was going to camp; his mom had already paid his fees. Sarah liked Colby; he was nice to her. Someday she'd like to find a man like Colby, get married, have children, and be a good mother. There was one thing though...she would not be getting Colby. Patti loved him more than life. Colby didn't understand, but Sarah was a girl, and she did. When you're in seventh grade, it's hard to know what the future may hold, but come hell or high water...Patti would fight for Colby...and Sarah would never stand in her way, Patti was her best friend, and best friends never stab each other in the back. Never.

School was ending, and the three musketeers were thinking about camp. Patti hoped the cloudbursts and floods would hold off until camp was over...then it could rain all it wanted. Sarah and Colby, who had never been to camp, were looking forward to fun and new adventures. Sarah thought it would be nice to learn to swim. A swimming pool was like a big bathtub, and Sarah was really into bathing but would miss the bubble bath.

Colby hadn't told anyone, but he was excited to be with Patti. Some of the boys at school kidded him about her...that she was his girlfriend...he didn't like that. Patti was not his girlfriend; he just liked her...a lot...well, maybe a little more than a lot...maybe he liked her very much...but he didn't love her, so she couldn't be his girlfriend. Of course, it was possible he did love her, just a little bit, but she was not his girlfriend. Nope, he didn't have any girlfriends, but Patti was special and he enjoyed being with her; they had fun together. They had gone to the park, gone to the movies, climbed trees. They had even kissed each other, more than once, but no, Patti was not his girlfriend. Girlfriends mean all that lovey dovey stuff; Colby wasn't into that!

Truth be told, it was Patti who was most excited about camp. First, she was going to be Counselor Dave's

281

assistant, a youth counselor. This was her first real job, and even though she wasn't getting paid, she was thrilled about working with Dave and the new kids. However, it was the next week that got her motor running; she would be with Colby and Sarah, but it was Colby that counted most. Patti thought about him a lot, and it finally occurred to her she truly loved him, but they were just out of the seventh grade and it was unfair to expect Colby or anyone else to wait for years to be married. If they went to college, it could be as long as ten years before they could really be together. No, she had to be fair. Colby liked her, but that was about it. For now, that was enough. But in the back of her mind she kept thinking how nice it would be to take a walk down one of the trails, find a quiet place to sit down, then maybe, just maybe, kiss each other again like they had in the park. That would be nice; in fact maybe they could kiss more than once. Maybe Colby would even kiss her on the lips. No, Colby probably wouldn't do that; kissing embarrassed him. He needed to get over that, and camp would be a good place to start.

⤞ Twenty-Four ⤝

School ended, and there was great joy in Muddville. The kids went wild and rioted in the streets...well, maybe not, but a lot of happy people were running around. The three musketeers had finished strong. Sarah had won the most improved seventh grader award, and all of them were on the honor roll. They looked forward to being eighth graders and hoped to once again share classes, but right now it was important to have their summer and be together as much as possible—camp was just around the corner.

Patti shipped out first to work with Counselor Dave at Fun Camp. The adult leaders met on Sunday morning with their assistants in the chapel for a short worship service, then they trained the youth counselors, explaining their duties. It was important for them to set a proper example for the younger kids and assist in any way possible. They figured the more eyes they had on the kids, the less likely anything bad could happen. It was important to account for everyone; with so much going on, it was easy to lose track of people, and while the camp was generally safe, no outdoor area is without risks. Last year's camp was a perfect example. It had been a perfect day for hiking and exploring, then suddenly in mid afternoon, a terrible storm arrived and nearly drowned the whole bunch of them. Had people panicked, a terrible tragedy might have occurred, but Counselor Dave had remained calm, kept the kids focused, and led them to safety; as bad as it was, a few of the kids thought the storm was kind of neat. Patti didn't.

Patti felt she understood...do what Counselor Dave said, and everything would be fine. On the other hand, make sure you kept your eyes open for potential problems. The adults needed both support and help to make things run smoothly; the youth counselors were there to provide that and have fun in the process. It made Patti feel important; she was the youngest counselor, but no one said anything because everyone knew Patti was reliable and responsible.

Patti wasn't required to, but she kept a journal for her first week of camp so she could share it with her mother. It could be summarized in one word, fantastic. The kids in her group listened to her and Counselor Dave, and everyone had a great time. Every single one of their group said they had to come back next year for Exploration Camp. Patti and Dave were pleased that everyone was so happy and there had been no problems...no poison ivy, no bears eating anyone, no one drowning in the pool...or on the trail. As one of their campers said, "It was awesome!"
.
When the kids were loaded in the bus and headed back to town, Counselor Dave came to Patti and extended his hand. Patti gave it a good shake. "Patti, you have been the best youth counselor I've ever had; you worked so well with the kids, and always did exactly what you were told. I'm very proud of you. Thank you for working with me."

"Counselor Dave, I'm the one who should be thanking you; you were great, and I had the most fun—we didn't get soaked this year."

"That's right, we sure didn't, and that's fine with me; we had way too much water last year. Oh, before I forget; I need your help. Do you know a smart, good looking young lady who could help us next year? We are always on the lookout for special people. Got any ideas?"

"Gosh, Dave, I'll have to think about that; I can't think of anyone off the top of my head. I suppose...well, maybe...I don't know...I might be able to help out again next year if you're in a bind. If you twisted my arm real hard, I'd have to give up and say, 'Uncle Bob.' I'd hate for you to shut this place down because I couldn't help."

Dave smiled and extended his arm again. They shook hands. "It's a deal."

Patti stayed and helped; then she and her uncle were off to town, but she would back in only two more days, this time as a camper. She and her uncle visited on the way home; she told him how mean old Counselor Dave had forced her into agreeing to come back next year. What was this world coming to if adults were allowed to abuse kids this way? Uncle Bob felt so bad he nearly cried. It ain't easy being a kid.

Patti got home almost the same time her mother did. Kathy was interested in her week's activities, so Patti produced her journal and told her she could read about it, but she'd had a great time, and best of all, the mean old adults wanted her to come back next year. Kathy felt bad the adults were picking on her sweet little girl; she would have a good talk with Uncle Bob and straighten things out. The conversation had to end because both girls got the giggles.

The weekend went quickly. Deb, Kathy, Sarah, and Patti had agreed to go to church. Uncle Bob would pick up the girls from Kathy's apartment and take them to camp. Patti and Sarah were so excited about camp it was hard to focus, but the church service was soon over, and they returned to the warehouse where Kathy had agreed to fix breakfast. The food was delicious, and they ate too much. They cleaned off the table, picked up in the kitchen, and finished everything by the time Uncle Bob arrived. They loaded the happy campers into his car and watched them drive away. Before they were able to get back into the apartment, Deb broke down, and Kathy had to assist her inside.

"Deb, what's wrong? Are you sick?" Kathy was concerned.

"Oh, Kathy, I wish it was that simple. I thought I could get through this...but I just can't."

Kathy was rather curious. "What do you mean?"

"Look, you and I know Sarah is just with me temporarily until she can find a good family, and Kathy, I love that little girl more than anything in the world. She is simply wonderful. You should understand; you have one too." Deb was still crying and wiping tears.

"I guess you could say that."

"I'm going to lose her. Don't you get it? Any day now the court will notify me they have found a home for her, and she'll be gone...just like today. I know Sarah will only be away for a week this time, but the next time I'll lose her forever."

Kathy was puzzled. "I thought you only wanted her for a short time. Wasn't that your plan?"

"Exactly, that was my plan; things have changed. I don't think you realize what I'm trying to say; I love Sarah...I love her. What if I came here and told you the court had ordered me to take Patti away?"

Fire shot from Kathy's eyes. "I'd kill you where you stand."

"Okay, you understand how I feel; I know she's not my child; she's not even related to me, but Kathy, I feel just like you. I don't want to give her up, and I'll have no choice. When it's time, she goes!" Deb still was having trouble with her emotions.

"Why don't you just adopt her?"

Deb sighed deeply. "Oh, Kathy, I just can't. Sarah deserves so much better than me. She needs a mom and a dad and maybe even some siblings. That's not in my future, at least, not now. She needs more than I can provide."

"I think you are being unfair. You have much to offer, perhaps not right now, but in the future. I'm sure Sarah would understand; you should talk to her."

"Kathy, that's the problem; I can't talk to Sarah about it. I just couldn't. It tears me up inside. Do I want to keep her? Yes, absolutely. Is it the right thing to do? No, I'm positive. It never occurred to me I would ever love someone else's child, or even take care of one. How could I know Sarah would make a home for herself in my heart and touch me so? I had to talk to someone about this; I hoped you might understand; I think you do, but you have no idea how it hurts me. Did you ever read the book <u>Old Yeller</u> where they have to decide the dog's fate? They have a choice between a beloved rabid dog or a dead one. I say, what kind of choice is that? I have the same problem. Do I keep Sarah because I love her, or do I let her go so she can have better home and family? You know the answer, and so do I; it breaks my heart, Kathy...it just breaks my heart."

Kathy stood, looking at her friend as tears began to flow and held out her arms. Deb walked to her with outstretched arms, and they hugged. Finally, Kathy lifted her head off Deb's shoulder and kissed her on the cheek; Deb responded by raising her head a bit and returning Kathy's kiss. As they separated, Kathy asked Deb, "Are you going to be all right? You'll be alone tonight."

"I don't know; I'd like to think so. Why do you ask?"

"I could stay with you if you'd like, or you could come over here; I want you to be okay."

"You know, I had this same conversation with Sarah."

"How did it turn out?"

"I ended up sleeping with her; she felt uneasy about her new home and environment; I wanted her to feel safe."

"Maybe you should take your own advice and be safe with me tonight."

Deb looked at her and they hugged again. After a few moments, Kathy lifted her head and pulled away to face Deb peering into her eyes; Deb did not notice the impish grin that crossed Kathy's lips just as she leaned forward and gave her a quick peck on the lips. Deb, taken by surprise, lifted her hand to her mouth. "Kathy, I'm not that way."

Kathy nearly beamed. "Oh, I know, neither am I...and if you'll remember, we've had this conversation before."

Deb looked at her, choked, then started to laugh, "Why you ornery devil; you're no better than our two crazy kids!"

"Hey, just remember, one of them is related to me."

Kathy was now laughing heartily. The girls embraced, then kissed each other on the cheek. Kathy knew Deb would stay with her tonight; she also knew Deb would be okay, but the pain would linger, and Deb might need more than Kathy or anyone else could give.

Patti and Sarah were headed for Exploration Camp, and Uncle Bob could not drive fast enough. The trip was not long, and they were soon at their destination. Fun Camp was named for exactly what it was, a week of fun. Fun Camp was also a hook; the leaders wanted the kids to have a good time so they would return next year. Exploration Camp was also intended to be fun, but the leaders wanted to extend its mission to include basic Bible study, the value of prayer, and various aspects of being a Christian. Generally, kids responded well. Many young teens were searching for meaning in their lives, and this camp was designed to get them thinking about it.

The camp followed a daily schedule. After breakfast everyone would meet in the chapel for a short service of mostly prayers and singing. Then a large group meeting featured one or more speakers presenting an issue. Following this, everyone would break into assigned groups with a leader, like Counselor Dave, to discuss what they had learned and its relationship to their lives. These discussions were often lively—the kids had much to share. When this session ended, depending upon the time, the kids were free to enjoy the outdoors, gab, or have fun. The afternoons were filled with outdoor and fun activities which continued until after supper. Chapel occurred again before bedtime, and the day was at an end. Sometime during the day there were journals to fill out, so they would have a record of their adventures.

Patti and Sarah were arriving early since Patti's uncle was one of those responsible to get everything underway. Patti thought camp seemed kind of bare with no kids around, but they would be coming soon, and she was anxious to see Colby. The two girls offered to help where they could as other counselors and their assistants began to arrive. Patti did a little investigating and discovered she and Colby were in the same group; she had hoped she would get Counselor Dave again, but she and Colby were assigned to one of the younger counselors, Barb. She was studying to be a youth counselor, so this experience matched her career. Sarah was assigned with Counselor Dave, and Patti was thrilled; she knew they would get along fine.

Patti and Sarah finished their chores, and Uncle Bob thanked them. They didn't mind helping because they knew it benefited everyone...including them. The bus arrived, and kids began to exit with backpacks and travel bags. Patti recognized several from youth group and middle school. Colby climbed down from the bus and surveyed the scene, no doubt looking for Patti. She gave a yell; he saw her, smiled, then walked toward his friends. Patti called out. "Hey, Colby, how was that bus ride?"

"Oh, Patti, I'm sorry you missed it; it was so quiet, and you, of all people, know how much fun it is riding on a bus. I think I'll just stand a while until my rear feels better."

Sarah quipped. "Well, at least you made it...and there's nothing wrong with standing; it makes you feel taller."

"Say, the bus was full, and apparently another group is coming in a van. I guess we have quite a crowd this year."

"That's good; I think it's better to have a larger group. The activities seem to work better with more people. I can show you guys where we are assigned; we can stash our gear and head back to the chapel for orientation."

The musketeers stored their things. Everyone was excited, and several counselors were trying to organize the confusion. It didn't take long before they had everyone headed to the chapel for their cabin assignments and other information. The orientation meeting took a while because there was much to explain. The main point was to not wander anywhere alone, always be alert and pay attention to the people around you. It was especially important to listen to and obey the counselors; they were there to help. All the leaders wanted everyone to have a great time.

When the meeting adjourned, the kids were encouraged to go to their cabins and unpack. There would be a time for them to look around and get acquainted with each other and the camp facilities. Patti already knew this, so she invited Colby to go for a walk; they wouldn't go far, and no one would disturb them. Patti wanted to visit. They hadn't gone far when they found a bench tucked into some large rocks by the trail. They sat down. "Colby, I'm so glad you came to camp, and we can be together for the whole week."

"Me too, it sure beats working at home; Dad is really keeping everyone busy. I'm looking forward to a rest."

"Colby, you know we're best friends, but I've been thinking maybe we're more than that. I want you to know you are very special to me. Even though it might sound silly, I want to say, 'I love you.'"

Colby moaned. "Ah, Patti, you know that bothers me; I know you really like me, and you're very special too, but I hate for you to say that. I mean, we're just a couple of kids. What do we know about love?"

"Well, this is what I know." Patti leaned over and kissed him on the cheek.

Colby pulled back. "Ah, Patti, cut that out! You know how

I feel about lovey dovey stuff."

"Colby Duncan, I think you like the lovey dovey stuff just as much as I do...but you're too embarrassed to admit it; you lean over here and give me a kiss."

Colby was quite shocked by Patti's bold behavior, but without thinking he leaned over and gave her a peck on the cheek. "Now, that didn't hurt one bit, did it?"

"Ah, Patti, come on...you know it's nice to be kissed; don't be mean...I guess...well, I...maybe I do love you."

Patti heard the "magic" words; she put her arms around Colby and kissed him on the cheek. Colby struggled in her grasp while she held him tightly and kissed him again. Colby seemed to relax and put his arms around her; they embraced for several moments, then peered into each other's eyes. Colby spoke first. "Now it's my turn."

He leaned forward and kissed Patti on the cheek, then kissed her again. Surprised, Patti said, "Let's do this right and kiss each other at the same time."

They leaned forward and kissed each other on the lips, then slowly pulled away, looking into each other's eyes, saying quietly, "I love you."

Lightning didn't strike, but perhaps it should have as Colby and Patti suddenly came back to earth and realized what they were doing and where they were. Sometimes angels, God, or somebody has to reach down and give us a swat to snap us out of our foolishness. They released each other, stood up, and scurried down the trail back to camp, arriving in time to go to the chapel with their comrades.

Each year's camp focused on a central theme throughout the week; this was presented on Sunday afternoon before their opening cookout and then into the evening after everyone had eaten. Several of the leaders were helping prepare the food as the kids filed into the chapel. Patti and Colby moved to a central location and sat down. The music director led the group in a few songs, which included some hand gestures, standing up, and sitting down. When the songs ended, Patti reached for Colby's hand holding it firmly; Colby squeezed her hand in return. The overall leader stepped forward and announced they had been fortunate to find a dynamic Christian speaker to kick off this year's central theme, "Helping Christian Teenagers Cope with Sex and Peer Relationships." Patti looked at Colby, Colby looked at Patti; Patti dropped Colby's hand; Colby blushed. Ouch! That angel wasn't satisfied breaking up their earlier romantic interlude; oh no, he wanted to dump a hundred gallons of water on it too. Darned old angel anyway; he ought to be helping someone who really needed it...but then, perhaps he was.

The opening session was enlightening. The speaker was funny and used jokes to get the kids laughing and thinking. Several points made sense. He told the kids they were in the midst of a great change within their minds and bodies. They were growing extra hair; they discovered that when they were active, they didn't always smell good. Girls were growing breasts and boys muscles; and finally, they were starting to have feelings, sometimes strong feelings, about the opposite sex. Suddenly, girls were pretty, and boys were handsome. All these things were new, some were embarrassing; it is difficult to cope with new and different things. However, whether they liked it or not, their bodies were becoming adult. Yuck! What kid wants to have an adult body? The kids all laughed. Adults are never happy with their bodies so why should a kid get stuck with one, but this was only half of it.

While it was obvious their bodies were changing, it was not so evident that their brains were keeping up. Their brains were in no hurry to grow up; they knew better! This could cause problems. The speaker asked the girls, "How many of you young ladies would like to have a baby right now?"

One girl started to raise her hand, but a friend next to her pulled it down. Otherwise, no one moved. "How come? Wouldn't it be nice to have sweet, cuddly little baby to hold and love?"

One girl almost jumped out of her seat. "No! I had to

babysit my little brother, and he peed on me. I only had to watch him for one hour, but he does that all day long."

Another girl responded. "Well, babies are fun when they're asleep or quiet, but my little sister had colic and cried all the time; it was awful. She drove us crazy!"

One of the boys added. "Hey, babies are full time, 24/7; you have to take care of them all the time. No kid wants to do that."

There was a general agreement that babies were better in pictures than real life. When the kids quieted down, the speaker asked, "How many of you girls could get pregnant today?"

The girls began looking at each other. One hand went up, then another, until only a couple of girls, including Sarah, kept their hands down. "Okay, if none of you want babies, and most of you could have one, don't you think we need to talk about this?"

The girls were embarrassed, and the boys looked mostly confused, but everyone seemed to think this was important. The speaker followed. "How many of you girls know how you get pregnant?"

The girls giggled, and the boys looked like they were lost, but hands began to rise, and it was obvious they all had ideas about sex. "Okay, there is only one way I know to get pregnant...except for our Lord's mother, Mary...it's not complicated. How do we prevent it?"

One girl shouted. "My sister says, 'Keep your legs crossed,' and she knows what she's talking about!"

Everyone laughed; the speaker replied. "Your sister has the right idea."

The kids laughed again. "Does anyone else have any suggestions?"

"Yeah, don't have sex!" yelled one boy.

The speaker looked up and smiled. "That's absolutely correct! Just say no to sex...but here's the problem. That twelve-to-thirteen-year-old brain has trouble working with its new adult body. We don't know how to handle our new feelings; we are growing up and away from our parents, but we are still kids in our head."

The speaker then asked if one of the girls would come forward and act out a scene with him. A girl on the front row stepped forward and approached the speaker, who moved from behind the podium toward her; he reached for her hand and knelt down on one knee. He looked into her eyes and smiled. "Oh, I love you so much; I want to spend my whole life with you." Then, from behind the podium, he produced a bunch of flowers and a box of chocolates. "You're the only girl I've ever loved; please be mine forever."

The girl looked at him, surprised by his boldness, but as he spoke, she seemed to relax, enjoying his comments. "Well, since you feel this way, I must confess I like you too...but I suppose I should talk to my mom about it; I don't want to get into trouble."

The speaker suddenly looked very sad, as if he might cry, then he frowned, his face hardened, and he took back the flowers and chocolates. "I need another volunteer."

The kids seemed to connect, laughing and clapping. One girl stood up. "Yeah, my sister says boys will do or say anything to get in your pants."

A few kids gasped, but most of them understood exactly what she meant.

While this was in progress, Patti kept looking at Colby; he seemed uneasy and embarrassed. Patti noticed she was feeling guilty about their earlier rendezvous. She was a woman now; she could get pregnant. She had seen firsthand all her mother had gone through trying to raise her with no dad. It was not going to happen to her; she'd keep her legs crossed, just say, "No," and even learn karate if she had to. Nope, it wasn't going to happen. Besides

Colby had just kissed her and only after goading him; Colby was a gentleman. He respected her; she'd be safe with him. Colby wasn't like other boys...or was he?

〜〜　〜〜

The first session ended, and the happy campers were dismissed for supper. Patti and Colby caught up with Sarah and headed for the Chow House, the kids were abuzz about the opening session. It was nice to see everyone so engaged and excited...but when sex is the topic, kids seem to pay more attention. Patti tried to listen to the comments of those around her, but there was too much confusion to understand anything. However, there was no doubt everyone was thinking about what they had heard.

On the way back to the evening session, Patti and Colby lingered; Patti reached for Colby's hand. He was tentative and nervous about it. "Patti, I'm sorry about this afternoon; I wasn't thinking. I hope you don't think I was trying to take advantage of you."

Patti poopooed him. "Don't be silly. It was just a kiss...and remember, I talked you into it."

"No Patti, it was more than that. I wanted to keep kissing you. I think I love you."

Patti almost stopped in her tracks; Colby hit that nerve again...and she knew he wasn't just saying it to make her happy. Patti wanted so much to kiss him, but restrained herself. "Colby, I forgive you; I love you too. You are the only boy I've ever kissed, except for Grandpa, and he doesn't count; I promise you I will never kiss another one until you release me from this vow. I hope you will kiss me again, and I hope it's soon. I'll keep my legs crossed."

Colby stopped, looked at her, and quickly gave her a peck on the cheek. "Thank you; I promise to be good."

〜〜　〜〜

In the second session, the speaker summarized the first by saying, "You girls told me you don't want to be moms right now, and I got the feeling the boys don't want to be dads. You also indicated you know enough about sex to get pregnant or make someone that way. In this session I want to explain how all of this fits in with our Christian beliefs. Let's get started. What does it mean to be a Christian?"

Patti jumped right up. "It means you have Jesus in your heart!"

"Very good. Have you accepted Christ as your Savior?"

"Yes, I have."

"Good. This young lady tells me she has Jesus in her heart...or we could say Jesus dwells within her. Right?" The kids nodded. "Okay, now you know we call this place a chapel or a small church. When someone mentions chapel or church, what comes into your mind?"

"It's a place to worship God," said one boy.

Another noted, "My father says it's God's house."

"So we could say the church is one of many places where God lives?" The kids nodded their agreement. "All right, then we agree God is here with us. Is Jesus here too?"

"Yes sir," replied one of the girls.

"Okay. In Biblical times a Jewish church was called a temple, and the Apostle Paul says our body is a temple. What does he mean?"

Patti got really excited. "Paul means Jesus is in us just like God is in the church, so that makes us temples of God!"

"That's exactly correct, young lady..."

Patti interrupted. "My name is Patti."

"Good enough. Patti is right. If we abuse our bodies with an excess of alcohol, food, or drugs, if we engage in promiscuous sex, if we make no effort to take care of ourselves, what are we really doing?"

One of the girls replied. "We are destroying our temple, God's home."

"Absolutely, the Bible says we are defiling the temple where God resides. Now I ask you, if you came home from camp and discovered someone was tearing up your home, how would you feel?"

Colby spoke up. "Hey, that would make me mad; my family has been working hard to fix up our house. All that for nothing!"

Patti smiled at Colby and gave him a thumbs up. The speaker went on. "That's right, it would make me mad too. How do you think God feels about it?"

A girl injected. "I'll bet it doesn't make Him very happy!"

"That's how I see it. I don't know about you, but I don't want God angry at me! I want God to love and care for me, to listen to me, to bless me and my family with His mercy. The Bible addresses times when God was angry at the Israelites, and believe me, it wasn't pretty...so I want a happy God, one Who looks at me and smiles...not one Who is shaking His fist!"

The kids sat, looking at each other. Most were nodding; others concerned. If this guy was right, maybe this year's camp motto should really be, "Don't Mess with God!"

The speaker took a break; the kids talked, responding to this message. Colby turned to Patti. "Gosh, I'd never thought about this. If I abuse myself, I'm insulting God."

"Yeah, and abusing yourself is bad for you!" Patti smiled.

Sarah chimed. "Believe me, I've seen enough self abuse from my mom and her 'friends' to last a lifetime; I don't want any part of it!"

Sometimes there is a deep well of wisdom within children. Why do so many adults stop drinking from it?

After the break, the speaker concluded by saying he hoped he had given the kids food for thought. He explained that throughout the week they would have a chance to discuss these points and other information in smaller sessions. He challenged them to think about what had been shared and ask as many questions as they needed to better understand these matters. Following further discussion, the kids were dismissed to their counselors, who headed them for their cabins and a good night's rest.

When they reached their area, a counselor directed them to their assigned cabins. Patti and the three girls in her cabin were busy putting their things away and getting ready for bed; they had to get up early in the morning. As Patti was finishing, a girl came into their cabin and walked up to Patti. "Excuse me; my name is Lisa; I would like to ask you a question privately. Could we please step outside?"

"Sure, we can talk." Patti was curious.

They stepped out under the overhang that shaded the door. "I'm sorry to bother you, but I can't go to sleep tonight until someone explains something to me, and since you talked about it this evening, I thought I'd ask you first."

"What do you need to know?"

"Well, you talked about having Jesus in your heart...I don't understand." Lisa seemed frustrated.

"Gosh, I don't know where to begin; have you ever read any of the New Testament?"

"Well, yes and no, I've tried a few times, but it's confusing. I get lost trying to keep it all straight."

"Yeah, I know; I used to have the same problem, but I've got an idea. Did you bring a Bible with you?"

"Yes, I brought the one my folks gave me in fifth grade."

"Okay, let's see if we can get permission to meet out here every night this week...we'll read the Bible together...and I promise to explain about Jesus before we go home Friday. What do you think?"

"That would be great...but one more thing; I have a friend, Julie, she would like to come too. Would that be okay?"

"I don't see why not. Be sure to check with your counselor so we don't get into trouble."

"Thank you." Lisa turned and headed for her cabin.

Patti went back in her cabin and crawled in bed. Somehow it had been a long day; she suddenly felt tired. She finally decided too much love can wear a person out; Colby loved her, Jesus loved her, a girl named Lisa, whom she didn't even know, loved her. Whew! On the other hand, despite this "terrible" burden, she really wished she could win over just one more heart. If only she could get her mother to love her, that is, really love her...then her life would be perfect...well, maybe not perfect...but good enough. She'd continue praying about it; God would know what to do.

⋙ Twenty-Five ⋘

Their study sessions continued discussions from Sunday. The kids were giving these ideas a lot of thought; they all had questions and ideas to share. The more everyone discussed their bodies and how they could be abused, the more Patti liked the concept of purity. "Just Say No," applied to more than drugs, and the idea of presenting herself as pure to her future husband honored them both.

Camp activities were always fun; especially when friends are there. Colby and Sarah were enjoying everything; Colby even liked the food...boys and their stomachs! Sarah liked her group; she had spoken up and had been well received. It helped her confidence. By evening everyone was slowing down and the chance to eat their evening meal was welcome. The study session that followed was cut short to allow more time to clean up and get ready for bed. Patti had okayed her time with Lisa and Julie at the "mini" shelter near her cabin.

Patti left her cabin and found them waiting. It turned out she knew Julie from grade school; she no longer lived in their community, but her grandparents, who did, had paid for her trip to camp as a birthday gift. The two girls were anxious to better understand the Bible and get to know Jesus. Patti started with a short prayer and asked God to open their minds to the mysteries of the Scriptures and help them better understand what they read. They started with the book of Matthew and read for a while; they were familiar with the early life of Jesus, but as they read, questions arose. Patti did her best to explain passages and answer questions. The girls responded positively and admitted everything made more sense when they discussed it together. They had a good session, and Patti suggested they continue reading as much as possible before they met again the next day. It was getting late so they adjourned for the evening. Patti went to bed feeling good; she hoped she could help the girls and give them what they most wanted, but she also knew they had to be ready...and they did not have much time.

Tuesday was another big day, especially for Sarah. She loved the bathtub, so it was no surprise she wanted to learn to swim. On Monday she had talked to some of the kids, who promised they would help her with the basics. During part of their free time they headed for the pool, and it wasn't long before Sarah was splashing around without sinking. With a little more practice, she would be doing well enough to be on her own. Colby also enjoyed his "vacation;" it was fun to be "wild and crazy" at camp. Patti almost enjoyed watching everyone else have fun more than doing it herself. This seemed to be a good bunch of kids; they interacted well during study sessions and played well together. Patti met again with Lisa and Julie. They read several more chapters and were making good progress. Everyone went to sleep quickly; it had been a busy day.

By Wednesday morning Patti realized she had not had any quality time with Colby except on Sunday afternoon. Wednesday marked the halfway point of the week, and if they didn't get together soon, the "last bell" would ring and they would be going home. Patti then remembered they had a free block of time right after lunch. She talked to

Colby during breakfast, and he agreed to leave this time open. The morning didn't rush by like a runaway train, but it managed to not creep. Lunch time finally arrived, and the kids were excited to have nothing scheduled. Sarah was going swimming. Patti and Colby were shocked. Everyone, except for Sarah, knew she was afraid of water. What was she thinking? Sarah refused to incriminate herself by not saying a word; she did manage a big smile. Colby and Patti said nothing about their plans to hike a "favorite" trail.

They reached their special spot amid the rocks and sat down. Patti reached for Colby's hand. Colby squeezed her hand gently in response. Patti spoke first, "Colby, I think I understand how we feel about each other. I love you and you love me. Don't you agree?"

Colby nodded.

"Our problem is we're just eighth graders; most adults would call us kids, I don't think we should get serious about each other right now; I think we should just be best friends. What do you think?"

"Well, It's hard to argue. You're right; we are just kids. I guess that's one thing I've learned this week. When kids try to make adult decisions, they end up with adult problems. I sure don't want to be a dad right now, and I know you don't want to be a mom, but please believe me. I've never wanted to have sex with you; I've never felt that way. I don't want you to think I'm trying to take advantage of you. I mean...I suppose this will sound silly, but I love you too much to ever want to hurt you, and it would be wrong if I tried. Does that make sense?"

"Colby, you are such a good person, and I am so proud of you. I can't explain it, but I have loved you since the first time I laid eyes on you. You are a handsome young man, and one of these days a lot of pretty girls are going to start paying more attention to you; I know I'm not pretty like some girls or even my mom, but I hope you will save a place in your heart for me and give me a chance to be with you forever." Patti started to cry.

"Oh, Patti don't cry, please don't think that way. You are pretty, in fact you're beautiful; I've always thought so. Your beauty is inside; there is a wonderful person in you. I see it all the time; other people do too. You've heard that saying, 'Don't judge a book by its cover.' My mom told me the best books are the ones with the worn and tattered covers; since everybody likes them, they get read the most. I think you are the best book ever...right up there with the Bible." Colby tried to smile.

Patti looked into Colby's eyes, crying even harder. "Colby, will you hold me?"

Colby moved closer and put his arms around her; Patti in turn wrapped her arms around him. They held each other for a long time. Finally, Patti pulled away a bit. "Colby, do you think it is okay for best friends to kiss each other?"

Colby grinned. "Gosh, I don't see why not." He kissed her on the cheek.

Patti returned his kiss and he kissed her again; she kissed him back. After a pause, Colby asked, "Patti, do you think best friends should ever kiss each other on the lips; I was just wondering."

"You know, I think if two people are best friends...that would be okay." Patti quickly kissed Colby on the lips.

Colby smiled. "We can do better than that."

Whereupon they embraced and kissed each other for a short time, then a bit longer. They were ready for round three when Patti heard voices. Whoops! That guardian angel was at it again...another bucket of cold water.

⤛ ⤜

Wednesday couldn't get any better after a good visit on the trail...and the kissing didn't hurt. It seemed the more Patti talked with Colby, the more she loved him. Why couldn't they both be about six years older?

Although Colby was a big distraction, Patti wanted to help Lisa and Julie. They met again that evening and continued their study and reading of the Bible. While they were making good progress, Patti was concerned they would not be ready in one more day. When they had finished for the evening, she asked, "What are you guys doing Friday afternoon when camp is over?"

"Lisa answered, "Well, we have a problem. I am staying with Julie and her grandparents for the weekend. Her folks are coming to pick us up on Sunday afternoon, but her grandparents are going to be out of town on Friday and we have to kill some time until they get home."

"Listen, I have an idea. Why don't you guys ride home with me and my friend, Sarah. We are going home with my Uncle Bob. That will give us more time to study, and when we get there, we can go to the park or stay inside and keep working. I want to do this right, and you do too."

"That's fine with me. Is it all right with you, Julie?" She nodded.

"Listen, that's great; it will be fun. See you guys tomorrow."

Thursday was set aside as a fun day with lots of activities; the kids could pick from a variety of events that would begin right after a shortened session in the chapel. Patti thought about it for a couple of days; she had asked both Colby and Sarah what they wanted to do and got only shrugs and "I don't knows." It was annoying. Finally, she looked at the schedule again and decided she would like to go on the day hike. Of course, it didn't need to rain and drown everyone; she had really enjoyed it last year until the "flood." Patti told Colby she was signing up for the hike; he had already assumed that and laughed when he told her he'd done the same thing. She tried to swat him, but he was too quick for her. Sarah had an even bigger surprise. No, she was not going swimming because the pool was not open until late afternoon. Sarah was going hiking! Patti nearly fainted, and even Colby was shocked. The three musketeers would all be together, and heaven help anyone who got in their way.

It was truly a beautiful day...a little warm, but June is like that. The air was dry and crisp, the sun shining, a breeze playing. The hiking group was fairly large, so two counselors went along, and they were soon on the trail. They hadn't gone far when Colby nudged Patti and pointed to a group of large rocks with a sheltered bench. "That's our bench." Patti blushed and nodded. This trail was rugged at times, and the kids found themselves puffing and panting as they climbed through rocky areas and scaled hills. The counselors made them take several breaks and drink plenty of water; it would be a while before lunch. The lunch break was welcome and long enough for everyone to feel refreshed and ready to go. The afternoon presented caves to explore, a rough area with many varieties of rocks, a valley containing a small stream, lots of vegetation, evidence of smaller animals, plus a good stop for refreshments mid-afternoon. Except for a few kids who wore the wrong shoes and got blisters, everyone had a marvelous time. There was one incident. Sarah wanted to jump into the stream and splash for a while; fortunately, Colby and Patti managed to restrain her and save the day.

When they got back to camp, they had free time; no one had to ask where Sarah was going. Colby had promised one of the boys he would play softball, so Patti was left on her own...but not for long. She started for her cabin to change clothes when she saw Julie running toward her. "Patti, I need to talk to you; it's really important." Julie's voice conveyed a sense of urgency.

"Hey, what's up?"

"It's Lisa; she's not feeling well; she needs to talk. Maybe you can help."

"What's the problem?"

"Patti, I'm not supposed to tell. Lisa's a wreck. She came here to get away from her boyfriend...I really can't say any more, but I think she'll talk to you. She needs help." Julie appeared concerned for her friend.

"Okay, lets go see her." Patti now shared Julie's urgency.

Lisa sat at one of the "mini" shelters, populating the camping area. She was obviously not herself. When she saw Patti, she began to cry. Patti gave her a tissue, and Lisa tried to dry her tears but was unable to keep up with the flow. After several minutes, she composed herself. "Patti, I wish Julie had found someone else; I'm so ashamed."

Patti looked at her curiously. "Why are you ashamed?"

"I didn't want to have to tell you because I will look like a liar and a fraud, but since you're here, I guess I will. I'm trying to get away from my boyfriend; he will be a sophomore next year. We have been dating for a about a year...and well, we've done quite a few things; he wants to have sex with me..." Lisa broke down, unable to continue.

Patti and Julie waited patiently. After a short time, Lisa continued, "I don't want to have sex; I'm afraid I might get pregnant. He tells me everything will be okay; he will use protection. One of my girlfriends at school told me to start taking birth control pills and enjoy the sex, but I have to get my mother's permission, and if I told her I wanted birth control, she'd kill me. When Julie told me she was going to this camp; I begged my mom to let me go too. She finally agreed. I didn't know what I was getting into, but after that first session about sex, it hit home. I knew I was playing with dynamite and could go out with a bang! Patti, I'm really scared, and I don't know what to do. Then when you talked about having Jesus in your heart. I thought maybe He could help me, but I know down deep Jesus doesn't want anything to do with the likes of me..." Lisa began to cry again.

Patti bristled. She took one of Lisa's hands and shook her hard on the shoulder with the other. "Lisa, you listen to me and listen good. What makes you think you're so bad Jesus won't love you? I think it takes a lot of gall to feel that way. Do you believe you are any worse than everybody else? Do you think Jesus doesn't care as much for you as He does for someone who commits murder? I want you to get a grip or I'm going to slap you so hard you won't know what hit you!" Lisa already looked that way; Julie's jaw dropped so low she had to pick it up from her lap. "Okay, what have you done that makes you feel so unworthy of God's love."

Lisa looked at her, tears rolling down her cheeks. "Well, you know, we've done things."

"Like what?"

"Well, we've kissed...you know, the French way; he's touched me on the breast and kissed me there; I've touched him...you know...things like that."

Patti demanded. "Are you still a virgin?"

Lisa looked shocked. "Why, yes...yes I am."

"Then you're not going to get pregnant as long as you stay that way." Patti was emphatic; Julie nodded.

"But, Patti, he is really pressuring me; I don't think I can hold out much longer!"

"Lisa, you can, and I'm going to tell you how but not right now. This is important; I need to know, do you trust me?"

"I don't know; what do you mean?"

"If you were an egg, would you let me hold you in my hand and trust I wouldn't harm you?"

"I...guess...so."

"Okay, here's what we are going to do. First, we're going to get our Bibles and read for a while, then we're going to go to supper; instead of doing any activities this evening, we are going to continue reading. Tomorrow, you are going to receive the peace only God can give...and finally we are going to decide what to do with your scumbag boyfriend!"

"But I love him!" Lisa was nearly crying again.

"I love carrots too, but if they were killing me, I could give them up. Think about it; you're the one that's miserable."

The girls got their Bibles and began to read; Lisa seemed
to calm down. Patti had discovered every time she read the
Bible, she learned something she hadn't realized before;
the other girls were also feeling better about their reading
and the life of Jesus. Both had questions and comments.
Patti didn't have all the answers and wondered if that was
even possible. Time flew by, and it was soon time to break
for their evening meal. Tonight they were to have a big
cookout and barbecue for their last dinner. Uncle Bob was
there, and Patti asked if it would be okay for Lisa and Julie
to ride home with him Friday afternoon; she also wanted to
see if it was okay to continue her Bible study before they
left. Sarah would be glad to help with some of the chores.
Her uncle insisted both the cleanup, and the Bible study
were God's work; he didn't want to interfere. It would be
fine, and he would deliver all of them to Patti's apartment
when they arrived in town.

After supper, Patti and her friends continued their studies.
As darkness began to fall, Patti went over their schedule
one more time. "Okay, tomorrow we are all riding home
with my uncle; we can study together until he leaves. He'll
take us to my apartment, and we can either stay there or go
to the park and finish our business. I know my mom will
be glad to feed us if you want to eat; you can stay as long as
you like, even spend the night if you have to. I promise I
will do everything I said I would do, and you will discover
something wonderful. I think you're both special. Lisa, we
are going to help you; please believe me."

"Patti, I do believe you. You're the greatest!"

Camp ended too fast. After breakfast, their chapel session
summarized the week's discussion. Overwhelmingly, the
kids agreed that adult things might be good for adults, but
not necessarily for kids. The girls didn't want babies; the
boys didn't want to be dads; and no one wanted to grow up
too fast. Everyone admitted it was fun being a kid, and one
of the young counselors said it was even fun to act like a
kid for the past week. The leaders wanted everyone to
know there were people who could help them and not be
afraid to contact someone in their church if they ran into
problems. Furthermore, they had friends from camp who

would gladly help them. Patti was impressed; she had enjoyed her week; it wasn't exactly what she had planned, but God had things for her to do, and sometimes He was too busy to give an advanced warning. She could handle it.

The morning ended quickly. The kids grabbed their sack lunches; the bus arrived and happy campers began to disappear inside it. Patti kissed Colby good bye and told him she loved him; Colby thanked her for helping talk his mom into letting him be there. As he turned to leave, he looked back and told her he loved her too. Patti almost cried, but thought it was pretty silly since Colby was just going home, and she would be there in only two or three hours. Love is strange sometimes.

Sarah headed off to find instructions on how she could help, and Patti's study group was back in session. Patti could tell that both girls were "fired up." After a while, Uncle Bob brought Sarah and told everyone it was time to go, so the girls loaded their gear, and they were soon on the road. Lisa and Julie wanted to finish the book in the Bible they had been reading, so it was quiet for a time. Finally, Uncle Bob broke the silence. "Well, did everyone have a good time?" He should have kept quiet because they all spoke at once. Bob was no dummy and quickly concluded camp had been great. "Are you coming back next year for Growth Camp?"

Lisa replied. "Yes, I'd love to come back; it was great to get away from home and have fun."

Julie added. "I want to come back too; everything was super."

Sarah seemed to hesitate and Patti asked why she didn't speak up. "Well, I'd love to come back, but only on one condition."

Uncle Bob was curious. "And what would that be?"

"I'll come back if you will let me spend the whole time in the swimming pool!"

Bob smiled then started to laugh. "Sarah I'm beginning to wonder if you have "water on the brain."

Sarah shook her head. "Now that you mention it, I do feel something sloshing up there." She flashed the biggest grin.

Bob almost had to stop the car; he was laughing so hard he couldn't drive. No thanks to Sarah, they made it safely to Patti's apartment. Sarah had instructions to call Deb. Sarah told Patti she had missed taking care of Deb and hoped she was okay; Deb wasn't, but that would have to wait. The other two girls couldn't believe Patti lived in an old warehouse, then were even more surprised when they got inside. "Wow, what a place...and really big!"

Deb came quickly, picked up Sarah, said hi to Patti and left. Patti went back inside with the girls, who already had their Bibles and were ready to go. They asked if they could just stay there; it all seemed so peaceful and grand. That was fine with Patti. After reading for a while, Patti stopped and turned to Lisa, "Please answer my questions carefully; they may sound silly, okay?"

"Okay."

"Lisa, are you a sinner?"

"Patti, you know I am; we all are, it says so in the Bible."

"Do you believe Jesus is the Son of God?"

"Yes, I do."

"Will you accept Him, now, as your Lord and Savior."

"Yes, I will."

"Are you being completely truthful, no reservations or doubts?"

"Yes, Patti, everything I've said is the honest truth."

"Okay, I want you to get down on your knees and pray

308

your ABC's backwards. C means to confess to God you are a sinner, B means you believe Jesus is the Son of God, and A means you accept Him as your Lord and Savior. What will happen if you do these things?"

"The Bible says my sins will be forgiven and I will receive the gift of the Holy Spirit...which means I will have Jesus in my heart."

"Very good, now I want you to silently pray your ABC's; God will hear you."

Lisa bowed her head, Patti placed her hand on Lisa's shoulder; there was complete silence. In a few moments tears began to roll down Lisa's cheeks and drip on her shirt and shorts; her body trembled and the tears continued. Julie was dumbstruck; she could not believe her eyes. Lisa cried and cried; Patti stayed with her and reached for her hand. Suddenly, Lisa lurched forward and grabbed Patti hugging her tightly. "Oh Patti, I feel something inside me; oh, Patti, it must be Jesus..Jesus loves me..Jesus loves me."

Julie nearly wet her pants. What had happened to Lisa? Patti embraced Lisa who continued to cry but now for joy instead of sorrow. They held on to each other, and Patti kissed Lisa on the cheek; Lisa returned her kiss. They separated and Julie could see Lisa was not the person she knew from camp; she had changed right before her eyes.

Julie begged. "Oh Patti, can Jesus save me too...please?"

Patti turned to Julie and asked her similar questions to the ones she'd asked Lisa. Julie got down on her knees with Patti, who placed a hand on Julie's shoulder, then told her to pray as Lisa had done. Julie had been so excited it took her a while to calm down. She bowed her head and prayed. Patti felt Julie relax as a calm engulfed her; she trembled a bit and a few tears rolled down her cheeks; she trembled again, and the tears increased their flow. Then with a look of absolute calm she looked up. "Oh Patti, I've never felt like this; it is like someone placed a warm hand around my heart. It's Jesus, isn't it?"

"Yes Julie, it's Jesus." Patti embraced her friend and held her; Julie returned the gesture.

Patti kissed Julie and Julie returned her kiss. Everyone was crying; these three campers had become three cry babies, but it hardly mattered. They had found God's greatest gift and if that wasn't worth crying over, nothing was.

One more thing. What were they going to do with Lisa's boyfriend? Julie was the first to address this problem. "How are we going to handle the scumbag in Lisa's life?"

Lisa was shocked, then realized what Julie was saying. Patti responded, "Thank you for asking. First of all, you are going to dump him like a load of hot asphalt. Lisa, I'm going to be blunt. Your boyfriend cares more about what's in your pants than he does about you; he ought to have his butt kicked...really hard! He doesn't love or respect you because if he did, he would never ask you to do something you don't want to do, and trust me you don't want to start down that road now or in the near future. This guy is poison and you don't need him. He is not going to change for you; he will just move on and take advantage of someone else, you mark my words."

Julie nodded, but said nothing. Lisa looked at Patti and Julie; she would have liked to cry but was either all dried up or able to restrain herself. "Patti I've been thinking about what you told me the other day; I've been a fool letting him run my life in a direction I didn't want to go. You're right; he doesn't love me. He only wants something I have. I've decided not to give it to him. When I get home I'm going to tell him we're through; I'll talk to my mother too. If he causes any trouble, we'll call the police."

Julie remarked. "Lisa, I'm proud of you; you're making a good decision. Maybe we can be friends again; I've always cared for you and wanted you to be happy...and you've been so miserable for the longest time. I'll stand by you."

Patti smiled. "I think we have your problem solved. Don't ever forget Jesus loves you and is with you always. Don't forget to pray; He'll listen."

Patti reminded Julie to try to call her grandparents, but no one answered the phone except their machine. Julie left a message and Patti's number for them to call when they got home. They had no sooner finished this task when Kathy came home from work and discovered two strangers in her apartment. "Who goes there?"

"Hey, Mom, guess what? I found a couple of lost kids at camp and decided to bring them home with me. I told them we could have them for supper."

"Oh, Patti, how cruel, you know we can't get them butchered in time for supper. Why, we couldn't eat them before Sunday night at the earliest."

At first the girls were shell-shocked, unable to speak. However, as these effects wore off, they realized they had landed in the middle of a joke. "Oh, Patti, please don't eat us. Is there anything we can do to save ourselves?"

Patti looked at her mother. "Mom, what do you think?"

Kathy walked over to the girls and gave each of them a hard look. "Oh, Patti, they look so delicious...but I suppose if they'd chip in and help me with dinner, we could spare them. I was thinking about frying a chicken."

"Hey, that sounds good." Patti smiled; the girls nodded.

Lisa and Julie appeared much relieved, and everyone was laughing. A fried chicken dinner is really special...unless, you're the chicken!

Julie continued trying to contact her grandparents, but no one answered. The girls enjoyed their dinner and Patti apologized for trying to scare them; they both admitted they were rather shocked by Patti and Kathy's comments, but it had been pretty funny.

After they got the table cleaned and the kitchen organized, Kathy told everyone she had rented two videos to celebrate Patti's return; the other girls were welcome to stay as long as they wanted. However, they could not stay indefinitely because Patti had been an only child for all these years and would probably be jealous at the sudden discovery of new "sisters." The girls laughed and agreed that Patti was a hard case...and their families might miss them; it would just cause too much trouble for everyone.

About halfway through the first video, Julie finally contacted her grandmother. There had been a car wreck, blocking the highway for what seemed like an eternity. She apologized over and over and hoped everyone was okay. Julie explained where they were and asked if they could finish the movies; Kathy had agreed to take them home when they ended. Julie's grandmother didn't see any problem and told Julie she'd see them later and to be good. Julie said they had to be good or they would end up on the menu for Sunday night's dinner. Her grandmother was confused; Julie told her not to worry, she would explain everything later. They might as well get as much mileage out of that joke as possible!

⤜ Twenty-Six ⤛

The movies ended. Patti and the girls made their farewells but hoped to see each other next year at camp. Kathy took the girls to Julie's grandparents and another year of camp was officially over. However, when Kathy returned, she was anxious to hear about Patti's week. Patti did her best to explain; she had not had time to write in her journal and had much to remember. Kathy was pleased with her report and glad Patti had been able to help Lisa and Julie. Kathy also thought the camp's theme on sexual issues was timely and worthwhile. Patti concluded her summary of activities by saying, "Mom, there is one more thing I should tell you; I hope you won't be mad at me."

"What is it, honey?"

Patti seemed tentative. "Well, it's about me and Colby; we...uh, we did some things at camp..."

Kathy interrupted. "Just what did you do?"

"Well, Colby and I are best friends." Kathy nodded. "For a long time I've felt maybe we were more than that...you know, more than best friends. While we were at camp, Colby and I talked about it, and I finally told him I loved him; it took a while, but he told me he felt the same way. Well, we were holding each other and I kissed him, and he kissed me back...you know, on the cheek. Then I kissed him on the lips and he kissed me back; we did this a couple times but were interrupted. Colby was kind of embarrassed, and he apologized to me and told me he didn't ever want to hurt me. He didn't want to get me into any trouble...you know, like...well, like getting pregnant. Colby cares a lot for me. I thought you should know."

Kathy sat there silently, trying to think of what to say and how to say it; she did not want to be angry at Patti for her honesty, and certainly kissing was no crime. The real issue was much more complicated. "Honey, you know how much I love you. I guess I need to talk to you about these things, and this is as good a time as any. First of all, I want you to know I respect you and Colby. He is a gentleman and you are a lady. I also want you to know I'm not mad at you or Colby for kissing each other. You both understand who you are and realize you have a lot of growing up to do, but I caution you to please be careful. Innocent kissing can ignite something that can't always be controlled.

"Believe me, the night your father and I parked to enjoy the evening air, the beauty of the stars, and each other's company, we had no intention of having sex or starting a family, but a few kisses and groping in the dark set my blood on fire. I was still a virgin, but I let your dad make love to me. It was so foolish. Neither one of us considered that just one moment of lust would result in a baby; I only thought about it after I got home and went to bed. Patti, I cried myself to sleep; I was so ashamed. I thought I loved your dad, but I realized later he didn't love me. It was a terrible mistake with no 'do-overs.' I can't control everything you do and don't want to; I want you to be safe and happy and not end up like I did...you deserved a dad. I know he would be proud of you."

Now it was Patti's turn to sit and look at her mom; Kathy

was crying. Patti stood up and moved toward her, holding out her arms; Kathy stood and they embraced. In a few moments Patti remarked, "Mom, I want you to know I understand. I have no intention of letting myself get into the mess you did. I promise to be careful. I'll keep my legs crossed. Thank you for being my mom and loving me."

Both of them were crying now; both of them knew their lives were changing. It wasn't easy being a mom and it wasn't easy being a kid, but maybe if they would work together...maybe they could get through this without anyone getting hurt. Love can be a very powerful thing, and teamwork makes the heaviest burdens lighter.

Meanwhile, Deb had taken Sarah out for ice cream, and they too visited about camp. Sarah had a wonderful time; she had learned how to swim; she had met new friends; and yes, she'd missed Deb. Deb was touched by her thoughtfulness. Sarah was a wonderful child, and Deb could not imagine how she could be that way, considering her previous environment. When Sarah finished her tales between bites of ice cream, Deb said, "Sarah, I really missed you, but I want you to know I took good care of the house and even fixed a few meals while you were away. I didn't want you to think I was completely helpless." Sarah smiled. "I'm glad you enjoyed camp and got to do some special things. You deserve your fun now. It's a lot harder to come by when you get older."

"I knew you would be all right, and I was only gone for about a week; you could live without me that long. I'm glad to be home; I'm looking forward to the rest of my vacation. I won't have to hide from anyone this summer!" Sarah sighed and looked relieved.

Deb laughed. "Just from me!" Sarah grinned.

Summer has a way of going too fast. Colby was home working with his dad; Patti had a few chores to keep her busy; and of course, Sarah had to babysit Deb. July brought Independence Day and fireworks, but other things were about to pop.

A couple from Patti's church had stepped forward to adopt Sarah. Neither Kathy nor Patti knew them. Their last name was Miller and they had two children, a boy who would be in the second grade and a little girl about four years old. Mrs. Miller had been given an opportunity to go back to work, and she did not want to leave her children. Her husband had suggested they could arrange to have an older child take care of their kids...then it occurred to them they could adopt someone, preferably a girl, to be part of the family and take care of the children. They were good people, but somewhat odd. Deb had gotten the word shortly after the Fourth; she was to meet with them, and if they met with her approval, they would meet Sarah. The meeting had gone well, although Deb was concerned they were looking more for a babysitter than a daughter; the Millers assured her while it might appear that way, they would not entrust their children to just anyone; an adopted daughter would be family and given these responsibilities as a family member, not as a servant or nanny. Deb thanked them for their candor and made arrangements for Sarah to meet them.

Sarah met with the whole family and talked for over an hour. She liked the children; they were polite and well behaved. Sarah agreed the parents were "different," but she sensed they had good hearts. She decided it was worth a try and didn't mind babysitting nor the responsibilities that went with it. These people were willing to provide her basic needs and much more. In addition, she would finally have a real family, one that would love and care for her. She would live with the them for thirty days. If everything was satisfactory, she would officially become a member of their family. Sarah became increasingly excited about this new prospect; Deb was devastated.

Deb and Sarah did their best to say goodbye, but it was not easy. Patti and her mother arranged to have everyone for a farewell dinner...big cake and all. It was both a happy and sad time. Everyone was happy for Sarah and her chance to have a real family, but everyone knew Deb was miserable. They tried to put on a happy face and enjoy their remaining time together. It wasn't as if Sarah was moving away or going to the moon; she would be right there in the community and in school just like before. The only difference was she would no longer be living with Deb. Everyone had agreed Sarah could visit Deb whenever it was convenient, but Deb knew Sarah's bedroom would be empty...and it was breaking her heart.

The day of transfer arrived. The Millers came and loaded what few things Sarah had into their car; Deb and Sarah hugged, then she got into their car and headed down the street to her new home. Deb had taken the day off; she watched the car until it was out of sight, then went inside. She walked into Sarah's empty room, sat down on her bed and began to cry; this must have continued for at least half an hour. She then went to the front room and picked up her service revolver, checking to see if it was loaded. She went back into Sarah's room, placed the gun on the bed, laid down and cried some more. When she finally composed herself, she got on the phone and called Patti. "Is there any way you could come to my place; I really need someone right now. Can you make it by yourself?"

Patti was not surprised to hear from Deb. "Sure; I'll get there, even if I have to walk."

Patti called her mother and asked if she could take her to Deb's; Kathy needed no explanation. Patti went to the hospital and met her mother, who drove her there. When they arrived, Patti's parting words were, "Mom, I may be here a while; I promise I'll call before I make any decisions; see you later."

Patti didn't bother to knock; she just opened Deb's unlocked door and went inside. The house looked tidy as Patti entered quietly; she looked around and thought she heard sounds from Sarah's room. She walked quietly to the door and surveyed the scene. Deb was on the bed crying, her revolver next to her. Patti approached her slowly. "Hey, Deb, looks like you're having a bad day; I hope you weren't planning to shoot me."

Deb seemed surprised, then looked at the gun. "No, Patti, the gun's for me; you're safe."

Patti quizzed. "So you're going to kill yourself, is that it?"

Deb replied rather casually. "I thought about it."

"Well, you're wasting your time. God doesn't want you to die."

Deb bristled. "Well, just what in the hell does God want from me?"

Patti appeared puzzled. "I wish I knew; I only know He loves and cares for you."

"Well, He's got a heck of a way of showing it! He gives me this delightful little girl to love, then takes her away. Does that make any sense to you?" Deb was angry.

"Nope, not one little bit, but something good will come from it. I know it."

Deb sat up and looked at Patti in amazement. "You really believe that, don't you?"

"Yes, I do. I don't know what God has planned for me, but He saved me in the park; I don't know what God has planned for Sarah, but He saved her in that alley; and I don't know what God has planned for you, but He saved you in your dorm room at school. I just know it, and maybe we're not supposed to know why. Maybe if we knew why, it would seem too scary or too much to deal with. All I know is you are an important part of God's plans, and that makes you special."

Deb sat looking at Patti; she didn't speak for the longest time. She finally held out her arms. "Hold me, Patti; I need someone close right now."

Patti moved toward her and they embraced; Deb was crying, and Patti struggled to hold back her tears. Finally Deb spoke. "You and your mother are the best thing that ever happened to me. I shouldn't ask, but would you do me favor. Would you be Sarah and stay with me tonight? We'll share her bed and maybe I can find some closure in this. Would you do that for me?"

"If that's what you want."

"Good. How about I put this gun away, clean up a bit and we go to the ice cream shop and enjoy our favorite flavors?" Deb licked her lips.

Patti made an awful face. "Oh Deb, you know how I hate ice cream, but since you've got a gun, I have no choice. I can't believe what I have to go through to be your friend."

⟫⟫ ⟪⟪

Patti and Deb visited; the ice cream was delicious. Deb had tasted a new and different life; it had scared her then became something special. She was now back where she had started, but something in her had changed; for the first time since she was little and wore dresses, Deb felt like a girl...a woman. She finally understood what love was...not romance and sex. She had experienced what it was like to love and be loved, and it was very good. Now these new feelings gnawed at her; they wanted out...to be part of her life, but she had lost the one person who had shared her love, and it was tough. Was Patti right? Was this just the beginning of something even bigger? Deb hardly believed in God; what could He possibly want from or for her? Sometimes life is bigger than everything else, and when that happens, we feel very small.

Patti called her mother and told her she would not be home this evening; she had to babysit; Deb was going to be okay, but it might take a while; she really needed their love, and Patti had placed her at the top of her prayer list. Kathy told Patti to offer whatever help or assistance Deb might need; it was the least they could do. Patti spent the rest of the day with Deb; they fixed supper, watched a little television, and finally went to bed. They held each other close; Deb cried for a long time; Patti kissed her on the cheek and told her she loved her very much. For the first in Patti's life, she actually felt like a mother, and it appeared for the first time in quite a while Deb felt like a little girl. As she fell asleep, she murmured, "Mama." Now it was Patti's turn to cry.

Sarah had lived with Deb for a little over ninety days, and Deb's life had changed. Patti assured her the next morning she and her mother would always be there for her; she was welcome to come by whenever she wanted. Deb was humbled and thanked Patti for her kindness. Deb was going to be okay; she decided she needed to get back to work and keep busy doing what she did best...solving crimes and getting scumbags off the streets. Work was cheaper than therapy.

Deb took Patti home, and life returned to normal, if there is such a thing. Patti was rather relieved about that, but sorry Sarah was gone. Peace and quiet was rather nice; it gave Patti a chance to collect her thoughts. Suddenly it occurred to her the end of July precedes the beginning of August. My gosh, school was about to begin; she would be an eighth grader. Patti reminded her mother they needed to do a little shopping for school related items; she would do an inventory to decide what she needed.

While this process continued, a few revelations occurred. Patti was not one to be vain; she didn't pay too much attention to herself. She knew she was not pretty, although certainly not ugly. She was plain and used to it. Even so, every now and then, it was important to check and make sure her nose was still centered between her eyes and one ear had not sagged below the other one. Patti was making such a check when she noticed something different; at least she thought it was different. Some of her freckles had disappeared; she couldn't remember washing her face any differently or using a wire brush to erase any grime, but some of her freckles were gone. Then there was this female thing; girls and their weird underwear. Patti hated wearing a bra; it was her mother's idea and she just could not understand why she needed to bother with it. She didn't have much to hold up. To make matters worse, the darn things felt uncomfortable. Sometimes, just to show her independence, Patti would skip that part of getting dressed in the morning; heck, some of the boys had bigger breasts than she did, and she was pretty certain none of them wore a bra. It was dumb! Lately her bras just didn't fit right; some of her other clothes didn't fit very well either. She and Mom needed to chat.

Kathy came home late and really tired. It had been one of those days when everything she started took too long and was much harder than it should have been. However, that didn't stop Patti. "Mom, I've got to talk to you; I know you're tired, but we need to visit. I'll help with supper if we can sit down for a few minutes and talk. Okay?"

"Oh, Patti, I'm afraid if I sit down, I won't be able to get back up...but sitting sounds like a good idea. What's up?" Kathy plopped into a soft chair.

Patti moved to her mother. "Do I look any different to you?"

"Oh, honey, I don't know; you look like my little girl, Patti."

"Ah, Mom, come on; take a hard look. I want to know."

Kathy gave her the once over. "I can't see anything on the outside. You're not hiding a tattoo under your clothes somewhere are you?"

Patti was annoyed. "Mom, I'm not that stupid; you'd probably kill me if I did something like that. No, look at my face. Don't you notice anything?"

Kathy tried to be funny. "Honey, everything is there...even both of your noses!"

"Mom, my freckles are disappearing. Can't you tell?" Patti was getting frustrated.

"Well, let me look; I think you're right, some of them have disappeared."

"What does it mean?"

"Honey, I don't know; remember when your Aunt Maggie was younger? She had quite a few freckles, but they disappeared. I'd say your freckled days may soon be over."

"Okay, Mom, there's another thing; all my clothes fit

funny, and my bra is awful. What's going on?"

"Well come here, and let's have a look."

Patti stepped up to her mother, who examined her closely, even checking for that tattoo. "Patti Linder, this isn't good."

"Oh no, Mom, what's the matter? Is there something wrong with me?" There was worry in Patti's voice.

"Yup, there is; you've got a dreaded teenage disease."

"I do? What is it?" Now Patti was really worried.

Kathy held a finger to her chin. "Well, it has a long medical name, but lay people call it...growing."

"Growing?" Patti's eyes got big.

"Yeah, I hate to tell you, but you're growing. That's why your clothes don't fit, and I'm afraid, dear child, that your breasts are growing too. Dolly Parton had better stand back and make room for another pair of big ones!" Kathy started to laugh.

"Sure, Mom...yeah, me and Dolly duking it out in the Miss USA Big Boobs pageant. You must have had a really bad day. I think you left your brain at work!"

However, Kathy was right; Patti had grown quite a bit since last year and was indeed filling out in the right places. It was kind of scary being a young woman, but eighth graders are only one year from high school, and a lot of high schoolers looked grown up, even if they didn't always act that way. One nice thing about growing bigger was getting some new clothes and even some new bras; they couldn't fit any worse than the ones Patti had now.

The new clothes did fit better. Patti called Colby to find out what he was doing and to remind him they needed to go to orientation and find out about their schedules. Colby had been so busy with his dad that he had not been very good about keeping in touch. His dad was planning a day off, so maybe Patti could come over and they could spend some time together and make plans; it would be fun.

Two days later they spent the whole day talking and trying to get back into school mode. Colby was anxious to find out about his schedule and hoped he and Patti shared several classes. He hadn't seen much of Geoff since May and missed him. In some ways, it would be nice to be back in school. Patti wanted to find out how Sarah was getting along with her new family. Everyone had good reason for school to start, but no one was in a great rush for it to happen; summer was just too much fun. Around mid afternoon, Patti convinced Colby to go for a walk. They soon ended up in the park and found their favorite bench. Patti then said, "Colby, I've missed you since camp; it's nice to be alone again."

Colby smiled and reached for her hand. "I missed you too; I was just thinking today how we haven't been together for a long time. Dad has been working us really hard; he wants to get all of his projects finished before school starts. I'm kind of surprised we aren't working today, but he had to be out of town. It's nice to be with you."

"Thank you, Colby. Do you still love me?"

"Do you have to ask? You know I do; in fact, I wanted to tell you earlier, but I don't like to talk about it at home. My mother doesn't approve of kids my age dating or going out; she thinks we're too young. I know she's right, but I still love you; you are special, and there isn't anyone in the whole world I would rather be with than you."

Patti leaned close to Colby and kissed him on the cheek; he returned her kiss. Patti put her arms around Colby and kissed him on the lips; Colby put his arms around Patti and held her tightly. They kissed again. Several moments passed. "Colby, how does kissing make you feel?"

"It makes me feel warm inside. How does it make you feel?"

Patti shivered. "Oh, I feel the same way; it even makes my

toes tingle."

"I would like to keep kissing you, but I don't think we should; Patti I'm afraid. I don't want to go too far; I don't want anything to spoil our friendship. We need to be careful."

"I know, Colby; I understand, but I would sure like to kiss you one more time. Would that be okay?"

Colby looked at her, nodded, and they kissed again. When they finished, they stood up, stretched, and started walking toward Colby's home. They didn't really say anything to each other until Colby's house was in sight. Patti slowed and spoke. "Colby."

"Yeah."

"I love you...and I wanted you to know..."

Colby injected. "Know what?"

"You're a good kisser."

"Ah, Patti..."

Patti, Colby, and Geoff arranged to go to orientation together; they hoped to meet Sarah too. Everyone was wondering about their schedules and even though thinking about school was painful, it was going to happen regardless of their feelings. Orientation was always the same. There was chitchat to welcome everyone; then someone talked about the new school year and rule changes. They picked up their schedules and took the optional tour of the building. Finally, there were treats and they were released for the day. Patti, Colby, and Geoff met at about the same time. After a while, they found Sarah on the other side of the building; she had just arrived. They discussed their summer...and yes, Sarah was happy with her new home although she had issues. The Millers were trying to work them out, but it would take time. She was looking forward to school and being with her friends.

The four companions agreed to meet as soon as they had their schedules; it seemed silly to take a tour of a building everyone already knew, so they would go to the cafeteria and talk schedules or other matters. When the assembly dismissed, the schedule lines formed, and they were soon headed for the cafeteria. They found a table, and the analysis began. Patti almost jumped out of her chair when she discovered Colby was in all but one of her classes, not counting PE, which they had decided was a good thing last year. Geoff shared most of his classes with either Patti or Colby, and Sarah had the same good fortune. There was one odd thing; Colby, Geoff, and Patti all had a question mark scheduled for their second semester exploration class. Geoff speculated it must be a secret class, so secret no one even knew what it was. Wow, maybe a class for learning how to become a spy or "secret" agent. Eighth grade was looking better all the time, and this gang of four was so distracted their treats seemed bland in comparison.

⤞ Twenty-Seven ⤝

When people reflect on their days in school, there are often memorable experiences: outstanding teachers, good friends, fun classes, special personal achievements, and even an embarrassing moment or two. Sometimes when we are lucky, a whole year turns out that way. For our four friends, this year would be their best, the one they would long remember, and for many reasons. None of them had ever hated school. Patti had always liked social studies and English, especially reading. Colby liked math and science. Geoff was a history nut and liked science. Sarah liked English and social studies but also liked crafts and wanted to learn to sew, cross stitch or knit.

As school began, the eighth graders had an assembly where the principal told them they were special, only one grade from high school, the oldest kids in middle school. As "big dogs" on campus, they were school leaders, helping set examples for younger kids. It was important they show good leadership. If they would cooperate and do these things, numerous bonuses would follow; they could make the whole school year better. The kids seemed to understand what he was saying, appreciating the opportunity to be rewarded for their good example.

The kids were also reminded they were not going to be in school much longer, and to begin thinking about what they wanted to do when they graduated. Eighth grade began what the school called career exploration; they would research and study careers, then in the tenth grade, and again when they were seniors. This would allow them to learn about different careers and to think about their future. Of the four friends, only Sarah had decided what she wanted to do, and that was to help abused and runaway kids; the other three had no clue, although Geoff thought running a crime syndicate would be exciting...which no doubt was true, but the question was how long he would live. Geoff bemoaned the fact he might have to give up this dream and find some boring job.

During the second week of school, Colby got a call to report to the office. It scared him; he couldn't think of anything he had done wrong, and his grades were okay. What was going on? When he got there, he was ushered into the eighth grade counselor's office where he was prepared to confess everything, even though he had done nothing wrong. Before he could speak, the counselor told him they needed to talk about next semester's exploration class. "You mean the secret class?" Colby was relieved.

"If you say so." His counselor appeared unimpressed. "Look, we would like to try something new this year; we'll call it an experiment; we are offering a limited number of students a chance to learn..."

Colby interrupted. "How to become a secret agent?!"

"No, not exactly, I think you've been watching too much television. We would like to offer algebra as an exploration class, and we tried to pick our best math students and give them first opportunity to enroll; we need your parent's permission." Had this counselor known ahead of time, he would never have used the "a" word around Colby. For Patti, the magic words were "I love you" and if that didn't earn a kiss then something was dreadfully wrong, but for

Colby, the magic word was "algebra," and that counselor came within a hair's breadth of being kissed; Colby was restrained by the fact that his counselor was a man, and the only man Colby had ever kissed was his dad. However, that did not keep him from standing up and offering to shake his counselor's hand. "Oh, thank you, thank you so much; my parents will sign the papers; this is wonderful!"

The counselor had never seen anyone so excited about taking any kind of class before and had to steady himself, but he managed to hand Colby the permission papers before collapsing in his chair. Colby headed back to class, but his feet never touched the floor.

The eighth graders had the last lunch period, a nice thing if the food was good; they were allowed to go back for seconds after everyone was fed. Patti, Sarah, Colby, and Geoff had agreed to sit together for lunch, so they picked a table and planned to meet there. On this day Colby was the first to arrive and had to wait for everyone else. When they did, he announced he had been offered a slot in the new algebra class...then was disappointed to discover Patti and Geoff had received the same offer, although he quickly realized this was a good thing because they would have the same class. He was so excited he could hardly eat.

During the first week of school, the eighth grade science teachers sponsored a contest for the kids to come up with slogans for the various science disciplines. Kids then submitted them to their teachers, who picked winners and awarded prizes. Geoff won a free pizza with his short but direct slogan, "Geology Rocks!" Another student won a free movie pass with his slogan on a Frankenstein theme, "Biology...It's Alive!" A girl won a fast food gift certificate with her slogan based on a song, "Let's get Physical. Levers Really Move Ya!" Another girl won her prize with a Shakespearean theme, "Fire burn, boil and bubble, Chemistry is Worth the Trouble!" Finally, another student won a gift certificate for writing a department theme, "Abandon all Hope for Those You Hold Dear. Only Weird Science is Practiced Here!"

In geography they were studying the United States,

reviewing names of the capitals, locating states on an outline map, and naming major rivers and lakes. One project was to find the name of an unusual town or city and write a slogan for it. The kids scrambled for their atlases and began to investigate. They found some very strange names. Geoff came up with, "Come to Gravity, Iowa, where Everything Is Down to Earth," Colby devised, "Always an Odd Moment in Peculiar, Missouri." Sarah invented, "Has Anyone Found Lost Springs, Kansas?" Patti created, "Nothing's Normal in Eerie, Indiana." Of course, the real topper was, "It's Always Very Hot or Very Cold in Hell, Michigan!" Geography can have its moments.

Shortly after school began, Sarah asked Patti if they could visit after school before her new mother picked her up. Patti quickly agreed; she was anxious to find out more about Sarah and her new family. A couple of days later, they met and sat on one of the benches under a large shade tree. Sarah spoke first. "Patti, I've wanted to talk with you for so long, but I just haven't had a chance; I know you must be wondering about my situation. The Millers are nice people; I know they care a lot for me, but Mrs. Miller spends entirely too much time worrying about everything. I think the poor woman might have a stroke. If she has to be gone and I'm supposed to babysit, she may spend an hour going over details of what I should or shouldn't do. I know she worries about her kids; I'd probably would to, but she drives me crazy going on and on. I know I've never taken care of kids before, but I'm not completely stupid. Like I'm not going to let them drink out the toilet or stick their head in the microwave. Her kids are not babies; four-and seven-year-olds weren't born yesterday." She paused for breath. "This sounds bad, but I'm not really unhappy. The kids are fun. We play games and do all kinds of stuff. Mr. Miller is nice, but I don't think he understands what is going on because he's gone a lot. I does help to talk about it, and maybe things will improve after Mrs. Miller gets to know me better."

Patti listened, not knowing what to say. "Sarah, I guess no place is perfect. Mom's not that way, but then she's gone all day and sometimes in the evening. It's hard for me to miss a dad I never had. You should go stay with Deb every now and then, just to get away. She really misses you."

"Oh, I know; I want to see her too; the court said they have to take me if I ask, but we've been so busy I haven't had time. I will soon...I promise; it will be fun. I miss Deb."

Just then Mrs. Miller pulled up. Sarah scurried to the car and was on her way home. Patti could tell Sarah was okay; it was too bad her new mother was a little crazy, but then maybe all mothers are.

Everyone looked forward to cooler weather. Patti took the bus home on hot days. A noisy, air conditioned bus was slightly better than a long, hot walk home, and Patti wasn't into sweating and being sticky, so a bus ride was tolerable. The beginning of fall brought little relief from the heat. The warm days may have caused other problems. Patti felt she had to compete for her mother's attention; it was hard to blame her, but Patti believed she could do better. Her mother often came home so tired she dozed off at the dinner table; she could not stay awake to watch television unless a show was very dramatic. She almost acted like someone who had drunk rather than eaten an evening meal. Patti did not understand why her mother didn't take better care of herself; she didn't fix her hair like she used to. She was sloppy around the apartment; Patti spent more time picking up after her than herself. Patti tried not to think about it because it made her mad, and since it persisted, that made it all the more annoying.

The weather finally cooled and seemed to help everyone get along better. Even school appeared to improve. As October began, some of their lunch discussions centered on the forthcoming Halloween dance. The middle school had no homecoming, so it had become a school tradition to have a Halloween dance as their social event of the first semester. None of them had ever gone to this dance, but this year Patti and Colby were giving it some consideration. Sarah didn't think she would be able to go, and Geoff wasn't interested in dancing. Of course, neither were Patti and Colby, but that was another matter; this would be their first "official" date, and the real shocker was that Colby had actually asked Patti if she would like to go. Talk about an offer you can't refuse; Patti was thrilled. Of course, they had to get permission.

Patti brought up the subject after supper. "Mom, Colby asked me if I could to go to the Halloween dance with him. Is that okay?"

"That's nice, but why do you want to go? You've never shown much interest in dancing."

"Well, it would our first real date. Colby's no dancer either, but it's a chance to be together. The dance will be chaperoned, so we can't get into any trouble. I think it would be neat."

"Okay, I guess it will be all right, but I want you to behave yourself and get right home when the dance is over. We don't want your first date to be your last!"

Colby fared about the same when he talked to his mom; she could not imagine why he wanted to go to a dance. He told her he had asked Patti to go with him...kind of like a date; he had never been to a dance, and now that he was in the eighth grade, his middle school days were about over. It would be fun. Mrs. Duncan had to agree his social life was nil. Perhaps the dance would be good for him; Colby's dad agreed. Whew, that was close; the first date was now official. The big question was what were the two lovers, who were not really dancers, going to do at a dance?

The Halloween dance was set, but life is more than a waltz, tango, or peppermint twist. Patti's Friday nights were still occupied with her youth group from church. Sarah tried to attend and occasionally came home with Patti after school on Fridays so they could go together. Patti had managed to get Colby to come a few times, but his Friday evenings were often planned for him. However, Patti was pleased that he enjoyed the group, and it did give them a chance to be together outside of school. Youth group was usually fun, and all the kids discovered the value of their Christian beliefs and working together to understand and answer some of life's big questions.

About the middle of October, Deb called to ask what Kathy and Patti were doing over the coming weekend; she had not seen them for quite a while, in fact, not since Patti had stayed with her. Deb had immersed herself in her work in order to forget about Sarah. It had not solved her problem, but it kept her from dwelling on it. Deb was no longer the same; she had found a soft spot inside but hardened on the outside. Patti could tell she was mad at God again; Deb was like that...angry at things she could not understand. Patti thought about talking to her, but realized she'd be wasting her time; Deb wasn't going to change, until Deb decided to change. Patti figured only God knew when that might be, and perhaps even God was confused. Deb was hard case.

They finally agreed she would come over late in the afternoon on Saturday. Kathy offered to cook dinner; Deb would bring a bottle of wine and a video or two; they would just relax and enjoy the evening. When Deb arrived, Patti noticed she looked a little different and when she inquired, Deb had to admit she had gained a few pounds now that she was cooking many of her own meals. When Patti asked her what kind of food she was making, Deb told her macaroni and cheese and wicked bologna sandwiches. At least Deb hadn't lost her sense of humor.

Deb wasn't talking much about anything; she and Kathy visited, but no big secrets surfaced. As the evening progressed, Deb seemed more relaxed and comfortable, even laughing a few times. When Kathy finally asked how she was doing, Deb told her she was fine although some days were tough; she had many mixed emotions and without warning would occasionally break out in tears. She tried to cover it up, but it was difficult dealing with her new feelings. Later in the evening, Patti and Kathy both discovered the real reason for her visit...and this time, it wasn't the food . Deb was rather embarrassed and it took several attempts before she finally asked, "Kathy, I was wondering if I could spend the night with you guys. I'm having problems staying by myself; I can't explain it. I get lonesome; I need some company. Would that be okay?"

Kathy looked at her surprised. "Deb, I've told you at least a dozen times you are always welcome here; Patti and I love you...you're almost family. If you would like to be here, then by all means please stay."

Deb hesitated. "Well, there's more to it than that."

Kathy had a curious expression. "Oh, I know."

"You do?"

"Yes, dear, I can read you like a book." Kathy smiled.

"You can?"

"Absolutely, you want to stay here and sleep with me; I think you'd like for me to hold you until you go to sleep...even give you a kiss good night."

Deb looked at Kathy rather surprised, saying nothing. She finally spoke quietly. "You're right; I need someone to hold me right now. I wish I understood what makes me feel this way. It's really strange."

"Deb, there's nothing strange about not wanting to be alone; I feel that way sometimes. I think maybe what we really need is a man...but what in the heck would we do with him if we had one?"

Deb quipped. "We could shoot him."

Kathy sighed. "Oh, yeah, what a way to treat someone you need for company. I worry about you."

Deb nodded. "Me too."

Deb spent the night and cried in Kathy's arms. Patti felt sorry for Deb, but believed her refusal to accept help from God was a mistake. Kathy's career in nursing was focused on healing, so supporting Deb was a natural response, but she had also seen a change. There was something softer, warmer; some of her rough edges were smoothing, and she seemed more like a person than a machine. Kathy liked the new Deb, but she wasn't so sure Deb did.

They had stayed up late, and there was no mention of early church or even getting up the next morning. Kathy woke first and noted how peaceful and relaxed Deb was. When Deb finally roused, she told Kathy she hadn't slept so well since summer. Kathy laughed and told her sleeping with her was better than a sedative, and Deb would benefit by taking advantage of the opportunity more often. Deb kissed Kathy on the cheek and told her she was surrounded by rascals; there was the little rascal, Patti, and the big rascal, Kathy, both trying to drive her crazy and ruin her life! Kathy swatted at Deb and told her to behave herself or she wouldn't get anything to eat.

Girls may want to have fun, but these girls were hungry, so they whipped up a late breakfast and enjoyed each other's company. Deb had to go to work right after noon, but before she left, Kathy made her promise to come back soon and not be a stranger.

During the next week, Patti came to a terrible realization. She had accepted Colby's invitation to the Halloween dance. However, this dance was not a costume affair, but a semiformal event; boys had to at least wear a shirt and tie with slacks, and girls had to wear a dress—not a formal, but something dressy. Patti had a lot of clothes but not one dress! Girls who climbed trees, ran through the park, and marched on day hikes at camp did not wear dresses. Nope, dresses were for pretty little girls, not for girls like Patti.

Patti approached her mother. Kathy was amused and told Patti they needed to go shopping. She needed more than a dress! Kathy explained nice clothes are more expensive, but she would get Patti whatever she needed—if she agreed to stay home and take care of her until she was thirty. Patti loved her mom, but sixteen more years at home seemed a bit much, and she had plans. Would Colby want to live with her at home if they got married? "Ah, Mom, are you sure you want me around that long? It's not all my fault; you're supposed to buy my clothes!"

"You make a good point. What say, we make it until you're twenty?"

Patti sighed. "I'll do my best."

So a shopping trip was scheduled.

Patti wasn't crazy about any of the dresses, but finally picked one she would wear; she then discovered she needed a new item of underwear called a slip. She would also look silly wearing her athletic shoes with a dress, so she needed dress shoes. Then there was the matter of stockings; most of the girls in the eighth grade wore panty hose, not socks. When Patti saw a package of panty hose, she flatly refused to even consider them. Just one slip up and a girl could get one of those long legs wrapped around her neck and strangle. Nope, no panty hose for Patti. If this wasn't bad enough, Kathy reminded her she couldn't very well wear a dress and expose hairy legs. Patti nearly had a heart attack; my gosh, she never paid any attention to her legs. They were inside her jeans! Was it too late to call Colby and cancel the whole affair? This was just more adult stuff getting dumped on kids. Why, it might even be against the law, and if not, it should be.

When Patti got home, Kathy made her try on everything but first checked those legs. Whew, they weren't too bad, just a little light colored fuzz; Kathy thought Patti could sneak by...especially, at night. To Patti's surprise, she liked her slip; it felt neat and as she put it, "It looked sexy."

"Why can't I just wear the slip and skip the dress, Mom?"

Kathy laughed. "Because you wear your underwear under your clothes, silly!"

"Oh." Patti was disappointed; she thought the dress looked ridiculous.

"Why, honey, you look nice; I think you'll be the belle of the ball."

"Mom, I don't know what that means, but if this was a real Halloween dance, I might win first prize for the scariest costume."

"Patti, you're a nut!"

The next week or two flew by and before anyone had time to think about it, the day of the dance arrived. Patti had a hair appointment about a half hour before school was out. Kathy picked her up and they headed for the salon. Patti was getting nervous, not just about the dance, but about her hair. Her mother or Grandma Bender had always cut her hair, and she was apprehensive about letting some stranger work on it. She had been letting her hair grow longer since summer; she didn't know why, but it turned out to be a good idea. Fortunately, Patti liked the lady at the salon, who made several suggestions about a new style; Patti was somewhat overwhelmed, but among the three of them, Patti, Kathy, and the hairdresser, they finally agreed on just one, and the work began. Patti was scared to look in the mirror while the stylist worked but was really surprised when she saw the final product. Was that really Patty Linder in the mirror or the image of someone they hired to make the customers feel good about their new "do"? Why, she looked nice; Kathy was impressed, and even the stylist remarked how pretty she was. Pretty? No one ever called Patti pretty, not even her mother. It was a good thing Patti was not wearing a hat; her head was getting bigger by the minute. No way it would fit!

All the way home Kathy kept telling Patti how sharp she looked, and Patti was embarrassed by the extra attention. She did look different, but she was the same old Patti with or without her hair. Kathy was still excited when they arrived at the apartment and asked Patti to try everything on again so she could get a good look at her. Patti was not impressed and grumbled about wasting time but complied because she knew her mother had gone out of her way to buy her clothes and fix her hair. When she showed Kathy the whole package, her mother was thrilled. "Oh, Patti, you look gorgeous; Colby will be so proud of you."

Patti was stunned; her mother had called her gorgeous. When Patti looked in the mirror, she definitely recognized who was there, but she was different...better. Fewer freckles, more figure, even taller. Patti began to wonder if she should have started this dancing business sooner. Kathy had her hurry around so they could show Grandpa and Grandma Bender the "new" Patti. They were very surprised and accused Kathy of trying to pass off some good looking stranger as their favorite granddaughter. Patti assured them it was her; on the other hand, it was almost Halloween. Their next stop was the Duncan's. When Mrs. Duncan came to the door, she too was quite surprised. "Why, Patti, you look so pretty in your new clothes." Patti blushed, but Mrs. Duncan went on and on, then took her to show Mr. Duncan, who winked at her and smiled. Patti liked Mr. Duncan; he was man of few words. When Colby came downstairs, he almost didn't recognize her. "Wow, Patti, you look great!" Patti beamed and told him he looked sharp in his jacket and tie.

The kids had arranged to walk to the middle school and then back to Colby's house after the dance. One of the Duncans would take Patti home. It had been a beautiful fall day, but the evening turned chilly. On their way, the two dancers held hands and walked quickly. Their first real date had begun. Kathy was right. Colby was proud of Patti. As they entered the school grounds, they slowed down, stopped, and looked at each other. Patti squeezed Colby's hand. "Thank you for inviting me to the dance."

"Hey, I wanted to do something special for my best friend."

They turned and walked toward the building. As they entered the door, Patti hoped no one could see the tears that ringed her eyes. Sometimes being with a best friend will do that.

The sponsors were aware that not everyone would dance the whole evening, so they partitioned one end of the lunchroom into a lounge area, so the kids could escape the music and noise to talk or enjoy refreshments. Patti and Colby made their way toward the lunchroom, Geoff's favorite place in the building. Strangely, as they entered the dance area, no one cheered or applauded. Of course, the room was darkened, and some kids don't pay attention to anything at school anyway.

Patti and Colby waited for the song to end, then moved

onto the dance floor. They did their best to keep up with the music and not look out of place, but the songs were shuffled and each dance was often different from the next. Patti liked the dances where Colby had to hold her close. Colby didn't care although he enjoyed being close to Patti. They realized after a few dances they were not likely to receive any awards. Colby had stepped on Patti's toes two or three times, and she had kicked him slightly once. Dancing can be dangerous, so they decided to give the lounge area a try. It was much quieter, and the soda was cold. There were firm rules also; students were allowed to only hold hands and no more. Patti and Colby sat for a while, enjoying their drinks and listening to the music. Soon they began to chat and time seemed to fly. Towards the end of the evening, they made their way back to the dance floor and finished the event in each other arms. Patti really liked that part.

When the dance ended, the two romantics headed for Colby's house. There was no hurry. In fact, even though it was chilly, those last two or three dances had worn them out; they needed to sit down and rest before they collapsed. At the far edge of the school grounds, a bench had been conveniently placed for such an emergency. "Colby, thank you for this evening; I love you."

Colby pulled her close to kiss her on the cheek. "You're very welcome."

They kissed again and held each other tightly. "Patti, I love you too; it's been fun and you look so pretty tonight. I guess I never realized you had legs until this evening."

Patti was a bit miffed. "Why Colby Duncan, we went swimming at camp together. What did you think those things sticking out of my swimsuit were, fins?"

Colby tried to escape Patti's wrath. "Well, I...er, I guess they must have been legs; I wasn't paying attention...uh, you know almost everyone has a couple of them."

"Well, I should think you would pay attention to the legs

of your best friend; I've seen your legs." Patti added to the drama.

"Gosh, I'm sorry; I won't make that mistake again. Besides, you have pretty legs."

Patti pulled Colby close and kissed him, then made a terrible mistake. She moved his hand to her bare knee and held it there as their kissing continued. Soon she began to feel strange; her body began to warm. It was cold outside, but she was heating up. What was going on? She realized she wanted Colby close to her; she was putty in his hands. Thankfully, he didn't know it. Then a terrible thought struck her; her mother had talked about how her blood was on fire the night Patti was conceived. Patti's blood may not have been on fire, but it was getting hotter by the second, and she was scared. She abruptly pulled away. "Why Patti, what's wrong?"

"Colby, I think we'd better get home; something's wrong with me."

"Are you sick?" He appeared quite concerned.

"No, I'm not sick. Do you remember our session at camp?"

"Yeah, I remember."

"Well, my mind and my body are having a fight, and my body is winning."

As Colby looked at her, the realization of what she said hit him. "Oh, my...okay, I understand. Has it gotten warmer out here since we sat down?"

A disappointed Patti spoke rather slowly. "Yes, I think so...a bit too warm."

Colby kissed her on the cheek and looked squarely into her eyes. "I love you, Patti."

"And I love you, Colby, with all my heart."

The two scurried to Colby's house, said goodbye, and Mr. Duncan took Patti home. On the way, he told her how nice she looked and that both he and Mrs. Duncan were proud of her. Patti thanked Mr. Duncan and told him he was special too; she thought he and Mrs. Duncan had really done a good job when they made Colby. Mr. Duncan acknowledged that Colby was quite a boy...not what he had expected, but remarkable nonetheless.

Patti hurried inside. Her mother was asleep. Patti slipped out of her dress and got ready for bed. She decided she would sleep in her slip; it made her think of Colby for some reason. Patti cried as she drifted away. Why does love have to be so sad?

The next morning when Kathy inquired about the dance, Patti told her it was fun and she would consider going again, but to be honest, the dancing was not important nor the refreshments grand. It was being with Colby that really mattered. He represented a part of her life, and yes, she could live without him, but it wasn't the same. Kathy understood but admitted her relationships with men had been extremely limited; she and Brandon had been together only about three months and even then had not seen each other often. However, Kathy had felt the same way about Sherry; life had always been more fun when she was around, and quite frankly, it had never been the same since she left. Patti omitted the romantic details of her evening; she did not want to get her mother worked up over something that never really happened, but it was her mother's example and warning that had restrained her. Despite their differences, Patti truly admired her mother's often frank conversations, and Patti had not forgotten that her own dishonesty two years earlier could have left her seriously injured or even killed. The thought of being raped and beaten in the park was abhorrent to her, and Patti was not going to make that mistake again.

With November just around the corner, the English teachers and eighth grade counselors initiated their unit on careers. The students were to pick a career, investigate it—which included a job shadow if appropriate—then write a term paper about that career and its various duties. Sarah was the only member of the four friends that even had a clue what she wanted to be. Geoff, Colby, and Patti were about to go crazy trying to decide. They even talked about it at lunch and finally determined rather than write about a career they might pursue, they would pick one to investigate and consider. Geoff finally decided to study geologists...since geology rocks! Colby chose to discover what chemists do. Patti remembered being with Sarah in physical therapy and how interesting it was, so she chose that career. They had been told they would all benefit from this investigation by learning not only what people do professionally, but also that many careers are extremely varied. For example, there are many different kinds of doctors, so that career choice created additional options. Their community did not have any geologists or chemists, but Sarah and Patti would be allowed to job shadow locally if they so desired. It was going to be a busy month for the eighth graders.

Patti was becoming more frustrated with her mother. Kathy had been working extra hours and odd shifts while the hospital tried to hire new help; she often volunteered for such duty because it was easier to adjust her schedule than for nurses who had families with younger children. Patti, however, resented this and saw it as neglect. Patti loved Kathy more than anything, even more than Colby. They got along well, had good visits, and rarely disagreed on anything. Sadly, her mother's neglect had encircled herself. She was increasingly messy around the house and acted as if the good fairy would show up to restore order. Sadly, the fairy's name was Patti, and she had her own messes to manage. Patti was becoming increasingly impatient, and issues that simmer often come to a boil.

Patti's research and writing continued as did job shadowing for an afternoon at the hospital, and a finished product began to emerge. Patti wanted to get her paper turned in before Thanksgiving break. Then she would indeed have something for which to be thankful...besides the food. Colby hoped for the same result, but he was not as gifted in the writing department, so his mother had to help him with his final draft; it all took more time. Neither Geoff nor Sarah was worried about getting the paper in before

December 1. Completing this project would remove a huge burden from everyone.

>~~~   ~~~<

Thanksgiving was special this year. Kathy had managed to get an extra day off so she would be home. Deb had agreed to come to Patti and Kathy's celebration. The Benders had never been "big" on Thanksgiving; they preferred getting everyone together at Christmas. However, they loved to eat, so they invited Patti, Kathy and any other family member, to join them. They always had a large traditional noon meal and then the men, or at least Mr. Bender, would cuss or discuss whatever football was on TV; it could get rowdy. The women adjourned to the kitchen or dining area to reminisce and discuss family issues.

While it was far from exciting, Patti still enjoyed being with her grandparents. She was their favorite, and only, grandchild. No one ever knew who would be there because Maggie and Jake were free spirits; they knew they would be welcome and no one made a big deal out of it. This year Maggie showed up and announced she had found a man—then admitted she wasn't sure if he had found her. They had dated and she really liked him, but they had issues, primarily related to Maggie's lifestyle. Maggie was a mess, nothing like Kathy; she had a good heart and Patti had always loved her, but she was goofy and unpredictable. She couldn't be depended upon, and her mother and Kathy had both warned her about it. Maggie understood but resisted their advice. Kathy figured one day Maggie would get "bit on the butt" and be forced to start acting her age. Sadly, it could be a painful lesson.

Jake came by in the afternoon to watch football; he was a lot like Maggie, but he was growing up fast lately and had been in a serious relationship with a girl who seemed well suited for him. He had eaten with her family, and she planned to visit the Benders later in the afternoon. Patti had never met her but was pleased the rest of the family was impressed; she had a good head on her shoulders and knew how to keep Jake in line. He had driven in the fast lane for two or three years at the end of high school but had calmed down a bit following a car accident. He had not been driving nor badly hurt, but it did "knock some sense into him" as Mr. Bender put it. He had met this girl at work, and she had him attending church and behaving almost like a gentleman. Patti had always enjoyed Jake; he knew how to have fun.

Jake told Patti privately he was going to ask his girlfriend to marry him at Christmas. Patti kidded him by asking if she would say yes. Jake felt confident she would; he really loved her. She reminded him of his mother; there were some things that were just no nonsense with her, and he respected that. His girlfriend was much the same way, and he admired her good sense and loyalty. Patti told him she would pray for him, and God would work things out. Jake responded with an, "Amen."

><>< ><><

Patti and Kathy planned their celebration on Saturday. Deb was coming over Friday night; they would have a light evening meal, watch a video or TV, and get to bed early for the next day. Deb actually wanted to help with the meal, and she planned to spend the entire day with them. They had debated for a week or two what to eat; everyone decided too much turkey can be fatal, so they finally chose lasagna, or as Deb called it, the traditional Italian Thanksgiving meal. Patti insisted they don't celebrate Thanksgiving in Italy, so Deb finally opined if they did, it would be lasagna. They would fix a big combination salad with garlic bread and pumpkin pie with ice cream for dessert. If anyone didn't get full, they deserved to die. Kathy could be very blunt!

Deb arrived at about mealtime on Friday evening in good spirits. Nasty crime was always down at Thanksgiving; domestic disputes arising from family and football issues were up, and then they had to deal with bargain-crazed shoppers willing to kill for a cuddly bear or electronic device. It could get pretty scary, and if it scared Deb, it was scary. They had a relaxing evening; everyone had enjoyed their holiday. Deb was looking forward to helping with lunch, and Kathy kidded her about her sudden interest in cooking. She had been experimenting at home and had expanded her skills to include deluxe macaroni and cheese and a special bologna sandwich. Wow, Deb was becoming quite the chef!

Deb asked to sleep with Kathy and they snuggled together; this time there was no crying. Deb was dealing with her loss, but every now and then she would kiss Kathy on the cheek. "Oh Kathy, I really need a man." Deb sighed.

Kathy groaned. "How about shutting up and letting me get some sleep?"

"Hey, you're no fun."

Kathy kissed her on the cheek. "I know. Good night, Deb."

They didn't exactly sleep in the next day, but no one got up early. Italian Thanksgivings do not require quite as much prep time as the traditional one; it is not necessary to thaw out a twenty-pound dead bird or make a washtub full of stuffing to fix lasagna. After a small breakfast, the happy chefs organized ingredients and started preparing their midday dinner; it required some effort to keep out of each other's way. However, once they got things figured out, the meal began to take shape. Pasta was cooking on the stove, hamburger browning nearby; vegetables being washed; and everyone was getting hungry. Deb insisted you cannot make Italian food without a little wine; she had already chilled the glasses and poured a small glass for everyone, even Patti. Patti was always willing to try wine but did not find it tasty; Deb and Kathy seemed to enjoy their occasional sips, and Patti was amazed anyone could really like the stuff. Sometimes she worried about adults.

Patti didn't think it was the wine, but Deb seemed to be having a lot of fun helping with dinner; in the past, Deb's only contribution to any meal was eating it. When Kathy kidded her about becoming a real cook, Deb laughed and said it was unlikely, but she did want to learn a few things and what better way than with her two crazy friends. Patti told her to be nice; Deb insisted she had given them the benefit of the doubt by not calling them "real" crazy. It was not long before one pile of ingredients looked like lasagna and another pile looked very much like a combination salad...and as Deb put it, "the only thing better than eating is...eating again." If anyone had not been hungry before, they were starved now. Deb asked if she could eat it raw, but Kathy insisted it would not be the same and had it in the oven before further complaints.

Lasagna doesn't bake forever, and it wasn't long before the hungry girls were at the table enjoying their meal. Deb thought she had died and gone to that great lunchroom in the sky. As she put it, "Those Italians really know how to celebrate Thanksgiving!"

Kathy observed, "I know how a turkey must feel this time of year; I'm absolutely stuffed." No one wanted to argue. Of course, there was still dessert, but the Thanksgiving pigs decided to forego this treat until later. One more bite could be their last, and no one wanted to die until they had eaten the pie and ice cream.

There's a chemical in turkey which makes us drowsy; while that may not be said of lasagna, it still had the same effect. The gang was more than a bit sluggish; they acted more like zombies than anything mildly alive. After a short time, Kathy, the resident medical expert, announced everyone was going walking in the park before they all died in her apartment. This proclamation was not received with the joy and enthusiasm it deserved, but by a series of moans and groans. However, it wasn't long before she had her two comrades on the way to the park. Deb estimated it would require at least one hundred round trips to burn off the calories from their first helping of lasagna, and she was certain this entree had been passed around three or four times. "My God, we'll be here all afternoon." These comments touched Kathy's sensitive side, demanding both of them to march or die. There was weeping, wailing, and gnashing of teeth, but the gluttons knew who put the food on the table, so they reluctantly complied.

Back inside, they spent half an hour or so picking up their mess from lunch and getting everything in order. They had several videos and decided to enjoy one before eating more. The afternoon and evening went well; the pie and ice cream was delicious, the first video enjoyable. Deb seemed more at ease, much more chipper than in October. It was a pleasant time and they had much for which to be thankful. After another movie, it was time for a good night's rest.

In the morning, Deb went out of her way to thank everyone for the wonderful time. Naturally, Patti and Kathy were pleased she was happy. They made a good team, and now that Deb had developed an interest in cooking, she could actually participate in preparing meals and learn a few things to apply in her own kitchen. She couldn't stay long this morning; she had to work a shift on Sunday to fill in for others who had family obligations. After Deb left, Kathy and Patti both noted how much she had changed and how much more fun she was. Sarah had transformed Deb in more ways than anyone had realized, and even though it had been tough on her, she had grown from this experience into a better person. Deb even admitted she was keeping her house cleaner and actually looked forward to taking care of it. No doubt about it, Deb was something else. Perhaps that's why Kathy and Patti truly loved her.

When school started, some of the kids were scrambling to get their papers done before the dreaded deadline. This paper was a major part of their first semester grade, and no one was likely to pass without finishing it. Colby and Geoff were done with all of their work; Sarah and Patty had turned in their papers before the holiday, and everyone was much relieved. All they had to do was survive about three full weeks of school and it would be Christmas vacation. It didn't matter if Santa was coming or not; they were anxious for a longer break. School seemed to fly by and the teachers were doing their best to finish the first semester, not too far behind; no one needed more work to do in the spring, so amazingly, everyone finished most assignments on time to end the semester.

However, while school was running smoothly, the home fires raged, or depending upon perspective, barely flickered.

ᗒᗒ Twenty-Eight ᗕᗕ

The weeks following Thanksgiving were difficult for Patti, watching the relationship with her mother slip away. Patti loved her mother more than anything, but Kathy was so wrapped up in her work that she had no time for anyone, including herself. Patti worried about her mother. Kathy looked tired and almost old; there was no question she came home exhausted, and in that condition had little to offer anyone. Patti had to take on more responsibilities, and she resented it. She didn't mind helping; she was glad to do that, but it was almost as if she had become the mother and Kathy her daughter. Kathy forgot things; it was impossible to visit with her because she could fall asleep at the drop of a hat. Patti worried about her driving home, especially when she worked nights. One thing for sure, Kathy did not want to talk about it, and that disturbed Patti about as much as anything. What could she do?

Patti had tried rebellion during the fifth and sixth grade and had been lucky to escape with her life. She had not forgotten her late night park experience and had no desire for a rerun. She had also tried the "get along and go along" approach, but her mother seemed to not notice. What else was there? Patti thought and prayed. No lights flashed, nor bells tolled, and she became impatient. After all, she would graduate from high school in four or five years and likely leave home. She didn't want to end up like Aunt Sherry and have no one to turn to if things got bad. However, an idea had been bouncing around; it frightened her because it might make things worse. Should she confront her mother head on, gloves off, and no holds barred? It could get ugly...perhaps so ugly that Patti would have to leave, and where would she go? Patti didn't want to think about it, but it was difficult to ignore.

The last straw landed about a week before Christmas vacation. New Year's Eve was on Saturday. The youth group had a tradition of having a New Year's Eve party for their group and any guests. This year there was a conflict; AFLAME met on Friday nights. The kids thought it silly to have their meeting on Friday, then the party the next day.

After considerable discussion, someone suggested they combine both events. Of course, the question then arose, which night...Friday or Saturday? After further discussion, the majority thought Friday would work best...so the event was scheduled. In and of itself, this was not a problem.

The conflict began when Kathy announced her parents had planned their year-end family gathering on the same evening as the youth group event. Kathy insisted Patti go with her; Patti wanted to go to the youth group party. Patti was not a fan of westerns but could envision she and her mother facing each other in the street, six shooters blazing. One of them would have to die! Patti didn't want to fight with her mother, but she didn't want to miss her party. After some thought and prayer, she laid down her gun and decided to make a deal. "Mom, we have a problem. I want to go to our youth group party, but it's scheduled the same night as Grandpa and Grandma's family event."

"Honey, I'm sorry, but I want to be with my folks, and you should be there too."

Patti complained. "Well, I don't think it's fair, but I'll make a deal. I'll go with you to see your family, if you promise to give me the whole afternoon the next day."

Her mother was curious. "Why do you need the whole afternoon? What do you want?"

"We need to talk about some things; it's very important."

"Well, we're talking right now. Why can't we take care of the problem today?"

Patti was getting impatient. "Look, I don't know how long it will take and I need your full attention." Kathy was puzzled but finally agreed; they even shook hands on it. Another battle was about to begin, and Patti was scared.

School ended, vacation began, and life seemed good. Even the weather cooperated; it was cold, but it was December. It always seemed like Christmas vacation roared through like an express train, but this year it held a dread in reserve. Each day moved Patti and her mother closer to the abyss; plus Patti had seen nothing indicating anything positive was about to happen. This train wreck was unavoidable.

Patti had fun at the Bender's party; she always enjoyed seeing Maggie and Jake; she loved her grandparents, and even Uncle Bob had shown up for a while. He was helping with the New Year's Party but wanted to say hi. Patti thought her mother had a good time; she also enjoyed her relatives, some of whom she hadn't seen for a while. On the way home, much later that evening, Patti reminded her mother about their "deal;" Kathy had not forgotten. They would visit after lunch.

Before school was out, Patti had made a bold move; she asked Colby to come over on Saturday afternoon. Colby wanted to know why. Patti told him she had to talk to her mother and needed a witness. Colby was puzzled, and if he had known what was about to happen, he would never have agreed to be there. In some ways Patti was ashamed of herself for deceiving Colby, but she felt his presence would give her extra courage to meet this challenge; she also knew if she told Colby to keep his lips zipped, no one would know what happened.

Colby remembered and arrived just after lunch; Patti hastily informed him she and her mother were about to have a confrontation. He did not have to say anything and if it turned ugly, he could leave; Colby was caught off guard but chose to stay because Patti had asked. When Kathy wanted know why Colby was there, Patti told her he was her witness. Kathy immediately became suspicious, but she had promised Patti and intended to keep her word.

They sat in the living area and Patti began, "Mother, I want you to know that except for Jesus, I love you more than all the world. You have always been good to me and cared for me. I don't think anyone could have done better. It's important you believe me."

"Why Patti, how nice of you to say so. Yes, I do believe you. I have always felt you loved me." Kathy was flattered.

"Good, I'm glad you believe me because I know what I am about to say may upset you. You are the only family I have; I don't have a dad or any brothers or sisters...no family, but you. If you were to die, I would be all alone, just like Sarah..."

Kathy interrupted. "Oh no, my family would take care of you if something happened to me; you don't have to worry. What makes you say this?"

"Mother, I'm losing you. I know you're not dying. I'm sure you're in perfect health, but have you looked at yourself lately? Do you pay any attention to our apartment? Do you ever think about who you are and who I am?"

Kathy looked at Patti, her expression became more serious. "I'm not sure I understand. What do you mean?"

"I mean when I was a little girl, I had the prettiest mommy in town, I had a mommy who took care of me and our home and cared about us. You don't care anymore. I come home from school and pick up your things and try to put them away. You don't fix yourself up to go to work; sometimes you don't even comb your hair. Mother, you are beginning to look old, and you're not even thirty-two."

Kathy's expression hardened and her look became more of a glare; she rose from her seat, looking right at Patti, who also rose. "Now listen here, young lady, I'll have none of this. How can you be so hateful to embarrass me in front of Colby when you know I love you..."

Patti interrupted. "No, you don't love me, and I don't believe you ever have."

Kathy almost shouted. "Why I never...I don't know what's got into you, but I'm not listening to any more of this...I should just slap you right across the mouth."

Patti was not nearly as big as her mother but stepped forward. "You mean like this?" She slapped her mother very hard on her cheek.

Fire shot from Kathy's eyes; Colby's eyes bulged; Patti stood her ground. Kathy had instinctively raised her arm to strike Patti; her hand started forward; Colby closed his eyes; Patti prepared herself for the blow. Then...something happened. Kathy's arm stopped; she gasped, sagged, and slumped down on her seat. Her face fell into her hands, her body racked with sobs. Tears began to flow through her fingers and drip on her clothes. Patti was crying too. Colby could not believe what he had seen; he knew if he hit his mother, it would be the last thing he'd ever do, but of course, he was unaware of the agreement Patti and her mother had made nearly two years earlier.

For a while, there was no talking, only crying, but as the sobs subsided, Patti, who had also sat down, began to talk softly. "Mother, can you hear me?"

Kathy nodded. "Yes."

"Can we finish our talk?"

"Do you still want to hurt me?"

"Mother, I've never wanted to hurt you. I want to help you; I love you."

"How is this going to help me?" Kathy sobbed.

"Mother, you have to face your enemy, and it is you."

"What do you mean?"

"Mother, the reason you don't love me, and I'm not sure you can love anyone, is that you don't love yourself. I'm sure of it. You cannot get over a mistake you made about fourteen years ago, and it is eating on you like acid. It's not your fault, but every time you see me, you are reminded of that mistake. I believe if you are to be truly happy, I will have to leave and that is what I am prepared to do. I love you too much to see you throw your life away..."

Kathy quickly injected. "Oh no, Patti, you can't! Please don't leave me; I don't think I could live without you. I do love you. Can't you see?" Kathy began to cry again.

"No, Mother, you don't love me; you want to love me, but you can't. You have to feel worthy to give or receive love and you don't feel that way. It is breaking my heart." Patti now started to cry.

"What can I do? How can I be worthy?"

"Mama, you've got to forgive yourself."

Kathy sobbed. "Oh God, how can I do that?"

"I'm not sure; that's the problem; I'm just not sure." Patti continued to cry. "But I want to help you; I want you to love me. You are a good mother!"

Patti sat there not knowing what to do; her mother was a wreck, crying and sobbing uncontrollably. After a few minutes, Patti got up and moved toward her mother. She managed to get hold of one of her hands, then leaned toward her and spoke softly, "Mother, do you think you could forgive yourself if God forgave you?"

"Oh, Patti, I don't know; I am so ashamed. You can see right through me, and I've been such a fool. I don't think even God can forgive me." Kathy tried to collect herself.

"You're wrong, Mama, God will forgive you; He loves you. I know He does. Can we try something?" Patti continued to hold her.

"Oh Patti, don't waste your time with me; I'm not worth it."

"Mother! Do I have to slap you again? Listen to me...let me try to help!"

"What do you want me to do?"

"Will you get down on your knees so we can pray? I have to ask you some questions."

Kathy moved forward, slipping off her seat, and knelt on

the floor; Patti was already kneeling at her side. Patti took her other hand away from her face and held it tightly. "Mother, I have to ask you some important questions and we need to pray, okay?"

"I'll do my best."

"Mama, are you a sinner?"

"Oh Patti, you know I am; I've failed you."

"Do you believe Jesus is the Son of God?"

"Yes, I do."

"Will you accept Him now as your Lord and Savior?"

"I don't understand; why do I need to do this?"

"If you accept Him as your Lord and Savior, He will forgive your sins and enter your heart. Now please, answer my question."

Kathy looked into Patti's eyes, her voice softened. "Yes, I will."

Patti squeezed her hands tightly and pulled her mother toward her; they were very quiet for several minutes. Patti pushed her mother away ever so slightly and asked her to bow her head and pray, telling God first that she was a sinner, followed by her belief that Jesus was the Son of God, and finally that she accepted Jesus as her Lord and Savior. Kathy bowed her head, and Patti placed her hand on her mother's shoulder while she prayed. Patti felt her mother tremble; her tears began to flow.

After a few moments, Patti said. "Now, Mother, ask Jesus to help you forgive yourself; ask for some sign so you will know you're forgiven. He will do that for you."

Kathy remained silent. Then suddenly she looked straight at Patti with a look that almost unnerved her. "Patti, I feel strange inside. I can't describe it. It's kind of like how I feel when I've had a glass of wine, only it's not in my stomach."

Patti looked at her, tears flowing from her eyes; she pulled her mother close and hugged her. Then she kissed her mother on the cheek and kissed her again. Patti looked into her mother's eyes. "That feeling comes from Jesus; He's in your heart now."

Kathy looked at Patti. "Oh, honey, you've saved me."

Patti shook her head. "No, Mama, Jesus saved you."

Throughout this episode, Colby had remained silent; he had never seen anything like what had just transpired, but right before his eyes, Patti's mother had changed. He couldn't explain it; he wasn't even sure what happened; but she was different. Colby didn't know much about miracles, but maybe he'd just witnessed one. From where he was sitting, Patti had started something that only God could finish...and it was truly remarkable.

Everyone remained quiet for quite some time; mother and daughter remained embraced, and Colby had no desire to disturb them. It was a strange silence considering what had just happened, and its peacefulness permeated the room. However, Kathy broke the silence and spoke in the kindest voice. "Say, why don't you and Colby find something to do; I have chores to finish."

Colby and Patti moved to her side of the apartment and began to share Christmas and holiday stories. Patti couldn't help noticing her mother was busily picking up and putting things away; she then cleaned and dusted; the apartment began to shine. Patti hadn't seen her mother work like this in ages. Patti decided to keep an eye on her.

Colby and Patti continued to visit but nothing was said regarding the confrontation. Patti asked Colby to not say anything to anyone about what had happened; she also thanked him for being there; his presence had made a difference. Colby was rather confused but told Patti he was glad she was pleased; he liked to make her happy.

Later in the afternoon, Kathy asked Colby if he wanted to stay for dinner; she knew it was New Year's Eve but had no idea what his plans were. Colby said his family had nothing planned, and if he called his mother, he was certain she wouldn't care if he stayed. She then asked what they would like to eat and Patti suggested pizza, whereupon Colby headed for the phone to get permission to stay. He really liked pizza and knew Kathy was a good cook. His mother said it was okay but wanted him home at a reasonable time; they had a few plans for New Year's Day, and he might need to get up early.

Patti and Colby decided to walk in the park. The fresh air smelled good and the cold was invigorating; the park was quiet and they enjoyed the sights of winter. Patti finally commented. "Colby, about my mom, I had to do something; I was losing her. I just couldn't stand by and let her go. I don't know if you understand, but I hope we've saved her; she's acting strange but hasn't done anything crazy. Thank you for being here; you're the best."

"Patti, you really scared me today; I thought for sure you and your mom were going to fight. I'm just thankful you got things worked out before anyone got hurt. I hope your mom is okay; I like her, and I want her to be happy too. I want the best for both of you."

Patti quickly leaned over and kissed Colby on his cheek; Colby was taken by surprise. "Hey, cut that out; you're getting awfully friendly."

"But I like to kiss you. Why don't you kiss me back?"

"You know, I think I will." He leaned over and kissed her on the cheek.

"Thank you; that was nice. We should practice it more often."

Colby smiled. "Patti, sometimes I think you're preoccupied with kissing."

"Yeah, sometimes I feel that way too...when I'm with you."

Patti smiled just like Colby.

When they returned to the apartment, it smelled of hot pizza, and both of them were instantly starved. Kathy had set the table and they each had a glass of wine...well, it turned out that Patti and Colby's wine tasted just like grape juice, but they called it wine anyway. Kathy brought the hot pizza to the table and sat down. "I think we should have a toast or two; Colby, why don't you start?"

Colby felt a bit awkward, but picked up his glass. "To my best friends in the biggest apartment in town."

Everyone tipped their glasses, sipping their "wine." Then Kathy said, "To the best kids anyone could ever have."

They tipped and sipped. Patti raised her glass. "To the best mom in the whole world."

They tipped their glasses for the last time. In the darkened room, it was hard to see the tears in the girl's eyes; even Colby felt his eyes watering. It had been quite a day.

They enjoyed their pizza, but there would be no leftovers for tomorrow; some pigs ate it all. The same pigs drank all their "wine" too. Kathy suggested they get some ice cream for dessert, and since she had to be out, she could pick up a movie to watch before Colby left. The kids gave her some ideas and she hurried off. While she was gone, Colby and Patti cleaned the supper dishes and put things away; the place looked reborn when Kathy returned, and she thanked them for being so considerate.

Kathy asked if they would be able to eat ice cream and watch a movie at the same time; some people have trouble multitasking. Patti and Colby thought they could handle it, so the ice cream disappeared as the movie ran its course. Everyone was having a lot of fun and Patti was happy that her mother was enjoying herself. When the movie ended, Kathy offered to take Colby home.

When she returned, she asked Patti if she wanted to stay up and bring in the new year. Patti told her she was tired and just wanted to go to bed. Kathy agreed. It had been a long day; a good night's rest would be welcome. Patti got ready quickly; her mother busied herself in the living room and kitchen for a few minutes, then turned out the lights and got into bed. The apartment was dark and quiet, but after a short time, Patti could hear her mother crying. Patti quietly got up and tiptoed to her mother's bed. She stood there for several minutes. "Mama, are you all right?"

Kathy was startled. "Oh, honey, I'm okay; go back to bed."

Patti held her ground. "Why are you crying?"

"I'm okay; I was just feeling sad, that's all."

"What about?"

"Oh, honey, just go back to bed."

Patti persisted. "No, I want to know why you were crying; you don't cry just for fun."

"Okay, I was crying because I feel bad I have not been a good mother to you."

"It's okay, Mom."

"No, Patti, it's not okay; you were right about me. I've been selfish and foolish; I've almost let one dumb mistake ruin my whole life and cause you needless pain. It was wrong and I should have known better."

"It's okay, Mom."

"Why do you keep saying that?" Kathy seemed annoyed.

"Because I forgive you, and I hope you'll forgive yourself; I love you." Patti started to cry.

"Oh, Patti, I love you too...with all my heart." Kathy was crying much harder. Patti pulled back the covers and slipped into the bed with her mother. She scooted close and did her best to put her arms around her; Kathy

355

returned the gesture.

Both of them were crying hard, but finally Patti managed to say, "Mother, I do believe you; I'll stay with you tonight."

The next morning was New Year's Day and Sunday. Patti was sleeping soundly when her mother nudged her. "Hey, sleepy head, you need to get up; we're going to church."

"What?" Patti groaned, still half asleep.

"You need to get up; we're going to church."

"We are? Now?" Patti was trying to get everything in focus.

"Yes, we are. The last time I checked it was Sunday, the day most people go to church; you need to get around."

Patti was still trying to wake up. "Mom, we don't usually go to church."

"That may be, but we're going today. You want to come with me, don't you?" Kathy was getting impatient.

"Sure, I guess so. Isn't this kind of sudden; I mean, you never want to go to church unless I threaten you with family secrets...like holes in your underwear or wearing your socks on the wrong feet..."

Kathy interrupted. "Patti, stop being silly and get ready; we'll have breakfast when we get home; I don't want to be late."

"Okay, I'll do what I can; I'm sure glad the early service is informal...cause informal is what I'm going to be!"

Since this was New Year's Sunday the service ended differently, the leader invited everyone to come forward and share their New Year's resolutions with God, thus strengthening their commitments. Without hesitation, Kathy stepped forward and knelt at the altar; Patti was shocked her mother had so boldly taken a place there. Patti hadn't thought about any resolutions but decided to step forward and say a prayer for her mother and was soon kneeling beside her. Shortly, they stepped back to their seats. The leader blessed everyone and dismissed them into a world much in need of Christian service.

On the way back to their apartment, Patti asked, "Mom, what did you pray about?"

"How about we talk about it when we get home, all right?"

"I'd like that."

When they got back to their apartment, Kathy put some things out for breakfast and directed Patti to the living area, where they sat down next to each other. Kathy looked at Patti. "I want to thank you for "knocking" some sense into me yesterday; I'm lucky to have you. I also want to thank you for sleeping with me last night; I needed company." Patti nodded. "Yesterday was the first time in my life I ever humbled myself before God and asked Him to enter my life. Now I believe God has spoken to me; well, maybe I should say God has ordered me to make some changes. It's only fair to share what I'm going to do. When I'm done, let me know what you think; it's really important.

"First of all, I'm going to attend church every Sunday from now on...no exceptions, unless I'm dead. I hope you will come with me. I want to see if we can get Grandma and Grandpa Bender to attend also; I hope you will help me talk them into it. I'm going to quit my job at the hospital unless I can get regular hours so I can be home with you as much as possible. You'll be gone soon and I want to spend as much time with you as I can. I'm going to start reading my Bible every night; I hope maybe we can read together. Finally, I'm going to be the mother you deserve. I want you to keep my nose to the grindstone and help me keep this commitment. It is very important to me. I also want you to know I love you with all my heart." Kathy fought to hold back her tears.

Patti sat stunned. One of two things had happened. Either her mother had lost her mind when Patti slapped her, or God must have talked to her. Patti hoped it was the latter, but this was quite a change. "Mom, I don't know what to say. We need to find that board the drug dealer used on Sarah and give me a whack on the head too. I can't believe it; this is wonderful. I want to help any way I can. It would be great to get your folks to go to church; Grandpa will be a tough sell, but I think we can do it. I would love to read the Bible with you. I like early church; I can go with you. I hope you don't have to quit your job; we need the money, but I'm glad you want to be with me. I love you."

Patti figured they had just started the new year in the best way possible. Yes, her mother had changed...but she had said good things in the past and been unable to deliver; the big question was whether or not she would come through this time. Little did anyone know that more changes were in the wind...and it would be more than just a breeze.

⤞ Twenty-Nine ⤝

Kathy was on a mission; she didn't know if it was a mission from God, but she was on a rampage...and no one was going to stop her. Monday morning was much like every Monday except Patti got to stay home while her mother went to work. Kathy said nothing about her plans to Patti, but she had rehearsed a million times what she needed to do when she got there. While she felt she was doing the right thing, she did sense, in the pit of her stomach, an uneasiness that definitely took the edge off her confidence. She got to work a few minutes early, went to the nurse's locker area, removed her coat, then added the finishing touches to her uniform. Other nurses and staff were arriving, and she could not help noticing they seemed to be paying a lot of extra attention to her. Her immediate reaction was to assume she had committed the grievous error of wearing only one stocking, buttoning her uniform crookedly or not at all, or something worse. She quickly checked to see if anything was amiss but found nothing. "What in the world are these people looking at."

Finally, one of the nurses on her shift stepped over to her. "Kathy, did you do something to your hair...maybe wear new makeup? You look really nice today."

Kathy was taken back. "No, nothing new...I did get up early and had more time in the bathroom, but I used the same old brush and curling iron I did last week. Hey, thanks for the compliment; they can be scarce around here."

Kathy was puzzled; she quickly checked again in the mirror of her locker; yep, it was the same Kathy Bender that stood in front of the mirror at home. Oh, well...

All the attention had momentarily distracted her, but she was now back on track; she must talk to the nursing supervisor before she did anything else. No one had better even think about dying for the next few minutes or she would kill them...well, perhaps not. The nursing supervisor was in her office, and Kathy marched in as if she owned the place. "Nurse Jackson, it's really imp..."

Nurse Jackson had looked up with a surprised expression, smiled and interrupted. "Kathy, I'm so pleased you came in; I really need to talk with you. I meant to say something last week, but the year was ending and I couldn't buy an hour of time for a million dollars. Something important has come up and since it involves you, I guess it's only fair to see what you think. I hope it's okay."

Kathy, caught off guard by her enthusiasm, replied. "Why, yes...sure, that would be nice."

"This is not a short story; please bear with me. Perhaps you know or have met our intern, Dr. Bradford." Kathy nodded. "Well, we have been very pleased with him and think he would make a fine addition to our staff. You may have also heard that Dr. Reynolds plans to retire in the next few months, and we need to replace him. We have offered Dr. Bradford a position here, and we think...keep your fingers crossed...he is going to accept. He likes our facility; he tells us he enjoys working with our staff; and he even likes the community. Now, I know you are thinking; what does this have to do with me? If Dr. Bradford accepts our offer, he will require a full-time nurse. Dr. Reynold's nurse wanted to retire two or three years ago, but she could not turn over the reins to someone else, and to be honest, it would not surprise me if they got married after they leave. I think they've grown quite fond of each other over the years and both of them have lost a spouse...so retirement cards and wedding bells may be in order.

"Anyway, we simply do not have a nurse for Dr. Bradford on staff. You are the best nurse in the building, but you have not worked in that capacity, and I would never ask you to make a change unless you wanted to. Personally, I hope you will consider the position; you would be invaluable to Dr. Bradford because of your experience here, and he would have a lot to offer you since he is young and just out of school. Please understand your salary would not be affected and might go up. You would have regular working hours every day, and finally, Dr. Bradford is single and rather handsome. I thought you might want the first crack at him." The glint of an "evil" nurse's smile crossed Nurse Jackson's face.

Kathy was aghast. "Oh my, you take my breath away; I assume you don't expect my answer today?"

"No, yesterday would have been better, but you didn't work...so how about by the end of this week? What do you think?" Nurse Jackson smiled again.

"The end of the week will be fine; I'll let you know. Thank you for this opportunity; I will definitely think about it."

"And, Kathy, you'll be a damn fool not to accept it. When you came in my office a few minutes ago, you started to say something and I interrupted. What did you need?"

Kathy stammered. "Why...I don't remember; nothing...it's all right...nothing important right now; it can wait until later." She started to leave.

"Kathy." Nurse Jackson spoke sharply; Kathy turned to face her. "You look nice today."

"Why thank you; thank you very much." Kathy moved quickly toward the door.

She left the office, walking briskly to the bathroom; once

inside, she quickly checked in the mirror. Thankfully, the lap and front of her uniform were still dry; she would have sworn she had just wet her pants. Isn't that what happens when someone drops a bomb on you? Talk about "right out of the blue!" Her mission had run into a herd of wild buffalo, leaving nothing but a cloud of dust. A thought did cross her mind. Was God messing with her today? Is this what it means to have God in your life? Kathy didn't know, but it occurred to her if she ever intended to win the lottery, today was the day to buy a ticket!

The rest of the day flew by. One of the lab technicians stopped and asked her if she had changed something and commented how nice she looked. At lunch several people who had said no more than hi in the past spoke to her. Even her patients seemed friendlier. One older gentlemen had offered a proposal of marriage...under the condition she would say nothing about it to his wife. During the afternoon, she was scheduled to meet with one of the administrative supervisors she did not particularly like. Surprisingly, everything went well, and he even responded favorably to several suggestions made by the staff. By the end of the day, Kathy was overwhelmed; it was darkness turned into day. As she was leaving the building, one of the custodial staff was mopping the floor adjacent to the exit walkway. The thought actually occurred to her that she could walk across the mopped area and not leave a single footprint. As she reached the exit, the security guard looked at her and noted she must have had a great day—it was written all over her face!

Kathy was just like a school kid rushing home to tell her mother she got an A on her math paper or the top score on a history test. She burst into the apartment. "Patti! I have wonderful news...or at least I think it is." Kathy looked around. "Where are you?"

"Mother, calm down; you could have a stroke or something. I'm over here on the floor sorting papers. What do you want?"

Kathy panted. "Oh, Patti, I've waited all day to talk to you. Is everything okay here?"

"Yep, quiet as a tomb."

"Come over here and sit down; I'm so excited. I have to talk with you."

"Hold your horses; I'm doing the best I can. You worked in a nursing home; you know how difficult it is to get off the floor when you get old."

Kathy flashed a smile. "Patti, I hardly think you're old; you haven't been sniffing Mr. Mitchell's paint thinner again, have you?"

"Ah, Mom, that stuff makes me barf. It's the toilet bowl cleaner that gets me going."

When Patti got to the living area, Kathy stood up, reached out, gave her the biggest hug. "Honey, I love you so much; you are my wonderful Patti."

"And don't forget, Mom, I like spinach too...but not as much as I like you!" Patti was trying to have as much fun as she could.

"Well, at least you're serious about things. Listen, I've had the most wonderful day. Everyone was so sweet to me. They told me I looked nice; they smiled at me; I even got a marriage proposal. How would you finally like to have a dad? The gentleman in question needs to get permission from his wife, but anything is possible."

Patti was curious. "Mother, how old was this gentleman?"

"Oh, I'd say around eighty, but he looks a lot younger."

"Maybe more like seventy-five?" Patti tried to be serious.

Kathy paused a moment. "Yeah, that's about right."

"Mom, I think you need to calm down; I thought we had your 'pep pill' addiction under control. I don't want you back in rehab!" Patti was really enjoying this conversation.

"Patti, seriously, the hospital has offered me a new job with regular hours; I would be our new doctor's full-time nurse...and Nurse Jackson, my supervisor, tells me Dr. Bradford is single."

Patti quizzed. "And how old is he, Mom?"

"Well, I think he's about thirty...but he looks a lot older."

"Do I need to ask?" Patti laughed.

"No, just trust me; I'm not sure I would recognize Dr. Bradford if he walked in the door."

"So you're not looking for a man...er, a doctor right now?"

"Honey, you know, I don't really think about it. I suppose it would be nice to be married and have someone, but I got burned and it soured me on men."

"Mom, I don't think you are being very fair; my daddy wasn't entirely at fault and he isn't like all men. Grandpa Bender and Uncle Bob aren't like that, and I'm sure you know other good men. I don't want you to let one bad apple spoil the whole barrel."

"Honey, you're right; I don't want you to think I would never get married; if the right man comes along, I'd give him a chance, but he'll have a lot to live up to. My standards are high!"

"Me too, Mom, me too."

"What do you think? Should I give this a shot?"

"Mom, you know more about it than I do, but if it's what you want, go for it. Pray about it; God wants you to be happy. He knows we do our best when we are content. Let Him speak to you...and Mom, think about this. In the book of Romans, Paul says, 'All things work together for good to those who love God and are called according to His purpose.' Could this scripture explain the great day you've had? God loves you, Mom, and I love you too."

363

Kathy was thrilled. "Oh, Patti, come here!"

Patti got up and went to her mother, who was now crying; they reached out and hugged each other, then Kathy kissed Patti on her cheek. Patti returned the gesture. "Patti, I am beginning to understand things long hidden from me. You told me I am all you have, that is, your only family. Just this weekend I realized you are my only family, and now I know how you felt. You are so precious...my little angel...I love you with all my heart. From now on we will be a team, and I promise to never let you down."

Kathy was crying; Patti was crying, but this team was building up a head of steam that might be unstoppable. "I love you, Mom; you're the best Mom on the planet. Thank you for all you've done for me."

The hugging continued and another kiss exchanged. Patti found the the same love and security as her head rested on her mother's breast that she had found there as a child. Yep, this was definitely the day to buy that lottery ticket, but all the money in the world could not buy what was being shared right there between a mother and daughter.

It was very clear Kathy was not the same person she had been only days ago. She had found something that would not let go, and it felt good; she realized she had value not only to others, but to herself. She also discovered the daughter who had been lost living in the same home with her. How could she have been so blind? But this was yesterday. Now she only wanted to make a future for herself and Patti. She had no idea what it might be, but for the first time in years, she was absolutely convinced it would be good, and her life would have meaning. Kathy Bender was a new person and loving every minute of it; other people saw it too.

On Tuesday morning she went to Nurse Jackson's office and told her she would accept this new position and break Dr. Bradford in right. She could not guarantee any romantic escapades but promised to never fist fight in view of the patients; fighting was inappropriate in the work place. She found out her new work would begin near the first of February. Nurse Jackson would schedule a conference with Dr. Bradford so they could visit and get acquainted. Nurse Jackson felt they would be a good match, and Kathy respected her opinion. Kathy asked if it would be okay to work a regular day shift until her new job began. The nurse saw no problem. Kathy thanked her for all she had done and extended her hand in gratitude. Nurse Jackson reached for it, held it very tightly and pulled Kathy closer. "Kathy Bender, if you ever tell anyone what I am about to say, they will find your body washed up along some river or lake. You are the best there is and don't ever let anyone tell you otherwise. If I believed in cloning, you'd be the only person I'd clone. We could use a hundred of you; you've got heart and drive like no one I've ever seen. I just want you to know that while your clones might look and act just like you...there would be one big difference. Kid, you've got soul, and that's what makes you who you are; don't ever forget it while I'm alive."

This blunt pronouncement precipitated a sudden stream of tears rolling down Kathy's cheeks. "Oh, thank you so much. If I didn't know better, I'd say you were an angel."

"Kathy, I'm afraid most people would call me a horse's ass, but thank you anyway."

Kathy turned to leave. "Kathy." Startled, she turned and looked back at Nurse Jackson. "You might need this." She handed Kathy a tissue.

Kathy nodded, wiping her eyes as she left the office. Why did good news have to be so wet?

Kathy had another good day at work. Nurse Jackson sent her a memo stating she would arrange a meeting with Dr. Bradford within the next week and they could cuss and discuss whatever might be on each other's mind. Kathy wanted to confirm her image of Dr. Bradford; doctors pulsed through the halls, offices, and back rooms all day. It was hard to keep track of them...and pretty soon no one even tried. Kathy did have some apprehension working specifically with just one doctor; she knew it was important for them to get along, and quite frankly, some doctors, young, old, or otherwise, were a pain in the backside. She knew their personalities would need to match; in addition, she did not want to step into something that did not improve her situation. Kathy decided to ask around and see what she could find out about Dr. Bradford; some of the nurses could give her their ideas.

Kathy discovered Dr. Bradford was a serious doctor who genuinely wanted to help his patients; he could be difficult if someone failed to meet his expectations, but he did not carry grudges or waste time reminding everyone of their past mistakes. The only negative that followed him was his lack of friendliness and cordiality, but some who worked with him felt he was so focused, wanting to make the best possible impression, that the real "doctor" in him had yet to surface. In other words, give him a chance to be himself. Kathy did not find this information at all threatening; it sounded as though they had much in common.

The scheduled meeting with Kathy, Nurse Jackson, Dr. Bradford, and one of the hospital administrators took place as agreed. Dr. Bradford admitted he had heard good things about Kathy, and Kathy acknowledged similar sentiments toward him. Nurse Jackson simply wanted both of them to determine if they would be a good match since they would be working together every day. The administrator wanted Dr. Bradford to know they were willing to let him have their best nurse. Her experience would be invaluable to him since she knew the hospital like the back of her hand. The meeting went well, and Kathy felt Dr. Bradford was pleased to have her on his team; Kathy felt she could work with him and provide the support he might need in his new position. When the meeting ended, Dr. Bradford asked Kathy if they might get together for coffee and visit more informally; he felt their personal lives were private and did not want to address those issues when others were present. Kathy agreed to meet him later in the hospital coffee shop.

They arrived at the same time. Dr. Bradford seemed more relaxed and apologized for taking Kathy's time. He just wanted to know a little more about her, and of course, he wanted to share part of his life. Kathy gave him her two-minute biography and then a brief rundown of her work experience. She could tell he seemed pleased with her work record and noted a tiny sparkle in his eye when she said she was single. When he asked about Patti, Kathy attempted to describe the indescribable; the doctor smiled.

Dr. Bradford was the baby in his family; he had an older brother who worked for a med tech company and a sister who was an RN. He was single and had never really been attached to anyone; he had dated a female doctor while in school, but they had different ideas about their futures, so they parted amicably. He admitted it had been tough, but he also knew he had to establish himself; that was more important than chasing after someone who really didn't share his plans. Kathy told him one of the good things about her situation was she did not have to worry about what a spouse might think, but she did admit it would be nice to have a man around. Dr. Bradford seemed to understand, acknowledging he did not wish to remain single but finding someone compatible with his lifestyle would not be easy.

Kathy saw many good things in Dr. Bradford, and she felt he was pleased with her; she was certainly willing to give him a chance if he felt the same way about her. There were a lot of pluses and few minuses. Kathy saw Dr. Bradford as no more than a partner in the healing business and hoped he viewed her the same way...but the thought did cross her mind: What would she say or do if he were to ask her out—dinner, dancing, movie? She guessed she would cross that bridge when she came to it, and nothing resembling a bridge was on the horizon.

⤞ Thirty ⤝

Kathy's sudden change not only sent shock waves through the hospital, but at home as well. She insisted Patti only do household chores when they could work together; this made less work for Patti, but more importantly, it gave them a chance to talk. Kathy came home from the hospital in much better spirits; she was still tired but now seemed to enjoy being home for more than just sleeping. The whole thing amazed Patti; she now had more attention than ever...in fact, maybe too much. However, Patti was thrilled to see her mother happy. Somehow the apartment seemed brighter, and that made every day better.

Others noticed too. Deb left a message for Patti at school and asked if she could pick her up and take her home. Patti agreed and waited for her after school. Patti got a kick out of being picked up by a squad car; the other kids nearly went crazy trying to figure out what "heinous" crime she committed. Patti always had a good story for them...and no one ever knew exactly what to believe.

When Patti got into the car, Deb told her she had been to the hospital that morning to visit an accident victim and had seen Kathy. "Why, Patti, she was glowing; I've never seen your mother so happy. She simply looks beautiful. What is going on?"

Unprepared for her comments, Patti hesitated. "Deb, I know what happened, but it's kind of complicated. Do you have some extra time? Maybe we could just go home."

"Sure, I've got time; I'd really like to know."

When they arrived at the old warehouse, both went inside and soon found themselves sitting comfortably in the living area. Patti did her best to explain the situation and what had happened between herself and her mother. Deb sat in amazement, much like a kid listening to a fairy tale. When Patti finished, she said, "Let me get this straight. You got her to accept Christ so her sins would be forgiven, and she could forgive herself?"

"Yeah, that's about it...and you've seen the results."

Deb was quiet for a long time. "It can't be that simple."

"Yes, Deb, it is; I know you don't believe it, and I guess I wouldn't believe it either, but when it happens, it's hard to ignore. Jesus could help you too if you wanted Him to."

Deb immediately bristled. "Damn you, Patti, you just can't let it die, can you? You're bound and determined to get me on my knees begging for forgiveness. Well, I'll have none of it! Do you understand?"

Patti was surprised by Deb's strong reaction. "Yes, I think I've always understood. You don't want to admit there might be someone out there bigger than you...and even if you did, you would see Him as a bully, making you do this or that and not letting you do your own thing. We keep having this conversation, and you'll remember I didn't start it. You asked me and I told you, plain and simple. Deb, next to my mom and her family, I love you more than anything. You helped Sarah, and her gift was the discovery of who you really are...a woman with real feelings. God loves you; He wants to help you discover even more about yourself. Don't be mad at me for being honest. I hope a time will come when I can help you, but it's your move, not mine!" Patti concluded emphatically.

Deb had calmed down and looked a bit sheepish. "I'm sorry I swore at you. You're right; I asked you and you told me. I love you and your mother so much; you are like family...the only real family I have. I walked away from everyone in my home...I don't want to lose you guys too. I'm sorry...can you forgive me for being so stupid?"

Patti, walked to Deb and took her hand. Deb stood up and pulled Patti close; they hugged. Deb was crying and Patti was tearing also. "I do forgive you...just remember you're special; I love you and God loves you...we'll be waiting."

Deb looked at her tenderly. "Thank you for caring."

"You're very welcome."

Some people don't see the light as quickly as others...that doesn't mean it's not shining.

Deb told Patti she'd better leave before Kathy caught them together and got jealous. Patti promised she wouldn't say anything...so their secret was safe as long as blabber mouth Deb didn't spill the beans. Once Deb left, Patti reflected on what had happened; Deb was a hard case, but she was important to God. Patti didn't know why and figured it was none of her business. Some things are better left up to God. That's why He's in charge. Of course, no one knew it then, but Deb's Godless days were numbered.

January was doing its best to freeze everyone. School and work were warm, but getting between the two was often cold and frustrating. It had snowed just enough to be messy but not enough to play. Kathy was about to end one part of her career and begin something new. The best part was that Dr. Bradford was also new, so if they made a mistake and kept quiet about it, no one would know any better. Kathy was apprehensive. She comforted herself knowing everyone seemed to feel she was up to the task. Patti had school under control—well, maybe not. There was this new class called algebra. Ouch!

The kids had not been told, but their algebra class was an accident. Math enrollment at West Wood High had been down, and one of the teachers, Mr. Wagner, ended up with no one in his second semester advanced math course. For some reason, the mean old school officials did not want him just to stay in his room and dance on his desk. After much discussion, everyone decided they would like to try an algebra class at the middle school, and Mr. Wagner agreed to teach it. Another teacher from high school had agreed to teach a class during his planning period, so these teachers would handle the two algebra classes during the exploration period.

Colby was assigned to Mr. Wagner's class while Geoff and Patti had the other teacher, Mr. Barton. Mr. Wagner had been around forever...or at least for a long time. Kathy told Patti he had been there when she was in high school, but she had never had him as a teacher. He had a reputation for being tough; you learned math in his class or you failed. Mr. Barton was much younger; he had taught at East Wood High for about five years, and no one seemed to know much about him. Colby loved Mr. Wagner and talked about him all the time. Patti and Geoff were not as excited about Mr. Barton, but he was okay. Math teachers are usually weird anyway, so okay was probably above average. Algebra had started off pretty well, but Patti found it confusing and complained to her mother. Kathy said she would gladly help her; it had been a while, but she could do math in high school and college, so she knew she could do it now. Patti asked if it would be okay to study with Colby; they had the same assignments, and Colby loved algebra more than ice cream. Kathy had no problem with that, but she did not want them moving in together and starting a new life somewhere. Patti promised she would show some restraint and not keep Colby hidden under her bed or in the closet. Kathy was relieved.

Colby was no teacher, but he could do the problems. The more he showed Patti, the more sense it made. It wasn't long before she could work most of the problems by herself, and sometimes when they studied, no one said a word. Patti began to feel much more confident and told Colby he was an inspiration to her. Why, just sitting beside him made everything easier. Colby thanked her for the praise but said it apparently didn't work for everyone because a couple of kids by him in class were really having a hard time with their work. Patti gave him a kiss. "Yeah, but they don't kiss you like I do."

Colby laughed and returned her kiss. "I hope they never do; they're both boys!" Patti nodded her agreement; she didn't want Colby kissing anyone but her...boys or girls.

With algebra under control, her mom's new schedule, and home life greatly improved, Patti thought she had the world by the tail. Life was good...no, better than that; it was wonderful. She could not imagine how it could get better.

Kathy started her new position on February 1; she reported it was challenging but enjoyed it. Dr. Bradford was pleasant, and the more she got to know him the more she liked him. They both had standards and wanted the best for their patients. That bond alone made them an excellent team. By the middle of the month, when Patti was kidding her mother about all the kind things she was saying about Dr. Bradford, Kathy admitted if he ever asked her out, she would accept his offer. Of course, she would not be able to let him meet Patti for quite some time; she didn't want her crazy daughter to scare him away. Patti quickly noted she was worried that if Dr. Bradford met her he would likely dump poor Kathy right on the spot! Kathy was concerned about that possibility until Patti noted she had always been attracted to older, more mature men...like Colby.

Shortly after this conversation on a Friday evening, Kathy picked up Patti from youth group; they chatted and discussed the news and views of the day, then suddenly remarked they were tired. It was time to go to bed and have whatever sweet dreams they could find. They had changed their clothes and started to bed when the peaceful evening was abruptly shattered by a thunderous crash. "What on earth?!" exclaimed Kathy.

One of the things they liked about their apartment was how peaceful and quiet it was; the building absorbed the street noise. On the other hand, no eye level windows made it impossible to see outside. Kathy thought about putting on a robe and checking the situation, then thought better of it. They were safe in their apartment and vulnerable outside. The idea had no more left her mind when a sudden pounding erupted on their door. Patti jumped out of bed and ran to her mother, who grabbed the baseball bat they kept for such an emergency. Kathy stood on one side of the door, and Patti prepared to open it as the pounding continued along with the muffled words, "Let me in." Patti threw open the door, Kathy pulled back the bat for a home run swing. "Mama! It's Deb...she's hurt really bad."

Kathy gasped, dropped the bat, and ran to the door. Deb was there, her face bleeding and hair a mess, with an expression of absolute terror. She held the microphone from her cruiser in her right hand, its cord trailing behind her. She looked as if she had just returned from Hell. "My God, Deb, what happened?" Deb just stood there wild-eyed and said nothing. Kathy moved closer. "Deb...Deb Johnson, are you okay? What happened?" The scene and silence were unnerving.

Finally, Deb came back to life and saw Patti in the semidarkness. Her voice sounded strange. "Patti...I've got to see Patti...I..." She collapsed in Kathy's arms.

Kathy instinctively lowered Deb to the floor and unzipped

her jacket, giving her a quick examination. There was no other blood except around her face. The left side of her head had sustained a blow. She had a laceration on her left forehead and temple, her cheek was scratched, and Kathy noted swelling. Deb had managed to get up the stairs to the apartment, so her motor functions and related body parts were working. Kathy felt around her left side and abdomen and was not sure, but suspected she might have broken ribs. Kathy was no detective, but it appeared Deb had been struck with considerable force, suggesting the crash they heard involved her squad car, and the microphone in her hand indicated she must have been calling dispatch when it happened. Kathy spoke first to Patti, "We have to get her to the hospital and make sure she doesn't have internal injuries. It's dumb to call an ambulance; we're only a few blocks away. Do you think we can get her to my car?"

"Mom, I think we can make it." Just then Deb seemed to rouse and again called out Patti's name. "I'm right here, Deb. What do you want?"

"I've got to see Patti...I've got to see Patti..."

Kathy ran to make herself presentable and Patti stayed with Deb, who continued asking for her. Patti could make no sense of what she wanted; she appeared to be regaining consciousness, which meant they might be able to walk her downstairs. Kathy came back to watch Deb, and Patti scurried to jump into some jeans and was back in a flash. They managed to get Deb on her feet and headed out the door; however, Deb did not want to leave and called out for Patti to help her. Kathy noted. "She must be out of her head; I don't think she knows what she's doing, maybe you'd better stay with me. If she snaps out of this, you'll be there." Patti agreed.

When they got downstairs, the street was swarming with police cars. An officer ran to them. They had lost Officer Johnson; Kathy assured him she was not lost. She was right here, and they were going to get her to the hospital. She was hurt and delirious. The officer volunteered to help get her in the car. In no time, Kathy pulled into the emergency entrance; the police had apparently called the hospital because several staff were waiting at the door. They got Deb out of the car and into the emergency room; Deb continued calling out Patti's name. It was spooky. Kathy and Patti went to the waiting room and waited for a report on Deb's condition.

Kathy finally asked, "Tell me, what does Deb want?"

"I have no idea...well, maybe I know, but you've seen her; she's out of her head."

"What's this maybe stuff? What are you not telling me?"

"Mom, I really don't know. Deb asked me about a month ago what had happened to you...so I filled her in as best I could. I told her God could help her find peace too, but you know how she is. It made her mad. I told her if she changed her mind, I would be there for her. I want Deb to be happy. She's been good to us."

Kathy paused, then noted. "Honey, there's a lot about Deb she doesn't like; I don't know everything, and I don't want to. I hope you're right. Maybe you can help her. I wish she had kept Sarah although she was probably right to let her go. Deb's no mother, but she did discover she has a little mother in her. She needed to realize that."

Just then a nurse came out of the emergency room and walked toward them. She confirmed Kathy's diagnosis; Deb had a slight concussion, two or three broken or cracked ribs, and bruising on her left side. However, if either one of them was Patti, she needed to come with her before Deb drove them crazy. Patti went with the nurse and Deb immediately recognized her. "Patti, where have you been; I've got to talk with you." Deb appeared desperate.

"Calm down; I've been here the whole time. They wouldn't let me operate. I wanted to remove your brain to make you smarter."

"Yeah, if only that would work. Patti, we have to go. Get me out of this place; I've got to talk with you...privately."

"Deb, you've been hurt; they need to take care of you."

"No, they don't; your mother's a nurse; she can watch me. Take me to your apartment."

Patti motioned to the nurse and told her to get her mother; maybe they could calm Deb down. After considerable discussion, they agreed to let Kathy take Deb home. Kathy was a nurse and lived only blocks away. They were concerned about internal bleeding and didn't want to sedate Deb to calm her since most sedatives thin the blood. Kathy thought they could watch her, and she would be all right once they got her home. They bundled her up, got her into Kathy's car, and were home in minutes. Deb was in pain, and the stairs went slowly; however, they finally made it inside and Deb immediately seemed more at ease. She was still out of her head but knew where she was. They put her in Patti's bed and were afraid Patti might have to sleep with her, but after only a few moments, she went to sleep. Whatever was bothering Deb had found peace; she slept like a baby.

Kathy and Patti took turns checking on Deb the rest of the night; she seemed fine. The next morning, everyone was exhausted, so no one got up with the rooster. It was mid morning before anyone roused. Deb woke up too; she was hungry, thirsty and grumpy. Her head ached...hmm, how odd. Kathy went to Deb and told her to lie still; she was broken up inside and she needed to be careful...she could puncture a lung. Deb seemed to have recovered her senses although she did not remember much about the previous evening after the accident.

The police department had been watching and following a suspicious gentleman who was probably selling drugs. On Friday night, she got her turn at surveillance; she watched him most of the evening. Shortly before the wreck, he had spotted her and made a run for it right up Broadway. However, he apparently had set a trap because the car that rammed her was driving with no lights, and she never saw it coming. There was an awful crash, a flash of light, and everything went black. She didn't think she was out for long; she had called for back up just before the accident, and no one had arrived. There were cruisers only a few blocks away. As soon as she got her bearings, she realized the car could possibly burn and explode; her driver's side door was wedged shut by the car that hit her, so she scooted across the seat and crawled out the other side. She went around the car to check on the driver that hit her; he was out like a light. She handcuffed him to the steering wheel. If the cars caught fire, he would be the main course at the next police barbecue. After that, she didn't really remember anything except...

After she lost consciousness, she awoke in a place that could only be described as Hell. Fires burned everywhere; it was hot; the air smelled of smoke, sulfur and burning flesh; she heard horrid screaming, weeping, and wailing, beyond anything imaginable. In the midst of this chaos, she heard a voice calling her name; it sounded familiar. She looked around and saw no one, then checked again. The voice continued calling, saying something like, "Look, look up." At first she saw nothing, but as she peered through the haze, she saw a shape in the cloud-like mist above her; it appeared to be a spirit or ghost hovering over her. The shape slowly materialized and took on human form, reminding her of Patti. "It pointed a finger at me and started to laugh, then just kept laughing and taunting. Then it stopped and for a moment there was silence. I watched it begin to rise and fade, calling out, 'too late' then eerily repeating it. The words echoed all around me. Finally, it pointed at me, laughed hysterically and disappeared. Honest to God, I thought I was dead and this sure wasn't heaven. Then I woke up in my squad car; I've never been so glad to be in a car wreck. I was alive and had the pain to prove it...but I've never been so scared." Deb trembled.

Kathy and Patti were stunned. What Deb was saying was unimaginable. Finally, Kathy concluded. "You must have come straight to our apartment; I suppose you thought we could help you. You kept calling for Patti and asking to speak to her."

When Deb heard this, she froze and was dead still; she looked at Kathy and Patti again with terror in her eyes, pleading. "Patti, you've got to help me; you've got help me...right now. I can't go to Hell; I don't want anything to do with that place. For God's sake, please save me."

Patti was shocked and rattled. "Deb, I don't understand. What do you want me to do?"

"Help me like you helped your mother; I don't want to go back there; please help me."

Kathy was nearly overcome; she had never seen anything like this. "Deb, do you think you were dead for a few moments...perhaps like Sarah?"

"I don't know, Kathy, all I can say is I was in Hell; I mean it...and I never want to go back. This is going to sound crazy, but I think God was giving me a preview of my afterlife and believe me, I took the hint. I don't want any part of it. Patti, please save me?"

"Deb, I can't save you; you'll have to do that yourself, but I can help you."

"What do I have to do?"

"The one thing you most don't want to do; surrender yourself to Jesus. Do you think you can do that?"

Deb nearly panted. "Anything, I'll do anything."

"Okay, we're going to have to get you out of bed and on your knees."

The girls helped Deb out of bed; she painfully knelt and humbled herself. Patti looked at her. "This is important. You must tell the truth, no fooling around." Deb nodded. "Okay, do you know what sin is? Are you a sinner?"

"Yes, I do. To sin is to go against God, and yes, I've been doing that all my life."

"Do you believe Jesus Christ is the Son of God?"

"Yes, I can believe that; I think it's true."

"Will you accept Him now as your Lord and Savior?"

"Yes, if that's what I have to do."

"Do you understand what will happen if you do these things?

"I'm not sure, but I assume you'll tell me."

"God will forgive your sins...everyone of them, and you will be filled with the Holy Spirit; that is, Jesus will be in your heart." Deb looked at her in wonder and disbelief. "I know you don't believe me, but if you have told me the truth, you will be saved here this morning. I want you to bow your head and pray silently. I want you to confess to God you have sinned against Him. Admit you believe Jesus is the Son of God; and finally, accept Jesus as your Lord and Savior. Do these things now."

Patti had Kathy place one hand on Deb's shoulder; she placed her hand on the other. Deb prayed silently, her body very still. In a few moments she trembled slightly; Patti could see tears rolling down her cheeks. She began to shake slightly as the crying grew into sobbing. "Oh, I'm so ashamed, so ashamed; Lord, please forgive me."

Suddenly Deb looked into Patti's eyes; her face seemed to glow. She stuttered and stammered "Oh my God, Patti, something's happening to me; Kathy, I feel something I've never felt before. God has forgiven me, I know it; I won't burn in Hell. I'm saved!" Patti and Kathy were crying; they wanted to hug Deb but were afraid they'd hurt her. They knelt together, rejoicing in God's love. God did love them, and that was worth more than anything in the whole world.

Despite the fact that joy filled the room, there was also a sense of uneasiness. Kathy couldn't get the picture of Deb's face and its horror out of her mind. Deb had been scared stiff, whatever she had seen and witnessed had frightened her, more than facing down some thug with gun, even more than the prospect of becoming a mother for Sarah or losing her. Deb was tough, both mentally and physically; she had been practicing it everyday for over ten years. Any fear she experienced had come from within; it was real to her and without question she had been genuinely terrified. Now Deb had found inner peace, but how would it affect her? What would the "new" Deb be like?

As the emotional state of the three companions began to ebb and tears ceased, a calm swept into the room. Deb's sore ribs were comforted and soothed by a warmth that flowed within her; her broken body felt revived. "Hey, we need to talk. How about helping me into a soft chair?"

"Sure."

Kathy and Patti helped Deb up, and they found comfort sitting in the living area. "I don't deserve friends like you guys; you mean everything to me. I've wanted to say this many times, but somehow I never got to it. You've helped me so much, and I have done so little in return. Thank you and bless you; you're the greatest."

"Deb, it isn't necessary to thank us; we were glad to help. That's what friends do..."

Deb interrupted Kathy. "I know that. There are things about me I've never shared because I was ashamed. I preferred to keep the dark side of my life a secret. Let's just say that I've acted like trash; I've whored around; I've used and been used, even abused; I've been drunk and had no idea where I was; I've made mistakes...lots of them...until right now. And there's one more thing, just to show you how bad things are, and this isn't easy to say, I have no friends except for you guys; I mean it. After Sarah left, I wanted to kill myself. I wanted to die; I had lost the only person that was part of my life. I sat at home with my gun trying to think of what to do or who to call for help, and there was no one I thought would help me. I know it's hard to believe; I'm not a bad person, ugly or disgusting; I don't smell bad or have gross behavior and manners. I think I'm a pretty regular Joe, but honest to God, I have no friends, except for you guys. So you are the ones I called, and Patti came to my rescue. She knew I wanted to die, but she saved me. Now she's done it again..."

Patti interrupted. "No Deb, Jesus saved you this time; I only assisted."

"Well, whatever, I'm giving you the credit anyway...God knows I'm confused. I'm going to change, and I pledge to you I will be a better person. Patti told me you guys were going to early church. Could I go with you? I'll come by or you can pick me up at home, and if you have to, I want you to drag my sorry ass out of bed. I want to go with you. I'd like to schedule a time...it won't be easy...to study and read the Bible with you. I want to better understand the Man I've been fighting all these years. I want to turn over a new leaf, but I know I'm going to need help. What do you think? Can we do this?"

Kathy was crying and Patti fought back tears. Finally, Kathy said, "Deb, you are a pain in the butt; on the other hand, you're looking at a couple of girls who would do almost anything for you. We'll help you...on one condition."

"Name it!"

"Can we count on you to be a member of our family? I know you feel alone with no place to go; your house is not a home. I want you to belong somewhere and have a family; we will gladly do that for you. Is that agreeable?"

Deb looked at Kathy in awe, unable to speak, but finally stammered, "You guys would do that? You'd adopt me?"

"Absolutely." Deb was crying again; Kathy and Patti joined her. If this continued much longer, they'd have to call a plumber to drain the building.

Deb had been injured in a nasty car accident; her body would not recover for several weeks; and her pain would not subside for many days. However, it was a small price to pay for what she had gained. Deb had found salvation on the floor of Kathy's apartment and with it a sense of peace and security; she had also gained a family, something she had secretly longed for. Recent events had hammered home her need for more than a job and a life dedicated to pleasing herself. She had gained a purpose.

However, one thing had not changed; Deb still liked to eat. "How about some breakfast? Even us cry babies need food; I'm starved!"

"You and your appetite. All you think about is food."

"Not true! It's all I think about when I'm hungry."

Kathy exclaimed. "But you're hungry all the time!"

Deb started to laugh, then held her side. "Ouch, no more humor. It hurts to laugh...and that's not funny!"

Kathy was already heading for the kitchen with Patti at her heels and Deb gingerly bringing up the rear. Perhaps being hungry at mid morning on Saturday was acceptable behavior, as long as they didn't eat the dishes.

Breakfast or brunch was delicious. Deb needed to get to the police station and fill out her report; she also wanted to find out if the police had apprehended the scumbag she was chasing when the accident occurred. Kathy warned her not to do anything too fast. She needed to rest and heal. Deb promised to take it easy and asked if she could borrow Kathy's car then spend the night; they could go to church together and her family could keep an eye on her. Kathy thought that was a good idea and complimented Deb on her good thinking. Maybe that wreck had knocked some sense into her after all. Deb was not terribly amused and bemoaned the fact her new family was already picking on her. Kathy reminded her "we always hurt the ones we love." Deb found little comfort in this wisdom.

After Deb left, Kathy and Patti marveled at what had just transpired. Their friend was now a part of their family; they had adopted Deb, and she was much in need of a place to find comfort and share her life. Kathy had always been close to her family; the Benders weren't perfect, but they loved and cared for each other. Then, of course, there was her immediate family, Patti, whom she had recently rediscovered. She and Patti had never been closer than in these last few weeks. Kathy had been just like Deb, so wrapped up in herself there was no room for anyone or anything else, but a slap on the face had brought her back to reality. Now there was Deb. It was important she felt like a part of their family. Kathy opined. "I guess we need to decide. Do you want a new sister or another mother?

"Oh gosh, Mom, why do you have to make everything so complicated. I don't know. I guess it would look better to have a sister than two moms; we don't want to encourage any more rumors. Two moms makes it sound as though you and Deb are married. I'll settle for a big sister—but I'm still the oldest child."

"We can handle that; you should be the oldest since you were born fourteen years ago, and Deb was born today.

Patti scratched her head. "It makes sense to me...I think."

The girls pitched in and got the apartment in order; they didn't want their "youngest" to be embarrassed in her new home. On the other hand, their place always looked better than Deb's old haunt. Of course, Sarah had changed Deb and everyone agreed she no longer lived like a pig. They had no idea when Deb might return but had everything in order before lunch. Kathy thought Deb should stay with them for a few days to make sure she behaved; it was hard to say what kind of patient Deb would be, but they knew she was bullheaded. On the other hand, perhaps she would be more obedient now that she'd "seen the light."

Deb returned shortly after noon, not in a good mood. She had been scolded for not being in the hospital; everyone at the station thought she needed to rest and take care of herself—not be at work. She insisted she was well enough to relate what had happened and figured it might be helpful. As it turned out, the "gentleman" she had been pursuing got away, but they were sure he was still around and would catch him soon. The accomplice that rammed her car was in jail and might be there forever. Assaulting an officer with intent to kill was not taken lightly by the authorities. They hounded her to go home; the department would survive without her. She acknowledged their point, but noted the place wouldn't be as pretty if she were gone; after all, the main reason she got her job was to have at least one good-looking face amidst all those ugly mugs. There were boos and one officer threw a wadded piece of paper at her, so she left before the violence escalated.

Deb returned hungry so it was obvious her injuries had not affected her appetite. She discovered she had gained the status of "big sister," provoking a cruel reply. "You mean I have to be a sister to Patti, public nuisance number one? How can I maintain any kind of reputation having a sister who's had more rides in a squad car than Al Capone!?"

Patti knew how to handle this nonsense. "Hey, doll face, how'd you like a punch in the ribs or a fat lip; we ain't gonna put up with your big mouth around here anymore. Do I make myself clear?" Deb immediately calmed down; she was no condition to spar with "bare knuckles" Patti.

Deb stayed the rest of the day. They all got up on Sunday morning to go to early church. By the time they returned to the apartment, life was back to normal. Of course, they had to take care of Deb, but she was hurt enough that the suggestion of a poke in the ribs was all it took to make her behave. She was in good spirits, and having her around for a while would not be a problem; it would also give them a chance to do a little bonding. Deb needed that.

Deb had to go back to the doctor on Monday; she had a good report although he was concerned about her ribs. He advised her to keep quiet and rest as much as possible for the next several days; he would notify the department and recommend she take the rest of the week off then see her again. Deb was unhappy about not being able to work. There was little for her to do at home or in the apartment. Patti did her best to get home early and keep her company; they worked on Patti's lessons from school and did a lot of gabbing. Patti had always liked Deb but didn't know exactly why. Deb was nothing like her mother nor anyone else Patti knew, but there was something about her Patti found fascinating. Deb admitted she had always cared for Patti. She liked Patti's honesty. Patti noted they had a good mother, and Deb quickly agreed. Kathy was remarkable, especially to be the mother of a daughter several months older than she was. Math and timelines can be confusing.

383

Living with Deb was interesting; she had lived alone forever...or at least since she had been in college, over ten years. At home she was a free spirit, admitting to running around in her underwear...and shock, shock...sometimes without it, especially in the shower. In simple language she lived much like a man; she made do and got by. However, around Kathy and Patti she was modest, embarrassed to act this way. Kathy and Patti were not free spirits but were practical about the fact they were both female, related, and naked under their clothes. In addition, the apartment did not provide convenient places to hide if you were caught with your "pants down." Kathy kept a robe near their door in the event someone should unexpectedly arrive; Patti used one of her mother's old flannel shirts for the same purpose. Deb was uneasy about this, and her mom and new sister thought it rather odd she acted this way.

When confronted, Deb was even more embarrassed, but after some kidding, finally confessed. "When I was in junior high, I was a mess. I had always been skinny; my brother called me toothpick, and some of the kids called me Popsicle, short for Popsicle stick. It didn't bother me because...well, it was true...I was a head on a stick. Anyway, when I was in seventh grade, the plumbing went haywire in the girls PE dressing room. They tried to accommodate us for a while by doing less physical activities, but our teacher was going nuts trying to keep us out of trouble.

"Finally they worked out a schedule where we could use the boys' dressing room every other day. Well, I can tell you it was a disaster that would put the San Francisco earthquake to shame. The boys' shower area had no stalls, only a large enclosure with multiple shower heads. You know how girls are, especially in the seventh grade. We had breasts and no breasts; legs with hair and others, smooth as silk; I could go on but it would be disgusting. Anyway, many of the girls refused to shower and we had nothing but trouble. I had never paid much attention to anyone in the girls dressing room because they were either in a stall or wrapped in a towel...but in this situation, everybody was naked as a jay bird...here I was tall, skinny, no curves, no hair...I felt like a freak. For the first time in

384

my life I realized how different I was from the rest of the girls. I used the shower, but it became more of a dread than death itself. I would have given my virginity to be out of there; it was awful.

"When they finally got the girls' locker area finished, I was in seventh heaven. No drug could make a person that high...and of course, I wasn't the only one to feel that way. Anyway, ever since I have been embarrassed to be naked around other girls or women; I would rather be that way around men because honestly, all naked women look the same to them. Yeah, they may like girls with curves and big boobs, but the cover means very little when what you are looking for is inside the book...if you get my drift."

Kathy was astounded. "Gosh, we never intended to embarrass you. It's hard to change our habits. Modesty has never been a big issue for me or anyone in my family, and Patti and I don't really think about it. You have nice features, a good shape, lean but not string bean, curves in the right places, square shoulders...a rather classic beauty. You're not cute or pretty, but attractive. If you were a man, I would call you handsome. What do think Patti?"

"Mom, I think my sister looks just fine; I'm proud to have her in the family."

Taken back, Deb blushed. "Do you really mean that?"

Kathy looked at her seriously. "Absolutely! Honesty is our policy." She then looked at Patti, who blushed and nodded vigorously.

Deb's expression changed; she was quite pleased to be complimented on her appearance. "Guys, I can't tell you what it means for you to say that. I know part of my problem is I've always thought of myself as a man; it's even better to be thought of as a woman. Thank you for your kindness; I love you more than anything. You're the best mom and sister in the whole world...and if you don't believe me, I'll kill you!"

The girls found comfort in a long hug but even longer to

stop laughing.

By the end of the week, several things began to gel. Deb was feeling better; her wounds were healing. Everyone felt like part of this new team. More importantly, Deb had changed. Like it or not, she was becoming a woman; it oozed out of her like honey from a comb. She was warmer, and a kindness began to show. She no longer thought only of herself; she was part of a family. Deb would never be the same; by finding love, she could now return it. The only question that haunted her was why it had taken so darn long to figure this out. On the other hand, she now had plenty of time to practice it the right way.

When Deb returned to the doctor, he released her to work on the condition she not overdo—no car chases, tackling escaping desperadoes, or using her body to stop oncoming traffic. She needed to understand that the right blow to the side could kill her, and he painted a grizzly picture of her lying on the ground strangling on her own blood to make his point. Deb was shaken by his warning, and understood what he was saying; she would take it easy. She was not happy with her new, temporary, desk job, but it was nice to get back to work. She had been bored to death during the last week or so with nothing to do but read and watch TV. On the other hand, she had read more in the last week than in the past five years, so everything was not necessarily bad. Her family had decided she should stay with them for a day or two while she made the transition back to work. Life was returning to normal as February surrendered to March on its journey toward spring.

Thirty-One

March was not a good or happy time for Kathy and Patti; bad memories of tragedy and near tragedy were hard to forget. As the winds of March whipped their way toward the end of winter, ominous thoughts and images appeared. What would March bring this year? Who might fall victim to its wrath? Of course, no one could know that this March would be different...in rather interesting ways.

At school everyone was looking forward to spring break. Patti and Colby's studies were going well. Patti discovered she could do algebra right along with the best of them. Colby was in hog heaven. Patti was tempted to throw cold water on him to calm him down. Another thing to consider was the eighth grade spring dance scheduled for the end of the month after spring break. Colby had asked Patti if she would like to go. Their love life had been on hold for some time although they had gone to a couple of movies. Colby had also gone to youth group a few times during the winter, but that produced no romance. An opportunity to actually go on another date was quite exciting. Patti told Colby she would like to go if he wanted to, but she did not want him to go on her account.

Early March held a certain intrigue while Patti and Colby decided what to would do. Of course, Patti's birthday was rapidly approaching. Somehow being fourteen sounded better than being thirteen. Patti had been cruising up the hill toward high school; the crest was in sight, and she could coast into West Wood High just like her mother. It sounded much more grown up to be a high school student. Granted, she would only be a few months older than she had been in eighth grade, but it didn't matter. Being in high school was special, and she could hardly wait. She sensed Colby felt the same way, and that connection only strengthened their relationship.

Deb decided she needed to be at her home for a while. However, she made it clear she would see them frequently, and they would be together. The Friday after she left, she called and caught Patti. Sarah was with her; they planned to go to youth group. Deb wanted to come by, visit everyone, then eat supper...possibly spend the night. Patti told her to come by soon so she could talk to Sarah. Deb arrived only minutes later. When she saw Sarah, they ran toward each other, but Patti quickly intervened, reminding Deb about her ribs. The wrong hug could hurt. She and Sarah shared a soft hug then sat down and talked like lost friends. Patti reminded Deb to share the news about her new family; Sarah flashed a big smile. "You couldn't have picked a better family, although..." She whispered. "You do know they're crazy, don't you?"

Deb went straight to the point. "Why else would I pick them?" Sarah laughed and the visit continued. When Kathy got home, Deb went to her and talked very quietly for a couple of minutes. Kathy changed her clothes and asked if Deb and Sarah wanted to get back into the cooking business and fix supper before youth group began. Sarah was thrilled, and Deb, caught by complete surprise, jumped at the chance to work with her old partner.

Patti wanted to know what Deb had been so secretive about; Kathy told her she would have to wait until she got home. It was a surprise. Poor Patti was fit to be tied; she hated to wait for things like this but knew her mother would not budge. She claimed patience was a virtue and Patti agreed, but it still drove her crazy.

Deb and Sarah concocted one of their famous mac and cheese variations and even Kathy was impressed. It was very satisfying seeing her new "daughter" excel in the kitchen at something other than loading a dishwasher. Deb was embarrassed by all the attention; she had always figured if what you cook doesn't kill you, then you've done okay. Kathy and Patti had higher standards and so did Sarah. After supper, Kathy took the younger girls to youth group while Deb cleaned up the kitchen.

Patti was so anxious to get home from AFLAME she nearly wet her pants. If her mother was even one minute late picking her up, she would die. Interestingly, her mother didn't pick her up; Deb did, and on the way home she was not talking. If she hadn't been carrying that darn gun, Patti would have beaten the news out of her, sore ribs and all.

Somehow they got home without any violence, and Patti rushed to the apartment to discover the news with Deb hot on her trail; she even had her handcuffs out in the event they had to restrain Patti. Kathy told her to calm down and sit in the living area, where they would talk. Kathy then told Patti, "While you were away, your sister and I talked about your fourteenth birthday and decided we should just skip it this year. What do you think?"

"Why Mother, how considerate of you and my sister to

ignore me like this; I assume we are going to forget about your birthdays too." Patti wanted to be fair.

Kathy raised her hand to her mouth. "Whoops, we didn't think about that. Did we, Deb?"

Deb's response was epic. "Nope."

"I guess we'll have to rethink the whole thing and let you know next week."

Patti jumped out of her seat and rushed to Deb. "Put the cuffs on me now; my dark side yearns for murder, and I don't want to kill anyone, especially in my own family!"

"Deb immediately complied, cuffing her to the arm of a chair. Kathy was disappointed in her children. "Whoa, hold your horses; maybe we need to reconsider this before any shots are fired. Patti, Deb and I want to do something special for your birthday. Do you have any requests?"

"Yes, I do; would you and Deb sing, 'Girls Just Wanna Have Fun,' all the verses...I really like that song." Patti flashed a big grin.

Deb remarked. "Oh, we have another smarty pants?"

"So it would seem." Kathy was amused.

"Okay, I'll be good. How about we go out on the town for an evening? Probably a weekend would be better than a weekday. We could go someplace nice to eat, then see a good movie—spend the evening together; it would be fun and something different."

An idea struck Deb. "You know, there's another possibility. One of the guys at work was telling us he had taken his wife to a dinner theater; he went on and on about how much fun they had, and they planned to go back. I could look into it. How does that sound?"

"What's a dinner theater?" Patti was unfamiliar with any such place.

"You go to a theater and eat a meal, then watch a live show. I'll bet you'd enjoy it. I think I've heard some people talking about it too; it would be fun." Kathy liked the idea.

"Okay, I'll give it a try, but would you consider letting Colby go with us? That would make it a perfect evening."

Kathy looked at Deb; Deb looked at Kathy; they both smiled as Deb said, "Sure, Colby can come, but no funny business or we'll put him in the trunk and cuff you to the steering wheel."

Patti was even more excited now; the big question was would Colby's parents allow him to go. Patti waited for a while and called Colby. She was shocked to discover what he told her. Colby had talked to his mother about the dance; she told him it was okay. However, she had another suggestion; she had heard about this same place and was excited about it. She and Mr. Duncan had gone to a dinner theater where they had lived before many times, and it was the one thing they really missed. She asked Colby if he would like to invite Patti to go along with them later in the month. Colby hadn't had a chance to mention it. Yes, his mother would let him go with Patti, as long as they would report on the evening and share any ups or downs. Patti was thrilled; she might actually be able to be with Colby twice on special dates. Of course, they wouldn't be alone, but perhaps that wasn't a bad thing.

March was looking up. Deb was able to get reservations at the dinner theater for all four of them in two weeks, just after Patti's birthday. She would be glad to wait. Colby was excited too; he had heard his folks talk about dinner theater, and if they were excited about it, it had to be exceptional. Of course, the best part had to do with the fine company he would be keeping. It was fun to be with Patti, but he also liked her mother. He did not know Officer Johnson, but if she was a friend of Patti's, she was okay in his book.

March plodded far too slowly to suit Patti, but it was still filled with surprises. School was approaching spring break and excitement filled the air. Many kids had special plans for their vacation. Patti had not even thought about it; Colby might be gone for two or three days to visit relatives, but he would be home the rest of the time; he and Patti hoped to get together. Then just before spring break began, Geoff made a big announcement. "I'm going to have a new neighbor; well, to be fair Colby will have a new neighbor too. Her name is Jennifer, and she is in the eighth grade."

Colby had no idea. "What? A new neighbor! I haven't heard anything. Where will they live?"

"Don't you know about that empty house down the street? It sold and the family that bought it will be moving in during spring break; they have a daughter our age. Like I said, her name is Jennifer, and I plan to welcome her into the neighborhood and show her around."

"Hey, Geoff, what if she isn't beautiful or weighs three hundred pounds?"

"Then you can show her around." Geoff grinned. Patti found this amusing since Geoff never talked much about girls or even showed any interest in them. What did he know he wasn't telling?

Patti's birthday came and went; she could not have cared less because she knew the coming weekend was going to be the best birthday ever. Her whole family would be there, plus Colby. Everyone agreed to meet at the warehouse about an hour before they needed to go. Once everyone arrived, Kathy announced. "I think we can forgo singing happy birthday; we wouldn't want to damage anyone's ears. In addition, I didn't bake a cake because Patti's sweet enough without it, but we want to give her a present before we head out for the evening."

Deb stepped forward with a nicely wrapped package and handed it to Patti. Patti was surprised; no one had said a thing, and she had not expected any gifts. "Why gosh, thank you; I had no idea you were getting me something."

Deb begged. "Go ahead, open it before we starve."

391

Patti carefully unwrapped and opened the box to find a finely bound copy of a student's study Bible. Patti was dumbstruck as she lifted the fine volume from its box. "Oh my, the perfect gift...thank you so much. I've wanted one but hadn't said anything about it. How did you know?"

"We have our ways." Her big sister, the detective, wasn't talking.

Patti opened the front cover to find the inscription, "To Patti, our real angel, happy birthday. We'll love you forever!" signed, "Kathy and Deb." Patti was so happy it came in tears. "Oh thank you again; this is wonderful. I'll cherish it always."

There followed a bit of chitchat; Patti introduced Colby to her "big sister." Colby was quite surprised; he didn't know she had a sister. Patti resolved this confusion by explaining Deb was her long lost sister. She had been lost for a long time, but had finally rejoined the family, much like the Biblical prodigal son. Colby was only slightly less puzzled by this explanation, and Patti didn't have the heart to tell him Deb was nearly a half year older than Kathy. Too many revelations can be dangerous, and Patti wanted to keep to Colby safe as long as possible.

Deb had agreed to take her car; it was bigger than Kathy's. As they headed down the stairs, leaving the apartment, Deb made a crushing announcement. "I know this is going to make Patti and Colby mad, but you have to sit in the back seat while Kathy and I sit up front. Colby, it's a family thing; if I sit back there with Patti we will fight all the time, spoiling the trip. On the other hand, if you sit with Kathy, she'll be flirting with you, which would make Patti jealous; we can't have that...too much tension. I hope it's okay."

Patti looked at Colby, smiled and kissed him on the cheek. "We have to behave because if we don't, Deb will make us ride in the trunk; she probably has a skunk back there."

Colby didn't have to say anything as he helped Patti into the back seat. His smile said it all.

392

Up to this point, no one had mentioned that Patti was wearing a dress. Kathy had found a less formal dress she liked for Patti to wear on special occasions. Patti had not been very excited but decided not to make it an issue. After all, the last time she had worn a dress, she had received numerous compliments, and young ladies enjoy such attention. When they got into the car, Colby noted he liked her dress and thought she looked pretty. Patti responded by scooting closer, laying her head on Colby's shoulder. Deb apparently was amused watching them in her rearview mirror. "Hey, I don't want any hanky-panky back there; Colby, if you mess with my sister, you're messing with me."

Colby almost jumped out of his seat, which knocked Patti sideways; Deb got so tickled she nearly had to stop the car. "Hey, that was mean. It's cold back here in this dress, and I asked Colby if I could sit next to him to keep warm."

"What did Colby say?" Deb was still laughing.

Colby winked at Patti. "I told her it would be okay; you can't have a hot date with a frozen girlfriend!"

"Colby, you're a man after my heart. Have you ever taken an interest in older women; you know, someone a little more mature?"

"Why yes, I sure have."

"And who, may I ask, was this lucky lady?"

"Why, my mom, ma'am; I've had an interest in her ever since I was little."

Kathy was now more amused than Deb, trying to suppress her laughter in the front seat. Deb was obviously beaten. "Ah, you just can't outsmart bright kids; we need to trade you guys in on a dumber pair."

Now it was Colby and Patti's turn to laugh, and laughing is so much more fun when you're sitting close to your best friend. Patti leaned on Colby and tightly grasped his hand.

The birthday party at the dinner theater was delightful. The food was tasty and more than enough to satisfy the hungriest of the group. Deb remarked more than once the meal alone was worth the price of admission, even if the play was a flop. However, the play was not a flop. While not a Rogers and Hammerstein, it was well performed and filled with surprises. Interestingly, it was one of those comedy dramas complete with a dead body and a little mystery. Deb howled frequently at the characters and the way they handled the crime. Patti and Colby delighted in the action sequences where someone was chasing someone else but never caught anyone. At one point an actor ran right past their table and nearly bumped Colby. Kathy chuckled frequently and enjoyed every moment. When the play ended and the actors came out for their final bow, the audience stood and clapped for the longest time even after the curtain closed. The enthusiasm was so intense that the stage crew opened the curtain again and the cast took a second bow, much to the delight of everyone.

On the way home, everyone raved about how much fun they'd had and decided they would definitely go back as soon as possible. When Colby mentioned that his folks hoped to attend near the end of the month, discussion arose suggesting they all might want to go and sit together. Colby liked the idea; he had enjoyed the company. He even liked Patti's big sister. Another plus was the drama company would be performing a new play starting the following week, so a trip at the end of the month would not result in a rerun. Kathy determined she wanted to go back for her birthday celebration in May.

In the meantime, Patti's dress was still a bit drafty and the weather even chillier; she definitely needed to sit close to Colby on the way home...to keep warm. Colby could probably make her hands warmer too and her face began to feel cool. Colby could not let Patti chill or freeze to death, so they held hands and exchanged a peck on the cheek every now and then. At one point, Colby's hand dropped on Patti's knee; he moved it away but she pulled it back. Her knee was bare and cold; she didn't want to risk getting "knee-monia." She rather liked the effect his hand made there. However, the kissing, innocent as it was, and the warm hand on her knee stirred a fire in both of them, and of course, spring was only a few days away, bringing its rites and fertility celebrations. Oops, that's how Patti had been conceived. Maybe it was good thing the familiar lights of their hometown were on the horizon and this ride was about to end. Timing means everything!

Deb took Colby home on the way to the apartment. He promised he would make a good report and see if they could all go again later that month. Patti kissed Colby goodbye, and the girls were soon home. The buzz continued about the fun they had. Deb decided to spend the night with them rather than go home so late; she hadn't brought anything to wear so Kathy loaned her some soft old clothes to use for pajamas; Deb was becoming much more comfortable there, creating less stress on everyone. If Deb was family, it was important she felt at ease when she was with them. Deb's conversion had affected the way she thought about things, especially how she viewed herself. She was more attractive as a female, but still had a few rough edges to smooth before the transition was complete.

The next morning they went to early church and returned for a quick breakfast. Deb had to be at work by lunch so could not tarry; however, she did have an announcement. "I hope I have this right, but isn't spring break the week after next?"

Patti thought a second. "Yes, it is."

"Well, I was wondering if we could set aside a day or two to be together. Maybe go somewhere or do something. I'd like to visit with you guys about a couple of ideas I've had, and I need some advice. What do you think?"

Kathy added. "You know, I was thinking the same thing. I promised Patti at the first of the year we would spend more time together, and spring break seems like a good time. It's kind of embarrassing, but we've never taken a vacation together. Maybe we could work things out and do something special. It would be fun, and if we beat Patti long enough, she'd probably go along with the idea."

"Oh boy, another beating! I can't believe you guys care that much for me. I can hardly wait!"

"Well, I guess we talked Sis into it. Kathy, you could sell needles to a porcupine; you're the best mom ever!"

"You are such dear children; I love it when we get along."

Patti was amazed. More was happening in her life than in the pit at the stock exchange; she might need to hire a personal secretary to keep up. When she got to school Monday, Colby had good news; his report to his mother confirmed her feelings about the dinner theater. They would definitely be going. In addition, they would be glad to share the evening with Patti and her family, including this older sister, although Mrs. Duncan was a bit suspicious about her. Then much to Colby's surprise, she even agreed to let him ride with Patti on the way there, but he would have to ride home with them. Colby was thrilled at her suggestion. His parents very much approved of Patti and her mother; Patti might not be as feminine as Mrs. Duncan had hoped, but she was "good people." Mrs. Duncan admired anyone with a strong character; Patti came by it naturally because she had a strong, determined mother. Mrs. Duncan would call Kathy and talk about everything.

Patti reported the news to her mother as soon as she got home and only a few moments before Mrs. Duncan called. They visited for the longest time, and Patti could not imagine what they were talking about. Even though Patti was starving, she begged her mother to fill her in on the details. Kathy told her everything was set for the end of the month. Mrs. Duncan would make the reservations; she confirmed the travel plans, and they visited about their children. Mrs. Duncan was anxious to meet this "older" sister and Kathy had explained it was a long story, Deb was not a blood relative, she was adopted...well, sort of adopted. Kathy assured her Deb would add extra spice to their evening, but Mrs. Duncan would need to keep an eye on her husband; Deb needed a good man. Mrs. Duncan had laughed and told Kathy she was such a remarkable woman Mr. Duncan didn't even dream about the opposite sex—and if he did, she'd cut him off at meal time—he'd starve in a week. Mrs. Duncan thanked Kathy for taking Colby to the play and giving him a chance to check it out; Kathy reminded her Colby was always welcome at their home and on any of their "adventures."

Patti was thrilled. Kathy also reported it looked like she could get a couple of days off. Dr. Bradford was to attend a conference next week and would be out of town. Kathy had the option of not working those days and had decided to accept it. They would have a long weekend at the beginning of spring break to do something special. When Deb called later that evening to say hi, Kathy updated her; Deb would work out her schedule and they would all be together. She was excited about the dinner theater too; it would be nice to meet the Duncans. That evening at bedtime Patti went to her mother. "Could I sleep with you tonight? I just can't tell you how happy I am everything has worked out so well for us lately; I love you so much."

Kathy was touched. "Honey, I brought you into the world and lived with you for nearly fourteen years. I am ashamed to admit it, but during that time I never appreciated what I had because I put myself ahead of you and denied you the love you deserved. I was such a fool. I can never make it up to you, but that doesn't mean I can't try. I've never met an angel, but if I did, it would have to be like you."

Patti was crying with her mother. They crawled into bed and held each other for the longest time. Finally Patti said, "Mom, we all make mistakes and you know I have forgiven you. Let's not talk about the past; let's just enjoy our future as long as we can. I wouldn't trade you for any other mother in the world; I'm sorry I don't have a dad, but I think we girls are doing just fine."

She kissed her mother on the cheek; her mother kissed her back; and they were soon asleep. As Patti drifted off, the thought crossed her mind that being close to her mother was much like being close to Colby; she felt safe and secure, yet not quite the same. Kathy's touch did not ignite any fire within her. Why did Colby's do just the opposite?

School wasn't over, but the week did not drag. It was

Friday before anyone realized it. Patti and Colby were both taking a short vacation; Sarah would be out of town the whole week; and Geoff was going to wait for the moving van. He was the most excited one of the bunch; he wanted to meet his new neighbor Jennifer and hoped she might find him interesting. One thing for sure, if Jennifer had any questions, Geoff had all the answers...and then some.

Patti came home to get ready for youth group; Kathy arrived an hour later. She told Patti that Deb might be over later and spend the rest of the weekend with them. Youth group was great; Patti showed off her new Bible. One of the leaders said it was a good choice because it held answers to many questions. Patti was pleased her mother and Deb had chosen well. She was a little surprised when Deb picked her up but was glad to see her.

When they got home, Deb was ready to visit. "Guys, I've been thinking about so much lately I can't keep it straight. I have some ideas to throw at you, and I want your honest opinion. I've been thinking about selling my house; I hate it there...I'm tired of being alone. I don't know what to do. If I sell it, I'll have to live somewhere, and honestly, I'd like to live with you, but I really hate to impose. You guys probably don't want me here all the time and, if either Kathy or I should find a man, we might not want to share him. Right now I'm just looking for ideas and not expecting answers. I want you to think about it."

No one was surprised by this announcement, but neither had any suggestions. Kathy said, "Deb, I'll think about this, but I have no idea. I want you to know you're welcome here as part of our family, and you're right, there could be complications. I'd rather not share my man, but we can cross that bridge when we come to it. If you need a place to stay, it might as well be here."

Patti added, "I'm with Mom; I'd love to have you here. Just keep your hands off Colby, and we'll get along fine."

Then it struck Kathy. "Wait a minute, Mr. Mitchell has been working across the hall on the other apartment; the front apartment was rented by one of the offices downstairs

398

for storage and kind of a lounge. He's been working on the back apartment for a long time; I swear the poor man will die working there. Maybe the back apartment is far enough along you could move in there; it would be hard to get much closer and not be living with us. We can probably check with him sometime during spring break and see what he says. It might be the perfect solution."

Patti could tell Deb seemed interested; they would find out and let her know.

It was getting late and the girls were sleepy. Deb had a short shift Saturday then three days off. After a short morning visit, the happy travelers had decided to leave right after early church and be gone at least through Monday. If they were having a lot of fun, they could extend their time into Tuesday with no problems. Patti and Kathy realized they really didn't have any luggage or travel gear, so they made a quick trip and found some inexpensive travel bags at a discount store. They returned home and began packing. When Deb arrived mid afternoon, Kathy and Patti announced they were ready to go. Deb had a bag packed at home, so these birds were ready to "fly the coup". Of course, it would be nice to know where they were going. That part was still in the air. By the end of dinner, they had concocted a plan, allowing them sight see, shop, and even fit in some entertainment.

Thirty-Two

Their timing was impeccable. The weather was balmy. They managed to find several good sales and caught the opening of a new movie. They had a wonderful time but noted on the way home the weather had changed. By the time they reached their apartment, snow flocked the air, worsened by a blustery north wind. They rushed from the car into the warmer stairwell and remarked it was nice to be home and not on the road. As they went up the stairs, Kathy heard noise from the apartment next door; she found the door ajar. Mr. Mitchell was finishing some work on the plumbing. Kathy apologized for bothering him, but he was glad to have an excuse to rest. She asked how the apartment was progressing, and he happily reported it would not be long before he could advertise its availability. Kathy brought Deb forward and told him she would love to rent the apartment to be close to her friends. Mr. Mitchell was pleasantly surprised, saying Deb could have the apartment if she didn't mind living around a few repair jobs and finish work. Deb noted she didn't mind because there was no hurry; she just wanted to have a place to live away from police station. Mr. Mitchell agreed the accommodations there were likely unpleasant; he'd do all he could to get everything ship shape, then contact Kathy when the apartment was livable; it wouldn't be too long.

Deb was thrilled; she planned to put her house on the market and if no one objected, she would move in with her new family until the apartment was ready. Everyone was excited that things were falling into place. Deb would be a great neighbor. As Kathy put it, she would be available to babysit Patti. Patti was not impressed; she figured she would have to babysit Deb!

Colby was still out of town, so Patti's love life was quiet. Deb was bringing over a few personal items each time she stopped by, storing them at the back of apartment. They had made a sleeping area for her and hoped to get her bed moved by the end of the week. On the other hand Deb was one of those people who could sleep anywhere, so it didn't matter if she had a bed or not. Patti found her amusing. For all of Deb's blustering, she was more a child than an adult. She was good at being a police woman, but helpless at everything else. However, her transformation into a woman had expanded her interests; she really wanted to learn to cook and take better care of herself. She even told Patti she was giving up excessive drinking. Deb made it clear she had drunk way too much way too often. She admitted she lost control when she was drunk and had gone way too far on more occasions than she cared to admit. Patti was proud of her; if Deb really meant what she said, she and all those around her would be better off.

Kathy had not talked much about her work but obviously was pleased. She had acknowledged that working for Dr. Bradford was different, but she loved the hours, and the job was no worse than her previous one. She did say she had caught Dr. Bradford staring at her on several occasions; she thought he was interested but had said nothing nor made any indication to support it. Kathy liked him although she felt she didn't know him very well. If he made the right move, she would give him a chance. On the other hand, the whole idea was unsettling; she had not dated since high school—that had not gone well. She had changed a lot since then...and was a lot smarter.

By midweek Patti checked to see if Colby was home and caught him as he was about to leave; he didn't know very much. He had not talked to Geoff, but there didn't seem to be any activity around the empty house so he assumed Jennifer had not yet arrived. In addition, he knew Geoff would call or contact him some way; Geoff couldn't be quiet about anything he was excited about, and he was definitely excited about Jennifer. Colby thought he and Patti could get together at the end of the week. He promised to call as soon as possible.

Patti had tried to help Deb with her belongings, and they had been enjoying time together in the evenings. Colby finally called. They could have the whole day Friday; Colby agreed to go to youth group with her that evening. She decided to go to his house in the morning then come back to the apartment in the afternoon. Deb had some boxes she wanted to move and Patti had agreed to help; it wouldn't hurt Colby to pitch in and haul a few too. Men have to be good for something!

Kathy took Patti to Colby's on her way to work, and Deb would pick them up later. Not too long after Patti arrived, Geoff called, reporting a moving van had pulled in front of Jennifer's new house and appeared ready to unload. Patty and Colby decided to steal some of Geoff's thunder and check out the situation. They strolled down the street, and as the house came into sight, a car pulled in the driveway. Two adults and a young girl about their age got out and perused the house and yard. The man turned, walked toward the van, and was soon talking to the driver and his assistant. As Patti and Colby got closer, Patti strained to get a look at Jennifer, or at least, who she thought was Jennifer.

The girl was taller than Patti, but not very tall; at a distance she looked quite pretty, but Patti noted something about her did not seem right. As they moved closer, Patti noted Geoff was headed down his driveway on his bicycle as fast as it would go; he passed them with a shout and was soon in front of Jennifer's house where he almost crashed into the van. Colby couldn't remember seeing Geoff so excited; he was off his bike and running up the yard toward Jennifer and her mother. It appeared they knew Geoff because he immediately began to talk to them like long lost friends. By this time, Colby and Patti had reached the edge of the yard, and Patti could clearly see Jennifer; she then realized what was odd about her. She had a look of unmistakable sadness that almost made Patti cry. Something was wrong here, and Patti intended to find out what it was.

Geoff brought Jennifer down to Patti and Colby and introduced her to them, then they introduced themselves. Jennifer smiled; she was very pretty. Geoff explained Colby and Patti were his friends and Jennifer would like them. Jennifer seemed pleased to meet some kids her own age and thanked them for stopping by. While Geoff was talking to Colby, Patti drew Jennifer aside. "Jennifer, I know it must be tough moving to a new location, being in a new school and not really knowing anyone. I've lived here all my life, and I still feel uncomfortable sometimes. I want you to know, if you ever need to talk to a girl, I can be there for you. We all love Geoff to death, but he's a guy and I'm sure you know about them."

Jennifer looked at Patti, surprised at her suggestion, but managed a smile. "Patti, thank you; thank you very much. I can't tell you how much it means to me. I would like to visit with you sometime; you might be able to help me."

Patti noted Jennifer's eyes were watering. "Listen, give me a call; Geoff knows my number. I can come over; we could take a walk; you name it. Call me any time, I mean it."

><del>⁓</del>   <del>⁓</del>×

Colby and Patti had no desire to improve their moving and unpacking skills, so they said good bye and headed back to Colby's house. Patti told Colby she felt sorry for Jennifer and didn't even know her. Colby had noticed she seemed unhappy. They hoped Geoff could cheer her up...or at least, not drive her crazy. Colby and Patti enjoyed the pleasant day, opting to walk for a while. They talked about school; they had already decided to skip the dance. The dinner theater would be more fun, and they would still be together. Patti asked Colby if he would be able to go to camp this year.

Colby told her he had talked to his mother; she was not opposed to it, but she and Mr. Duncan had not finalized their plans. However, she assured him they would take his situation into consideration and not intentionally make it impossible for him to go. Patti said she would keep her fingers crossed. She was going to be a counselor at Fun Camp again, and her mother had promised to pay for eighth grade camp if Patti wanted to go. Patti was pleased by her mother's generosity, but Kathy had been a different person since their confrontation in January. Patti felt bad about it but realized it had been for the best. When they got to Colby's house, they spent the rest of the day enjoying each other's company and waiting for Deb.

When Deb arrived a little after 2:00, they went with her to load boxes; it wasn't a big deal, and they were glad to help. Once Deb's things were safely tucked away, they decided to walk to the park and further enjoy the nice weather. However, once there, they found a bench and sat down. Patti scooted close to Colby and held his hand. A few moments later Colby said, "Patti, I don't know if I should tell you, but I enjoy being with you more than anyone else. I don't really understand love very much, but I guess I love you. I don't know why, but you make my life complete."

He leaned over and kissed Patti. "Colby, I've told you how I feel about you and nothing has changed; you are the greatest guy in the world, and I love you more every day."

She returned Colby's kiss; they embraced then kissed on the lips. Patti felt a tingle inside and Colby must have felt it too. "You really like it when we kiss, don't you?"

"Oh, yes, I do; it makes me feel all warm inside."

"Well, I like it too." Colby kissed her again.

They kissed a couple more times, then Patti said, "Maybe we'd better get back before we end up spending the night here. Mom might worry and send the cops after us."

"You're right; my mom would probably call out the National Guard."

Within minutes they were inside the apartment and thinking about something to eat. Lovey dovey stuff can make people really hungry.

Deb was there, sorting and repacking. "Hey, Patti, you had a call while you were out; it was a girl...I think her name was Jennifer. She would like for you to call her back; I wrote her number by the phone."

"Why thanks, sometimes you can be so sweet; I won't mention the other times." Patti grinned.

"Well, I love you too! I think."

Patti went to the phone, called the number, and asked for Jennifer. They visited for a few minutes. Patti put the phone back in its cradle and came back to Colby. "What did Jennifer want?"

Patti looked serious. "Oh, she'd like to visit; we'll meet tomorrow and spend some time together. I'll let you know more after I talk to her."

Patti and Colby helped Deb, watched a TV show, then helped get supper ready so they could eat before youth group. It had been a wonderful day, and Patti dreamed of a time when she could spend more days with Colby—not just two or three each month. Kathy picked Colby and Patti up from AFLAME and took Colby home. On the way, she asked about Patti's new friend. Patti briefly explained what she knew, noting she and Jennifer could hardly be called friends when they had only just met, but if Jennifer was a friend of Geoff's, she could be Patti's friend too.

Saturday morning flew by before anyone realized it had arrived. Deb was working and Kathy was tired, so Patti slept in for a while. Jennifer called again later in the morning, and they arranged to meet after lunch in front of her house. Patti was anxious to get to know to her. Kathy needed to run an errand, so she dropped Patti off near Jennifer's house and Patti walked the rest of the way. It was warm in the sun with a cool spring breeze. Just as planned, Jennifer was waiting outside. When she saw Patti, she walked quickly toward her, motioning for her to stop; it appeared she wanted to get away as quickly as possible.

Patti finally got within listening range. "Patti, thank you for meeting with me; I really need to talk to someone and I don't know why, but I feel you can help me."

"I'll do what I can."

"Is there someplace we can sit and visit?"

"Well, we could could go by the middle school; there are some benches along the walks, or I guess we could go by the park. Whatever you think."

"Okay, let's go to the middle school; I guess I'll be going there Monday, so I might as well know the way."

They finally got to the middle school and comfortably situated. "Patti, this may seem weird. I mean, you must be wondering why I want to talk to a complete stranger..."

Patti interrupted. "Jennifer, sometimes, we need to talk; it doesn't matter who listens."

Jennifer nodded. "Well, thank you...here goes. I know you saw my folks yesterday. Well, my mom is not my mom; my real mom passed away when I was little. She got sick and after a short time, she died. I loved her; she was special. My dad had lots of problems about six months after she was gone. He wrecked the car; he had been drinking, and some witnesses said he tried to kill himself. He wasn't hurt very much, but when he recovered, he went through a period of being very angry. One time he even hit me. Then he started crying, telling me over and over how sorry he was, that he was no good and everyone would be better off if he were dead. Finally one of his friends at work took him to a doctor and they put him in therapy; you know, kind of like rehab. I lived with my grandparents and started school there. I stayed the whole year.

"My grandparents, my dad's folks, were nice people, but I wasn't happy living with them. When my dad got better, he came by their house, and we talked for long time. He didn't want me anymore; he told me I reminded him too much of my mom, and he just couldn't think about her every time he saw me, so we agreed I would live with my mom's sister, my Aunt Mary. She and her husband didn't have kids; they both worked and didn't get along. They just lived together. It wasn't a bad place, but there was little happiness. After about two years, they got divorced. Aunt Mary said she wanted to keep me, but it was really hard for her to work and take care of me, so she called my dad and asked if he could do anything to help. About a week later, he showed up and told me how grown up I was and how much he had missed me. He cried for a long time and told me he was sorry for abandoning me; he wanted to know if I could forgive him. Well, it's hard for a kid to hate her dad, so I forgave him. He asked if I would like to come live with him; I figured, 'what the heck,' it couldn't be any worse than living with my aunt. I was wrong.

"My dad was still a mess; he didn't take care of himself. The apartment he lived in was more like a pig pen than a home. I told him I wasn't going to stay with him if he lived like that, so he told me to clean it up and make it the way I wanted. Patti, it took me all summer to get the place in order. I can't tell you how many times I threw up cleaning up his messes. I had to do the cooking, laundry and cleaning; I felt like a slave. Well, in third grade, I made a big mistake. I told my teacher about my situation one day after school; she told the counselor, who told the principal, who reported us to social services. They made a surprise visit and almost arrested my dad. I guess he admitted some of things he was doing, and they told him they were going to take me away if things didn't change, pronto!

"When my dad came home, he was really mad and wanted to know how they found out about us. I told him I had no idea but figured out later it was probably my big mouth. I never told my dad; I was afraid to. Anyway, something weird happened; the next day my dad told me things were going to change; he had a plan. As soon as was school out, we moved. He got a better job and really straightened up. He helped me around the house, learned to do some of the cooking, and our place was really nice. It was kind of spooky. I figured it wouldn't last, but by the end of fourth grade, I actually began to like my dad. We were best friends. He told me I was his girl and no one would ever come between us; I believed him and for two years, I was in heaven. Dad always helped me at home; we would get dressed up and go out on the town...almost like a date. He would joke about his "younger" girlfriend, and Patti, I really felt special; it was nice to get the attention.

"Then he dropped me like a hot potato. He met my 'new' mom at work. His company had this big celebration, and he was to help get it organized. My 'new' mom, Katie, worked for the catering company in charge of the food. They had talked on the phone, then met once or twice. Dad was smitten; she was young and pretty; they had things in common. So they started dating; that's when he dumped me...and Patti, I know why. It was the sex. My dad never so much as touched me except for a pat on the back or a kiss on the cheek; he told me one time if anyone ever touched me, you know, in a bad way, he would kill them. I think my dad is a good man, but once he started having sex with her, it was over. They got engaged and then married a year ago. I can't be angry at him; he is still good to me, but he only pays attention to Katie...and she has been good for him. However, right before we moved, they dropped a bomb on me...well, actually several bombs.

"Dad came home from work and told us he had received a promotion and we would be moving. No, it couldn't wait until I graduated from eighth grade. Katie got all excited and said she could have a baby; that's all she ever talks about. I swear she wants a dozen kids. She must be nuts! I expect her to announce any day that she is pregnant; she has a whole box of those pregnancy kits in her bathroom.

Patti, if she gets pregnant and has a baby, I'm done for; I might as well be dead. They won't even know I exist."

Patti studied Jennifer; she wanted to cry because she felt so sorry for her. Jennifer's story made sense even if it didn't make sense. Her father was simply erasing the hurtful part of his life, and Jennifer right along with it. Patti reached for her hand. "Jennifer, you don't know anything about me, but I can tell you I understand everything you've said. I guess we could sit here and cry about it all afternoon, but that would solve nothing. I think what you need is a new family, not at home, but away from home. I will be your friend; you've already met Colby and Geoff; I have another friend, Sarah. We're all crazy, but we're good people. You're welcome to be with us and we will care for you. If you don't mind walking for a while, I'd like for you to meet some other friends. Would that be okay?"

Jennifer perked up. "Sure, it's a nice day to be outside."

They walked past Patti's home. She wanted Jennifer to see the park. Then they headed back toward the apartment. "You actually live in this big building?"

"Yup, upstairs."

When they entered, Jennifer's eyes bulged. "Wow, this place is huge!"

"Everyone says that."

Patti introduced Jennifer to her mother, and they exchanged a few words. Then Deb suddenly appeared, so Patti introduced her "big" sister. Deb shook Jennifer's hand. Patti briefly explained to Deb and her mother that Jennifer was in need of a family. Kathy told her she had come to right place; she was welcome anytime. Deb informed her if she ever needed the police, she was her man...er, well, woman. Jennifer laughed. They visited for a while, got a drink, then headed back to the park. Once outside, Jennifer commented, "Your sister looks almost as old as your mom."

"You're right. She's six months older than Mom."

Jennifer looked shocked. "What?"

"You heard me."

"Well, how can that be?"

"She's adopted."

"Oh...I see...I think." Jennifer scratched her head. "Where's your dad?"

"Never had one."

"Never?"

"Nope...never."

No other words were spoken until they found a bench at the park, then Patti spoke. "I told you there was a lot about me you don't know, and someday I promise to share more; however, there is one thing we might as well settle right now." Patti leaned over and gave Jennifer a peck on the cheek. "I'm from a family of kissers!"

Shocked by Patti's kiss, Jennifer almost jumped off the bench but managed to compose herself, and did something she had never done. She leaned over and returned Patti's peck. Patti held her hand; they hugged and whispered, almost simultaneously, "friends." The circle was growing.

They stayed in the park for some time enjoying its beauty. As the sun began to go down and the weather cooled, Patti finally said, "I suppose we'd better get you home before someone gets worried."

"I doubt they even know I'm gone, but you're right; I don't want to get in trouble on my second day in town. That would look bad."

They headed back to the apartment, where Deb offered to take Jennifer home; Patti rode along for company. After

Jennifer had been safely delivered, Patti and Deb chatted. "Hey, I like your new friend."

"Me too. I think she's a good kid." Patti paused. "Why do some people work so hard to screw up their kids?"

"You've got me; I don't know, but it happens all the time. It seems like kids are the innocent victims in lots of crimes. The sad thing is the crimes are not necessarily illegal. Kids just get caught in the crossfire, and that is no place to be even if you're grown up. Is that Jennifer's problem?"

"It looks like it."

"Do you think you can fix her?"

"I'd like to try. She deserves to be happy; I'll do my best."

✐ Thirty-Three ✐

Spring break was almost over. Patti, Deb, and Kathy went to church and came back for a late breakfast. School would be starting Monday, and the following weekend would bring the end of March and a second trip to the dinner theater. So far, March had been good to everyone. Deb was happy, Kathy had another child, Patti had a big sister and a new friend, Colby still loved Patti. Eighth grade was almost over, and Patti would be in high school in less than six months. How could things be any better?

When school started on Monday, Patti was glad to see Jennifer; their lockers were right across the hall from each other. Jennifer was in most of her classes; she even had algebra. Apparently, Jennifer was a good student and fit right in with Patti's friends. Of course, Geoff was sticking to her like velcro, but she appeared to enjoy his attention, and he could certainly answer her questions. Jennifer liked Geoff; he could make her laugh, and she needed all the laughter therapy she could get.

The last week of March went well. Toward the end of the week Jennifer told Patti she liked her new school, missed

some of her old friends but had made new ones. They all
ate lunch together and had time to talk every day. Of
course, they also had to eat. Geoff had noticed he could
eat faster if he didn't chew his food, so his friends were
often forced to look the other way; watching Geoff could
bring on a severe case of indigestion. His habits would
have killed a normal person, but then...enough said. On
Friday Patti almost invited Jennifer to youth group, but
decided she'd had enough excitement for one week. There
would be plenty of time later.

Patti had gotten a sturdy book cover for her new Bible and
decided to carry it at school; if she had it with her, she
could sneak in a verse or two at the end of class or after
lunch. In addition, she felt carrying it made a statement. If
God is with you, why not carry His Word. A few kids
questioned her, and it wasn't long before some of them
referred to her as "Patti the Preacher" because she carried
the Bible. At first, Patti ignored the title, but the more she
thought about it, the more of an honor it became. Perhaps,
when kids had questions, she could offer help. That's what
Jesus would do.

Sarah went home with her that Friday and they went to
youth group. Sarah had changed. She was more confident
and just seemed stronger. Having responsibilities at home
had been good for her. She stood taller and was even
prettier when you could see her whole face and not just the
top of her head. Patti was very happy for her. Sarah had a
good sense of humor and could be really ornery. She
brought sunshine into every day.

This Saturday was extra special because it meant another
trip to the dinner theater and an evening with Colby. They
got to sit close and even sneak in a kiss or two on the
way...well, it may have been just a couple of pecks, but that
was better than nothing. The dinner seemed better than
before, and the play was another comedy, which delighted
everyone. Deb sat next to Mrs. Duncan; they joked and
wisecracked all evening. Poor Mrs. Duncan would get
tickled and laugh until she cried. Patti and Colby enjoyed
watching the adults almost as much as the play. Kathy and

Mr. Duncan were the only ones that remembered anything about it the next day. Mr. Duncan told Kathy it was fun to see his wife happy; she often took life too seriously and needed to laugh more often. The Duncans planned to attend as often as possible and even bring Caitlyn along; she had stayed with a friend, but Mrs. Duncan was pretty sure she would have liked the play.

On the way home, Deb told Patti to hang on to Colby; the Duncans would make good in-laws. Patti informed Deb she completely agreed but didn't want to marry Colby while they were still in middle school. Besides Colby hadn't asked her yet and it didn't seem fair to marry him without his permission. Deb told her she wasn't suggesting they get married, but if the time ever came, she had picked a good family. Patti did not argue but noted she hoped Colby would ask her fairly soon—before some other girl stole his heart. Kathy injected she didn't need a son-in-law right away; she already had two crazy girls who talked too much. She was soundly booed!

The week and March ended gracefully. It wasn't until Deb read the church bulletin that she realized it was not only a day to honor her new Lord, but to honor her as well. She drove home, noting, "There are many holidays throughout the year, some well known like Christmas, and others not so well known like Flag Day; today, April 1, is celebrated to honor me and so many other fools who have alienated their families, squandered great opportunities, and become so self absorbed that they are the only person in every room. We honor these fools today; they deserve a day of glory. As for me, I have seen the light with help from two of the most wonderful people on earth. I mean it, guys; I always partied hardy on this day, but never again because I no longer feel like a fool. I thank you from the bottom of my heart." Kathy and Patti were taken back by Deb's remarks and said nothing for some time.

Finally, Kathy said quietly, "Deb, I don't say this as your mother, but as a friend. I will be honest. You and I are so different...and yet, in some ways, very much alike. I have always loved your honesty and straightforwardness; you call a spade a spade. Just now I realized one of our

412

common bonds. Until my youngest child knocked some sense into me, deep down I think I hated myself. I had the world by the tail; when I looked in the mirror, I thought I saw perfection...not so much in the physical sense, but as a person. Then I met, or perhaps I should say, discovered, a young man who was attracted to me and made my heart dance. I'm ashamed to say this, but I think if Brandon had asked me to drink drain cleaner, I would have done it and never asked why. I may never understand what happened, but just one night of sex...one mistake...doomed me.

"The ironic thing is this same mistake saved me. Most children would admit they owe their parents their life, but for me it's the other way around. I owe my daughter everything. Patti saved me from myself. How can I ever repay her? However, right now I realize you too have hated yourself all these years; I can't say exactly why. It doesn't really matter. You have fought tooth and nail to avoid being a woman; you came to hate God for the things that went wrong around you; you let yourself be treated like trash because that's what you thought you were, but Deb, I hope you understand we were both so wrong and so stupid and such fools. I hope you never feel that way again. I love you, Patti loves you, and we will never abandon you."

Deb had now parked in front of the warehouse, and it was probably a good thing. She and Kathy were crying so hard no one could see the road. Patty was crying too; she hated to recall the pain her mother had endured all those years. Her big sister had also suffered terribly. They sat in the car for a long time until Patti suggested. "Let's go fix something warm for breakfast and be together; I'm hungry."

Deb took note. "Me too."

"Me three. Come children, let's go upstairs and figure out what to eat before you guys chew up the seats."

"Yummy," added Deb; Patti injected, "Yuck." It's hard to make everyone happy!

Today these fools and ex-fools had discovered what bound them together, and it appeared nothing and no one was likely to break those ties.

⥥⥥⥥⥥

April is known for its showers, but this April roared by like a raging fire and expired before anyone knew it. Mr. Mitchell reported some of the materials he had ordered were on hold due to shipping problems, but he was working to get the apartment ready for Deb and had made good progress. Kathy's work continued to both interest and challenge her; she noted Dr. Bradford was more relaxed and at ease. He had even made a few jokes, although his humor needed some polish. It was still a move in the right direction. Deb seemed happier every day; many of the guys at the station had commented she was almost human and quizzed her about this transformation. Deb had told them she had found new meaning to her life, and a Man that truly loved her.

This information instigated the investigation of the century to discover who this Man might be. Anyone who loved Deb was an honest threat to society and needed to be found and put behind bars. After work one day, one of the older detectives observed he needed no investigation to determine this culprit. Only one Man could love the likes of Deb, and He was God. Deb smiled and told him old detectives didn't need to learn new tricks; they were good enough without them. He placed his hand on her shoulder and congratulated her. Deb remarked she should have found Him a lot sooner and was surprised when the detective responded, "No Deb, it had to happen at the right time, and sooner was not that time; God is like a good running back in football. He waits for the holes to open; He doesn't try to make them all by Himself." Deb told her mother about it when she got home, and Kathy noted this old detective was nobody's fool.

At the end of the month, Deb began to make plans for Kathy's birthday; they had already agreed to go back to the dinner theater. However, Deb wanted a big bash and hoped they could get more people involved. She talked to Patti about it. "Do you think your grandparents would like to go; I'm sure the Duncans would if they can, and I was thinking about a surprise guest."

"What do you mean, a surprise guest?"

"I thought I would ask Dr. Bradford; Kathy thinks he's kind of dull. Maybe we could give him a good time and get some laughs out of him. What do you think?"

"Oh, gosh, I don't know. I bet Grandma Bender would love to go, but Grandpa is another story; it's hard to get his butt out of his favorite chair in front of the TV. You're right about the Duncans; Mrs. Duncan loves the theater, and Mr. Duncan does too. As for Dr. Bradford, I have no idea, but it would be nice to invite him and give him an idea of something Mother likes. I would like to see her go on date. It would be good for her."

"Okay, you ask the Duncans, and how about we both go talk to the Benders. Why heck, do they even know they have a new granddaughter?"

"Whoops, I don't think so."

Patti called Colby and lit the fuse there. The next day, on the pretense of running an errand, they went by the Benders and dropped their bombshells. Mrs. Bender was shocked to discover her family had grown without her knowledge; Mr. Bender said he already knew his kids were crazy, so nothing surprised him. He was pleased to meet his new granddaughter and even happier to discover she was gainfully employed and would not be coming around begging for handouts. Deb instantly liked Mr. Bender; he didn't fool around. Mrs. Bender thought the play would be fun, and Mr. Bender liked Deb's description of the food, but he had been thinking about having his appendix removed and might schedule it then. Deb told him he could postpone the operation long enough to go to a birthday party for one of his crazy kids. If he was going to get nasty about it, she would cuff him and take him to jail—the food was less savory there. Given this choice, Mr. Bender began leaning in favor of the better food. Deb assured him he had made a wise choice, but she could tell he would grumble about it for the next thirty days. Mr. Bender noted his grandkids were a lot smarter than his children. By this time, everyone was laughing, and it was obvious Deb was a big hit with Kathy's folks. They would make themselves available. Mr. Bender's last question more or less summarized his feelings. "Do I have to dress up for this darn thing?"

"No, just look nice; we don't want you to embarrass the rest of the family."

Mr. Bender smiled. Happiness is casual.

Deb made an appointment with Dr. Bradford. She made no effort to explain her relationship or lack thereof with the doctor. She simply asked him if he would like to get away for an evening to celebrate Kathy's birthday; it was to be a surprise. Dr. Bradford was caught off guard but quickly recovered. "Why, yes, I think I would like to do that; Kathy is a great nurse. Would I need to bring anything?"

"Nope, it's just a fun night with family and friends. I hope you can come. I'll get back with you on the details, but you might give me a home phone number so I can leave a message. I don't want Kathy to get suspicious."

The doctor gave her what she needed and Deb left. Later, when Kathy asked Deb what she was doing in the hospital, Deb's curt reply was, "Police business." Kathy seemed satisfied.

A few days later, Deb reminded Kathy about their plans and that she had already made reservations. Kathy had forgotten and was pleased to be reminded...not necessarily that she was having a birthday, but that she was going back to the dinner theater. Kathy asked if the Duncans would be there, and Deb told her she did not know for sure, but she had reserved enough seats for everyone. She promised she would get everything arranged and all the plans in order; Kathy would not have to worry about a thing...except being available; it would be a shame to miss her own birthday party. Deb talked to Patti about the trip; it appeared everyone was going, even Colby's sister Caitlyn.

The birthday plans obscured the fact that eighth grade was about to end. The middle school had given up eighth grade graduation years ago, but they did have an evening assembly to honor their eighth graders and present awards. Most of the students were excited about the end of school, but Patti was so distracted it didn't really occur to her until they announced plans for the honors assembly. Patti was shocked and told Colby she couldn't believe school was almost over and summer vacation on the horizon. Colby admitted he was surprised too and then remembered to tell Patti he was going to camp again. Patti was thrilled; she could hardly wait, but decided to calm down and take one big event at a time; they had to surprise her mother.

Patti had checked periodically with Jennifer to make sure she was okay and not having problems. She was adjusting well and actually liked her new school. She enjoyed Geoff's friends and had generally been well received by her new classmates. However, unlike the rest of the students, she was not looking forward to summer and vacation. Jennifer was not happy at home. She knew her new mom could turn up pregnant any day, making her life more miserable. Patti told her to keep in touch, and they would do some things. Jennifer promised she would contact Patti if necessary. At least being ignored meant she could be gone, and no one ever know it.

Just a few days before Kathy's birthday party, Deb laid out the details. The Duncans would be going to the play, but Colby would be riding with them. She had reserved a big table and they would all sit together...and yes, Patti could sit next to Colby...if she was nice. After the play, they would stop for coffee or a drink and find out whether Kathy had enjoyed her birthday. If she hadn't, they'd kill her. Deb had a way of making things fun.

Patti was disappointed she could not go with Colby but recognized it was for the best. She and Deb really wanted to surprise their mother. The week ended quickly and before anyone realized it, they were dressed for the theater and on their way. Kathy was excited; she not only enjoyed the plays, but also the chance to be out and about. Deb was the last person anyone would have thought to be a patron of the arts. On the other hand, given the right circumstances—multiple killings, stacks of dead bodies, a villain to hiss, or heroine to kill—Deb was in seventh heaven. These plays had none of these qualities...but Deb liked them anyway. Maybe people can change. Patti enjoyed the plays and being close to the action. She even told her mother she would like to be in a play sometime, and if Colby wasn't in it too, that was his misfortune.

When the girls arrived, they quickly moved toward the building. Once inside, they made their way to the table. Kathy was not paying any special attention but noticed Mrs. Duncan, who seemed particularly happy. Then as she focused on this panorama, she noticed more familiar faces. Her parents were there and even Dr. Bradford. What in the world? Kathy grabbed Deb's arm. "Is this your doing?" Deb smiled but said nothing. "I should have expected something like this from you! When we get home, you'll get a good spanking!"

"Oh, Mommy, I hope so! I just love it when you beat me." Deb gave Kathy a hug.

With that the guests stood and applauded, with a round of laughter.

Deb had arranged the seating, and by coincidence Kathy sat next to Dr. Bradford; she glared at Deb, knowing full well what she was up to. Deb sat next to Mr. Bender so she could be close to her new grandpa; the two of them hooted all evening, and Mrs. Bender kept having to quiet them. As dinner ended, the waiters brought Kathy a small birthday cake, announced the occasion, then sang happy birthday. Kathy was embarrassed by all the attention but managed not to cry. Everyone enjoyed the play for one reason or another. Best of all, Mr. Bender told his wife they would definitely be coming back; she was thrilled. They spent too much time at home; it was nice to get away and have fun.

At the coffee shop, the buzz continued. Dr. Bradford told Kathy he was jealous. Her birthday party was better than any he ever had. Kathy promised they could come back for his birthday and even the score. Dr. Bradford was pleased. As they got ready to leave, he pulled Kathy aside. "I want you to know you have the most wonderful family and friends; please tell Deb thank you for inviting me; I had a great time. I would love to come back...on one condition."

Kathy's attention piqued. "And what would that be?"

"You must come with me. The play is out late and I'm scared of the dark." The doctor smiled.

"So you want Nurse Kathy to come with you and keep you safe from the bogeyman?" Dr. Bradford nodded with a sheepish grin. "It's a deal." Kathy reached for and shook the doctor's hand. "Would it be all right if I bring my kids? I have an awful time finding a sitter. Deb gets carried away with her handcuffs and Patti likes to swing on the light fixtures; they go nuts when I'm not home."

Dr. Bradford started to laugh. "Sure, you'd better bring them; we can slip a sedative in their water and really enjoy the play. You know what they say, 'some people's kids.'"

"You know, for a guy without children, you sure know a lot about them."

"Hey, it's been awhile, but I was one once; some things are hard to forget!" The doctor smiled.

A connection had been made and a few lights were shining...even in the dark.

As soon as Kathy and her two girls got into the car, she dropped a bombshell. "I'm not sure, but I think I just got asked out...and worse yet, I'm almost positive I accepted."

Patti yahooed and Deb remarked. "All right! It's about time you get in on the action and some rich man buys you nice things and treats you first class. You deserve the best!"

"Deb, I hardly think Dr. Bradford is a rich man; he'll probably be paying off his school loans until he's fifty."

Deb seemed overjoyed. "Be that as it may, you've hooked a good one!"

419

"I hardly think I've hooked anyone; he probably wants me for my money, the poor man."

"Okay, at least he's a nice guy."

"I agree, and I find him more interesting all the time."

Patti injected. "I'm glad to hear that, Mom; you never talk about men. I'm glad you found one."

Kathy pointed at Deb and Patti. "There is one more thing."

Deb quickly noted. "What might that be?"

"I told him I would have to bring my kids; no sitter will put up with you guys."

"You're kidding?" Deb paused to think. "Well, at least you didn't lie to him."

"I'm not kidding, and the good doctor agreed; that's why I said, 'yes.' It's one thing for the guy to look good, which he does; it's even more important for him to have brains!"

"If you say so." Deb shook her head as her voice trailed away. "If you say so."

On Monday, Colby told Patti that Caitlyn had enjoyed the evening. He was surprised because normally if everyone in the family was for something, she was against it and vise versa. It made Colby mad because he knew she only wanted attention...and if that was what she wanted, then there was something down by the railroad station she should see. It was lying on the ground between these two metal rails, visible at only at a certain time of the day. There might even be a whistle blown to alert her to its location. Just wait a moment and...POW! She'd get a whole train load of attention. Sometimes Colby didn't like his sister. However, in this case, she told her mother the play was fun and the food good; she had especially liked the soft serve ice cream. Colby agreed with this point. Even Caitlyn wasn't stupid all the time! Anyway, the evening had been a great hit for his family, and Mrs. Duncan wanted

Kathy to know she hoped it was worth being one year older. When Patti delivered the report, Kathy told her to tell Colby yes, it was worth it. Adding a one to her previous age could not spoil a delightful evening.

Kathy had spoken to her mother, who reported her dad had a great time with his new granddaughter. He told her he looked forward to going back, just a romantic evening for the two of them. Mrs. Bender was shocked at his brashness and rather embarrassed, even more so when she realized he was serious. "Why, Kathy, I don't know what's got into your dad. He's acting like a teenager again."

"What's wrong with that, Mom; it's not like he wanted to go with someone else. You should feel pretty special he still wants to be with you."

"Heavens! I never thought of that. Maybe the old fool is a better man than I thought. I think I'll fix him something special for supper tonight; maybe you'd better not come over this evening...er, we might...well, you know, be busy."

"Mom, I'll stay away and keep the grandkids at home; you and Dad have...well, have fun. I love you."

Dinner theater seemed to spark all kinds of romance; no wonder it was always sold out!

It's hard to beat live drama for real excitement, but the younger members in this group had to shift gears and ready themselves for the end of eighth grade. The honors assembly was just around the corner, and it was difficult for them not to be thinking about "graduation." Patti's family, including the Benders and her big sister, were coming, and Colby's family would be there. The assembly was indeed a gala affair and every attempt was made to honor as many kids as possible. The only problem was it had been scheduled on Friday, so Patti would miss youth group.

The eighth graders had been asked to arrive about a half hour early; they would sit in the front of the auditorium to make it easier to come forward when their awards were presented. In order to keep everyone interested, none of the students knew for sure what awards or honors they might be receiving. In the past, people had complained the assembly was too long, so the principal had changed the format; many awards would be distributed to the students where they sat. Patti and Colby both had perfect attendance so they knew they would be honored, but everything else was a surprise.

Once the program began, Patti and Colby were named as top scholars; both had made the honor roll every grading period and were in the top ten percent of their class. Geoff received similar honors, and Sarah was named the most improved student. Jennifer was acknowledged as a top student, but she could not be included in certain awards because she had not attended their school for more than one semester. At the end of the assembly, the principal announced the final award, a special honor. The teachers had been asked to choose four students they felt best represented the qualities of scholarship, citizenship, and school spirit. The administration then chose two boys and two girls to receive this honor.

When the names were read, one had a very familiar ring, Colby Duncan. Poor Colby nearly had a heart attack; he never dreamed he might be picked. His mother had to be restrained by Mr. Duncan when she jumped up out of her seat. It came as a complete surprise. Patti gave Colby a big thumbs up; it was hard for her to disagree with such a wise choice. Colby was indeed the "perfect" student; it was nice to see him get credit for it. On the other hand, little did either Patti or Colby know this honor would be the source of a poison that would weaken and perhaps destroy the bond they had for each other; relationships must be tested, and this event caught the eye of another eighth grader—not any run of the mill eighth grader. No, it was one of the two girls who stepped forward with Colby to accept this award. This young lady was used to getting what she wanted, and if she had to run over someone to get it, well, they should not have stood in her way. Some of the clouds on the horizon were growing dark; this was not going to be an April shower but a full blown thunderstorm. The big question was who would still be standing when the wind calmed and the rain stopped.

➤➤ Thirty-Four ➤➤

For all practical purposes, school was over for the eighth graders even though the last bell had not rung. All they had to do was keep their noses clean to be paroled for the summer. Colby was ecstatic; his family had so many plans, plus he was going to camp. Of course, Patti had camp, then more camp; she was anxious for it to begin. On the other hand, her circumstances had changed; she had a big sister now, and it had changed her opinion of being at home. Deb was a lot of fun, and Patti felt she was good for her mother. They had spoken about it a year or two ago. Kathy had been down and they had gotten comfortable on the sofa; Kathy had sipped on a glass of wine and Patti had tried to cheer her up. In the course of the conversation, Kathy had remarked she was lonely. Yes, she very much enjoyed being with Patti, but it would be nice to interact with someone more her own age. Patti had understood; she liked being around friends her own age. Patti had realized her mother was occasionally sad; she felt bad about it...sometimes blaming herself. Deb had changed that.

➤➤   ➤➤

Sarah had a busy schedule planned and almost had to miss camp but finally convinced her parents to let her go. Patti wanted to talk to Jennifer about it, but the opportunity never seemed to present itself...until almost the last day of school. Jennifer had asked Patti if they could chew the fat at the end of the day or on the way home. She wanted to talk to someone besides Geoff. They met and walked to the park. On the way, Jennifer expressed her concern that summer was going to be especially difficult, new town, new environment, and few friends. She wanted to know what Patti was doing. Patti indicated she had nothing planned except camp. "You know, Jennifer, do you think your folks would let you go to our church camp for eighth graders? It's called Growth Camp."

"Gosh, I don't know; I assume you have to pay?"

"Well, yes, but if you really wanted to go and money was a problem, I might be able to help. My uncle is one of the people in charge, and I have some influence. I probably should have asked you sooner, but I hate to meddle in other people's business; I have enough trouble taking care of myself." Patti grinned.

"Oh, I know how that goes; I don't have much influence in my family, but I don't want to be in charge of them. They have their lives to live. I think they would be better off with me out of the way. I don't mean they want me dead...just gone; It sounds awful, doesn't it?" Jennifer sighed.

"Well, camp is a good way to get rid of you for a week. Why don't you see what they say?"

"I'll do that; it would be fun, and I could meet new people. I'll see what they say and get back to you."

They continued their discussion, spent a long time at the park, then headed toward Patti's apartment. When they arrived, Kathy was already there and offered to take Jennifer home if she could wait a few minutes. It was not a problem; she and Patti chilled until Kathy was ready.

Interestingly, that same evening Jennifer called and told Patti she could go to camp. Her folks were going to be out of town on business and had been wondering what to do with her; it might work out almost perfectly although she might need a place to stay for a night or two. Patti told her not to worry; she wouldn't have to sleep under a bridge or live in a dumpster. They would take good care of her. Jennifer was pleased, and Patti was excited.

As May ended, Patti realized it was almost time for Fun Camp. By now she was a veteran. Uncle Bob had talked to her about helping full time next year, and Patti had been thinking about it. She really loved camp; there was nothing she didn't enjoy. If she worked full time, she would get paid. Patti had never had a job where she was paid. It would be neat to make and have her own money, although she couldn't think of anything she wanted to buy. Of course, if she worked, she wouldn't have as much free time. She couldn't decide and finally turned the matter over to God; if He needed her at the camps, then He would just have to let her know. After all, it was His job to help with big decisions. He knows what's best. Patti knew this; she'd read it in a book someplace.

One bad thing about Fun Camp was that Patti was more or less alone; none of her friends were there. Of course, she knew most of the adults and counselor Dave, but she even missed her mom while she was gone. However, it was fun to work with the kids. They were full of energy. By the end of the week, Patti tried to take stock of everything. First of all, no one died. Counselor Dave had told her dead kids and camp don't go well together, so this was a good thing. Everyone seemed to have lot of fun and Patti had enjoyed this bunch of kids; they had followed directions and been easy to work with. She also realized these kids were having good, clean fun even when they were getting dirty; it was important for them to have positive alternatives to fill their free time. Too many kids had no one to keep them out of trouble, but at Fun Camp there was no time for mischief.

The more Patti thought about it, the more she realized how important it was to help at camp; it was her youth ministry. However, Patti was worn out; they had done some extra activities, and Patti's feet were tired.

When Patti got home, she and her mother visited about the week and accepting Uncle Bob's offer to work full time. Kathy told her it was a good idea; Patti could get paid for doing something she enjoyed. Patti began to wonder if her mother was working for God because what she said sure made sense. When Deb got home, they went out to eat pizza and celebrate Patti's return. Kathy had no news, but Deb had heard from Mr. Mitchell that the apartment would be ready in about two weeks. Deb also had several nibbles on her house. On the way home, Kathy and Deb told Patti they were planning another short vacation for later in the summer and wanted to know if she wanted to come. Patti said she would rather spend time on the streets and live like Sarah; it would be like...well, like being at camp, living off the land from one trash bin to another and never knowing which molester might be around the next corner. Deb was not amused, threatening to run her in as a vagrant; she could spend a week in jail. Patti complained the mean old adults didn't want her to have any fun.

Patti was glad to get a week off and relax at home. She had some reading to finish and looked forward to being lazy and doing nothing. Mid week Deb came home early, and they talked a long time. She no longer worried Patti might entrap her and turn her into some "radical" Christian. Deb was curious. "Patti, has your mother said any more about Dr. Bradford; I sort of hate to ask. It's none of my business, but I am curious."

"Well, not really, I know they get along, and I think she likes him, but I'm not sure it's any romantic thing. I do know she agreed to go with him to the dinner theater for his birthday. We have to go too."

"When is his birthday?"

"I'm not sure anyone knows, but I think Mom said he was born in the summer; I'm guessing July."

"That won't be long. Are you going to go with her?"

"If she wants me to. I think we had better play it Mom's way; she knows what she's doing, and I think she wants to send the message that if the good doctor wants her, he will get us too. I appreciate her thinking; she's not trying to hide anything, and I figure if he knows what he's getting into up front, we will all be better off."

"Yeah, I guess you're right. He's going to get the combo platter, not just an entree."

"Deb, since we're on this subject, I was wondering how you really feel about men; I know you've dated and gone out, but what are your plans?"

"You know, I've been thinking a lot about that lately. My life has been a mess. When I was in college, I was used by a man, and I hated him for it. After that, I didn't want anything to do with men; then I decided to get even and use men the way I had been used. I'm ashamed of it now; I was wrong. I realize I blamed everyone else for being stupid when it was my own fault. You helped change that.

I'll be honest, I'd like to have a good man in my life. I'd like to settle down, get married, and have a couple of kids. Don't laugh at me; I mean it. I'm not getting any younger. I keep hoping the right man will come along, but I'm not jumping at anyone. I've decided to let God lead me; He knows what's best. I'll let Him pick one."

Patti stepped over to Deb and reached for her hand. "Deb, I know we've had our differences, but I have to tell you something. If I had a real sister, she couldn't be any better than you. You are special and I love you very much. I know God will take care of you, and I think you would make a good mother. I want you to know where I stand."

Deb began to cry; they hugged and kissed on the cheek. After a few moments, Deb said, "Patti, you are the best there is. I'm humbled for you to accept me as your sister; I love you more than anything."

Deb looked into Patti's eyes, leaned forward, and kissed her again. Deb's kiss felt good and Patti knew she was trying to express something she could not put into words; she did love Patti as a sister and friend. Patti returned Deb's gesture; they held each for a long time. Deb noted. "You know, maybe we don't need a man after all; we've got each other and our mom. For now, that's enough."

Patti looked at her and smiled. "It's enough, but I'm still not taking a shower with you."

"Party pooper!"

At the end of the week, Jennifer called and visited with Patti. She needed a place to stay Saturday night before going to camp. Her parents had to leave after lunch on Saturday, and she was on her own until they returned. Patti asked if Jennifer's parents could drop her off at the apartment on their way out of town. She could stay with them the rest of the day and evening. The girls would leave for camp on Sunday morning. If Jennifer's parents were still not home when they returned on Friday afternoon, Jennifer was welcome to stay with Patti until they got back. Jennifer thought that would work and told Patti she would see her Saturday afternoon.

Kathy wanted to do something special for Patti before she left for camp, so they decided to have a taco feed. Patti liked Mexican food, but they didn't have it very often. Deb would eat about anything, so it was easy to keep her happy. Deb promised she would get some beer for herself and soda for Patti if Kathy would get the tacos ready. When they finally got together, Deb told Kathy she simply had to drink beer if she was going to eat tacos; Kathy thought Deb was crazy but finally decided to have one to make her happy. Patti was content with a soda and enjoyed watching her mother make faces trying to drink her beer. However, after a while, she admitted the beer tasted better; it just took some getting used to. Deb laughed and noted beer is one of those drinks that needs company. Never drink it without other food or by yourself and you'll be fine. Kathy didn't need any convincing, but still managed to drink two bottles before the meal ended. Deb also had two and said that was her limit; she no longer believed drinking too much was a proper example. Kathy praised her "oldest" for making better decisions. Deb thanked her for the encouragement; it meant more than anyone realized.

After supper, they watched a video, and Patti laughed as the older members of her family kept burping. Deb told her to watch the movie and noted that beer is supposed to make a person burp. Patti could not help being tickled by them until she managed her own soda burp. Sometimes it's hard to be a lady.

They slept in Saturday morning and had a late breakfast. Deb had to go to work, but would be back early in the afternoon. Kathy and Patti worked to straighten up the apartment and get ready for Jennifer. They visited about life in general and Patti's forthcoming trip to camp.

Jennifer arrived about 1:00; she was happy to be away from home. She felt rather alone since school had ended. Geoff would come over and they would talk, but she didn't know any of her neighbors, and none of them had kids her age. She tried to entertain herself but got bored. Her parents were gone a lot, so she was often by herself. Patti could relate to this situation and told her she was welcome to come by any time; she enjoyed having company too. They visited and decided to walk in the park. Jennifer spoke first. "Patti, I really like your mother and thank you for allowing me to stay with you until camp begins."

"Jennifer you are very welcome. Mom and I have had our differences, but she is really special. She's even better since she found new meaning to her life."

"What do you mean, new meaning?"

Patti briefly explained enough of the situation for Jennifer to make sense of it. "Life is empty without a purpose. It's one thing to go to work every day and do your best. It's quite another to come home and be fulfilled. God gives you direction and helps you realize true satisfaction comes from putting others ahead of yourself."

"Patti, I know you and God are on good terms. My real mom was a Christian. When I was little we went to church almost every week, but after she died, my dad became bitter. He couldn't understand why Mom had to die; he didn't blame God. He just couldn't make any sense out of it. I don't think he has been in church since Mom's funeral. My new mom is so goofy; I don't think she believes in anything. She is nice and treats me okay, but she doesn't care one bit about me; she does love my dad and he loves her, but she is so self-centered. It's really been hard for me to live with them. Anyway, I know the kids call you the 'preacher;' I would like to know more."

Patti walked slowly and waited to reply. "Jennifer, I know they call me the 'preacher,' but I don't do any preaching. I like to read my Bible so I carry it at school. I know quite a bit about the New Testament, and I could share it with you. Our camp is a church camp and we will be doing some Bible study; if you don't have a Bible, the staff will give you one. Let's see what they do at camp and if you like, I'd be glad to read the Bible with you. Then when you're ready, I can help you find a friend that will always be with you, and you'll never feel lonely again. You also might enjoy coming to our youth group; it starts again in

July on Sunday nights until school starts. I go all the time; sometimes Colby and Sarah come with me. It's a lot of fun and keeps us out of trouble; you might even talk Geoff into going. I know it must be difficult living in your situation, but don't give up on yourself or your family; things change. Don't forget my family loves you too."

Jennifer looked at Patti with sad eyes. "Patti, thank you for sharing; I've never met anyone quite like you. I know you care for me, and I can tell your mother does too. I won't forget; and yes, I am interested in knowing more about God and going to youth group. I think it would be fun, and we can be together."

She reached for and squeezed Patti's hand then they hugged. As they parted, Jennifer observed, "What, no kiss? I thought you were from a family of kissers?"

Patti looked at her and smiled. "It's true, but too much kissing can wear out your lips, then it would be over."

Jennifer gave her an astonished look. "Oh no, then you'd be ruined." She leaned over and kissed Patti on the cheek. "I'm willing to risk it."

Patti returned her kiss. "Me too."

Jennifer and Patti returned to the apartment about the time Deb arrived. Deb greeted Jennifer and asked how she was getting along. Jennifer replied that as of about 1:00 today, everything was great; Deb caught on and gave Jennifer a big hug. They visited for a while, then decided to eat. Jennifer pitched in to help, and Kathy noted she was an old hand in the kitchen. Jennifer laughed and told her when you are in charge of the household and no one else can cook, you had better learn fast. Jennifer knew this from experience, but she had not been satisfied eating anything; she tried to make food taste better. After many trials and errors, she began to master what she called good cooking and was reasonably proud of her results. Kathy told her she was wise beyond her years; good cooking takes time, and only the cook can make it special. Even Deb agreed practice makes perfect. She had macaroni and cheese down to an art, and figured even Leonardo DaVinci would rave over it!

The girls had a delightful evening; they watched a video, fixed a big bowl of popcorn, and were disgustingly lazy. Jennifer raved she hadn't had so much fun in years and thanked them over and over for the good time. Near bedtime Patti asked Jennifer what she wanted to do about a place to sleep. With Deb living in the apartment, there was less extra room; the sofa was a possibility; or she could sleep with Patti. Jennifer was surprised Patti offered to share her bed; Jennifer had never slept with anyone since she was very little. She had slept with her real mother sometimes when her dad was gone. Her mother insisted they would be safer if they slept together, then she would laugh and say two girls are tougher than one. Jennifer resolved to sleep with Patti and give it a try; Patti warned her to keep her cold feet to herself. Jennifer laughed and noted good advice works both ways; Patti agreed, but insisted her feet were always warm.

The next morning, no one got up early. Jennifer and Patti were already packed for camp. There had been one conflict. Uncle Bob was out of town and would not arrive until Monday. The girls would have to ride the bus or go on their own; Deb and Kathy finally decided to take them, then run around the rest of the day. Church had been changed also; many people had gone to a conference, so the leaders decided to combine the two services and start midmorning. They would go to church, eat a quick lunch and be on their way. The morning flashed by, and they soon found themselves heading to camp. Jennifer remarked she had enjoyed church and would like to go back; she also wanted to go to youth group when it resumed in July. Patti praised her for this decision and said they would be glad to take her.

They arrived at camp a little early, so Patti showed Jennifer around to acquaint her with the surroundings. Jennifer was impressed; she liked being outdoors unless the weather was nasty or too hot. It was fun to explore and see new things. Growth Camp was similar to Exploration Camp. They would have speakers and learning activities followed by outdoor events and recreation. About the time Patti finished her tour, the first bus pulled in the drive. Patti expected to see Colby and Sarah, but was surprised to spot Lisa and Julie, the girls she met last year. She rushed toward them and gave everyone a big hug. Patti could tell Lisa had solved her problem; she looked so much happier. Julie remarked she was glad to see Patti and thanked her again for helping them. Patti and Sarah introduced Jennifer to the other girls, who in turn introduced themselves. Poor Colby, the only male in the group, stood by somewhat disappointed no one was paying any attention to him. Here he was in all his glory, a dashing young man, and these girls acted like he wasn't even there. He could have cried or made a scene but thought wiser of it and acted like a real gentleman; he'd put a thumb tack on their seats or a snake in their beds. Boys can be like that!

The theme of this year's camp was putting Jesus and others ahead of yourself. The first speaker talked about how, as a Christian, each person had a responsibility to others as well as himself. He emphasized the history of the church and its obligation to care for the poor, sick or suffering. Churches cared for those who were unable to care for themselves. This outreach fulfilled the mission Jesus had given to His disciples, the same mission we have inherited from them. When we fail to consider others, we fail in our ministry and our Lord. The speaker noted caring for others was not easy; some people are hard to like, and we almost enjoy watching them suffer, but it is our obligation to care for all of God's people, whether we like them or not.

When the session ended, considerable discussion followed. One girl felt they had been told to not be selfish and admitted it was hard not to think first about yourself. Another boy observed Jesus told us to love our enemies; he thought that was very hard to do—loving someone who hated you. However, as the kids talked and thought about it, they realized it would be very hard to expand the kingdom of God if we only think of ourselves. One student noted if we fail to grow the Kingdom, our enemies will overcome us. The world is often an evil place, and we are to shine light in all dark places so evil will have no place to hide. Colby may have summed it up best when he said,

"We all have a lot of work to do if we ever expect to leave the world in better shape than we found it." Another boy followed with, "Amen," and it echoed around the room.

Camp was going to be fun; the kids were being challenged to think but would also have chances to get outside and be crazy. Patti wanted to be with Colby, but there were so many friends around it would be difficult to be alone. Patti kept thinking how they could arrange a rendezvous. They had their evening meal and returned for another session in the chapel. The speaker continued to challenge them to place others ahead of themselves and work to further God's kingdom. As they left, Patti managed to grab Colby, and they more or less sneaked away before anyone realized they were gone. They hurried down their favorite trail and found their seat. Colby tried to catch his breath. "Patti, I've been wondering when we might get together; I've really missed you." He leaned over, kissing her.

"I've been thinking the same thing; I thought maybe we could get away without anyone seeing us. I guess we did."

"Patti, there's something I've wanted to tell you, but I wanted to do it when we were alone. First of all, you're getting taller. Have you noticed?"

"Gosh, I hadn't paid any attention, but that might explain why my jeans seem shorter. Maybe I am growing."

"I think you are, and I just wanted you to know you look pretty lately; I don't know why, but you do. When we went to your mother's birthday party, I noticed you looked really nice. I like it when you wear a dress; somehow you look better that way, you know, more feminine. I wanted you to know. My dad tells me women like it when you notice good things about them."

"Your dad is a pretty smart guy; that's great advice." Patti leaned over and kissed Colby.

They held each other and kissed on the cheek. "Patti Linder, I love you; I don't know anyone quite like you. When I think about you, it makes me feel good."

"Colby, you know I feel the same about you; I also know things change; I can't expect you to love me forever. All I want is for you to give me a chance. If things work out, so much the better; if not, I hope we can always be friends."

Colby looked into Patti's eyes. "Cross my heart and hope to die. I promise I will never let anyone steal my love for you. You're right, we can't guarantee what the future might bring, but right now no other girl means anything to me. You are my best friend, my girlfriend."

Patti started to cry. She held Colby close and they softly kissed again. They sat together for quite a while, holding each other and exchanging an occasion kiss. Patti felt she had died and gone to heaven. How could anything be better than being with Colby?

Time and the lovebirds soon noted it was getting dark; they didn't need the attention of a search party, so they walked quickly down the trail to the cabin area for the night. It had been a great day; it would be a great week. Happiness is friends and family.

When they returned to the cabin area, members of their party inquired what happened to them. Patti explained she and Colby had decided to take a walk and get some fresh air; she omitted the details of their adventure. Sarah commented privately she knew what had transpired and didn't need any help from Sherlock Holmes to "deduce" it. Patti told her to keep quiet; they had done nothing for which to be ashamed. Sarah noted she had not accused them of anything, but it was obvious her two friends were not just walking. Patti admitted she and Colby had sat together and exchanged a few kisses, but that was as far as it went, and more importantly, it wasn't going any farther. Sarah understood and told Patti she would keep quiet, and if she could do anything to give them another chance to be alone, she would be glad to help.

Patti knew no one in her cabin; Jennifer and Sarah were both in her group of cabins; Julie and Lisa shared the same cabin in a different group. Patti didn't mind; she was tired and wanted to sleep. A new day was coming, and she wanted to greet it well rested.

The first two days of camp were pleasant, but uneventful. Everyone was having a good time, and Jennifer was impressed; she enjoyed the outdoors, and their studies made her think about who she was and how to better treat others. On Wednesday, they had a schedule change and ended up with two hours of free time before lunch. Colby, Sarah, Jennifer, and Patti gathered to decide what to do. Jennifer suggested they might take a hike, and the others were agreeable. Patti knew a shorter trail they could take, so they picked that option. Along the way, they marveled at the trees, wildflowers, and various rock formations. At one point Sarah led Jennifer on a side trip while Patti and Colby rested under a large tree. They waited for the girls. "Colby, do you like camp this year?"

"Yes, I do, especially since you're here."

"Yeah, it helps to be together; I like camp, but I enjoy being with you."

"Patti, I've been thinking after all the time we've been together...well, we...you know, we've never had a real date. I mean gone somewhere by ourselves and been together. I know I don't have to ask if you would like to go someplace because I know you would, but I'd like to go out after we get home, sometime this summer, just the two of us on a real date. I'll even pay your way."

"I'd love that. Where do you want to go?"

"I don't know; let's think about it and decide when we get home."

"Okay, I'll give it some thought and we'll talk later; it will be fun." Patti seemed pleased.

Colby nodded. "I think so too."

These words were no more than spoken when Sarah and Jennifer returned. Sarah grinned. "We hurried back because we didn't want you guys to get into any trouble."

Colby looked at her rather curiously. "What do you mean? Patti and I were resting and holding up this tree. How could we get into any trouble?"

Sarah winked at Colby. "Hey, you know how kids are when left unsupervised."

"Well, thank you Mother Sarah for your concern. Me and Brother Colby were about to practice huggy bear and kissy face. Now you show up and spoil our fun."

"Patti! Keep your big mouth shut; she'll never leave us alone if you share all of our secrets."

Patti covered her mouth with her hand. "Oops."

Sarah got tickled, and Jennifer simply shook her head. Some people's kids...

The hikers were quickly back on the trail and the conversation lingered upon the "not to be trusted alone" Patti and Colby. Before long their laughter had frightened away any wildlife in the area, so only plants and rocks remained to be studied and enjoyed. As they neared the end of the trail, Colby noted they had arrived right on time; he admitted all this hiking and laughing had made him hungry. Apparently, he was not alone because everyone picked up the pace and headed straight to the Chow House for lunch.

Thursday was the big event day. Sarah had signed up to go swimming, and after some thought, Jennifer decided to go with her. Patti and Colby had no idea what to do. Colby wanted to play softball in the late afternoon and evening but had not decided about the first part of the day. Patti didn't really care; she just wanted to be with Colby. They finally decided to take another hike, then Patti would go swimming with Sarah and Jennifer; Colby could play ball.

Patti and Colby enjoyed their hike and during the rest periods they visited about school issues, especially being in high school. They had pre-enrollment the first of August. They were allowed to pick their own classes, but all courses had to be approved by their counselors. Colby and Patti had generally chosen the same classes. Kathy wanted Patti to be in choir, so she had agreed to try it. Colby was no singer so he would not be in choir, but his mother had urged him to take a cooking class. The home economics department offered a class called Home Survival, where students got practical experience in cooking, cleanup, washing dishes, and even doing the laundry, plus tips on shopping for food. Colby wasn't crazy about the idea, but agreed it would be good to know some of these things. PE in the high school was coed, but the boys did not always have the same activities as the girls. Geoff had been particularly excited about the coed PE program until he discovered the boys and girls had different dressing rooms.

Patti and Colby had been thinking about what they might do on a date, and thus far no light bulbs had flashed. Patti did think it would be fun to go together to eat, and Colby, who was not shy around food, could hardly disagree. Beyond that, they were stumped and resolved to give it more thought over the next several days.

Talk also revolved around their friends, especially Geoff. Colby noted how he had changed since Jennifer arrived. Geoff had always been a loose cannon; he would do or say anything to get attention. While he was harmless, he sometimes crossed the line between funny and just plain crude. Patti and Colby liked him, but he could be difficult. However, he had mellowed since Jennifer had entered his life. Patti figured he was trying to impress her, and Colby agreed but felt it was more than just Jennifer. Maybe Geoff was growing up and beginning to realize acting like a fourth or fifth grader in the eighth grade was no longer chic. Geoff had always been popular but had few true friends; he usually annoyed most people after five or ten minutes. He had changed. Patti and Colby agreed it was a real plus, and Jennifer had been partly responsible by simply arriving on the scene. She liked Geoff too, which surprised Patti, but Geoff could make her laugh, and laughter had been in short supply for her; they made an interesting couple.

Sadly, the hike offered no time for romance, but the lovebirds didn't mind. One thing for certain, they loved being together, and perhaps that was more important than anything. Right now, these best friends could not have been happier. The hike ended with no causalities and everyone anxious to further enjoy the day. Patti went swimming and soon found Sarah and Jennifer. When asked how the water was, Sarah replied, "Wet."

Patti accused her of talking too much and poor Jennifer had to step in before blows were exchanged. Sarah had a quick wit, and she and Patti knew how to work it. Jennifer restored order. "Stop the violence."

By this time everyone was out of breath; laughter can be exhausting. They splashed and enjoyed the water until the cookout, where they ate more than they needed. Colby wanted to go to his softball game, and the girls decided to stroll around the campgrounds. Sadly, camp was ending.

⌒ Thirty-Five ⌒

Once they were home, life returned to normal, if that was possible. It appeared Deb would be able to move her things into her apartment at the end of the month. Kathy continued to enjoy her work and noted that Dr. Bradford was paying a more attention to her; it bothered her, but she was flattered he found her interesting, pretty...whatever. Deb told her she should feel good about it and observed Kathy had not been paying attention to men all these years so this was "new" to her. Kathy admitted Deb was right, observing she did not think the doctor was "undressing" her. Rather, his attention seemed to come from genuine admiration; he truly respected her as a nurse and a person. While Kathy was pleased he felt that way, it embarrassed her. Patti was glad to be home; she had missed her family.

Near the end of the month, two events transpired that would have future significance in the lives of Patti and Colby. The first seemed trivial, but would have important consequences before the end of high school. The second appeared to be no more than a flash in a pan, but would have lifesaving consequences only a few years hence. Colby called Patti and asked if they could get together and talk about their date. Patti quickly agreed, and they decided Colby would come by the apartment so they could talk at the park. Colby arrived a half hour later. Once at the park, their conversation turned toward their first date. Colby spoke. "Mom told me Il Spazio's makes good Italian food, and I know you like pasta. Would you like to eat there?"

"Yes, that would be okay; let's go Italian."

"Good, they have this festival at the park close to town. It's called "Art in the Park;" they have local people displaying various arts and crafts, and there's music, including an evening concert. A lot of people will be there, but it might be fun to go and look around. What do you think?"

"It sounds like interesting; I've never been there, but I think Mom might have said something."

"Now, I asked my mom if we could go to my house later and sit on the front porch and talk...and I didn't tell her, but maybe we could be close...uh, well, you know." Patti looked at him and smiled; Colby appeared embarrassed. "Mom says I need to be in by 10:00, and she will take you home. What do you think?"

"I think your mother has a wonderful son." Patti leaned over and kissed Colby.

Colby blushed. "Gosh, I'd never thought of it like that; your mother has a wonderful daughter."

"Which one?" Patti grinned.

"Why, you, silly."

Patti pretended to be annoyed. "You don't think my big sister is wonderful too?"

Colby tried to weasel out of trouble. "I didn't say that. Sure Deb is wonderful, but she's a couple years too old for me, and I don't want you getting jealous and trying to hurt her; I was talking about you."

"Okay, I think we've got great plans; you did quite well."

"Thank you." Colby kissed Patti on the cheek.

"You're welcome."

Colby then told Patti he would get information about the event at the park, and they would get everything planned as soon as possible. Patti agreed to talk to her mother and make sure it was okay. Both were looking forward to this grand occasion and the opportunity to be on their own.

Colby learned the "Art in the Park" festival was held just before the first of July. It was advertised as a week-long event, but the first night was reserved for setting up exhibits; by the last night, many participants were packed and gone. It started on a Tuesday; Colby and Patti decided to go on Friday. Patti talked to her mother about her date and was quite surprised by her reaction. Kathy told her it was okay to go with Colby, to have a good time and act like a lady. Kathy had no problem with their plans and was pleased Patti had a way home. Patti had expected more of a hard time, but everything seemed okay. Patti was relieved, but curious why her mother had been so accommodating.

Before anyone had time to think, it was Friday afternoon. Colby called and told Patti he would be by around 4:30 to pick her up. They were going to walk to the restaurant, eat early, and enjoy the festival. Patti dressed up, and Kathy had a chance to compliment her on how nice she looked before Colby arrived. Colby made the same observations, and Patti felt embarrassed by the attention...although when she was getting ready, she had noted she looked nice.

The weather was warm, so the lovebirds walked slowly, enjoying the afternoon; they did not speak for a long time. Finally Colby noted. "Thank you for going with me; this is really special; and we haven't even done anything yet."

"Well, thank you for asking; I wouldn't have gone with anyone else. I love you, Colby."

Colby blushed. "Patti, I love you too; I hope we have a

great evening."

"We will." Patti seemed very happy.

As they walked, it was not long before the restaurant came into view. "Patti, I've never done anything like this before; I'm kind of scared."

Patti looked at him and smiled. "You'll do fine; you're a gentleman."

As it turned out, they had no problems. Mr. Duncan's party of two was seated in the nonsmoking section, and he very politely turned down the offer of cocktails and wine to the smiling waitress, who noted what a handsome couple they made. They did opt for iced tea, with lemon, and perused the menu, which seemed way too big for the undersized guests. Colby lamented everything looked so good; he wished his mother was here to pick for him. Patti had no problems finding what she wanted to eat but insisted on a cold salad. Colby agreed and finally, chose chicken Alfredo; he liked the creamy sauce. The waitress noted they had made excellent choices.

Patti and Colby felt a bit out of place, but both of them were thrilled by this opportunity; it made them feel grown up. The salad was delicious and Patti noted she could have eaten three or four more; Colby wasn't sure he wanted that many, but agreed he could easily eat another. However, the waitress soon brought their entrees, and both decided an extra salad might have been good, but they had plenty to eat without it. As they were eating, Colby noticed an older lady and her husband seemed to be giving them a lot of attention; he almost said something to Patti, but they got up to leave. The lady walked to their table and excused herself. "I just wanted to say what a nice looking couple you make. Have a good evening and enjoy yourselves."

As she turned to leave, Colby and Patti stammered. "Thank you...thank you very much."

It then occurred to them they had received quite a compliment. Kind words are nice.

The waitress took good care of them. When she asked if they had enjoyed their meal, she received a resounding, "Yes." Colby paid their bill and the waitress invited them to come back soon. They assured her they would. Colby wanted his parents to come, and Patti knew Deb and her mother would love the food too. They would definitely be back...as soon as possible.

Colby complained on the way to the park that he was too full to walk. Patti laughed and told him it would take more than a walk to the park to burn off all they had eaten; if he wanted to feel better, he'd better keep walking. When they arrived, the park was a beehive of activity. They strolled through the exhibits, admiring the paintings, arts, and handicrafts on display. Patti wished she had a lot of money and could buy some of everything; Colby agreed, but noted it might be a while before either of them had much money. Patti sighed and acknowledged it would probably be a long time, but someday she would like to have unique things for her home. Colby reached for her hand, smiling. "You'll have me and I'm unique."

"I suppose, but you'd look pretty silly hanging on the wall in my living room. I'd probably have to get you stuffed to keep you quiet." Patti started to laugh.

"I'm already stuffed...just not so quiet." Colby laughed too.

"I love you, Colby...stuffed or otherwise!"

Colby found a gift for his mother; Patti found something for Deb and her mother. They strolled and got closer to the music; however, the band was loud and not playing anything they wanted to hear. They couldn't talk with all that noise. Colby noted he was feeling better; the walking had helped. He suggested they swing through a different area of the exhibits and then head home. They meandered through the various displays and marveled at all the work that must have gone into some of these projects. Patti told Colby she would like to learn to paint someday; it was a way to preserve the beauty around her with a personal touch. Colby observed he too would like to learn to paint because he hated the color of his bedroom. Patti took a swipe at him, but missed.

As the evening cooled, they finally found themselves at Colby's house, sitting on his porch. "Patti, thank you again for being with me tonight; I had a wonderful time, and I, well...I mean...I bought you a present. Mom and I went by the park the other day and she saw something she liked, so while she was looking at it, I did my own shopping"

Patti was taken back. "Colby, you didn't need to buy me anything; I mean...well, you know what I mean."

Colby looked at her. "I didn't intend to buy you anything, but when I saw it, I thought of us and had to get it."

He reached into his pocket and pulled out something folded in tissue paper; he held it in his hand and unfolded it carefully. As he did, a small bit of silver chain slipped from beneath the folds, followed by another piece of silver chain. When the last fold was undone, it exposed two oddly shaped silver charms, each attached to a silver chain. Patti looked curiously at them and could not figure out what they were. Colby held them firmly in one hand and his other hand reached for Patti's. He looked at her with an expression she had never seen before; at this moment it appeared Colby was trying his best to be a man. "Do you remember last year in math when we talked about circles?"

"I guess so."

"Do you remember what the teacher said? He told us the Greeks believed the circle was the perfect shape and thought it was special, even magical. Sometimes, I think life is a circle. My mom runs in circles and doesn't really get anywhere, only frustrated. My dad isn't like that; he just goes around one time and whatever he was doing is done. I think my life is a circle that can never be complete without you." Colby arranged the two charms and showed Patti how when properly placed, they formed a perfect circle.

Patti looked at Colby and began to cry. "Oh, how I love you; you are so sweet."

443

Colby held her close and once she composed herself, gave her the charm representing the missing piece of his circle. "I want you to have this so you will remember that you make my life complete, and I will wear mine to show that I'm not complete without yours." Colby gave Patti her pendant and placed his over his head and around his neck.

Patti carefully put on her pendant, then reached for Colby and kissed him rather passionately on the lips. Colby was surprised by her response. He returned her kiss, embracing her; they held each other tightly and kissed again. Patti groped Colby's back, and his hands moved around hers; soon they began to feel different. The temperature was rising. Finally, Patti pulled away just a bit. "Colby, I think we need to stop; I'm scared."

"My gosh, why are you scared? There's no one here to hurt you." Colby was confused.

"Yes, there is; there's an animal inside me that wants to tear off your clothes and consume you. Do you understand?" Patti felt disappointed.

"Is it the animal that's inside me with the same idea?"

"It probably is...and it scares me. I don't want to end up like my mother. It's not fair." Patti was almost crying. "It's just not fair."

Colby held her close. "Patti, I hate to say this, but you are right. We have to be careful, but our time will come; I know it will."

"It doesn't change anything, Colby; I still love you and I always will. It doesn't even mean we'll get married; it just means I will always love you...no matter what!"

They sat together and held hands for a long time before Colby noted it was almost 10:00. It was the best night of Patti's life; the charm felt warm around her neck, a reminder of what Colby meant to her.

When she got home, Kathy asked if she had enjoyed her

"first" date. "Mother, I was in heaven."

It had been a long time, but Kathy remembered that feeling, the great joy, soon followed by great pain. She looked at Patti and smiled. "I know the feeling. I hope it lasts a long time. Just be careful."

"Mother, I know there's a monster in me that wants Colby more than anything; I also know Jesus wants me to resist that monster and enjoy my life. Colby and I will not do anything stupid, I promise."

"And, honey, I want you to be happy; Colby's a good man...er, boy."

"I know, Mom. One more thing, could we go to the park for a little while tomorrow? There's something I have to buy if you will let me. It is really important."

"Sure, we can do that in the morning. Maybe Deb would like to come too."

Patti had trouble going to sleep that night; she thought about Colby and the future. She decided it wasn't easy being a kid...even though she enjoyed her life. It seemed there was always something over the next hill you had to wait for. It was so frustrating. Why couldn't she be four or five years older? She and Colby could get married; they could go to college and be a family. Finally, she decided to turn it over to God; she prayed He would direct her and make everything turn out all right. It must have been a good plan...because she soon fell sound asleep, and there was peace in the world.

The next day, as agreed, she and her mother went to the park. Deb had worked late and wanted to sleep in. Kathy wondered what Patti wanted, but Patti didn't want to say until she found it. She asked her mother to keep her eyes open for a place that sold jewelry, specifically silver jewelry. It took awhile, but she located the exhibit, but not the item she wanted. She finally asked the gentlemen in charge about a pendant. Yes, he had that item; it should be on display, but he could not find one, so he checked and discovered they had been packed in the wrong box; he soon showed her several and she spied the one she wanted. It was not cheap, and Patti was afraid her mother would not spend so much for it. Patti drew her aside and briefly explained why she needed this particular piece. Kathy smiled and gave her approval. Patti hugged her, which may have made it easier for Kathy to go along with the purchase; Patti rarely asked for anything special.

The following Monday, the second event took place. On Sunday afternoon the weather changed, suddenly still and sultry. Kathy, Deb and Patti were in the park and noticed it almost immediately. Deb thought for sure a bad storm was brewing, but the sky seemed no more threatening than before. The three scurried home to seek the comfort of air conditioning. On Monday, the ominous weather persisted, and later in the morning Patti was certain she heard fire sirens. Within minutes the phone rang; it was Colby. He was calling to tell her that a house in his neighborhood was burning—or at least, trying to burn. Thick black smoke hung everywhere and smelled awful. Colby had started outside to check it out, but the hot weather and the smoke almost bowled him over. He decided to watch from inside. It was strange; the humid air combined with a complete lack of wind created a vacuum. The smoke did not rise; it just wormed its way through the neighborhood. No one knew it then, but the smoke would linger for days until a storm passed, dumping enough rain to cleanse both the air and much of the smell. Poor Mrs. Duncan was fit to be tied; even after the rain, their house still reeked, and she was going crazy trying to wash and clean everything to remove this repulsive odor. Colby talked about it for the rest of the summer; even Geoff thought it was disgusting, which is saying a lot from someone who once ate catsup on his jello at lunch!

Having received word it was okay for her to begin moving things into her apartment, Deb would move a box there then grab of few loose things and carry them across the hall. Both Patti and Kathy helped, and it didn't take long before her new apartment was a mess. Deb moaned she would have to find places to put all of her stuff. Her mother and younger sister vowed to help if she would behave and cooperate. Deb complained they didn't want her to have any fun, and they agreed she could only have fun when she was with them or vice versa. Deb commented she didn't really know why she was moving everything; she would probably be spending most of her time with Kathy and Patti anyway. Kathy insisted that was fine...but there might be a few things Deb wanted to do privately; sometimes a big sister can get away with things little sisters dare not try. Deb insisted she had no idea what Kathy was talking about. Patti was amused by their bantering.

While Deb was busy moving out, Patti was anxious to get back to youth group. Jennifer had asked about going with Patti, who had agreed she would do what she could to get Jennifer there and back. Jennifer was anxious about the first meeting; she hoped to meet new friends but was hesitant about something new. Patti explained everything would be fine. She would be there, plus Sarah also tried to attend. Thus assured, Jennifer became rather excited about her first trip to AFLAME. Patti enjoyed Jennifer, but told her mother Jennifer always seemed so sad; it took a lot of energy to raise her spirits. Kathy admitted some people need a lot of encouragement to keep going, but she felt Jennifer would get better as she became more acquainted in her new surroundings.

By mid July Deb was moved, and Jennifer had gone to youth group twice; she had liked it, and Patti was pleased she had something to look forward to. On the third Sunday of the month Jennifer called Patti and asked if she could visit during the afternoon, then go to youth group that evening. Patti told her to come by; she had no other plans. About a half an hour later Jennifer arrived; it appeared she was upset. They decided to go for a walk and ended up in the park. Jennifer spoke first, "Patti, thank you for letting me stop by; I needed to talk to someone."

"I've told you I want to be here for you; I'm glad to do it."

"I know, I just want to thank you for being such a good friend. I feel so alone sometimes. I think it helps to talk about your problems...get them out in the open. My dad hardly knows I'm alive, and my step mom has no clue; she's such a dork. I think if he asked her to jump off the house, she do it in an instant. I feel sorry for her. She wants a baby so bad, and they are trying; I've heard them from my room. I want her to be happy, but I wonder if she has even the slightest idea what to do with a baby; I can see her planting it and waiting for it to grow." Patti laughed. "It's so difficult to be in that environment all the time. I mean they're gone a lot during the day, but I still have to put up with them a night. It's like a bad dream, but I never wake up! Do you have any ideas?"

After a short time, Patti replied, "Jennifer, I'll be honest; I don't know what we can do for your folks. Adults can be a tough nut to crack; we can only hope they will wake up and realize how foolish they've been. I don't know you real well, but you are special to me. You are pretty, smart, and wise for your age. You have been blessed. Jesus loves you, and my crazy friends like you. Maybe all you need to do is heal inside and feel better about yourself. I know you've been reading your Bible. Do you know what sin is?"

"Why yes, yes, I do. To sin is to go against God."

"Do you believe in Jesus...that He's the Son of God?"

"I do; Jesus is the Son of God."

"Would you be willing to accept Him as your personal Lord and Savior?"

"Yes, I would do that."

"Okay, I call this the ABC's backwards: confess, believe and accept. Do you understand?"

"Yes, I understand."

"Okay, Jennifer, get down on your knees and pray all of this to God; go through your ABC's and tell Him what you've just told me. Will you do that?"

Without saying a word, Jennifer knelt in front of Patti and

bowed her head. Patti placed her hand on Jennifer's shoulder and waited quietly beside her. Patti could tell Jennifer was praying, and in a few moments Jennifer began to tremble with an occasional quake; Patti could see she was crying as tears dripped on her shorts. After a short time, she looked up at Patti with an expression of awe and joy. Patti had never seen Jennifer like this; she peered up into Patti's eyes. "Oh Patti, I feel so wonderful. What's happening to me?"

Patti looked down at her. "You've allowed Jesus to come into your heart; He is with you now, and your sins are forgiven. I hope He fills your heart with joy."

"Patti, that must be it; I feel so warm and happy. I don't feel alone anymore."

"No, you'll never be alone again."

"Patti, thank you; I understand now why some of the kids call you the preacher..."

Patti interrupted. "No, Jennifer, I may have told you what to do, but you need to thank Jesus for this, not me."

"Oh, I understand, but you helped me find Him; you led me in the right direction."

Patti was insistent. "I assisted; He did the work."

Jennifer stood up and moved toward Patti. "I love you, Patti; I'm not sure I've ever told that to anyone since my real mom died, but I love you."

Jennifer kissed Patti on her cheek. Patti returned her kiss and they hugged for a long time. "Jennifer, Jesus and I both love you."

Jennifer again kissed Patti, who returned her kiss. The park was warm, and it was time to escape the heat. Once back at the apartment, Kathy noted. "Why, Jennifer, you look so happy today."

"Thank you, I found a special friend this afternoon and my heart is glad."

Kathy looked at Jennifer, smiling. "That special friend...is He a good friend of Patti's too? I think I know Him."

Jennifer beamed, nodded, then accepted a big hug from Kathy. Not wishing to be left out, Patti rushed to embrace her mother and friend. It had been a delightful afternoon.

As summer vacation wound down, one loose end needed tying, and Kathy was able to make the announcement the next day. Dr. Bradford had made it official; he had asked Kathy out to celebrate his birthday. The day itself had already passed, but he had been unable to get tickets at the dinner theater and decided a few days late was far better than no celebration at all. Kathy was secretly pleased; obviously she did mean something more to the doctor than just a nurse, and while she did not expect any marriage proposal, the prospects of having a man in her life were rather exciting. Dr. Bradford insisted she bring her two daughters, and they would go out for the evening. When Kathy told Deb, she was almost as excited as Kathy; Patti was thrilled...because she wanted her mother to be happy. If anyone deserved a bit of happiness, it was Kathy Bender. Patti didn't know the doctor well, but he seemed nice and that was a good start.

He had purchased tickets for Friday evening. Everyone was on edge waiting for the happy day. Deb was so excited she came over every night to talk about it, nearly driving the rest of her family crazy. When Friday arrived, the girls were dressed and ready to rumble, or so Deb said. Dr. Bradford, right on time, quickly seated Patti and Deb in the back seat and Kathy in front with him. Deb whispered to Patti that the good doctor was thinking romance; Patti motioned for her to calm down and not spoil everything. Deb responded by settling down. She and Patti talked while Kathy and the doctor chatted in front of them. When they arrived, Dr. Bradford got quite a few stares as he escorted three "lovely" ladies into the theater; once inside, Deb grabbed Kathy and headed for the ladies room; she wanted all the "buzz." Kathy told her to be still and act like someone older than Patti. Deb fired back, noting Patti was older than both of them, and she didn't want to get any older than she already was. Kathy had no response other than to say Dr. Bradford was really nervous.

As usual, the food was delicious and everyone ate more than necessary. Dr. Bradford ordered wine, and the adults managed to get through a whole bottle. Patti ordered ginger ale and called it champagne—without the ill effects. The audience roared at the comedy, laughing so hard they could hardly breathe. This broke the ice. Deb noted the doctor kept his eyes on Kathy the entire evening; he definitely had feelings for her. He seemed to enjoy Patti and Deb, careful to include them in his conversations and comments. Toward the end of the play, Patti noted her mother seemed relaxed and comfortable with the doctor; she was truly having a good time.

When the play ended, the audience begged for more, but the cast was exhausted and cried for mercy. Reluctantly, everyone headed for the exits. The doctor suggested they go to the coffee shop to continue the evening. They lingered, visiting and laughing; no one wanted to go, but the prospects of staying the night there were bleak, so they loaded themselves in the car and headed home. Patti was tired; it had been a long evening. Deb was so charged up she could have gone on for days, and it was easy to see why she'd had trouble in the past; parties that never end often end badly. When they got to the apartment, Deb maneuvered Patti out of the car, leaving the doctor and Kathy alone.

Deb nearly went wild when Kathy came into the apartment, demanding to know what had happened after she and Patti left. Kathy attempted to quiet her, saying nothing had happened; Deb didn't believe her. Finally Kathy said, "Okay, after you left, Dr. Bradford reached for my hand and told me how much fun he'd had. He hoped we could do it again sometime. I told him I had enjoyed the evening and would be glad to go another time. He was really nervous; I know he wanted to kiss me, but he held back, and I'm glad he did. I have come to the conclusion Dr. Bradford is a gentleman; he truly respects women. I think the reason he and his med school girlfriend broke up was that he was not aggressive enough. I think she wanted a "take charge, throw me on the floor, and have your way with me" kind of man. Dr. Bradford is not like that. He'd be worried I'd break. I'm not looking for a wrestler; I am looking for a companion, someone to love and take care of me. I'm going to say something I may regret, but if he were to ask me to marry him, I'd say yes so fast he'd faint dead away. I don't love him, but I easily could. I don't expect you to understand, and it doesn't matter. I've thought about the kind of man I want, and he is such a man."

When Kathy finished, Deb sat stunned by her comments. Finally, she looked at Kathy. "I know you won't believe me, but I do understand; I can't tell you how many men I dated or slept with; I'm ashamed of my past, but I can tell you not one of them ever respected me, and I'll be honest, I didn't deserve any respect. I was no better than a whore; I know it and admit it. You and I are as different as night is from day, but thanks to you guys and my good friend JC, I've changed. I want a man that loves me for who I am; I know I'm not much, but I'm a hell of a lot better than I used to be. Kathy, I hope it works out for you; I know I speak for Patti. We want you to be happy; if we can do anything to help, please ask. Dr. Bradford is a good man; if you want him, don't let him slip away—and whatever else you do, don't sleep with him before you get married. He will never respect you if you do."

Now it was Kathy's turn to be quiet, but she finally spoke. "Guys, I've got the best daughters in the world and I love you more than anything. Let's go to bed and enjoy tomorrow together. I promise to hold on to my doctor as long as I can; I think he's worth it."

><del></del> <del></del>><

Summer vacation was nearly over. Romance hovered in the air. School was about to start, and everyone's prospects looked good. Patti was thinking about what challenges she might face in high school. Other girls would soon notice Colby; he wasn't Mr. Excitement, but he was handsome and smart, and he definitely had potential. Patti wasn't stupid; she knew Colby was a good catch, and she wanted to hang on to him every bit as much as her mother wanted to hang on to Dr. Bradford. The future looked bright, but very often there are clouds just over the horizon. It was hard to say what the future might hold. Only God knew, and He wasn't talking.

～ Thirty-Six ～

"Patti, thanks for coming to see me; this place is driving me crazy. I guess I'm a little messed up. This morning I would have sworn it was Saturday, but Mom convinced me otherwise. I lost a whole weekend. It's kind of scary. I guess someone tried to run me down, but Deb's on the case so the poor slob driving that car is in real trouble; she'll never rest until she gets him." Colby sighed deeply.

"You're right; Deb can be very single minded...and she doesn't forget. She'll find this guy and it won't be pretty. I'm really sorry you got hurt. I tried to catch you all weekend, but I had no luck; then I didn't find out you were in the hospital until your mother called this morning and asked me to pick up your assignments. She was really worried about you. Everyone at school was glad to hear you weren't seriously hurt; we missed you."

"I'm sorry to cause so much trouble, but it's nice to know everyone was concerned. The doctors tell me I'm fine; I had a little trouble walking, but I've managed to improve that. I guess I'm on the mend, but I'm kind of sore and my head aches. They may release me in the morning, and I might get to go back to school on Wednesday; I really hope so. If I get far behind, I'll never catch up!"

"You'll be okay; I know you will. I've been praying for you, and Sarah told me to tell you she knows exactly how you feel; she's praying too. I think you're in good hands. I know it's no fun being here, but it sounds like they're going to kick you out to fend for yourself."

"It can't happen anytime too soon. I..."

"Hey guys." Deb interrupted. "I just wanted to tell you the good news; we've got a suspect, and I think we have her by the throat. I'm going to question her tonight and we'll see what happens. Colby you're looking a lot better. I like that bandage on your head; it makes you look...important, distinguished. If you only had gray hair, we could pass you off as some dignitary—or maybe someone who escaped from a nut house—someone special. I can't stay; I've got to get back to work and keep this town safe from all the crazy people that can't drive. See you later." The detective turned and rushed out the door.

Colby observed. "Whew, Deb is crazy enough to be your real sister; no wonder you guys get along so well!"

"Yeah, It's true; we love her very much." Patti shook her head. "I really feel sorry for the girl that hit you."

"Me too; I ought to be mad at her for putting me in here!" Colby shook his fist and grinned.

About an hour later, two policemen escorted a young, dark-haired lady into Detective Johnson's office. Her name was Melanie Adams. The detective introduced herself. "Miss Adams, we are investigating a hit-and-run accident that occurred last Friday around 10:00 pm near the juco library. I have evidence that places you at that location about that time. In addition, the left front fender of your car is noticeably cleaner than the rest of the vehicle, and we found traces of cloth attached to the trim. If this cloth matches the clothes or belongings of the young man who was hit, I will have to arrest you for attempted murder, and you may end up spending the best years of your life in prison. How does that sound?"

Miss Adams had seemed somewhat indifferent to the detective's comments although nervous; however, as the detective concluded her remarks, the suspect gasped. "Oh no, I didn't do anything; I didn't hit anyone. You can't send me to jail!"

"Miss Adams, I don't think you understand; it doesn't make any difference what you say or even think, if we have the evidence, rest assured you're going to prison. We don't take attempted murder lightly in this community, nor will any judge I know give you a pat on the back and tell you to drive more carefully next time. You are in trouble, and to make matters worse, the young man you hit is a friend of mine; his mother and I are not inclined to show mercy."

The suspect gasped, only louder than before. "Oh my God, you can't do this to me; I didn't hurt anybody...no, no, no...I just bumped into the curb. I didn't hit anyone!"

"Calm down, Miss Adams. Why don't you just tell me everything that happened after you left the library?"

"Okay, sure, I have nothing to hide. I checked out a couple of books. I left the library and headed straight to my car; I get scared being out alone late at night. I've been having trouble with my car; it doesn't want to start. Anyway, I got in my car and couldn't find my keys; they had slipped out of the pocket in my purse and fallen to the bottom. I was getting frustrated, but I found them and the car started fine. I backed out of my parking stall and headed down the driveway toward the street. Just as I got ready to turn, my purse slipped off the seat, and I tried to grab it. When I did, the car swerved and ran up over the curb. It scared me. By the time I got it under control, I was already into my left turn and headed down the street. I swear I didn't hit anyone or anything; I just ran up over the curb." Miss Adams seemed honest and sincere.

"So you're telling me you didn't see anyone on or near the driveway and sidewalk going out of the library."

"That's correct...not a soul."

"Okay, if evidence shows your car hit this young man on the sidewalk, how did this happen? Did you loan your car to someone? Was your car stolen, and you failed to report it? You are responsible for your vehicle unless it was not in your possession. What do you have to say about this?"

"I don't know. I didn't let anyone use my car Friday. The only thing I can think is someone might have been walking on the sidewalk that I didn't see; I mean, it's possible. Then when I bumped into the curb, I suppose I could have hit him and not realized it."

"What if I were to tell you I believe you; that is, that you didn't see anyone...that you didn't realize you hit anyone...and yet we have this young man, a friend of mine, in the hospital, unconscious for two days rather banged up. What should I do?"

"Well, I guess if I hit someone and hurt him, I should be punished, but I didn't do it on purpose; I didn't even realize it. Please don't send me to jail; my dad will kill me!"

"What punishment do you deserve? What do you think is fair?"

"I don't know; I'm sorry, I didn't mean to hurt anyone." Miss Adams started to cry.

"You say you're sorry. Would you be willing to go with me and apologize to the young man you hit? His name is Colby. I think he deserves that much. Don't you?"

"Yes, yes, he does." Miss Adams sobbed.

"How about his mother? Do you think she deserves an apology?"

"Yes, she does; I would want one if my son were hurt."

"Okay, how about we do that right now so I can tell the judge you have apologized, you didn't realize you hit anyone, and you deserve leniency. How does that sound?"

"It sure beats prison!"

Deb nodded with a slight smile. She excused herself, left the room, and called the hospital. As it turned out, Mrs. Duncan was there. Deb talked to her for several minutes and returned to her office. "Let's go take care of this before I change my mind."

In no time at all, Deb and Miss Adams appeared in Colby's room. Colby was sitting in bed looking rather forlorn; he didn't like being in the hospital...when he was conscious. Melanie looked at him, gasped a bit, then looked away. Deb took charge. "Colby, this is the young lady who tried to kill you Friday night. I realize this sounds ominous, but she insists she never saw you. She drove away without realizing you had been hurt and subsequently offered you no assistance. She tells me she is very sorry about the accident and feels bad you were hurt. Isn't that correct?" Deb turned, giving Melanie a stern look.

"Yes, ma'am, that's correct." Miss Adams then turned to the patient. "The detective told me your name is Colby. Is that right?" Colby nodded. "Colby, as God is my witness, I want you to know I never saw you; I was messing with my purse and let the car get away from me. I guess I hit you...but honestly, I never saw you; I didn't realize I hit anyone, and I'm so sorry you were injured. I don't know what to do to make you feel better, but I'm so sorry..." Melanie began to cry again, unable to continue.

She stepped forward to Colby's bed and extended her hand; Colby reached forward and took her hand. He felt sorry for her. "I believe you. I know you're sorry; I forgive you. Thank you for coming to see me; I know it wasn't easy. May I ask your name?"

"My name is Melanie."

"Well, Melanie it has been nice to meet you; perhaps someday we can meet under better circumstances."

Melanie looked at Colby with teary eyes. "You're a nice boy; I hope you're much better soon...and yes, I would like to meet you under different circumstances. Thank you for forgiving me."

Colby squeezed her hand and she turned to Deb. "I guess I'm ready to see his mother now. Where is she?"

"Mrs. Duncan is down in the waiting room; we'll go there." The detective led Melanie away.

Mrs. Duncan was sitting with Caitlyn. She was immediately touched by the look on Melanie's face; it was obvious she had been crying, and Mrs. Duncan's motherly instincts took over. Melanie told Mrs. Duncan the same things she had told Colby. However, she was unable to hold back her tears and was visibly shaken as she attempted to recount the details of the incident. When she finished, she was surprised by what happened. Mrs. Duncan approached her. "All weekend, all I could think about was what dirty so-and-so tried to kill my son; I can tell you I was angry, very angry—I would have extended no mercy. However, now that I've met you and you've so graciously apologized, I bear you no ill will. Will you please forgive me for my bad thoughts? I had no way of knowing the truth."

Tears still streaming down her face, Melanie looked at her. "Yes, ma'am, I forgive you, but you must forgive me; it was my fault Colby got hurt. I was driving the car."

Mrs. Duncan did not need to say anything; she held out her arms and moved toward Melanie, who in turn moved toward her. They embraced and held each for a long time; both were crying. Even Deb found herself wiping a few tears. Caitlyn sat amazed at her mother's kindness and pity. When they finally separated, Mrs. Duncan turned first to Deb. "Detective Johnson, I don't want to press any charges against this young lady; I realize you can't let her off scott free, but I will not press any charges against her. She has suffered enough."

She then faced Melanie. "Young lady, I don't know anything about you, but if I can ever be of assistance while you live in our city, please come see me; I mean it." She then handed Melanie one of her business cards.

Melanie was genuinely surprised by her offer. "May I say the same thing; if I can ever be of assistance, I would like to help. Thank you for being so kind. I don't deserve it."

"Perhaps not, but that's for me to say, and that's all there is to it; thank you for being honest. Accidents happen. I'm sorry things got messy."

Melanie tried to smile and nodded. The day had ended well for everyone. However, Colby's butt was still sore.

>̃∼ ⌢∼̃<

After Deb and Melanie left, Mrs. Duncan went to tell Colby the doctors confirmed he could go home in the morning assuming there were no problems during the night. Colby welcomed the news but was concerned that perhaps he was not as well has he appeared. He could deal with his sore body, but it bothered him that his head still ached despite the pain medication. He had asked one of the nurses, who reassured him it was not unusual for head pain to persist following a solid blow like he'd received. While her report was comforting, he was not completely convinced. Colby never had headaches, and it was not easy dealing with this nagging throb. His mother was to keep a close eye on him all day Tuesday, and then decide if he was ready to go back to school. That was one thing Colby really wanted, but he didn't want to have any problems and call unnecessary attention to himself. That was more Geoff's style.

The evening passed quickly. Colby had a few visitors and was secretly pleased people wanted to see him. On the other hand, if a friend of his had been hit by a car, he would have been concerned, so it did make sense. Colby finally decided he simply was not used to all this attention; he liked to function under the radar, so to speak. It was safer there. One thing did amuse him; his sister had actually seemed worried about him, and Caitlyn was not one to get excited about anything Colby did. They had never gotten along; she was so wrapped up in herself she rarely considered other people. Colby resented her lack of compassion, and it was hard for him to be nice to her. However, his mother told him Caitlyn actually cried when she heard Colby had been hurt and had asked, without being told, to go see him. He couldn't say anything to his mother, but maybe Caitlyn did have a heart...somewhere.

>̃∼ ⌢∼̃<

Colby had a good night; the nurses more or less left him alone. He slept well and felt much better when he finally woke around 6:00 am, way too early, but it didn't matter; he felt rested and even his headache was better. One doctor who made early rounds came to look him over. "Well, good morning, how are you feeling today?"

Colby seemed pleased by his question. "I must say, I'm feeling better, especially, since I was dead for two days!" His doctor laughed. "I shouldn't have to tell you, but you need to be more careful about playing in the street. You could get hit by a car!"

I'm afraid you're right. When I was growing up, I can't count the number of times Mother warned me not to play in the street and always look both ways before crossing."

The doctor smiled. "Your mother is a wise lady." Colby nodded. "Well, I've got good news for you. Everything looks fine. I want you to stay active at home today to make sure you have the strength to handle a full day at school. If you begin to feel strange, I want you to come home immediately and rest. We want you back on your feet as soon as possible, but we don't want you to have a relapse."

Colby looked at the doctor. "I promise to take good care of myself and not overdo; I sure don't want to end up back here." He and the doctor shook hands.

It wasn't long before his mother showed up and he was being wheeled down the hallway toward the parking area. He felt silly being in a wheelchair—when the doctor had told him to be active. He considered standing and jumping up and down in it but then thought better of it. That sounded too much like Geoff. His mother was overjoyed he was coming home and the doctor's report had been so good. She was excited to have him back under her wings. Colby worried about her sometimes. What would she do when he left home to go to college? He could imagine her wanting to go with him and even be his roommate. His mother was very attached to him.

At home Mrs. Duncan offered to make Colby anything he wanted to eat; he told her to decide and surprise him. He wasn't sure he could handle such a big decision in his present condition. His mother didn't argue. Colby decided to work on school assignments. Patti had brought

Monday's work, and he still had things he had not done when he was "dead." Around 11:00 am Colby asked his mother what she was making for lunch. She told him she hadn't started anything yet but was going to fix him a breakfast meal because he loved that kind of food and she had not eaten all morning. Colby didn't say anything, but he had been smelling pizza or Italian food for at least half an hour. He couldn't understand why he would be smelling something that wasn't there. He decided not to say anything to his mother about it. It was probably just his imagination—or the "hungry teenage boy" syndrome.

Lunch was scrumptious. Colby felt good but decided to take a short nap after eating. When he awoke around 2:00, he noted the distinct smell of coffee. Without saying anything, he went into the kitchen, discovering no evidence of coffee whatsoever. Why in the world would he be smelling coffee? He didn't even like it. In fact, he rarely drank any hot drinks. What was going on? Once again, he refrained from saying anything; it was no big deal...just his mind playing tricks on him. Sure, that was it; after all, he'd had a nasty bump on the head. There were bound to be side effects; there was nothing to worry about...besides, he felt fine, even better than yesterday.

Very soon Patti called and asked if she could stop by and bring more assignments. They could catch up on school news. Patti arrived about a half hour later. She thought he looked better than yesterday and asked how he was feeling. "Patti, don't say anything to Mom, but something weird is going on; I keep smelling things that aren't there."

Patti glanced at him with a "what in the world" look. "Smelling things that aren't there; I don't understand. What are you talking about?"

"Okay, this morning I smelled pizza; my mom fixed me a big breakfast for lunch—no pizza. Then I took a short nap; when I woke up I could smell coffee, but there's no coffee around anywhere...I checked." Colby was frustrated.

"It must have been your imagination."

"Maybe so, but it seemed so real; I mean, I really smelled those things...but they weren't there."

"Well, you know; you've always been...kind of crazy. Maybe that bump on the head pushed you over the edge." Patti smiled.

"Look, it's Geoff that's crazy, not me, but this is strange."

"I'm sure it's nothing; you'll be fine."

"Well, I hope so; I don't want to go around smelling things that aren't there; I have enough trouble with things that are."

Colby and Patti visited about school and fall activities. The junior and senior years were loaded with events, primarily for fund raising. Juniors needed to earn money to present a quality prom for the seniors. The school had modified prom in order to inspire the juniors to go the extra mile and put everything they had into this grand event. The rules had changed even before Patti's mother graduated. The old junior-senior prom was no more; the prom was held to honor the seniors and was financed by the junior class. The extra twist was brilliant; if the juniors raised enough money and committed themselves to the work, they were invited as honorary guests of the seniors. However, if they failed, they paid the bills and got to spend the evening with friends and family, anywhere but at prom. This modification had proved quite effective.

The big fund raising event in the fall for the juniors was the "junior" play; they received all the proceeds less any expenses. Anyone could audition for a part, and often the whole school was involved. This year the juniors had gone all out and picked a musical, which required the choirs, so Patti was involved. She had urged Colby to try out; he didn't want to and told her so, but she insisted, and he finally agreed to audition. He never dreamed he might be asked, but the committee in charge of tryouts liked what they saw, so Colby was asked to join the cast. It shook him up, and he delayed his response as long as he could. He finally decided he would do it for his class. He asked for a small role and got a part to fit his style. Patti was thrilled because they could attend practice together part of the time. Colby was not thrilled, but had grown into the idea more after play practice had begun. Colby's accident did not cause him to miss any practice, but he not been able to study and learn his lines while in the hospital.

Patti got him up to date, and Colby was pleased she came to see him; she had other things to do, so she could not stay long. However, as she left, she did kiss Colby goodbye; he returned her kiss and told her it made him feel much better. Maybe she should stay longer and they could kiss some more. Why, just a few more kisses, and would Colby be completely healed, leaping tall buildings in a single bound like that guy in the movies, the one with the big S on his chest. What was his name? Patti told Colby to calm down, maybe take a cold shower. There would be plenty of time for kisses later. Too much romance can be fatal, and who would want to risk it, especially when he was just out of the hospital and back from the dead.

Colby was feeling better; it was nice to see Patti, but shortly after she left, he started smelling things again. What was the deal? He couldn't imagine what in the world was going on. This time he could not identify what he smelled; it seemed familiar but he couldn't place it. The sensation seemed to come and go; that is, one moment he would sense it distinctly, the next moment it seemed to fade away. This was crazy. Why would he be smelling things that weren't there? So far the odors were not unpleasant, but smells are smells, and not all of them are good. He remembered how the whole neighborhood stunk to high heaven when the house down the street burned. It almost made him gag. Wait! It was coming to him. He was smelling vanilla; it smelled good, but it didn't make any sense. Colby began to worry something was definitely wrong; this had never happened before nor had he ever heard of someone who smelled things that weren't there.

The smell soon disappeared and Colby could hear his mother working on the evening meal. His dad was to be home tonight, and Colby was anxious to see him and show him he had completely recovered. Well, except for his nose—and it hadn't been hurt at all!

Colby felt he could go to school on Wednesday. His mother must have asked him a dozen times if he would be okay. Yes, he could do it, and no, the odors had not gone away. If anything, they might be a little worse. It obviously was not life threatening, but by the end of the day, Colby decided to tell his mother about his "problem." Very surprisingly, Mrs. Duncan took the news well; that is, she didn't grab her heart and have "the big one." However, later in the evening she became more concerned. Mr. Duncan asked her not to worry. All things considered, Colby had come out of the accident virtually unharmed. This was a small bump in his recovery. Nevertheless, Mrs. Duncan was on the phone the next day to schedule an appointment at the hospital. By pure coincidence, a neurologist would be there. His doctor from the hospital was not terribly concerned, but agreed it wouldn't hurt to have someone give a second opinion. Colby was not very happy at the prospect of going back to the hospital, but if they could figure out why he kept smelling weird things, he was willing to take the chance.

It had been a good day at school although Colby admitted it was tiring and he had trouble concentrating. His headache came and went, a distraction, although the pain reliever seemed to work. His mother picked him up a few minutes early on Thursday and they headed for the hospital. The doctors ordered several tests and took more X-rays. The technician offered words of comfort, reporting that Colby still had a brain. Colby was thrilled to hear this news, now knowing he was not some "brainless teenager." When the examination was complete, the specialist met briefly with Colby and his mother. Colby still had a little swelling on the left side of his head, which explained the headaches, but not necessarily the smelling issue. The doctor did explain the swelling might be putting minor pressure on other parts of Colby's brain, but there was no reason to believe it would affect his olfactory senses.

On the other hand, the doctor did not believe the smells were all Colby's imagination; there was no reason to think he would have recurring episodes affecting his senses, except for the headaches. However, the doctor would review the results of Colby's tests and give a full report as soon as possible. In the meantime, he told Colby to keep his nose clean and not sniff out any trouble. Colby confirmed that placing items in his nose was becoming stressful and he was not going to put another pizza there until it sufficiently cooled. Spices are one thing; too hot is over the line! The doctor offered to pray for him. Medical science can only do so much. Maybe God could help.

Colby's mother was relieved he checked out okay, but she was also anxious about his tests. In the meantime, Colby was smelling what he thought might be cigarette smoke, and he hoped it was short-lived or he was likely to sneeze; he said nothing to his mother. She didn't like cigarette smoke either.

Colby's dad was pleased with their report, and even Caitlyn seemed relieved. She had been hit hard by the realization her brother might have been killed and seemed to have a new appreciation for him. Colby was not completely convinced Caitlyn had really changed but was willing to give her a chance to be a better sister. Colby called Patti and told her the news; she was happy everything appeared okay. She had talked to her mother, who was just as stumped as everyone else; Kathy had even consulted Dr. Bradford, who also had no explanation. Everyone wanted Colby to be one hundred percent again; Colby had heard how people only use ten percent of their brains. He questioned whether he would ever make one hundred, maybe fifty percent.

Friday, Geoff and Jennifer walked home with Colby after school; Patti had to go somewhere with her mother before youth group. School was going fairly well and Colby had caught up most of his work; he did get tired during the day, and by Friday he was getting so used to all the various smells he hardly noticed them. The headaches seemed to get better also. Life was returning to normal...sort of. Colby's mother told him to go to bed and sleep in on Saturday morning and get a good night's rest. Normally Colby might have argued with her, but this time he was agreeable. He went to bed early and fell right to sleep.

The next thing he knew, he was lying in bed with light streaming through his windows, and he was really hungry, especially since he smelled the heavenly aroma of frying bacon. Colby loved breakfast, and bacon was a hot button on his menu. His mother often fixed it when they had a fancy breakfast. This morning the smell overwhelmed him; he threw back his covers, grabbed his old house shirt, and was downstairs faster than the speed of sound. The kitchen was quiet as a tomb. No one was there. Where was his mother? What was going on? He called for her and she quickly answered from the front room; she was reading the newspaper. Mr. Duncan and Caitlyn were running errands, and she was going to start breakfast when they returned. She was thinking about fixing French toast and sausage. Colby almost cried; he had his heart and stomach set on bacon; now he'd have to reset and go with sausage. This nose thing was getting to be a curse; it might have been funny at first, but now it was messing with more than his head. It's not wise to get between a hungry boy and his breakfast...not wise at all.

After breakfast, Colby went to his room, closed the door, and sat quietly at his desk. There was much to reflect on over the past week, and he decided he needed to get things in a proper perspective and make an effort to restore his routine. He had begun this process when a knock sounded at his door. He invited his guest inside. It was Caitlyn; she looked rather sheepish as if she might have been caught doing something she wasn't supposed to do. "Colby, have you got a minute? I'd like to talk with you...please?"

For a second or two Colby felt sorry for her; she looked woebegone. "Sure, I have a few minutes. What do want?"

"Well, Colby, I just wanted to tell you I'm sorry."

"Sorry for what?" Colby noticed she had started to cry.

"I'm sorry you got hurt. Mama was so scared; she rushed out of here like the place was on fire. I think she thought you might have been killed. Whoever called said you had been in an accident and they had taken you to the hospital. You know how Mom is, she gets all worked up over things, but she was really scared. Dad was gone and I had to stay here by myself although I did spend one night with a friend. I thought about how lonesome it was without anyone here, and then I began to think what if you had died. You're the only family I have, and I didn't want to lose you. I guess what I am trying to say is, I love you, Colby. I'm glad you're my brother." Caitlyn was now crying harder and having trouble talking.

Colby surveyed this scene with complete astonishment. He could not remember his sister expressing any love or concern for him other than a casual remark. He could not recall her ever saying she loved or even liked him. Colby wondered if perhaps Caitlyn was the one who had been hit in the head because she was really acting strange. However, Colby got up and opened his arms; Caitlyn ran and threw her arms around him tightly. Between her crying and sobbing, he was sure she kept whispering over and over, "I'm sorry; I'm really sorry..." and Colby even got a few tears in his eyes.

He looked down at her. "Caitlyn, I know you love me, but you have a hard time showing it; I love you too. I know we're not much alike, but you're my sister. I hope we can always be friends. It's nice to have friends at home because then you have someone to talk to. Thank you for being concerned about me. I guess I was okay, but no one really knew, and I feel bad everyone worried about me; it's nice to know people care."

After Caitlyn left, Colby began to take stock. He had a great mom and dad who loved and cared for him. He had a sister who could be nice when she wanted. He had a girlfriend who would die for him; he also had several friends whom he liked and trusted. He was a good student and well respected by his teachers and classmates. He obviously had a future, even though he was unsure what he wanted to do. Could a seventeen-year-old boy really have the world by the tail? How about a seventeen-year-old boy who could smell things that weren't there? Not everyone can do that. And how does a seventeen-year-old boy know if he has the world...or a tiger by the tail? Surely, it would make a difference, and surely it would be nice to know.

Too much excitement can be dangerous. Why, it can even be tricky just going to the library...or at least, leaving it.

Finally, if Colby was going to have some kind of extra sensory perception, why couldn't he see the future? Now that would be really handy, time saving and profitable. On the other hand, did he really want to know? Wasn't it awfully nice to discover, just moments ago, that his sister, of all people, actually cared for him? Don't surprises make life more exciting? Gosh, being a seventeen-year-old boy can be tough; it probably isn't any easier for a seventeen-year-old girl. After the better part of the morning, Colby concluded he was thankful for the blessings he had, and as for the things he didn't have...well, he would just have to get along without them. Maybe this was what adults meant when they talked about growing up. Maybe taking stock and looking honestly at life is what growing up is all about. He could always ask some adult about it, but they might not have an answer. Life is like that sometimes...too many questions, not enough answers...and often the answers don't match the question. No wonder some people drink to stay sober. Colby smiled and nodded; life is a mystery, and where is Sherlock Holmes when you really need him?

✎ This book is dedicated to ✎

Elvin H. Beemer, my father,
who explained to me the real meaning of romance,
and to
Rush Limbaugh,
who encourages listeners to pursue their passion.

✎ Acknowledgments ✎

It is impossible to acknowledge all those who have inspired
and led me throughout my life; many have no idea of the
subtle and not so subtle ways they have encouraged me to
pursue my dreams. Certainly, I want to thank my wife,
Judy, for reading and correcting my less than perfect
grammar; the same goes to my daughter, Christa, who
helped edit and offered encouragement. My son, Jud, is an
engineer so he knows nothing about spelling and grammar
but still offered ideas to improve the final product. I want
to thank my readers for their advice and opinions, positive
and otherwise. I cannot make everyone happy, but it
helped me write a better book. A special thanks goes to
many of my former students who, without knowing it, kept
my heart young and spirit free. Also, a special thanks to
those at AuthorHouse, especially my consultant, Chelsea
Downham, who convinced me to make this "leap of faith."
You are all wonderful; thank you so much.

✎ To the Reader ✎

I hope you have enjoyed this book and have come to love
the characters as much as I have, perhaps shed a tear or
two for them. I invite you to continue the story of Patti and
Colby in my forthcoming novel, *Lunch Table 37*, second
in a series of three books. My hope is to touch the hearts
then the minds of readers to better understand the meaning
of life and to love it's simplicity. Thank you for purchasing
my novel. A portion of the proceeds will be donated to
charities whose mission is to care for the less fortunate,
especially young people.

❧ About the Author ❧

Chris E. Beemer was raised in Southwest Iowa and attended Northwest Missouri State University, majoring in mathematics education. Following his graduation, he married Judy Osburn, who has put up with him for longer than either of them care to remember. In 1973, they moved to Kansas where their two children, now adults, were born. Chris has worked as a banker and a math teacher, with a short stint at Home Depot.

He has many passions, including listening to classical and Christian music, enjoying classic movies, reading, eating and solving household problems. Writing is something new for Chris; it is both humbling and inspiring, causing him laugh and cry, often at the same time. He wishes the same for his readers, especially the laughter.

Printed in the United States
215848BV00001B/2/P

9 781438 960180